INTO
THE
LIGHT

INTO THE LIGHT

THE

LIGHT

MARK OSHIRO

Tor Publishing Group New York

INTO THE LIGHT

Copyright © 2023 by Mark Oshiro

A Tor Teen Book
Published by Tom Doherty Associates / Tor Publishing Group
120 Broadway
New York, NY 10271

www.tor-forge.com

Tor® is a registered trademark of Macmillan Publishing Group, LLC.

The Library of Congress Cataloging-in-Publication Data is available upon request.

ISBN 978-1-250-81225-4 (hardcover)
ISBN 978-1-250-81226-1 (ebook)

Our books may be purchased in bulk for promotional, educational, or business use. Please contact your local bookseller or the Macmillan Corporate and Premium Sales Department at 1-800-221-7945, extension 5442, or by email at MacmillanSpecialMarkets@macmillan.com.

First Edition: 2023

Printed in the United States of America

0 9 8 7 6 5 4 3 2 1

To all the teachers, coaches, librarians, guidance counselors,
admin staff, students, parents, best friends,
and strangers who helped a young, in-the-closet kid
navigate a nightmare—

Thank you.

You were my light in the darkness.

Note: This will be a difficult novel to read. Please consult the
author's note at the end for content warnings if needed.

2:27 p.m. Sunday.

The diner is packed. Not surprising. It's off a long stretch of the 5. Lots of campers. Families heading out to hike or visit relatives. There isn't a big city for hundreds of hundreds of miles in any direction. Even fewer places to grab breakfast. All of the booths are taken, so after I push through the glass door connected to the motel lobby, I slide into a seat at the end of the counter. Glance up at the TV.

And wait.

I ignore the din. The sound of joyful voices. The scraping of utensils on plates.

I wait.

A waitress sidles up to me. "Good afternoon, honey," she says, her voice thick. There's a little twang in it.

I glance at her. Brunette hair, a nice orange hue in her lipstick. She smiles.

I point to the TV. It's a rerun of some old sitcom I vaguely recognize. "Is that on channel 19?"

She looks to where I gesture. "I don't think so. Why? You want me to change it?"

I nod. Press my left hand against the front pocket of my jeans, feel the few folded bills in there. "And I'll take an orange juice. And a side of waffles. Extra syrup."

She drifts away for a moment, then returns with a remote. Flips a few channels, then drops the remote next to me. "I'll be right back with that OJ," she says, then winks.

I wait for the cartoon to switch over to a commercial. I don't prefer this, but I don't have consistent access to a smart phone or a computer.

So I wait.

My heart thumps as the animation fades to black.

There's an off-white clock hanging over the door I came through. I twist round, glance at it.

2:30 p.m.

The music swells, and even amidst the countless conversations around me, I recognize every note, every beat of the drum, every wordless harmony sung as the words appear on the screen:

CHRIST'S DOMINION
WITH DEACON THOMPSON

And then he's there. On the screen. Deacon Thompson, his eyes always as blue as I remember them. He smiles.

I shiver.

There are five children surrounding him. I think it's a good sign. He's done so many broadcasts by himself lately. I scan quickly for any sign of her.

I see three kids with light brown skin, dark hair. A Black girl with her hair to her shoulders, straightened, her lips stretched open wide in a smile. An Asian boy beaming at the camera.

The children are close, almost as if they are vying to be on camera with Deacon.

And she's not one of them.

I lean back. Heart sinks. Familiarity creeps in because . . . well, this is a rerun, too. I don't hear the words Deacon says, though I can probably guess what they are. He's talking about the children: how important they are. How he's saving them. How broken the world is that week, with a long litany of sins.

And everything he and Christ's Dominion have done to repair it.

I know he's not reading from a script. I know that he probably means it all.

The waitress sets a glass of orange juice at my side. Lingers for a moment. I peer up at her.

"You know, I might just go to hell for saying this, but that Deacon guy is kinda cute."

I don't respond.

"You know, in a spiritual way, I guess."

I nod at her, offer a weak smile. "Yeah, I guess."

She shrugs. "And he wants to save the children! Put God back in our lives. Can't say the same about most people."

She doesn't wait for me to respond before she heads to one of the booths.

I have gotten good at biting my tongue. At holding it in. I can't say what I want to say because . . .

Well, she won't believe me.

No one will.

But me, I don't believe a word he says. Not anymore.

So I halfheartedly eat the waffles when they arrive, dousing them in syrup, knowing that they're empty calories but they're calories all the same. I only have twenty dollars in my pocket, and this will draw me back eight bucks. Nine with a tip. Not sure where I'm going to make more money, and the thought creeps back.

Maybe it's time to leave.

The music swells again. I look up. Watch the number flash at the bottom of the screen, the one you're supposed to call to give money to help all the children that Deacon is rescuing. Images flash forward: a toddler walking jerkily toward an adult couple. The kid has the same deep brown skin tone as me. Same black hair. His parents are pale and grinning and that's the dream they sell you: Give us money. We'll save *them*.

It changes. A group of kids—not one of them white—sit in a classroom. *The* classroom. Harriett Thompson—Deacon's wife—is there, lecturing to them, and they nod, attentively.

And for a brief moment, my sister is on the screen.

She's tall. Long black hair. Beaming with gratitude. In faith. I don't know when this was recorded, though. It's been hard to guess. Deacon's show is broadcast over this tiny network throughout the week. It's a recent thing, and most of these are the same as the ones that appear on his YouTube channel. His church . . . it's all online. No place of worship. Just an online "movement." So these videos are how he reaches people.

I think I've seen them all. Have most of them practically memorized. Maybe he's trying to reach people who don't use YouTube though. Thus: these public broadcasts. Always at the same time every week in different local markets across California.

I wonder if that means I'm close to them—close to *her*. I still don't know. I've tried calling in on that number they list between the sermons. Ask them where Reconciliation is, how I need to find my way. Say that I want to visit as soon as possible.

They always hang up on me.

So I watch for her, whenever I can.

Elena.

My older sister.

She isn't in the rest of the episode. Not in the background, not in one of Deacon's devotional messages, not in shots of all the loving homes of good, American Christians, where all the saved children are placed. The one glimpse of her—from that shot in Mrs. Thompson's classroom.

It's the only thing I've gotten in the last three weeks.

I place the dollar bills next to my empty plate, then leave the diner. It's too loud. I pass a few booths. Families. Couples. All deep in conversation, all unaware of me. Which is how I like it. It's easier for me to disappear that way. Easier for me to shove down the bitterness that rises in me during moments like this, when the desire tries to claw its way up my throat.

Because truthfully, I want what they have.

But I don't get that. Not someone like me.

I've taken a lot of rides from strangers this past year. Learned that when you need to get somewhere and you can't drive *and* don't have money, you can't be too picky.

Also means that sometimes you ride with bad people.

Some of the truckers are creepy. Not all. Not even most. Most are kind. Have seen lots of kids on the road. Don't know why, but that part surprised me. After I was cast out, I always assumed that there wasn't anyone else like me. But I've met some kids who've been rejected. Thrown away. Discarded.

I always think of Cesar, though, whenever I'm getting into a new car with a new stranger.

I met him in Las Cruces at the travel center. First one I ever spent time at after they broke me. He found me scarfing down the remains of a burrito some bougie family tossed in the garbage because their daughter took a bite and didn't want it anymore. Gave me a bottle of water, a change of clothes. My first belongings.

Then he gave me advice.

Cesar was scrawny. Brown like me. Had a shaved head. Rough around the edges. He wore torn denim jeans and a gnarly leather jacket with punk patches glued to it over a tattered Discharge tank top. It struck me that his clothes looked like they were falling apart not because it was an intentional style, but because he was real. His life was real.

And he knelt before me. Said he could tell I was new. Could smell it on me, see it in the way I devoured food. He told me not to be so open. So desperate. "People like us *are* desperate," he explained as I continued eating. "But don't show it. Don't let them know."

I swallowed. Eyed him suspiciously. "Know what?"

"Anything about you. I can see your whole story on your face."

I looked away. No, he couldn't. No one could.

"Someone hurt you," he continued. "Badly. Probably threw you away."

When I looked back at him, my vision blurred.

"See? I knew I was right. You gotta cut that shit out."

I rose and walked away from him, but he followed. "I been at this longer than you," he called out. "And if you're gonna survive out here, you have to hide it all."

"Why do you care?" I sneered, rounding on him.

"Because I'm just like you."

No, you're not.

"At least, I once was."

No, you weren't.

"And no one else is actually going to help you."

I suddenly had no appetite. Tossed the remains of the burrito in a nearby trash can, very aware of what I had just been eating. Leftovers. A stranger's leftovers. No one had offered me this.

No one else was going to help.

And so I sat there, on the curb outside a travel center in Las Cruces, New Mexico, and Cesar told me his rules. They worked for him. Work for me, too.

Before he left, he said he was sorry.

"For what?" I said.

"Whatever happened to you, man," he said, shaking his head. "It shouldn't have happened."

No one has ever said that to me since.

When you're like me, you have to lie all the time.

The motel we're at is one of those low, flat buildings. Looks like it was smashed down from the top. The gray paint is peeling in places. It's sad and old, like so many others I've scrounged up money for. They all blend together after awhile. But right now it's a roof over my head that I don't have to pay for, so I don't mind. Most of it could be on fire, and all I would care about was whether I could take a shower or get a few minutes of sleep.

I can still hear the water running inside. Carlos has been in the bathroom for the last thirty minutes, and I know I'm running out of time. Don't want that. Don't want to make the Varelas even one minute late, because that's when you start down the path to becoming a thorn in someone's side. I've been with them for weeks. Longest I been with anyone since I left.

Was forced to leave.

Whatever.

The end is still the same, so it doesn't matter how I describe it.

I know what happened, but a lie will always come out of my mouth. I think about what lies I'll have to tell them today. The Varelas haven't asked about the TV thing yet. They aren't as nosy as the other people I've traveled with.

It's weird. I'm not used to that—people not wanting me to tell them things. Or not expecting all that much from me. Or not acting in ways to make them feel better about themselves.

The door to my left creaks open. A man with a long beard and a thick mustache pokes his head out. Hair on top of his head is bushy and curly, too, and he's trying to dry it with a white motel towel.

"Manny, is he *still* in there?" Ricardo asks.

I nod.

He curses in Spanish, then gestures to the filthy, empty swimming pool beyond the metal gate just ten feet from us. "Coulda filled that up with all the water he's wasting."

I shrug. "No big deal. I can be quick."

Ricardo steps out of the room, and his button-down shirt is still open, and the lapels spread like wings at his sides as he moves. His chest is bare and a little damp, and I avert my eyes quickly. Shouldn't be thinking those things.

He pounds on the door. "Carlos!" he calls out. "Please hurry up! We have a long trip to make today, so we need to get going soon!"

The door swings inward, and I realize I didn't hear the water shut off. Carlos scowls at his father first, then at me. He's shorter than I am, with hair just as bushy and curly as Ricardo's. Got the build of a running back. Wouldn't be surprised if he'd played football before his parents pulled him out of school. He's only got on a pair of boxer briefs, and bottom part of his stomach hangs over them. I guess he gets his size from Ricardo, too.

More thoughts I shouldn't have pop into my head. I push them away, too.

"It's not that big of a deal, Papi," Carlos says. "We'll get there when we get there."

Ricardo sighs. Shakes his head. "Never said it was a big deal."

Another argument lingers there. It's been happening a lot. Heard Ricardo tell his wife the other day that he suspects it's because Carlos's seventeenth birthday is looming. It's making him "disagreeable."

I start to back away. Don't want to be a part of this. As soon as you're inserted into the affairs of others, you become a risk. Traveling with the Varela family has been less chaotic than what I'm used to, so I don't want to lose this window of calm.

Even though I know I will eventually.

Carlos catches me, though, looks me up and down. Steps back, pulls the door open as wide as it goes.

"Shower's all yours," he says to me.

Ricardo sighs again. "I didn't realize I had raised the world's moodiest teenager."

Carlos offers a sarcastic smile. "And I've still got another year to perfect it."

This is my only opening. I duck inside past Carlos as the two keep bickering and picking at each other. I quickly nab the pouch of toiletries tucked into my duffel, as well as a change of shirt, socks, and underwear. The bag is fairly small, but it has to be. One of the many rules I have, the ones that keep me moving, that keep me alive.

Don't own a lot. Keep it all organized. Be ready to leave at a moment's notice. A living situation can always go toxic or unwelcome faster than you think. Make the bag as inconspicuous as possible so it's easier to tuck out of sight. You want people to functionally forget you're there. And if they forget you, you might get to stay with them longer.

But not that long. No one *actually* wants you around.

I shut the bathroom door quietly. Can still hear Carlos and Ricardo.

I don't belong here.

It's not a surprise thought. Or an unfamiliar thought. It's the truth.

I don't belong *anywhere*.

I'm a boat, adrift at sea. No oars. No engines. Just letting the waves and the current take me where they may. Right now, that place is . . . this. With the Varelas.

I strip out of my clothes, fold them neatly, and place them on the back of the toilet. Turn on the water. Wait for it to get hot.

Is today the day I leave? Or do I have more time with these people?

Four weeks. It's been four weeks since they met me outside of Fresno and asked me to join them on their journey. Monica and Ricardo have reassured me that I can travel with them in their ridiculous van as long as I need to, but I'm still awaiting the moment it all falls apart, just like it has so many times before.

The water runs over me. I scrub quickly, intensely. This might be my last shower for a while. Can't ever presume to know what my future holds. A year ago, I was with my sister. A year ago, they cast me out, and I been on the road since then. Drifting. Found weird jobs, hitchhiked a lot. Made some money down in Santa Barbara for a while working for a guy named Hernando who ran a landscaping business. Job gave me mean calluses. I can feel them now as I rinse away the soap, as I run my fingers over my face.

I lasted two weeks. Ten days of paid work straight, but that ended when he couldn't pay me at the end of a shift. Asked if he could pay another way. Pulled down his pants and started rubbing himself.

I couldn't help shirking away. Or laughing. And I ran when he picked up a shovel, his face red with fury, and swung it at me.

My own cheeks burn as I wrench the water off. Because if he hadn't gotten mad at me, I probably would have said yes.

I don't know what that makes me.

I dry quickly using the last clean towel, then rub lotion over my skin, moisturize my face. Another rule: Never use a shared bathroom longer than necessary. I've got the whole routine down to under ten minutes, because most people won't notice an occupied bathroom in that amount of time. Thankfully, we're checking out today, so I don't have to clean up the water or any errant body hairs.

That's part of the routine, too. Don't leave anything behind. No proof that you exist.

It's easier that way.

I dress, then head out into the room to pack up. Carlos is dressed now, and he's lying down on his stomach, the TV remote in his hand, some reality TV show blaring loudly. I ignore him as I roll up my sleeping bag, then stuff it in my duffel with the dirty clothes and my toiletries.

"You know you're allowed to sleep in beds, right?" he says. "You don't always have to be on the floor."

"It's fine," I say, zipping up my bag. "I'm used to it."

He changes the channel. "You're weird."

Can't argue with that. I'm reminded of it regularly, and in that moment, I try to remember the last time I slept in a bed.

Damn. Long time. Nine months? Maybe?

Don't wanna think back too far. There's a big hole there. Black and terrible and painful. It's like they cut a part of myself from my body. Can't spend too much time dwelling on it.

So I don't.

I sit at the foot of Carlos's bed as he flips from one channel to the next, so fast that I'm not sure how he catches anything. How does he know what all these shows are?

Right. He probably grew up with this.

Elena and I hopped from foster home to foster home. Meant I never really grew up watching TV.

Guess I didn't grow up with much of anything.

So I sit there in my unfamiliarity, and I wrestle with the question I always keep in my mind.

Is it time to go?

Haven't decided yet.

They're nice people. Carlos doesn't really like me, though. He doesn't *hate* me, but he's certainly not my biggest fan. I think he sees me as competition or something when it comes to his parents. Don't know. Don't really have proof. Just instinct at this point, a feeling based on experience. Kids don't want to have to compete for attention from their own parents.

So I sink into my own hollow reality. The images flash on the TV: a family touring a home. A couple getting married. A car commercial. A superhero movie.

All a fantasy to me.

Another cartoon. A judge in a courtroom yelling. A basketball team on the court. A news broadcast. A dog running on a—

"Go back," I say.

Hair raises on the back of my neck.

I saw *his* face.

"Go back?" Carlos keeps barreling through channels. "Why?"

"Just do it!" I say.

My tone is sharp, forceful. I feel Carlos shift on the bed. He goes back. Back past the comedy set, past the dog on the beach, and then:

It's a shot of a forest. Yellow tape strung between trees. People standing around, one hunched down, staring at something. There's a banner along the bottom of the screen.

BODY FOUND OUTSIDE RELIGIOUS CAMP

A newscaster with a deep, clear voice speaks over the next image:

It's him.

Deacon Thompson.

It's a still from one of his YouTube videos. One of the ones I've seen a million times because . . . because *she* is in it.

I watch. I listen.

"Local authorities have not confirmed any details aside from reiterating that the body was found *outside* property lines."

Heart is racing. There's bile in my throat.

The broadcast cuts to an officer. Crop-cut hair, baby face with reddened blotches on pale skin, beige uniform.

"We're a little shaken up," he says, frowning. "We're just a little mountain town. Idyllwild doesn't really get stuff like this."

Idyllwild.

The news anchors are saying something about the successful Christmas toy drive that Deacon organized last year, and I don't care. Doesn't matter. Can't really hear any of it anymore.

A body.

There's a body in Idyllwild.

Is it her?

Is it her?

They tell me that I'm not ready yet. That it's been too soon since my miracle, since reconciliation came for me.

I sit in classes with Mrs. Thompson. I study with Deacon in his home. He tells me everything: what reconciliation does. How it is to be achieved. We rehearse my story. We rehearse scenarios. The Thompsons prepare me for every possibility.

My parents are trying to be encouraging, and I can tell they expect a lot from me. It's in the way they gaze at me over dinner in the lodge, or the way they watch me from the couch in the evening when I come back to the cabin after a long day. It's in the hesitant touches, as if I'll disappear if they do anything but graze my skin with their fingertips.

And it's in the hopeful gaze of my sister Elena. She watches me, too, not just in class, not just in the garden, not just on our morning hikes amidst the tall, lanky pines.

I think she believes I'm going to disappear.

But still, I'm not ready yet. "Soon, Eli," Deacon tells me. "Soon, we will reopen this place for the others. Then you will show your miracle to the world. You will create others."

It's all I want.

To love these people. To *be* loved by these people.

And to make Deacon Thompson proud.

I wouldn't be here without him, of course. Elena found me, the Sullivans took me in as their own, and Deacon . . . well, I'm evidence that this place is real. That it is blessed.

I can't let anyone down.

"Yo, you good, Manny?"

Carlos taps me on the top of my head, and I startle, my body a tightly wound knot.

"Why you so jumpy?"

I shake it off. Push myself upright. I'm vibrating. My skin is on fire.

A body. They found a body.

I know who it is.

It's her.

It can't be.

It's her.

An abyss opens in me, one I have long kept shut. It aches, threatens to pull me into it. The thing I always avoid thinking about . . . it's right there.

No. Not here. Not now.

I steel myself against the tide. Memories are flooding back, and I can't stop them.

Why now?

Why *now*?

"Manny, what's going on? Are you okay?"

I snap to attention. Turn around. Carlos is staring at me, his dark brown eyes wide.

"What?"

"You just like . . . zoned out. Went somewhere else."

I blink at him.

Shit.

He saw it all.

Lies form easily these days. My brain spits them out, smooth like oil, and they slither off my tongue.

"Sorry," I say. "That news story . . . just reminded me of a bad dream I had last night. About . . . finding a dead body."

"Oh."

He looks away.

I don't know if he believes me, but I don't care.

I can't be here.

I rush to the door. Close it softly behind me. It's getting warmer out. A thick humidity clings to my skin.

So does the terror.

And the *rage*.

They separated us. Took her from me.

I tell myself that she's fine as I pace outside the motel. That there's no reason to believe that's her body. It could be anyone. It could have been there long before Deacon Thompson bought the land.

That body can't possibly be her.

Lie lie lie lie lie.

My heart thumps. I'm pouring sweat. That shower I took was pointless.

I'm spiraling.

This is all I am anymore. Panic and terror and fear and bitterness. It's all I can be. They took the rest from me. All I know anymore is survival. I control what I can: the stories I tell. Who I tell them to. The people I stay with. The strength and power of being alone.

I want to grab my duffel bag.

Leave the Varelas behind.

Wouldn't be the first time I disappeared. Won't be the last.

I am soon to overstay my welcome anyway. That always happens. At some point, this family will tire of me. They'll pull away. Talk to me less. Make comments they don't think I can hear about how I am a burden. I am stress-inducing. I'm so complicated.

All things I've heard before.

So maybe I should just go now. Go . . .

Go *where*?

Idyllwild.

Wherever that is.

I should just go. Go and find out. Go and chase that certainty.

A year of calling that fucking hotline, and here it is: the location of Reconciliation. Idyllwild. I don't know where that is. But it doesn't matter. It's somewhere here in California.

I can get there. Hitchhike. Save up for bus fare. Doesn't matter. I can go.

I *should* go.

But I don't know if I can. If I can go back to the place where they broke me into pieces.

I don't know that I should. She chose them. She is part of the problem. If the body isn't her . . .

Why should I assume she wants to see me again?

But it was always supposed to be me and her. That's how it used to be.

God, I fucking hate this already.

Carlos startles me again when he bursts out of the motel room. He glances over at me once, then darts to the adjoining room where his parents are.

The thought blooms without hesitation: *Is he annoyed with me already?*

I want to believe that. It is easy to, because it provides me with an exit. A reason to leave this behind.

But I have no plan. No means of reaching her, other than a name: Idyllwild.

She's in Idyllwild.

Alive or dead, that's where my sister is.

We leave Redding shortly after.

As I approach the van, Monica asks me the same question she does each morning. She's standing there in a summer dress with bird-of-paradise flowers on it, her arms crossed, leaning up against the black van.

It's a big van. Fancy. Has a couple TVs in it. I'd never seen that outside of semitruck cabins. The seats fold down in the back so that there are beds, and there's a box mounted on the roof where the Varelas store all their clothing and belongings. Well, the stuff they keep with them. Most of what they own is still in storage in San Jose.

"So, Manny," she says. "Do you want to come with us today?"

This is her thing. She told me that I should never feel like I'm being forced to join them. I do appreciate it, but . . . I can't tell her why. That would require that I tell her the truth.

And she won't believe me.

I hoist my duffel bag up on my shoulder.

Part of me is screaming to leave them behind. But I don't even know where Idyllwild *is*, and at least I'll have some food and a place to stay for another night.

"Yeah," I say. "Sure."

I drop my bag in the back row of seats, and then Ricardo invites me to sit shotgun. I don't think it's because he wants the company. I am not terribly good company these days anyway. But it's a study morning for Carlos. He's graduating soon, but he still has more of his homeschooling to do with Monica until then.

Before they leave, though, they go check on Yvonne.

She rode with us yesterday. Seemed to be a close friend of Carlos. They were chatting away the entire time. We picked her up outside Eugene, Oregon, a couple days ago. It's what the Varelas do. Travel. Monica and Ricardo whisper about it. Consult their tablet or laptop. Make constant phone calls. They are hopping around California for now, but there are tentative plans to head into Nevada, too. These people seem to be old friends. They're all really young, though, so sometimes I think that they're from where the Varelas used to live before they uprooted their lives.

Yvonne has a deep voice. Shaved head like mine. She talked to me a bit the day before and told me that there's a great punk scene in Oregon that I should check out someday. Didn't have the heart to tell her I can't really plan for the future like that. I liked her. She spoke to me like there was a secret she was holding close to her heart: hesitant. Weary. I liked that. Recognized it in me.

They got her a room here at the motel, and I wait in the passenger seat while the Varela family says their goodbyes. I wonder if this is what they do: pick up young people who need things. Am I more like Yvonne than I know?

Probably not. No one is like me.

Monica sits in the middle row with her son. She's got her curly hair pulled back out of her face and a math book in her lap. They're splitting a set of headphones connected to a tablet, where an instructor is guiding Carlos through a lesson.

I haven't been to a school in a long time. Didn't ever graduate, either, and I wonder then if I'll ever fix that.

Not important. Gotta get through the day first. That's all that matters.

I disappear into the view. I disappear into myself.

We head down the 5. Supposed to eventually cut west so that we can end up in Mendocino by the afternoon. No one has told me *why*, but the Varelas are looking for people. I never ask who, either.

Yesterday, I was considering going with them. Haven't been to Nevada in a while.

But now . . .

Idyllwild.

I have a name.

A place.

This is my favorite part, though. Cruising down the highway, I can drown out everything. Look out the window. See the world. It's a silver lining of my own making, and it's the only thing I have left of Elena. No home, no family, not much to my name, no proof that I am a whole person. But she gave this to me first. That thing she does, where she grasps on to joy wherever she can find it. I always envied that, but now I have it, too.

It's pretty up here. Lots of rolling fields with pale green grasses blowing in the breeze. Scattered, scraggly trees. Farms and houses dot the landscape.

Sometimes, I like to pretend. I pretend I have things: a home. A car. A bike. A record collection. Maybe even a boyfriend or a husband. I do it then, wondering what it would be like to live in one of these homes, have rescue dogs frolicking in the backyard.

Right now, I can't keep my thoughts together.

Is it her?

The fantasy crumbles.

It can't be her. The world isn't that cruel.

It is. You know it is.

I miss her.

I despise her.

Both these realities live inside me. Two truths. One body.

Because I wouldn't be where I am now if she hadn't listened to that man.

Ricardo clears his throat. "You doing okay, Manny?"

I give him a quick glance, then gaze back out the window.

"Just in my head a bit."

I know he sees me as a fortress. Impenetrable. They all must. It's by design. I don't say much. Have to keep it that way. The less they know, the better. How would they feel if they knew I missed someone who ruined my life?

I drift.

Down the highway. Through the fields. Lost in the encroaching darkness.

Is it her?

Two realities.

One question.

I don't want to disappoint anyone today.

I'm dressed as neatly as possible in black slacks and a white, short-sleeved button-down dress shirt. Mom and Dad had me tie my long, curly hair in place so it wouldn't get in my eyes when I met the others.

The others.

After months of training with Mrs. Thompson, it is finally time to meet the others.

My sister is behind me, and I step out onto the porch to a warm summer evening. I hear the finches and sparrows call out as the earthy scent of the pines and firs hits my nose. I inhale. I let God's love fill my lungs, and I imagine it spreading to every part of my body.

Because I need this. I need this to work.

"Hurry up, Eli," Elena says, and she gently nudges me forward. "We don't want to miss their arrival."

I twist to gaze up at her.

My sister.

Her hair is tied back, too, though it's much longer than mine. I don't ever forget how rare it is to see a bit of myself in her face; I know that most of the kids who come through Reconciliation don't get this kind of experience. Another sign that we're blessed, that we were meant for this. What are the odds that God would give me a sister who looks so much like me? Because I was abandoned here, left at the front gate by . . . well, I don't know. I was in terrible shape. I don't remember much before that. Just vague images and feelings.

This is my new life.

And it's better. That's the promise of Reconciliation.

I watch Mom and Dad rush across the clearing that separates our cabin from the lodge. We're on the farthest edge of the semi-circle of homes, a deliberate choice so that all the visiting families get those that are closest to the lodge. Well, at least when they're all built. Most of the ones to the north are just cement foundations. Skeletons of cabins sit to the south. They'll be finished someday, and I think about the transformation that awaits those who will come to this place, who will experience the unification of body and spirit that once changed my life. That gave me a family of my own.

I'm scared.

I don't want to mess this up.

Dad smiles widely as he comes up to us, and then Mom embraces me. Even though it's a quick thing, I still cherish it. The affection feels so real, so genuine, as if I am their real son. I guess I am, even if it's hard to accept that some days. Everything is still so . . . new. Fresh.

"You two ready?" Dad says.

I nod.

Because I have to be.

Elena links hands with me.

"Yes," she says.

Then she guides me forward, across the low-cut grass in the clearing, and I try to ignore the sweat beading on my forehead, running down my sides from my underarms. I try to ignore the fear mounting in my heart. I try to remind myself that I have been reconciled, that God has chosen to work through me.

At the edge of the clearing, just feet from the enormous lodge, we stop, and our timing is perfect, because the white van is finishing its climb up the incline beyond the cabins. It approaches, and inside are the first kids who will attend Reconciliation since I arrived. They are my first real test. They are my chance to prove that I am not going to botch this miracle.

Reconciliation worked on me.

It's going to work on them.

The van slows. A woman swings open the passenger-side door and steps out. Mrs. Thompson. She's pale-skinned. Brunette. She glances at us—smiles at me, too, and my heart leaps—then slides open the side door.

As the newcomers exit, Deacon Thompson comes around the front of the van. Gives his wife a kiss. When he turns to me and my family, he looks overjoyed. Maybe a little nervous, which isn't like him. But there's happiness there in his light blue eyes, in the way he rubs his hands together, then smooths back his blond hair.

"Welcome, my children," he says, then gazes at each and every one of them as they leave the van, clasping his hands tighter.

The last three remove blindfolds and adjust to the light. An Asian girl with fine black hair to her shoulders and light brown skin. A Black girl with locs down her back. Another is Latinx, his skin tone lighter than mine, his hair cropped short and a contemplative look on his face. He removes his glasses. Cleans them on his shirt, then puts them back on.

They gaze around at the towering trees. The lodge. Then at us.

"Your parents will be joining us shortly," Deacon announces. "For now, though, I'd like you all to meet your two counselors for this weekend's retreat."

My heart stammers. Feels like it's going to explode. Counselor. I'm a counselor. Do I even know what I'm doing?

Yes. I've been trained. That's what all this preparation has been for.

"I'm Elena," my sister says, raising a hand. "Elena Sullivan. And I'm so glad you're all here."

They mumble hellos. Don't seem all that excited to see us.

So it's my turn to make sure they're welcome.

"I'm Eli," I say. "Elena's brother."

They look to me.

"This place is going to change your life."

I say it because it's true.

I say it because I *need* it to be true.

The Latinx boy raises an eyebrow at me.

"I doubt it," he says.

"Let's go," Deacon says quickly, and he gestures for the newcomers to follow him, and Mom is telling me to go, too, but I feel like I've already failed them. This isn't going to work. I'm going to disappoint them all.

Elena reaches out to hold my hand. She squeezes it.

"Deep breath," she says to me. "You got this, Eli."

It brings me back. Reminds me of what has occurred here and what's going to occur here.

We are blessed. We will show the others what life is like on the other side.

Elena and I walk hand in hand toward Deacon's home, toward my destiny.

Carlos has to pee a lot. I think he's got to be made mostly of urine.

We've pulled off the highway in a town called Corning. Weird name. We're at one of those massive travel centers, the ones for truckers that are littered along highways in this part of the country. They kinda became my beacons of hope while traveling. Got cheap food and showers, and sometimes, I've found work in them. Spent a lot of time at one in Las Cruces back at the beginning.

They're familiar.

Dependable.

Not a lot in my life is.

Monica runs inside with Carlos. I get out and start to clean off the dirt and dead bugs from the front windshield. That's another thing Cesar taught me: It's okay to be noticed when you're useful. It's best to be unseen, but if you must be perceived, do something good with it.

People tend to like that. Makes them feel better about helping you. Plus, there's the debt, both financial and emotional. You can accumulate it to keep a situation going. Maybe that's cynical of me, but it's the truth. Kindness can be a currency, and I'm investing in this journey with the Varelas for the moment.

Buying myself more time before it finally comes to an end.

"You really don't need to do that," Ricardo says after topping off the gas. "I promise. We're fine."

"It's okay," I say. "Besides, I'm just following through in the tradition of my people."

Ricardo raises an eyebrow. "Your people?"

"I'm homeless."

He rolls his eyes. "Seriously, Manny?"

"Hey, I'm *allowed* to make that joke."

And then he laughs, and it feels like a victory.

Another thing: Make people laugh. Keeps them easy and comfortable.

For a while.

Ricardo walks around to the open side door of the van, then does push-ups off the step. I think muscles come easy to him, and he certainly passed that down to Carlos. They're both bulky in an effortless way. I've only seen Ricardo do push-ups and pull-ups before, nothing else. I wonder what that's like. To actually keep weight on.

"You ever been out to the coast up here?"

Ricardo hops up and dusts off his hands, then takes off his button-down shirt. He's got on that tight-fitting white undershirt.

I glance away as heat rushes to my face. Probably bad to have a crush on Carlos *and* his dad, but it's not like anything will ever come of it.

"Nah," I say. "Hadn't even been to Northern California until I met you guys."

"It's wonderful up here," he says. "I haven't been since I was a kid, so I'm looking forward to it. You're not ready for the views. How dramatic it all is."

"I like the ocean," I say. "It's . . . calming."

He smiles gently. "Yes. It is."

There's an awkward silence. Then:

"We're thinking of heading north again after we're done in Mendocino. Up to Eureka for some business."

"Cool." I trace the cement beneath me with the toe of my shoe. Don't know what "business" entails.

All I care about is the word he said: *north*.

Is Idyllwild north of here? South?

"You're still welcome to come with us."

"I know." I then give him a short smile. "I appreciate it. Thank you."

He hesitates again. "Manny, is there . . . is there anywhere *you* want to go?"

My heart jolts in my chest.

Idyllwild.

Find her.

I take a risk.

"Do you know where Idyllwild is?"

He seems taken aback. "Uh . . . yeah. I do. It's in Southern California. Pretty far from here." He narrows his eyes at me. "Is *that* where you want to go?"

I shake my head.

Then lie.

"Nah," I say. "Maybe some time in the future, but for now? Just going where life takes me."

He sits on the step into the van. "Do you ever think about what you want to do with your life?"

When I finally open my mouth to say something, probably some joke to stop this conversation, Ricardo puts his hands up. "I'm not going to lecture you about college or your choices or anything. I just mean . . . did you have dreams you wanted to fulfill when you were younger?"

Younger. Weird idea to me. I don't feel young anymore, even though I'm seventeen. Still a teenager, but . . . I feel like I'm a hundred.

I try, for the sake of Ricardo's interest. But . . . there's nothing there. Wasn't thinking of jobs as we bounced from one foster home to another. No careers. No plans to start a family. No desire to get married. All of that was for other people, not someone like me. I just wanted to get out on my own.

Then Reconciliation happened.

"I don't think so," I say, and as the words leave my mouth, I can see that it's not what Ricardo wanted to hear. It's in the way he looks away. The silence that falls. The gap between us.

So I press on. Give him a little more.

"It's just that . . . it was hard for me to imagine those things when I was younger. We didn't really have those sort of options. I just had to do my best to get through each day."

He nods, and a warmth returns to his eyes. I'm thankful that Monica returns then, because the timing is perfect. Ricardo looks somewhat satisfied, and he reaches out and places a hand on my left shoulder. Squeezes it.

"Carlos is getting something to drink," she says.

"That seems like a bad idea," Ricardo offers. "Given how frequently we have to stop for him."

"At least he's hydrated?" Monica says, shrugging. She glances over at me. "Everything okay?"

"Just talking to Manny about his future," he says before I can answer. "That's all."

"Your future?" Monica narrows her eyes at me. "Are you leaving us soon?"

Yes, I think. *I have to.*

"No, not like that," I say. "I'm staying for now."

"Well, we like having you around," she says, smiling. "All of us, even if Carlos doesn't make that obvious."

"He just deeply dislikes everything and everyone right now," Ricardo adds. "Equal opportunity hater."

"It's the whole college thing, I think," says Monica, and she runs her hand up and down her husband's arm. "My theory is he's acting out because he's about to be very, very far away from us when he goes to college next year."

My skin bristles. "Where's he going?"

"Either M.I.T. or Carnegie Mellon!" Ricardo says proudly. "He wanted to go somewhere for computer engineering, and he managed to get into both of his top schools."

They both are beaming at this. I can't blame them. Those sound like important schools. I don't know anything about them, but . . . they're far away, apparently. Far from here. Far from this van.

Far from you.

I have no part in this. I am nowhere in this future, am I? There's no way these people will want me sticking around once their son is gone. What then? What am I supposed to do?

Ricardo heads inside the travel center to check on Carlos and Monica asks me to watch the van as she goes after him.

And I know that I only have a tiny window of opportunity.

They won't miss me. Not really.

I hop back into the van through the side door. Open the console in the center between the front seats. Dig around and pull out what I can. At first, it's too many bills. I put some back until I'm holding five twenties. $100. That should get me through a week or so.

I shove aside the voice telling me not to do this because the other voice is louder. *There is no future here.* I have to leave. It's time. If I don't do this now, it will only get more awkward in the future.

I can't let them know what I did, how I ruined everything already.

I climb into the back row of seats and grab my duffel bag, which I had forgot to close up. I zip it shut. Close the doors to the van—don't want anyone else stealing shit from the Varelas—and start walking away from it as quick as I can. I avoid the entrance and veer to the left, cutting through the bays where the regular cars are getting gas. Head to the far end of the massive parking lot.

There are a few semitrucks parked along a chain-link fence.

Some use this space to rest. Take mandated breaks. Sleep. Call friends and family back home from the road. Wait for repairs or their turn in the travel center's showers.

It's one of the only things close to a certainty. I can find someone, slip them some money that might get them some food or a longer shower. I get to ride in the cab, get to a new city, start over.

I am a blank slate. Empty. Hollow. It's best that way. Erase erase erase.

Always easier than the alternative.

Three semis sit side by side. Two red. One bright blue. I don't see any truckers lingering by them. Don't want to risk pounding on a door and frightening anyone. Found out the hard way once when I had a shotgun pointed at my face.

I glance behind me. There's only one other semi refueling.

Shit. Not many options. Soon, the Varelas are going to come out. Realize I'm gone. That some of the money is missing.

And I don't wanna be around for that.

Can't let panic overwhelm me. There are other gas stations nearby; we passed a few once we got off the highway. I've done this before, and sometimes it takes a day or two to find a person willing to take me on.

I don't have a day or two to get out of here, though. So I double back, then cut to the left to stick close to the building.

But then I see him: Carlos. He's still got his headphones on, and he's walking *back* toward the travel center. I curse and duck down behind a dumpster before he sees me.

Shit shit shit.

"¿Necesitas ayuda, joven?"

I look up. There's an older man there, his skin brown like mine, wrinkles around his eyes and forehead, a thick mustache sitting over his mouth. His stubble is white and gray, and his face is shadowed by a cowboy hat.

He looks like he could be my grandfather.

Another fantasy. I wonder if other people like me—orphans and foster kids and the adopted—do this, too.

But then I remember there's no one like me.

I stay crouched and shake my head. "No, señor," I say, and my tongue sticks to the roof of my mouth. Spanish still doesn't feel comfortable. Had to learn it to survive, but it's a clumsy thing. An approximation. A part of me is thrilled, though: He *thought* I was just like him. But he makes that face—the same one Ricardo wore a few minutes ago—and I know he's disappointed in me.

A fantasy. That's all this is.

But the man doesn't leave. He removes his hat, and his thin gray hairs are pressed down against his scalp. "You don't look fine," he says, his accent thick, heavy. "Te escondes."

Takes a moment for the word to filter through my brain.

Hiding.

You're hiding yourself.

I frown. Watch as Carlos heads back to the van. When I think I'm clear, I rise up. Dart over to the red pickup truck next to me and hide behind it.

The man *still* hasn't left.

He stands at the front bumper. Staring.

"Estoy bien," I say, annoyed. Is he one of *those* men? The ones who see boys like me and try to act out their own fantasies?

He doesn't budge.

"Adios," I add.

"Te escondes detrás de mi coche."

I wince. Look down at the truck, then back at him.

"This is yours," I say.

He chuckles. "Sí."

Then:

"¿Necesitas ayuda?"

I see them: Ricardo and Monica. Heading to the van.

They'll know soon.

"I just need to get somewhere," I say quickly, my voice low. I grimace, because I should be using Spanish. "Necesito . . . necesito llegar al sur."

"¿El sur?" He rubs at his stubble. "¿Dónde vives?"

Fuck.

"No tengo . . . casa." I pause. No, that's not how you say that. "Estoy sin hogar."

His eyes go wide. He gets it now.

I've seen this too often. People don't expect someone as young as me to say they're homeless. I'm used to it. The shock, the condescending offers for help, the backhanded advice, the way adults sometimes do things just to make themselves feel better.

But this man isn't moving. Doesn't push me out of his way and leave. Doesn't ask a thousand invasive questions. Doesn't treat me like a charity case. He puts his tan cowboy hat back on his head.

"Vámanos," he says. "I can drive you."

I give the van a quick glance.

And I think Carlos is staring right at me.

"Okay," I say, and I move. Round the back of the truck and make for the passenger door. Open it, jump in, stuff my duffel at my feet. His car smells sweet, like cinnamon. There's a deodorizer hanging from the mirror. The Virgin Mary. The leather on the seats is worn and split in a few places. Cozy.

He starts the truck, then points at my feet. "¿Eso es todo?"

"Es todo," I say, nodding.

He gives me a concerned look. Or maybe it's pity. I have to look pitiful right now, all my belongings in one bag, hiding from someone, hopping in a stranger's car.

But that's good. If he feels sorry for me, maybe I can use that for a while.

As he's reversing, he sighs. "Lo siento. No AC." Then he rolls the window down.

"Está bien," I say, then point at myself. "No car."

He laughs at that, his mouth open wide. I see silver-capped teeth. Remember a woman named Em. She helped me once. She was nice.

I hope this man is nice.

He drives. Past the semi pumps. Past the van.

Carlos steps out the side door. Looks around.

Sees me. His mouth drops open, and I turn my head away.

We leave the travel center. Head left. There are more gas stations. Fast-food restaurants. A Denny's. We hook another left, cross over the 5. We wait at a light to join the cars rushing south.

He sticks his hand out in front of me.

"Guillermo," he says.

I take it. His hands are rough and callused. He squeezes, but not too hard. Doesn't linger.

"Manny," I say.

We head south in silence.

It took me nearly a year to break one of the rules that Cesar taught me.

Ironically, it's how I ended up with the Varelas.

I was in Bakersfield, a hot armpit of a city. Big place. Felt like another planet at times. I don't remember how I got there. Have forgotten so many of the trips along the way. They blend all together most of the time.

But not him.

I was leaning against the side of a gas station, watching a family get out of a station wagon. I hadn't been there long; maybe a few hours. But the sight of them tripped me up. I'd gotten good at hiding in plain sight, just like Cesar had taught me. And yet . . . the image of them was so unfamiliar to me. Not because I hadn't seen it before. I see it everywhere. More because the experience is something I've never known.

Two parents. Three kids. They all looked similar in that way that people take for granted. The younger boy was practically a copy of his mother. He argued with the older brother, and the daughter—she looked like the middle child—was totally uninterested in everything. She busted out a jump rope and started jumping behind the bumper of the car.

Do other kids like me do this? Watch a family exist and ache for it to be their life?

I was so focused on the family—the oldest son was trying to grab hold of the gas pump while his dad was using it—that I didn't notice the man staring.

Cesar told me that when the voice in my mind starts screaming—tells me to abandon ship, to get out, to get away—that I need to listen to it. Things will never go well when I ignore it.

I felt it first. You develop that sense, too, because you have to. I slowly looked up.

He had on dirty jeans that rested on brown cowboy boots. They came to a point on the end. Dusty, too. His pudgy stomach strained the light blue button-up shirt. Long, graying beard. Sunburned face.

He examined me.

"Hi," I said.

He stared some more. The thought appeared: *He is undressing you.*

It felt so extreme at the time. So irrational.

So I just looked away.

And he didn't budge.

"You need anything?" he asked.

There was a drawl to his voice, his vowels drawn out.

I swallowed. "What?"

"You by yourself?"

"Clearly."

"You got somewhere you need to be?"

I walked away without a word, slinging my duffel bag behind me. This wasn't a surprise. Men did this sometimes. Talked to me like that, like they were trying to be all fatherly. It didn't work on me.

Or, rather, it wasn't *supposed* to. As I headed toward the front door of the gas station, I heard his footsteps.

He was following me.

"I guess that's a yes," he called out.

I didn't say anything. Kept walking.

"You don't need to be afraid. I won't hurt you."

I shouldn't have taken the bait. Should have ran away.

Instead, I turned quickly.

"That isn't as comforting as you think it is," I snarled.

"It's the truth," he said, spreading his arms out in front of him.

"I don't know you at all."

"No, you don't." He grinned. "But I know *you*."

"Come *on*," I said. "You can't possibly *not* know how creepy that sounds."

He shook his head. "I mean kids *like* you. Who eat like they don't know where their next meal is coming from. Who cower when people come near them."

I snorted. "You don't know a thing about me."

Started to walk across the parking lot. His pointy boots clacked on the cement behind me.

"Hold on, that's not what I meant!" he yelled. "I spend a lot of time on the road, so I see a lot of kids like you."

"I doubt that."

"Strays. Abandoned. Forgotten."

I stopped just past one of the pumps and groaned. "I'm not a dog."

He took advantage of the pause and suddenly, he was there, right in front of me. "The name's Stan," he said, and he stuck his hand out. "I'm not trying to intimidate you or anything, but if you need help, I can give it."

"No."

"So you're just going to wait here and . . . what? Hope someone else comes along?"

"Sure," I said, then shifted my duffel to the other shoulder.

He threw his hands up. "Suit yourself, then."

"Why do you even want to help me?"

"These are trying times, brother," he said. "I'm just doing my part."

I twisted my face up. What was with this guy?

He saw that look. "Just tell me where you need to go," he said, then pointed behind him. "I got a big one over there. State-of-the-art cab. Freshly laundered sheets and blanket. For however long you need it."

I pressed my lips together. Hated that I was considering this. This never happened this easily. I always had to pursue a ride; it never *came* to me.

But . . .

No. Don't.

But I didn't want to be there. I didn't like Bakersfield or the heat or the way the people there stared at me as I waited outside the gas station. I had to leave.

I thought that I could just ride with him for a few hours. Get what I needed. Then get out.

"North," I said. "I need to go north."

"Just north?" Stan ran his hand through his long beard. "No specific place?"

"Never mind, then," I said, and I turned away, but he leapt forward. Grabbed my arm firmly. With purpose.

"I can do that!" he said. "Sorry, I just was asking for clarification."

I yanked my arm free from his grasp. Should have left then and there, in that very moment where he revealed exactly who he was. Someone who would hold onto a child like that.

But I broke the rule.

I was desperate, and I ignored the chorus of voices screaming in my mind.

"Let me show you," he said, then stepped away from me as if to give me space. "If you don't like it or don't feel comfortable, we can just go our separate ways."

No. No, I shouldn't do this.

I followed Stan.

He led me to a semi with a bright blue cab. Climbed up and unlocked the passenger door. Hopped back down.

"Air conditioned," he said. "Sleeping area behind the two front seats. You've seen a cab before, yes?"

I nodded.

"Well, this was just updated last year. New upholstery. Better padding. You'll be impressed, I know it."

But I didn't check it out. I gazed up at his sunburned face.

"What do you want from me?"

"Nothing."

"People always want something. It's weird to me that you *don't*."

"I'm not like other people."

Go. Run away.

The heat bore down on the back of my neck.

I reached up. Hoisted myself up. Peered inside. Even with the truck off, I was hit with cool air. Felt so good on my sweaty face.

That's all it took.

Air conditioning.

"Fine," I said.

I saw Stan grin as I swung my leg in, set my bag on my lap, and he closed the door, then dashed around the cab to his side.

I knew I shouldn't be doing this.

I did it anyway.

The AC blasted me in the face as we pulled out of the gas station. Wasn't sure if I believed in God or god or anything, but someone created air conditioning, and they were absolutely holy in my mind.

I sent that thought out, a prayer of sorts to the patron god of homeless boys riding in trucks with strangers. *Keep me in close proximity to an AC unit. Get me safely to my next destination. Some food would be nice, too.*

I didn't speak as Stan drove, at least not for the first fifteen minutes or so. Stan was right; his cab *was* much nicer than any of the others I'd been in. I peeked behind the curtain he'd installed to separate the main area from the sleeping bunk. Also much bigger than I had expected. Smelled good, too.

You never know what you get. Some guys are extremely neat and hygienic. Most aren't. Lots of smells can develop while sitting in a truck for hours. They fade into the background if you're used to them. I've ditched rides early because of the stench.

I let the silence grow. Put my bag at my feet. Watched as Stan reached into a bag of sunflower seeds in the middle console. He kept doing this thing where he split the shell with his teeth, perfectly spat it out, then ate the seed. It was seamless. Kinda mesmerizing.

We cruised along.

"So where are you from?" he asked, then tossed another seed into his open mouth. "I assume you don't live around here."

The rules: Don't tell anyone the truth. Give as little as possible. Cesar said it's because most people don't want the truth, but you also don't want to give anyone ammunition to use against you.

I altered his rule. First time I was in Nevada, I watched the slot machines in some shitty roadside diner. They blew my mind. A game that always cost money to play and rarely gave you that money back.

I have one of those in my mind. When a question comes up, I flick the lever. Pieces fall into place. Reels spin. I let it happen. I pick things at random.

"Hemet," I said. "At least that's where the foster home was."

"A foster kid, huh?" He shook his head. "Met a lot of y'all on the road." He grunted. "Most have been thrown out."

"Yeah," I said.

"Is that your story?"

Lie lie lie lie lie.

"Yeah," I answered, then added: "It's a rough system."

He nodded, his eyes still on the road. "So what was it? Drugs? Disobedience? You fall in love with someone or something? Or ran away because you couldn't stand it? I hear that one a lot."

His questions were daggers, each of them piercing a different part of me. Presumptuous. So I went for mystery rather than let him get to me.

"It just didn't work out."

We fell silent again.

And then I couldn't resist myself.

"So . . . you pick up a lot of kids?"

"I do what I can," he said. Then dug in the bag of seeds. Popped one in his mouth. Crunched. Spat.

Over and over again.

"So how did you get to Bakersfield?"

I got why he was curious. They all are. Sometimes, leaning into the mystery pushes them away just enough; they feel too awkward to pry. But most people want all the details. They want to know how I survived. They want to be part of the story.

But the more questions a person asks, the more lies I have to tell.

"A family," I lied. "They were coming from east of here."

I gazed out the window, hoping he got the picture.

"It's all desert east of here," he said. "California desert is beautiful. Haunting, too. I'm from down in Blythe. You know where that is?"

I shook my head.

"It's down south, out near Arizona. Doesn't look a whole lot different than this." He gestured at the monotonous landscape around us. "Less hills, though."

"I heard it's prettier up north."

"Definitely. Some places are harder to drive. Smaller highways, too many narrow mountain passes. I like driving in the wide-open desert."

Pop. Crunch. Spit.

"What's your name?"

I decided to give him that. Maybe he'd shut up.

"Manny."

"How old are you?"

My skin prickled. I didn't look at him. Regretted giving him my name instantly. "Nineteen. Just turned it last month."

"You look pretty young for nineteen."

"I get that a lot."

"But that means you're an adult, and you get to make your own decisions."

Goose bumps rose all over me again. I didn't like the way he said that. We crawled along the highway, stuck in a patch of traffic, and I couldn't say anything. The air was on, but I was sweating.

And Cesar's rule came back to me then.

My body had told me to get away from this man.

I tensed up.

Stan shifted in his seat. Took his right hand off the wheel. Reached across that space and put it on my left leg.

I didn't move at first. Couldn't. Didn't know what I was supposed to do. He wasn't the first man to make moves on me, but this had never happened *inside* a cab.

He moved his thumb back and forth over the denim of my jeans.

There was no oxygen in that truck. His touch was a terrible electricity, and I shuddered when he moved it higher.

Stan jerked his hand back. "You okay, Manny?"

"Sorry, I just . . ." I swallowed hard. "I just feel tired, that's all."

"It happens, kid," he said. "Why don't you head into the back and get some sleep?"

It could have been an escape from his wandering hand, but I worried about feeling trapped. "Nah," I said. "I'll get through it."

He started talking. I didn't hear the words.

Because his hand was back on my leg.

He moved his hand higher.

I twisted away, crossing my left leg over my right.

He brought his hand back to the steering wheel.

I thought he finally got the hint. For the next hour, he didn't touch me. Kept his eye on the slow-moving traffic. I was turned almost completely sideways, my eyes searching for any sign to read and keep myself occupied, distracted.

Keeping the rage at bay.

There's very little good in the world, at least when you're like me. Yes, people have done nice things. But they come with restrictions, with strings attached, with a price to pay. If it's not the pity or the sympathy, then others see me as a piece of their puzzle. A means to an end. A way for them to achieve a prize in their afterlife. A thing they can control because they know, deep down, that no one actually cares about me.

I could disappear tomorrow.

(I *have* disappeared on people. I do all the time.)

And no one would try to find me.

That's a sobering thought. No one is looking for me. They never will.

The traffic crawled. I did actually think of jumping at one point when we came to a stop. But we were on a stretch of the 99 with nothing on either side of the highway. Nowhere to go in the most literal interpretation of that phrase: no home, no family, but also, there was nowhere to walk to. No gas stations or restaurants or diners or strip malls. Just . . . dirt.

I folded into myself. Deeper. Deeper. Counted the threads coming loose on my duffel bag. Then I counted the billboards until I reached eight. Hoped a half hour had passed by.

Been only five minutes.

I was pouring sweat. Under my arms, my crotch, down my temples. It was boiling. I glanced over at the dash console.

"Had to turn it off," Stan said. "Sorry about that. Didn't top off in Bakersfield, so I don't want to put a strain on anything."

I struggled to keep my eyes open. A headache brewed as a dull pain behind my eyes.

I shouldn't have done this. Shouldn't have taken the risk.

"You can head in the back for a nap," he said.

I shook my head. Blinked. Started dozing off again.

Truthfully, I don't sleep as much as I should. Hard to find a consistent place. Even if I do, I don't sleep in or sleep late. I'm always up and gone or being useful before anyone else.

One of those rules, you know.

But then I thought: Sleep will pass the time. He needs to get fuel. You can leave at the next stop. Thank Stan for his help. Never see him again.

"Yeah," I said. "I should get some rest."

I popped off my seat belt. Grabbed my duffel.

"You can leave that up here," he said.

My response was immediate. "No. I like keeping it with me."

Stan's face fell.

I realized he probably thought I was insulting him. Insinuating something terrible.

(I was.)

"I've lost my stuff too many times," I added. "Just a habit."

He smiled.

I pushed myself up. Started to move to the back. He reached out to me. Thought he meant to help me.

I twisted out of the way of that, too.

The back sleeper cab smelled as sweet as the front. Stan kept it clean. There was a stack of blankets, pillows, and towels on the floor behind his seat. The shades on the two small windows were pulled up. Thankfully, it wasn't as warm back there.

"Not bad, right?" Stan called out.

The cushioning was firm. I kicked off my shoes and stretched out.

"Yeah," I said. "It's nice."

I picked up a pillow. Grabbed a blanket from the top of the pile. Smelled like floral detergent. I curled up under it, and even though I shouldn't have been there, my body let itself go.

I fell asleep quickly.

In the back of Stan's cab, I dreamed.

I was in the Greene house. San Bernardino. Elena and I were there back when I was eight. It was the longest we spent in a single location. Two years. The Greenes were the only foster parents I liked. Or maybe I was just too naïve to notice anything to dislike about them, but I suspect that isn't the case. Elena liked them, too. Robert was Black, and Junie was Korean. I remember how surprised I was when I moved in because . . . well, almost all my foster parents had been white. All the parents I knew through kids in school were always the same race. And yet here was a married couple who looked utterly unlike every other one I'd ever seen.

I dreamed of his breakfasts. He loved making waffles, and it's where I developed my obsession with them. Twice a week—Thursdays and Sundays—Robert made a plate stacked high with them, gave us butter, syrup, and jams to spread on them, and his were perfect. Crispy on the outside, soft on the inside. Seasoned with a bit of vanilla. He ate his with just butter and a cup of coffee (splash of oat milk inside). Junie piled eggs and bacon on top of hers, poured syrup over the whole thing, then drizzled gochujang at the end.

In my dream, Elena and I were at the table. Eating. Every time I took a waffle, a new one would appear and replace it. But I couldn't get full. I couldn't satiate my hunger. So I kept eating them, one after another, and every waffle made their smiles bigger and bigger until it began to tear their faces apart.

And I ate another.

Another.

Another.

I sensed something.

Deep from my slumber, I felt a presence. In my dream first, looming over me as I devoured another waffle, gazing to Elena, desperate for her to tell me to stop. It was a shadowy figure with impossibly long arms, and they bent over, bringing themselves closer and closer.

I stirred.

Then I smelled him.

I was in darkness. Could hear the hum of the engines. It was cold, so the AC must have been turned on.

I shivered, pulled the blanket tighter over me. Opened my eyes.

And he was there, just feet from me, staring.

I froze. Couldn't move a muscle. He stared at my legs, curled up underneath the blanket, and I watched as he lifted a hand. Hovered it over my leg.

He didn't touch me. Pulled back. Moved back to the front cab, and the curtain fell closed behind him.

I breathed out slowly so that he wouldn't hear me. My whole body was rigid in terror.

We started moving again a minute later.

"You awake back there?"

The light spilled through a gap that he left in the curtain, and it fell over my legs, and I shuddered. Once. Twice.

I had to get out of this cab.

"How long has it been?" I asked, my own voice rough from sleep.

"Just a couple hours," he said. "There was an accident north of us, so we've been at a complete standstill for almost an hour. Just now getting back up to speed, and I didn't have the heart to wake you up."

Nausea tore at my stomach. How long had he been watching me?

"I have to pee," I said.

"You're in luck," said Stan, and his face loomed in the sleeper cab. "I'm at another travel center. Do you need any snacks? Any more water? I can pick it up while you're in the bathroom."

An opportunity had presented itself.

So I took it.

"Yeah," I said, then scooted forward. "Yeah, I should probably eat something soon."

"A burger? A sub? This place has some pretty good chili cheese fries, actually."

"Fries," I answered. Forced myself to look him in the eyes. Smiled. Like so many things, it was a lie. A necessary one, of course.

But they're all necessary to me.

He reached over with his left hand. Placed it just above my knee. Squeezed. "Anything for you," he said, then smiled.

He thought he was being warm, but his touch chilled me.

"I'm glad you decided to come with me."

I wanted to shove him out of the way. Kick him in the dick and escape. Instead, I put my hand on top of his.

"Me, too," I said.

Lie lie lie lie lie.

He let go and turned to get out of the cab. I grabbed my duffel and slid into the passenger seat, then flung the door open. Hot, dry air rushed in, and as I swung my legs out, I could tell it was late in the afternoon.

Stan was right there. "Here, lemme help," he said, then he grabbed my free hand, and his was clammy and wet, and somehow, *that* was the thing that undid me.

I had to get away from that man. Immediately.

Yet I refrained from sprinting off. I let him guide me down and then shut the door behind me. We were near a couple of other semis, and the massive travel center loomed ahead of me. Otherwise, it looked the same as the last one, from the expansive parking lot to the endless expanse of land around it.

The cars zipped by on the nearby highway. If we were in Fresno, then Fresno must not be very big. Or maybe we're just outside of it. Either way, it was clear: There was nowhere to go.

Fuck. How the fuck was I going to get away from Stan?

Didn't matter. I had to try. Couldn't be in his presence one more minute.

"You can leave your bag here," Stan said, then tapped the side of his truck. "I'll lock it up."

I clutched the duffel to my chest.

"Right, right," he said. "You have a thing."

Good. He remembered.

He held out a hand, gesturing toward the travel center. I started walking.

And he reached down.

Grazed my hand with his fingers.

I wanted to scream. To gouge his eyes out. To break every one of his sweaty fucking fingers.

I glanced around, tried to see if there was anyone else I could hitch a ride with.

There were only a few families. Guess Fresno wasn't a big travel destination. Four trucks in total were in the diesel fueling lanes, so perhaps there was a chance there.

Or not.

Because all around the center was ... dirty. Dry shrubbery. More dirt.

Shit. I didn't like this.

Stan held the door for me, and the cool air hit me in the face. *Focus*, I told myself. *You have to figure this out.*

"I'll meet you here at the entrance when you're done, okay?" he said.

"Gimme a few minutes," I said.

"You don't need me to come with you?"

A spike of fear jolted my heart. "No, no," I said, but then I saw the disappointment hit his face.

He's going to follow me in there, isn't he?

So I added a new layer.

A new lie.

"You'll still be here when I get out, right?"

It had just the right amount of innocent. Just the right amount of terror and potential disappointment.

He caressed the side of my face. "No, Manny," he said. "No, I won't leave you like the others."

I granted him one last thing he wanted:

A smile.

Big and wide and completely untrue.

I dashed off to the right. Saw a glass door that led to some sort of restaurant. Fast food, maybe. I hooked a left down a long hallway with multiple doors on either side. There was a small medical clinic, as well as a laundry facility and showers, and then I found the men's room and ducked inside, and I couldn't breathe. Could barely get the stall open, could barely lock it behind me.

I had to get out of this place.

But I had no phone. No other means of travel. And now, no place to hide.

I wondered if I should just suck it up. Go with him. Let him touch me and lurch at me and insinuate all that weird daddy shit that he thought was hot but just made me want to shove him into oncoming traffic.

No.

No, I couldn't do that.

I unlocked the stall. Pushed past a group of rowdy teenage boys who were just coming in. One of them hissed something at me.

Pretty sure it was a slur, but I couldn't care. Didn't really hear it. Used to things whispered as I pass by. Used to stares and names and things muttered under someone's breath like a curse.

At the end of the hallway, I chose not to head into the store toward Stan, but to try my chances in the fast-food joint. I shoved open the glass door, and the smell of fried food and oil made my mouth water. It was much more populated in here. There was a small family to my left who all turned to look at me as I came in. I ignored them. Headed to the counter. Looked up at the menu, then gazed around me to case the options.

A lone man with a cowboy hat behind me at a table, chewing with his mouth open. He glared at me once he realized I was looking his way.

Two young women. Maybe a few years older than me. Both with blond highlights streaked in brunette hair. They looked like they were in college. Would they listen to someone like me? Help me in a time of need? Maybe. But I had never traveled with people that young.

Didn't think it was worth the chance. So I looked to others: the middle-age men in three-piece suits.

Nah. What the hell were men like that doing here?

The family with four kids, two who were toddlers.

No. Too risky, too chaotic.

An elderly couple walked in the far set of doors. No. Never. Wouldn't happen.

"Do you know what you want?"

I turned back to the counter. A woman with thick brown curls smiled at me. Her voice had a little twang in it.

I reached into my front left pocket. Still had some bills crumpled up in there, but wasn't sure I had time. Any second, Stan could walk in, and I didn't know what I'd do then.

"If you need a moment, could you step aside?" the woman behind the counter asked. She wasn't rude about it, and her smile seemed genuine, but it shattered my confidence. I had no idea what I was doing.

I didn't say anything. I turned around, past the rows of booths and tables behind me, and I instead headed toward the family in the back, curled myself into the booth opposite them, my back to the glass door behind me, my duffel at my feet.

I glanced at them. Three of them. They kinda looked like me. Brown skin, dark hair. The father and the son were bulky. Looked like they worked out or maybe played football or something. The mom was gorgeous, with curly hair in ringlets that bounced as she chewed.

A mom, a dad, a son.

The envy raged. Why wasn't that me? Why didn't I get something like that?

I looked away from them. Buried my face in my arms. Tried to make myself as small as possible.

I heard the door to the restaurant open.

Heard boots on tile.

I stilled, my heart racing.

The boots moved away, and I raised my head up. Risked a look behind.

He wasn't there.

I caught them looking, though. All three of them were staring at me.

Shit.

His voice echoed over.

"I'm sorry to bother you," Stan said, "but I'm looking for my nephew. I think he ran in here. Have you seen him? Short Hispanic boy, about five-foot-five, shaved head?"

My eyes went wide.

And they all saw.

I slid farther down in my seat. Refused to look back. Maybe he wouldn't notice me. Maybe he would go search for me elsewhere.

There was a squeaking sound. A sneaker on tile.

The man sat down across from me. The man from the family. He was clearly much taller than I was, because even sitting down, he towered over me.

The first thing that struck me—aside from the boldness of what he was doing—was that he smelled nice. He was wearing something that had a floral scent to it. His hair was curly, too, but in a different way. Maybe more wavy than curly.

"You don't have to say anything," the man said. "Just nod."

What?

"Is that man trying to take you away from here?"

That man?

Oh.

I didn't hesitate. I nodded at him.

"Tell me your name," he demanded.

I grimaced.

"I promise, we won't hurt you," he said. "Just tell me your name and play along."

"Manny," I blurted out in a whisper.

The man smiled again. And unlike Stan's smile, it *actually* felt warm. "I'm Ricardo," he said. "I'm sorry if this is going to be uncomfortable."

And then he reached over and grabbed me by the forearm. "Manny!" he said loudly. "Oh, it's been so long since we've seen you!"

I didn't know what to do. My mouth dropped open.

"Where have you been traveling these days?"

"I—uh . . ." The words sputtered out. They felt uneven on my tongue. "I came from Bakersfield. And . . . other places before that."

Surely not my finest work, but Ricardo seemed unfazed by it

all. "That's amazing, man. I'm so glad you're getting out in the world!"

"Manny?"

I gazed into Ricardo's soulful eyes. Couldn't bring myself to look at Stan, but I saw his boots out of the corner of my eye.

"Let's go, Manny," Stan said.

His fingers looped around my upper arm.

And just like that, Ricardo stood up. "Excuse me, sir, but who are you?"

"Who are *you*?" Stan shot back.

Ricardo gestured at his family. "We met Manny years and years ago. Just happened to run into him here. And he was telling us about maybe traveling with us again."

"Was he now?"

I could feel Stan's eyes burning into me.

"That true, Manny?" he said. "I thought we were traveling together."

I wrenched my arm out of his disgusting grasp. "I'm good," I said, fixing a murderous gaze his way.

Stan frowned. Stepped away. Glanced at the others at the table across the way. And without another word, he bolted, his stupid fucking boots clacking on the tile.

Long ago, I learned to hide it all. To never reveal desperation, to never reveal vulnerability, to never reveal my truth. Cesar taught me that. He was right. It has served me time and time again.

And yet, I erupted into tears of relief as soon as Stan was gone. Rested my head on the table and just cried, ignored the burning shame that appeared then, too, because I should not have allowed myself to get emotional in front of these strangers.

I lifted my head. Saw that Ricardo was staring at me, not with annoyance, not in irritation, but . . .

It was like he'd seen this before.

"You can stay here as long as you need," he said. "Get a meal. It's on us."

"Thank you," I said between sniffles.

"If you need a ride . . ."

He paused. Glanced over at his wife and son.

"We can take you where you need to go. Where do you need to go, Manny?"

I don't think Guillermo is like Stan.

His energy is different, first of all. He doesn't leer. What little he says is always laced with a distant sadness, as if there's more to share, but he can't bear to do it. I wonder if his sadness is a reaction to me. I have that effect sometimes.

It's like the world's shittiest superpower.

But his questions are gentle. I don't know why, but they seem more genuine, too. When he asks where I'm from, I tell him I don't know. Instead of arguing or pressing further, he nods his head. Says, "Es así."

It's like that.

It is a simple but effective answer.

He then starts talking. Softly at first, in short sentences, switching between English and Spanish. Says that he came to this country thirty years ago. Left what remained of his family behind. He'd lost a lot of people over the years, so it was just him now. He lived in Ripon—about three hours south—with a bunch of other workers, all of whom escaped life in Mexico, Guatemala, and El Salvador, who were trying to earn what they could and send money back home to support the rest of their families.

"Most of the time, estoy solo," he says. "Like . . . like you."

He isn't wrong, but I don't know how he knows that. Perhaps I'm simply *that* obvious.

Because I have been alone for a long, long time. Over a year now. Am I *still* alone? Am I venturing south and pursuing a pointless end? Is she already dead?

Are you?

The silence returns. I try to remember her face. I can see the images from Deacon's videos, but most days, that is not enough. I am forgetting how she sounds. What she smells like. How her hair falls over her face. The cadence of her words. The memories are distant. Hazy.

I need to see her.

I need to know if she remembers me, too, if she still recalls how I talk with my hands, how I love corn roasted over a fire with butter and lime juice, how I am quick with a joke.

Was.

I don't think I'm all that funny anymore.

We go an hour without speaking before Guillermo reaches over. I assume the worst—my mind goes back to Stan again—and jerk away from him. But he merely opens the glovebox with a gentle hand.

It's full. Candies and granola bars and other treats.

"Toma uno," he says.

I pull out a wrapped candy that's shaped like a small puck. There's a red rose on the wrapper.

"Mazapán," Guillermo says.

I shake my head. Never seen it.

"¿Nunca lo has tenido?"

Never. I know that word. I can guess what the rest means.

"No. Never."

"Ohhh," he says. Draws the sound out, then grins. "It's very good. Pruébalo."

I unwrap it. Take a bite. It crumbles when I hold it too hard. But the taste is sweet. Like almonds.

"It *is* good," I say.

"Yo comía eso," he says. "When I was a kid. I always keep some around for . . . for the bad days."

A burst of envy strikes me. I immediately shove it away. Compartmentalize it. If I let myself go every time I felt that kind of jealousy, I couldn't function. The truth is that I don't have those kind of memories. My childhood between all the various foster homes is one enormous blur, and honestly? I'd like to keep it that way.

I finish off the Mazapán, and then Guillermo holds out his hand. I put the wrapper in it, and he stuffs it into a bag in the side of the door.

"¿Puedo preguntarte algo?"

He grips the steering wheel tightly.

"Sure," I say.

"¿Qué pasó?" He blurts it out instantly, then twists the steering wheel cover again and again.

"What happened?" I repeat back to him in English. "With what?"

I know what he means, though. It's what everyone wants to ultimately know about me. It's almost like they can't help themselves.

"Why are you here?" he asks after a moment of hesitation.

"Porque me ofreciste un paseo," I say. I'm not trying to be smart, but then he laughs. Hard.

Good. Means my Spanish was decent. Means I can continue to disarm him.

"Sí, sí," he says. "Yo sé eso. Pero . . . you were in the middle of nowhere. Hiding."

I sigh.

I have to tell him something. Offer him just enough to keep him from asking more.

And a story is better than nothing, even if it is just a story and not reality.

"I've been on my own for a while," I say. "Don't have anyone."

Is it her?

"What about your parents?"

I think: *I don't have any.*

Then: *You used to.*

The edge of the abyss flares.

"They gave me up," I say.

I didn't know until later that they'd been in contact with Elena for months.

She found out about Christ's Dominion through the Internet. YouTube or something. We weren't really the church-going types. I mean . . . it was hard to keep that up. We bounced around a lot. Some families made us go to church with them, others didn't care what we did with our free time.

Guess I was surprised that Elena was into anything spiritual or religious. She never spoke about it before she started showing me those videos on her old tablet a few months before they came for us. The videos . . . they didn't mean anything to me. It was just something she was into. Spent a lot of time watching them. That's all. Nothing more.

Until it wasn't.

We'd always had each other. Elena was a year and a half older, and somehow, through all the chaos, we were always kept together. It was her, honestly. She fought for it. But as stringent as she was about this, she dedicated an equal amount of energy to a fantasy:

She thought we'd still get adopted.

I remember saying that we were ancient. Kids as old as us don't get adopted. No one wants teenagers who have spent their entire lives in the system. Parents always want younger kids, ones who are more malleable. It's a way for the adults to feel like they made an actual difference in some kid's life.

Not us. One of our guardians—a woman in Moreno Valley named Jaclyn, whose breath smelled like wet dogs, who chain-smoked on the back porch at night, who never seemed all that interested in raising us for the year that she had us—spelled it out for me.

"You're already set in your ways," she explained. "Where's the fun in being a parent to that?"

So it was just me and Elena. Biological siblings, always handed out as a unit, always returned as a unit.

I looked up to her in a way. Her positivity frustrated me some days, but there were times I respected it, I guess. She was so steadfast. I didn't see myself that way. Everything was a joke or a dark thought, and maybe that's because she somehow got all the good parts of being a person from our biological parents (whoever they were) and I got none of them.

So sometimes I was hard on her, but . . . she was my sister. She loved me. I complained while going along with whatever she wanted, but . . . I wouldn't have had it any other way.

Just me and Elena. Nothing else mattered to me.

Until they showed up and took us away.

If I'd been paying attention, I would have noticed that Elena was already being changed.

We were living in Riverside at the time. Apparently, there was an actual river somewhere in the city. Don't know where. Never saw it. We were in the part of town ringed by these enormous hills that towered over the dingy apartment complex our foster parents lived in. Sam and Gertrude. Those were their names. Don't even remember their last ones. We'd been there about six months, and most days, I really only saw one of them. Gertrude was a nurse, I think. Or maybe she worked in a retirement home. Or both. She was older, too, and when we first met her, I whispered to Elena that it didn't seem likely she'd be alive long enough to stay our guardian.

She had smacked me on the arm. Told me to stop being so mean all the time. "They're trying," she said.

I didn't think they were. On the whole they were better than some of our previous guardians. Worse than most of them, though. There's a stereotype that a lot of foster parents are only in it for the money that they get from the government. It's not really true, but with Sam and Gertrude . . . yeah, it actually felt that way.

I went to yet another new school while we were with them. La Sierra High. It felt as big and sprawling as the city of Riverside. I got lost a lot in those initial weeks. No one talked to me, but that wasn't out of the norm for me. I usually kept one of my earbuds in, music blaring fast and loud on a shitty MP3 player while I drifted through classes, barely paying attention to anything. I'd gotten it and the earbuds as a Christmas gift from Silvia one year, and I think she found it at the swap meet in the old drive-in in San Bernardino. It worked. I used library computers—either at school or a public branch—to download songs and stick 'em on there. It was enough to get by.

We didn't have phones. Not enough stability to have them, and the foster system wasn't going to get them for us, either. Don't remember when I lost the earbuds and the MP3 player.

So we made the best of our circumstances more often than not. Usually within a year, we'd move somewhere else. My life was impermanence. The only constant was . . . Elena. I don't know how, but she seemed to always excel wherever we were. Top grades. Occasionally, she'd join a sport or one of those extracurricular clubs they advertise all over campus with cheesy posters, and then, when we inevitably moved on, people would be gutted to see her go. They'd beg her to stay. We couldn't control that, of course.

But I never forgot that no one seemed to miss me. Never seemed to want *me* to stay. At the same time, I didn't really try to *make* friends. I might get to know some punk kid every once in a while, but I mostly stuck close to Elena.

She tried to get me involved. Tried to get me to make friends.

I don't know that I ever told her that I appreciated that. All these years, and she could have just given up on me, but she didn't. She always fought for me. Always tried to include me. Always tried breaking through my darkness.

And then she stopped.

She started disappearing a few months into the school year. At first, she would ask me if it was okay if I walked home alone. I assumed she'd found some new club to be in that kept her around until long after school ended. I liked being by myself, and I had walked to whatever foster home we lived in plenty of times before. We shared a room in Gertrude and Sam's apartment, so I used the solitude to sit at our shared desk to do homework.

But then Elena came home later and later. Sometimes, Sam—who worked as a mechanic—would come home with bad Mexican takeout. Ask where my sister was. I'd shrug because I didn't actually know. He'd scowl at me, then disappear into the living room, leaving the soggy tacos on the counter. I'd pick through them. Wonder when Elena would come home.

I thought maybe there was a guy. Maybe after all this time, she was the first of us to fall for someone. She was seventeen after all. I knew she liked boys because we *both* did. We sometimes compared crushes, but we never really entertained the notion of a serious relationship. Still, it wasn't unrealistic that someone had caught her eye.

And when she *was* around, she was . . . secretive. Constantly distracted. If I asked her where she'd been, she'd laugh. Tell me it wasn't a big deal. Just after-school clubs and stuff.

Until eight or nine at night? *Every* day?

She also constantly asked to use the house computer after her tablet died on her. Gertrude wasn't too happy about that; she liked to spend long hours on forums and on Twitter arguing about whatever terrible TV show she watched. But Elena convinced her it was for schoolwork, and Gertrude couldn't argue with that.

I stayed up late one night. Snuck out of our shared room. Peeked around a corner to see what Elena was doing.

They were YouTube videos of a man on a stage. Talking. He sat there, in between some other people, moved his arms about wildly. The camera cut to a close-up. Blond hair. Piercing blue eyes. Elena had headphones on, so I couldn't tell what he was saying.

I didn't understand any of it, so I wrote it off as a weird obsession of hers. Maybe she'd found a bunch of self-help videos, and that's why she'd been even more cheerful than usual.

But then, a week later, Elena didn't come home from school. It was a Thursday night. Sam had left some fast-food burgers behind before he went drinking with his friends. Gertrude was on the computer. I paced our bedroom, waiting for her. Wishing I had a phone. Wishing she'd walk through the doors and apologize because she'd had a wild day, but she was back, and everything was fine.

I ended up passing out from exhaustion.

She wasn't in her bed when I woke up.

And she wasn't at school the next day, either. I probably should have told someone, but who? Who would have even cared about us? Gertrude or Sam? They barely spoke to us most days.

Friday passed. So did Saturday. No Elena.

It was the single longest period of time we'd been apart. We had spent practically every waking day alongside each other for as long as I could remember, and I had no idea what to do when she wasn't around. We had no contingencies, no plans if we ever got separated because . . .

Well, we never *had*. It was always Elena and Manny.

I brimmed with anxiety. Walked from the apartment to the Galleria at Tyler, the big, ostentatious mall that didn't feel like it belonged in a city like this. Paced from one side to the other, buying nothing except a smoothie. Watched the other families. Other kids my age. All the people who seemed to have such full and busy lives and probably weren't worrying about where their missing sister was.

I walked the four miles back to Gertrude and Sam's. Neither of them were home, and I scrounged up some stale cereal in the pantry.

Couldn't even finish it.

Elena strolled back into our room on Sunday evening. I remember leaping up. Grabbing her. Hugging her, then realizing she *smelled* different.

I backed up. Saw that she wasn't wearing the same clothes as she had been on Thursday when we walked to school together. She had on a new shirt. New jean shorts. New shoes.

"Where have you been?" I whispered harshly.

She shook her head as if my question was absurd. "Don't worry about it," she said. "I've just been . . . out."

"Out *where*? I haven't seen you in days!"

Elena caressed my face.

Then sat down at our desk. Put her backpack aside. Pulled out some homework and started working on it.

All like nothing had happened.

Still, I didn't worry like I should have. Elena was seventeen. Why shouldn't she have her own life outside mine? She probably had friends. A boyfriend. Something like that, you know?

Maybe she was finally growing away from me.

I wondered a lot those days what she would do when she graduated a year ahead of me. Would she go off to college? Leave me behind? Leave me in foster care?

I thought to ask her.

But she seemed so *happy*.

She didn't disappear on me like that again.

Instead, she asked me if I wanted to live with another family.

It was a Saturday. Late in the morning. Gertrude was getting ready for a shift at the hospital and puttering around the kitchen, mumbling to herself as if we weren't around. I'd made Elena and myself some waffles, and once Gertrude scuttled back to the main bedroom, Elena nudged me.

"Let's go somewhere else," she said, her eyes alight with joy.

I shook my head. "Not today," I said. "I'm going to that backyard show, remember?"

I had been craving it: the anonymity of a punk show. The energy. The way I could lose myself in the crowd, in the distorted rage.

She smiled ear to ear. "No, that's not what I mean. Somewhere away from *her*."

Elena gestured toward the back bedroom with her head.

"What's that supposed to mean?" I asked, then shoveled more waffle in my mouth.

"Do you ever want to live with just *one* family?"

I rolled my eyes. "Sure, but . . . if it hasn't happened yet, then it's never going to."

"Well, not with that attitude," she shot back, and her face soured. "If you have hope, God will reward you."

"God?" I scoffed. "Didn't take you for the religious sort."

Her frown grew. "There's a lot about me you don't know."

She pulled away. I felt the chasm widen.

And the pit in my stomach grew then. That was the first moment. Deep down, I knew *something* wasn't right. Plenty of foster kids I'd met over the years were religious. I didn't have anything against that. But the two of us . . . it just never worked out. Elena and I didn't talk of God. Guess I assumed that like me, he didn't really fit in her life.

So why then? Why did she suddenly speak about God with such certainty?

Because they'd already gotten to her.

It was too late, and I hadn't even known it was happening.

"Gave you up?" Guillermo crinkles his forehead. "Cómo . . . they abandoned you? As a baby?"

I don't answer him. I am not sure he would believe what happened, but even if he would . . . the story is too long. Too hard.

He shifts in his seat. "Did they . . ."

He presses his lips together.

"¿Te dejaron . . . ?"

"No, no," I say quickly. "No, this happened a long time ago."

"So . . . that is why you are with me."

I guess. I have no plan. Just a desire to get to her, to find out the truth.

"Yes," I say. "I don't have anyone else."

And I don't know why, but in that moment, I take a risk.

I tell him a truth.

"I'm trying to find someone."

"¿Quién?"

I hesitate. "Mi hermana."

Guillermo nods as if this makes sense to him. "It is good to find family. Does she love you?"

"She did," I say. It isn't a lie. I know that what she chose to do was out of love, even if that love was corrupted. "I don't know if she does anymore. I hope so."

"Will you . . . ?" He struggles with the words again. "¿Estarás seguro con ella?"

He won't believe the truth.

So I tell him a lie.

"I've always been safe with her."

His mouth twists to the side. "I wish I could take you to her. The whole way."

"No te preocupes," I say. I probably should be using the formal conjugation, since he's an elder to me, but I feel too comfortable for that. "Whatever you can do, it will help."

"Tengo que trabajar en Stockton," he says, as if I know where that place is.

"Okay. Stockton is fine."

He resumes his silence. Stares ahead. Grips the wheel at ten and twelve.

I question why people help me all the time. I have to. So many of them have ulterior motives, have terrible reasons for performing kindness. My doubt is a shield. A weapon.

But I question Guillermo because he seems *kind*, not nice. It is easy to play at niceness. It is not so easy to reveal kindness to others. I don't see that often. Maybe from Em. Cesar. The Varelas.

And now this stranger, who gave me a ride, who speaks delicately and with purpose, who keeps glancing over at me every few minutes as if I'll disappear if he doesn't check to see that I am there.

"Can I ask you something?" I say.

He nods. "Por supuesto."

"¿Por qué me ayudas?"

He does not answer. Not at first, that is. He taps on the steering wheel, his eyes focused on the increased traffic on the 5. He merges to the right-hand lane, lets a bunch of cars pass him.

"Perdóname, Manny. Pero . . . es difícil decirlo en inglés."

"In Spanish, then. I'll try my best."

He smiles again. Flashes those teeth.

"La gente cómo nosotros . . . necesitamos estar juntos."

I know some of those words. "People like us . . ." I begin.

His face lights up. He briefly lets go of the wheel, uses his knees to keep the truck steady. Then he links his hands together.

"We need to be together."

"Together?"

"It is . . . hard," he continues. "To be here. In America. Y es importante cuidar de nuestra gente."

He pauses.

"Were your parents white?"

His question sends a jolt through me. "What?"

"It's okay," he says, lifting his right hand in a gesture of innocence. "I was curious."

I swallow hard. Reach over and open his glove box, then pull out a granola bar. As I'm chewing on a bite, I nod. "Yes," I say, trying to push the nerves away. "Yes, they were. How can you tell?"

"Conozco a un chico como tú. You . . . you seem like him."

I am not sure how he knows so easily.

No.

That's not true.

I always feel like it is obvious that most of my foster parents have been white. It's not just the language barrier, though that's a big one. There was a Mexican kid at La Sierra High who once told me that he knew my parents were white because of how I acted. How I shrunk away from everything. How English sounded on my tongue. How little I knew about the world around me.

Even now, however many hundreds of miles from the Sullivans I was, how far I was from all the white foster parents I'd had, I was still defined by them.

"You still have time," Guillermo says.

"Time for what?"

"To discover who you are," he says. "To discover where you came from. Your parents . . . they don't have to be the end."

The end. I like that idea. I am not sure I know how I would even begin to pursue that, though. Because I don't know my beginning, either. All of it is a mystery.

All I ever had was Elena. And as we cruise down the 5, I think about asking Guillermo where Idyllwild is. I think about how much easier my life would be if I had a phone, something with GPS on it. I think about how everything would be different if I had an ID card. A birth certificate. Something to prove that yes, I am a person in this world.

Maybe Guillermo is right. Maybe I can figure out who I am. But it's just a fantasy to me. Because I'm not anyone to this world anymore, so . . . where would I start?

"Gracias por ayudarme," I tell Guillermo softly. He does not know that it is one of the first sentences I learned in Spanish after they abandoned me.

Shit. My first sentence in another language was about other people.

His eyes are soft when he glances at me again. "De nada," he says, so quiet it is almost a whisper.

He drives.

I gaze out the window.

Maybe people are not all bad.

I think it's hard for me to accept that because . . . well, practically every person I've spent time with has revealed some terrible ulterior motive in dealing with me. Especially after the Sullivans . . . but then there *was* Cesar. The few hours I spent with him in Las Cruces helped me to survive to *this* moment.

And the Varelas. I was with them for weeks. Never treated me with anything but kindness. Which really doesn't make sense. What did they get out of it? Why help someone who can't ever give anything back?

And now . . . Guillermo.

He goes silent for long stretches during the two and a half hours that I'm with him. Then he starts talking away, telling me more about what his life has been like these past thirty years. Like the man he worked for in Santa Nella, who worked him and his friends for thirteen, fourteen hours a day, paid them all under the table, then threw his workers under the bus when his farm got raided. Guillermo barely escaped Immigration that time, so now he keeps moving. Rarely establishes roots. Has to always be prepared to pack it all to leave again.

I tap my duffel bag with my foot. "Yo también," I say.

He gives another one of those smiles. The ones that feel like he truly gets me.

I don't know why my luck has turned. Two nice people in a row. Maybe that just means something terrible is going to happen.

We're on the highway for a bit more before the sign for Stockton appears. Population 307,000. Okay, so not a small town, but not a big city. Guillermo passes through all of it, then goes another ten miles or so before he exits the 5, then navigates to yet another gas station off a small local road. It's not as busy as the last one we were at, but it'll do.

He turns off his truck in the parking lot. "Lo siento. Tengo que dejarte aquí."

I shake my head. "Don't apologize." I reach down and grab my duffel. "You helped me. A *lot*. Gracias, Guillermo."

He points through the windshield at a tiny window in the side of the building, near the front door. "El autobús para ahí. Greyhound."

I see a few people sitting on the ground near the window, their bags and suitcases scattered around.

"Puedes comprar un boleto. Usualmente son baratos. Maybe . . . Maybe that can get you to her."

"Maybe," I say.

"¿Dónde está ella?"

"Idyllwild."

He scrunches his face. "Eso está muy lejos."

Far. It's very far.

Fucking great.

"I'll find a way," I say.

"It's south of here," he says. "South of Los Angeles."

Then he reaches in his front pocket. Extends his hand toward me. I can see the wrinkled hundred-dollar bill there.

"No," I say. "No, I can't take that."

"Tómalo, mijo," he says. "Tú lo necesitas más que yo."

I shake my head. "I can't, Guillermo. That's too much."

His eyebrows arch. Pity floods his face.

I know I can't be too picky when I have almost nothing to my name. So I take the bill, and guilt rages as I stuff it next to the twenties I lifted from the Varelas. Turns out I would have been fine without stealing from them.

I'm not a good person.

But I can't really afford to be.

"Thank you," I say softly.

"Don't give up," he says to me, but he's not looking in my direction. He stares out the windshield.

I don't know what he's thinking of, but the moment is too intimate. I shouldn't be here. So I open the passenger door. Hop out with my bag. Thank him again before shutting the door and leaving him behind.

I look back once.

As he's pulling away, I think he's crying.

Maybe we're all more alone than I thought.

I mill about near the Greyhound window. Not sure I should do this. I don't take buses. Usually it's because I don't have the money or an ID. Guillermo is only partially right; they are cheap most of the time, but when you buy things last minute, the price shoots up. Makes no sense to me. Still the same seat, still the same destination.

So I usually hitchhike. Truckers are my go-to, both for work and a ride. Been hired to help unload in places. Other times I just ride along. Met a guy named Bert—never knew his last name, which is how I like it—out in Arizona. He was the one who got me to California. We were together for weeks. Up and down the state, out into Nevada, then up the 95 into eastern Oregon. Was pretty over there, but I didn't feel safe. Lots of weird people in that part of the state, many who don't care for brown dudes like me.

I keep moving. I keep an eye out. I keep myself first.

But maybe this bus will get me there. Back to her.

Is that what I want to do? Maybe this was too impulsive, even for someone like me. Despite that my brain keeps needling at me, insisting that it's her body, I don't even know if she's there. If she's with *them*. What if she left? What if I travel south and find Reconciliation and she's been long gone?

Is that better or worse than being dead?

You know who they found.

The other terror rears its head again:

What if she doesn't want you?

I swat it away. No. Can't even entertain it.

I walk over to the window, but stop short of it. There's a schedule posted next to the window. Not many departures or arrivals
during the day. I look at the destinations. Did I expect to know
what cities and towns these were? Apparently. We're in Stockton.
There's Manteca. Modesto. Turlock. Delhi. Livingston. Atwater.
Fergus.

Fergus? Who names a city that?

I see Los Angeles as the end destination for this route, but I
need Idyllwild.

The window opens. "You need a ticket?"

There's a blond woman with flashy eyeshadow on smiling at me.
She's got a matching set of dangling earrings. Red hearts. They're
cute.

"Gimme a second," I say, and I'm flustered. Can feel frustration
building in me. I walk away from the window, my duffel over my
shoulder.

I should have stayed with Guillermo.

No.

I should have stayed with the Varelas.

Why did I make this choice? Why did I think I had to leave?

Because this is what I do. I was abandoned. So now I abandon
others. No sense getting close to anyone.

So why am I allowing myself to think I can find her?

I don't know what I want anymore.

Yes. Yes, you do. You know exactly what you want.

I do know what I want. I know it is impossible, but I still
desire it.

Why not now? Why not try?

I turn back. Make for the window. I have at least $200 on me.
Should be enough to get me *somewhere*. And in the meantime, I
could come up with a plan, some way to find her. To find myself.
To find the truth.

I tap on the window with the back of my hand. The same woman opens it. "Can I help you, hon?"

"Uh . . . I need to get somewhere," I say.

"Okay."

She waits.

Oh, right, she's waiting for me.

"Uh . . . Idyllwild?"

She looks away, types something into the computer in front of her. "Do you know the zip code?"

"I don't," I say. "I just know it's in the mountains."

"Lots of places are in the mountains," she says, still staring at her screen.

Types some more.

"We don't have a direct service to Idyllwild," she says. "Best I could do is . . . three, maybe four transfers, and that will get you to either Palm Springs or Banning, and then you'd have to find local or connecting service there."

Man. Sometimes people speak with words I know separately, but together it sounds like some weird ritual spell or something.

"So . . . how would I do that?"

"Do which part?"

"Find the connecting service."

She finally looks over to me. "Sorry, hon. I can only do so much from this computer. You have someone you could call once you're there?"

I don't even own a phone, much less have any person on the planet I could call. "No, not really."

She sighs, but I don't think she's annoyed with me. It's that other emotion I know well.

Pity.

I always see it. Pity. People pity me. Which is fine for them, but pity often doesn't do anything for me but make this shit worse.

"Well," she continues, "a one-way trip from here to Banning would run you $188 before tax and fees, so you're looking at probably close to two hundred. If we do Palm Springs, that's an even $205, and $219 with taxes and fees. Both buses have transfers in Bakersfield and in Los Angeles. The bus leaves at 6:25 a.m. tomorrow."

My head spins. Don't even process that time because . . . almost $220? "For a bus?"

Too late, I realize I said that last part out loud.

"For a bus," she says, raising an eyebrow. "It's a long, long trip. You could cut down on the time by taking Greyhound to a city with an Amtrak connection, maybe think about Metrolink, too, but I'm not sure they go out as far as you—"

I hold up a hand. "It's okay. I'll think of something. Thank you, though."

She eyes me up and down. "No problem. Have a good day, hon."

The window is closed.

I head to the side of the building with the most shade. It's baking out here. Making it hard to think. I plop down. Rest my head against the wall behind me.

I don't know what I'm doing.

I've been here so many times before, though. Shouldn't be so hard on myself. Always find a way out. But this time . . . it grates on me.

Maybe it's because this is the first time I have an actual destination.

I'm good at wandering. Going where the flow takes me. But now . . . south. I need to go south. And the universe has no interest in letting that happen.

A car pulls away from a pump. Turns and parks at the front of the store. I watch a woman get out of the passenger seat clutching a book. She's tiny. Mousy. Older than me, but much smaller. Her sandy blond hair is pulled back in a ponytail. Has thin-framed glasses.

She walks up to me, and I'm ashamed I didn't recognize her earlier.

Don't know her. Never seen her. But I know her type. They're everywhere.

"Good morning, young man," she says, and she does that smile that white people do where they press their mouth flat, don't show their teeth. Do they all learn that shit somewhere? "Can I sit with you?"

"No," I say. "I'm busy."

She stills. Then shifts her weight from one foot to the other.

"It will just take a moment to—"

"You're wasting your time," I snap.

"God's time is never wasted," she offers, then crouches down. "Do you need His help? Is there anything I can do?"

Smile. A sarcastic thing, not a genuine one.

"Sure, you can."

Her green eyes light up.

"Give me a thousand dollars."

Those same eyes go wide.

"Better yet, take me to Los Angeles. Or Idyllwild, more specifically. Buy me food. Buy me a house! Never had one of those. You got any extra?"

She stands up. "I'm sorry. That's not what I meant."

"I know," I say. "That's why you're wasting your time."

Can tell she wasn't expecting this answer. Wasn't prepared for it. Maybe I'm being too mean, but her timing couldn't be worse.

"I'll pray for you."

"Please don't."

"God loves you very much."

She practically whispers it.

I rise suddenly. She rears back.

"I very much doubt that," I say. "He didn't care to save me when I needed him. The thousands upon millions of times I asked him for help, he ignored me. So I really don't think your fucking prayer is going to help me at all."

"You don't know that."

"Why would he listen to *you* about my life but not *me*?"

"The Lord works in mysterious ways," she says, nodding.

"Well, could he stop being such a fucking mystery to me?"

I say that too loud. Too harsh. Shame hits me. Does she even know what she's saying? Or is she merely repeating what she's been taught?

Shit.

She reminds me of Elena.

She's backing away. Turns away from me and bolts to the car. When she's in the passenger seat, she doesn't look at me. Keeps her head down. The driver—a young man who looks like he might be her older brother—is saying something to her, but I can't watch them anymore. I don't care.

I'm hungry. Thirsty. Pissed off. Embarrassed. My nerves frayed. Probably shouldn't have yelled at her, but I don't like people who offer prayers and nothing else. I don't even really have anything against them. It's just that . . . God can't be listening to us all. And he's certainly not going to listen to me. It makes people uncomfortable when I say something like that, because I think prayer is a balm for them. A form of meditation. It relaxes them. I don't want to take that away from anyone, but someone *offering* prayer? Does nothing for me. Ever.

Keep it to yourself.

Inside the gas station, I browse the aisles. I want a meal. They don't have those here. Sure, they've got burritos and taquitos that have been sitting under heat lamps for god knows how long. Hot coffee that's probably watered down. I see a case of donuts. But I want a meal.

I had those with the Varelas.

Damn it, what have I *done*?

I swing my duffel bag behind me. Head to the aisle with snacks and grab some trail mix. Don't feel like something super fried or salty at the moment, but I need to get food in my stomach soon.

After paying, I head back outside. Find the shade on the side of the building not facing the sun. Slump against the wall and slide down. Eat a few handfuls of granola and nuts, and just like that, my appetite is gone.

I've made a mistake. A huge one.

No way to get to Idyllwild. Still don't even know where it is. I left a good thing to chase after this impossibility, knowing full well I can't actually go back there, that I can't return to Deacon and the Sullivans and to Elena. They didn't choose me. Who do I think I am, believing something different?

A shadow falls over me.

"Manny?"

My heart skips.

Eyes go up.

And I'm looking directly at Carlos.

"Say something," Carlos says, and his words have a sharp edge to them.

How? *How?*

"Why are you here?" I ask.

Carlos *scowls* at me. Says nothing. Reaches down and yanks my duffel bag toward him. He kneels down, then peels it open.

Sitting on top of my belongings is his tablet.

"*This* is why, asshole," he sneers. "I tossed this in the backseat when I went into the gas station, and I guess it fell in your bag."

"Oh, Jesus," I say, and I'm trying to push myself up, but he shoves me back down.

"Why did you just *disappear?*" he screams. "What's wrong with you?"

This time, I manage to get upright. "I'm sorry," I say. "I—I can't—"

Ugh, I just want to disappear. But instead of answering his question, I furrow my brow. "Wait, that still doesn't explain how you found me."

Carlos gives me a vengeful stare. Flicks on the tablet. Swipes a few times, then shows me the screen.

It's a map. There's a blue dot blinking in the center of it.

Fuck. Tracking. He always knew where it was.

"The tablet has cell service," he says. "So we've been chasing you down the freeway to get it, and we've been driving in the wrong direction for *hours* now."

His face is twisted up. I'm sure he hates me.

"I'm really sorry, Carlos," I say. "I promise. I never would have left if I'd known your tablet was in there."

"But if it wasn't? Then what? Would you have left then?"

My mouth drops open, but nothing comes out.

"I can't believe you," he says, and he storms off, his tablet in hand. I'm standing there as he rounds the corner, then calls out, "He's back here!"

A few seconds, I see the others:

Ricardo.

Monica.

"Hi, Manny," Ricardo says. He has his eyebrow raised. Monica won't even look at me.

Shame burns my face. I hate this. I've done something terrible to some of the only people who have been genuinely nice to me. I'm in debt to them, too, because of what they've had to do to get Carlos's tablet back.

Debt twists people up. Makes them think weird shit about who you are as a person. I made that mistake early on outside Las Cruces, despite that Cesar had warned me to borrow nothing. I met a woman named Joana at a job I picked up bagging groceries for eight bucks an hour. I wanted to get a hostel for a few days to have a bed to sleep on because I was tired of collecting old cardboard from behind the store to fashion a mattress. Joana was my only friend there, and she wore these big hoops in her ears. I remember her hair was bleached from all the time she spent under the sun.

I borrowed a few hundred dollars from her. And when I didn't pay her back in a week, she lied to our boss at the supermarket, and I got fired. Don't even remember what the lie was. But the whole thing made no sense to me. How was I gonna pay her back without a job? Didn't she want the money?

And now I owe these people. They've driven a couple hundred miles out of their way, and I can't do anything about it.

"Manny . . ." Monica says.

Her voice is gentle, but heartbroken.

Fuck.

They hate me. How could they *not*? I ruined their trip. Stole their son's tablet. Wasn't even on purpose, but does that matter? Panic ripples over my skin. Heat in my face. Fear in my gut.

I brace for the worst.

"What's going on with you?" asks Ricardo, looking down at me. "I know you weren't with us for long, but you'd never done something that . . . *impulsive*."

"I'm sorry," I say. "Didn't know his tablet was in there."

"It's a genuine mistake," says Monica. It surprises me. I expected coldness, not . . . this. She reaches over. Runs her hand up and down my arm. Sends chills.

I flinch.

She backs off, but continues talking. "And we just want to understand more than anything. Is everything all right? Is there something we can help with?"

I glance from one of them to the other. Wait for a raised hand or a sharp lashing of the tongue.

"You know we like having you around," says Ricardo. "You're not a detriment or a burden; you aren't diverting us from anything."

"Except I just did," I say softly.

"Okay, yes, in a literal sense," he says, grinning. "And it was an accident. We can accept that. But . . . why? We just want to know *why*."

I can't speak at first. Don't get it. Why aren't they angry? Shouting? Telling me how awful I am? I ruined their whole day. It's been hours since I left them, since I fucked everything up.

But they just look at me. Expectantly. No anger, no rage in their faces.

"I can't," I say. Soft. Quiet. Like I'm invisible and I'll startle them if they hear me.

"Can't what?" says Monica.

"Can't tell you. Any of it."

"What happened before, you mean," says Ricardo. He rubs at the stubble on his chin. "Is it because you're unsafe?"

I shake my head.

The abyss is awakening. Growing. Gnawing at the edge.

Don't. Tell no one.

Lie lie lie lie lie.

"Not unsafe."

"Then what?" asks Monica.

The image flares in my mind.

The forest.

The prayers.

The moment of separation.

"I don't belong here," I say. "Or back there. Or anywhere."

"I'm sorry you feel that way," says Ricardo. "Does it help you to hear that we think you belong with us? That you're supposed to be here?"

"Supposed to?" I shake my head. "That can't be true."

"I think so," he says.

I look to Monica.

She smiles. "My husband is a lot more . . . spiritual than I am. I don't know that I believe in anything like destiny or fate. What I know is what I feel, and I feel good having you around, Manny. So does Ricardo. So does Carlos."

I scoff. "There's no way he does. I stole his tablet."

"And I'm sure he'll get over it," Ricardo says quickly. "I don't believe that he thinks you did anything on purpose."

"So . . . what now?" I say. "Are you inviting me back?"

They both hesitate. Glance at each other. I think, *This is it. They're going to leave me here.*

Because everyone always leaves me.

"I would like to redirect that question," says Monica. "Manny, are you trying to head to somewhere specific?"

My heart thumps. "What?"

"You are going south," she says. "And in the four weeks you've been with us, you've never once picked a direction. Never once asked us to go anywhere. And then, after freaking out over a news program this morning, you ditch us, hop in a truck with a stranger, and start heading south."

My face burns. "Shit. You figured all that out already?"

"Well, not exactly," says Ricardo. "It's more that . . . well, we'll tell you. We'll trade. One day, when you're ready to share more, we'll tell you why we're on the road, too."

"And until then . . . yes, please, travel with us," says Monica, her face soft, gentle. "No strings attached. No caveats. As far as we're concerned, all is forgiven."

I don't want to press the issue with Carlos because I'm convinced it won't be that easy with him. But then I'm thinking of Guillermo, about how he told me that my parents didn't have to be the end.

The Sullivans can be something else.

It is a wild, terrifying thought. But standing before the Varelas, a light of hope ignites in me. I have never been shown this kind of grace before.

Maybe they *actually* mean it.

"Okay," I say. "Thank you. And I'm sorry. I won't do that again."

Both of them are all smiles, and Monica asks for a hug. I let her embrace me, and it feels good to have someone want to touch me. But then I pull away. Something is burning in me.

A possibility.

"Idyllwild," I say. Soft at first, then again, louder. "Idyllwild."

"You mentioned that earlier," says Ricardo. "Is that where you were headed?"

I nod.

"What's in Idyllwild?" Monica asks.

I breathe deep.

And I tell the truth.

"I think that's where my sister is."

I'm sitting in the back row of the van. Monica and Ricardo are up front, and Carlos is leaning his back against the side window, his legs stretched out over the seat. Still isn't looking at me. There's silence, because they're waiting. Waiting for me to start. Waiting for me to say something.

They just told Carlos that their itinerary is changing. They're not heading up the coast. We're not turning around. We're going south. Carlos pouted. Demanded to know why.

I don't know where to begin. Don't know how to do this. Don't know how to talk about what I've been hiding ever since it happened.

I regret it. I regret telling them even a shred of the truth about Elena. It's pointless. They can't do anything. I can't, either. What made me think I could go back there and face what was done to me? To face *him*?

Sitting in that van, a thought occurs to me. The door is open, and a cool breeze wafts in. If someone passed by and glanced in, to that outsider, I would look like I fit here. I resemble these people enough. We've all got the same shade of brown skin. Black hair. My nose is pretty similar to Monica's. They might assume we're a family.

It's just a fantasy, though. A fantasy I once had when I first met them.

But Elena . . . she *is* my family, isn't she? I used to hate that word, but now that I don't have anything, I crave it. I had long accepted that I'd given up on her because . . . well, I had to. She gave me away. Chose Deacon Thompson. And I needed to let go to survive.

But what if I don't have to? What if there's something more out there?

What if it's her?

"I have a sister," I finally say. Practically blurt it out, and Carlos actually jerks away before staring at me, his brows furrowed together.

"A sister," he says, his voice in an even tone.

I nod.

"Would you tell us her name?" Monica asks softly.

I gulp.

Then utter the name I haven't said aloud in the last year.

"Elena," I say. "My sister's name is Elena."

I watch Carlos look to his parents. Ricardo nods. I don't know what just transpired, but Carlos turns back.

"I didn't realize you had a sister. Where is she?"

"I think she's in Idyllwild," I say.

"Idyllwild." He repeats the word. Raises an eyebrow. Then raises both as his eyes go wide. "Idyllwild. Oh, *shit.*"

"Carlos!" says Monica, and she reaches over and gently smacks his leg. "Why are you reacting like that? What have we taught you?"

Taught you? What does *that* mean?

"Mami, I'm sorry, but . . ." Carlos gazes back at me. "That news story. Idyllwild. Is *that* where she is?"

He pauses.

And for the first time since I've joined them, Carlos looks at me . . . differently. It isn't pity. Not really sadness.

It's more like . . . like he can finally see me.

"Do you think it's *her*?" he asks softly.

His parents are reacting. Demanding to know what he's talking about, what he meant, but my mind reels. Spins. I'm sitting down, but it's like I'm afloat. Drifting. Anchorless.

Am I doing this?

Is this happening?

Carlos touches me. It's a brief thing. Just puts a hand on my shoulder. "Hey, Manny, I'm sorry for reacting like that."

He jerks his hand away. "Sorry, I should have asked, too. Is it okay if I touch you?"

Heat flares in my face. "Yeah," I say.

And he puts his hand back on my shoulder. "I didn't mean to come on so strong. You don't have to tell us anything. But . . . I'm right, aren't I? About that broadcast?"

Still can't form words. His hand feels so heavy on my shoulder.

And it feels so good.

I nod at him.

"Can Carlos tell us about the broadcast?" Monica asks. "All we know is that you saw something on the news that triggered you. You don't have to relive it if you don't want to."

But what she doesn't know is that I relive it every day. I try to shove it down, I try to forget, but how can you forget an experience like that? How can you forget that kind of abandonment? That kind of damage?

I close my eyes.

Lean my head back.

Start talking.

"I saw a story on the news," I say, and the words are so clumsy in my mouth, but I have to keep going. "About . . . about where I came from."

"Where you came from?" Ricardo rests his chin in his hand. "What do you mean by that?"

I gulp down the rising fear.

I'm doing this, aren't I?

"Before," I say. "Before I was on my own, I went to this . . . thing. It was a part of my parents' church."

Terror climbs up my throat.

"Christ's Dominion."

Monica frowns, presses her lips together. "Why does that sound familiar?"

"Mom," Carlos chides gently, then squeezes my shoulder.

She raises her hands up in concession. "You're right. Continue, Manny."

But how?

How do I tell them what they did to us?

What they did to *me*?

I can't tell them everything.

So I keep it light. Stick to the bones of the story.

Elena and I were in foster care all our lives, depended only on each other—but then she met Caroline, the woman who manages the YouTube for a group called Christ's Dominion. And then there was the offer—Caroline would take her in, she'd always wanted a daughter. It was Elena's dream, to finally be part of some huge family, but I couldn't just let her go without me.

The adoption happened. And then they sent me to Reconciliation when they decided I needed to be saved, long after Elena already had been. It was supposed to be a chance for me to make friends, to learn to believe. And once I was there . . . well, it was pretty bad, in the end. It was good until it wasn't, and it became so very quickly.

So they cast me out.

I pause on that one. It sounds a little too passive. The reality is much worse, much more violent. But I can't tell them *all* of the truth. And how it still hurts to think about it.

So.

"She chose them," I say.

Carlos fidgets in his seat.

"She chose them," I repeat, quieter, because the reality is settling in.

Elena had said that I would never accept her. Those people. That place. It just couldn't happen.

So she chose them.

Carlos's hand is still on my shoulder. He squeezes it. Lets go.

Then he stares at his parents. They're communicating like this again, and I still can't penetrate what it means.

"When you say that they cast you out, what do you mean?" Ricardo asks. I can tell he's trying to be delicate about it. He clearly wants to know more, but he doesn't want to push too far.

I'm not ready for that part.

I shake my head. "It's not important," I say. "But I've been on my own since then. Never knew where Reconciliation even was, and never knew what happened to Elena. Until . . ."

This time, I glance at Carlos. Nod my head slightly, granting him permission to finish.

"There was a story on the news this morning," he says. "About a property owned by Christ's Dominion in Idyllwild."

He hesitates.

It's not even his story, and he doesn't want to say it aloud.

I wonder if he now knows how hard this is for me.

"They found a body near it."

They look away. All of them. It's so synchronized that I actually laugh. A nervous thing at first, and then it spills into a manic burst of elation and terror. I double over in the backseat. They're so perfect as a family, so completely all on the same page, and I can't believe I am here.

God, I will never belong with these people.

"Are you okay?" Carlos asks. "That seems like the least funny thing I've ever said. Easily."

"Sorry," I say, sitting back upright. "But all three of you turned away at the exact moment and—"

They're staring at me. Confusion on their faces.

"Never mind," I say. "I'm mentally ill, that's all you need to know."

"Whatever," says Carlos, scowling. "But . . . can we talk about this? Do you think that's *her*?"

Well, that moment didn't last long. I come crashing back down to reality. Right. We're talking about my possibly dead sister.

"I don't know," I say. "But . . . well, you know Deacon makes videos, right?"

Monica snaps her fingers. "That's why I knew the name," she says. "I've used some of his videos before."

"Used them?" I grimace at her. "For what?"

"One thing at a time," says Ricardo. "What about the videos, Manny?"

I make a mental note to bring that up again, because I want to know what Monica was talking about. "He has a whole You-Tube channel. That's how Elena found him and the Sullivans initially. And he does these updates from the compound. Films them inside the lodge. And . . . well, Elena hasn't been in one for a while."

The silence is painful. Because now I'm seeing them put together what is already a possibility for me.

She might be dead.

That might be her body.

"Jesus," mutters Ricardo.

"Doubt he has much to do with this," I say.

Carlos actually chuckles. "Man, you're kinda funny, Manny. Who knew?"

"Carlos," Monica says, her voice a warning.

"What? He never talks. How was I supposed to know he got jokes?"

She rolls her eyes. "Manny, thank you for sharing that with us," she says, and her gaze is kind. "I know it's scary telling a bunch of people something like that, especially since we're practically strangers."

"Not strangers," I say. "I mean, I know a little bit about you."

"A very little bit," Carlos says softly.

"And we will share more about us if Manny wants to know more," Monica says quickly. "But for now, this is about *him* and what he wants to do."

"It's okay," I say. "I mean . . . it's not like we can do anything."

"Not with that kind of attitude!" Ricardo says brightly. "Besides, this is kinda what we do anyway. Travel around. Help people. See where life takes us."

I highly doubt that helping people involves finding a religious sect's secret compound and determining whether someone's sister is alive or dead, but I don't say that. I curl up. Bring my knees to my chest.

"I don't know," I say. "It's too much."

"Mami, Jamal can wait," says Carlos. "We know where he is. We know he's safe. Can we find Elena first?"

"Jamal? Who's Jamal?" I ask.

"An old friend of mine," he says. "It's not important. It's just . . . I didn't know that's what you've been dealing with this whole time. You never asked us for anything, and you could have."

I'm not so sure of that. No one helps me like *this*. Why would I have thought the Varelas are any different?

I don't know what to say to him. Or to any of them. There's a part of me that's relieved to have said *something*. I don't know that I feel better. Or lighter. They still don't know the whole truth.

"Honey," says Monica. "You gotta stop with the guilty puppy dog thing."

"Huh?"

"That thing you do with your face," says Carlos. "Like . . . your eyes get all sad and you look like you've disappeared inside your head."

Shit. Guess I am more obvious than I thought I was. If it's not one thing, it's another. Another sign I don't belong.

"So . . . what would you like to do first?" Ricardo asks.

"First?" I say. "No, there's no first. We shouldn't do anything. We *can't* do anything."

"And we don't have to," says Monica. "Need I remind you, Ricardo, that we can't force people to do what they don't want to? Especially in matters like this?"

"Okay, the whole mystery thing y'all are doing?" I say. "You have to stop. What the hell do you keep referencing? What is a 'matter like this'? Who's Jamal? Why are you traveling around in this van?"

"Wow, someone's got a lot of questions now," Carlos says, smirking.

"Shush, Carlos," says his dad. "Monica, it's late in the afternoon. We can't reliably get anywhere today, so let's travel tomorrow and get a motel tonight."

She sighs. "Yes, of course. That okay with you boys?"

Carlos nods, but I cross my arms in front of my chest. "No one answered my question," I say.

Monica doesn't bat an eye. "We're traveling around to find all the kids who were ejected from our church," she says plainly.

And then it's my turn to sit there in shock, unable to say a word. She stares at me for a moment, then smiles at her husband.

"Ricardo, would you find us a place to stay for the night?"

The moment passes. They all start talking, and I slip into the background like I always do.

Who *are* these people?

Last night, Deacon had sat me down on his porch. Gave me one last pep talk. Said that I couldn't tell them everything up front.

"No one more than you knows how special Reconciliation is," he had said. "But it will be hard to believe if they hear it right off the bat, okay?"

"I guess," I'd said, still unsure what I was supposed to do.

"Your miracle takes a lot of faith, Eli," he said. "We need to build theirs up, and that can't happen without companionship. Kindness. Respect. Build that with them, and God will ensure that the rest will follow."

Now, I remind myself what I was taught:

Interact with the new kids. Get to know them. Show them that I care about their future. Demonstrate what it means to be reconciled.

So I sit across from the kid with the light brown skin who had stared me down and expressed his doubt. Try to smile at him. He gazes at me for a moment, then looks away.

Okay. I was trained for this. It won't be easy, so I sit there. Smile wider. Project calm and certainty. It will work.

Deacon sits at the head of the long wooden table. The chandelier above it sparkles, and soon, a door opens in another part of his house. Mrs. Thompson practically floats into the room carrying a tray with a pitcher of lemonade and a bunch of empty glasses. She passes them around as Deacon clears his throat.

"So, let's start with introductions, if you don't mind."

There's an awkward silence. The six of us glance around at one another.

"I'm LaShawn," the Black girl says, and she offers a shy wave. "Hi."

"How old are you, LaShawn?" Elena asks.

"Thirteen."

"And where are you originally from?" Deacon says.

She gulps. "Uh . . . well, I was born in Mississippi," she says. "Adopted when I was eight."

"Mississippi!" Deacon says excitedly. "That's very far from here. But your life is so much better now than it used to be, right?"

She smiles, but . . .

I don't believe it. I think she's forcing it.

"It's . . . different," she says. "I remember some of it and—" She shakes her head. "My parents love me very much, so I'm happy."

Julian is next. He's seventeen. Originally from Mexico. Adopted by another local family—the Carsons—who are in Hemet.

"Wonderful," says Deacon. "Welcome to Reconciliation."

Julian doesn't react to that. Just stares impassively at his lemonade.

Annie is shy at first, mumbling her name. "No need to be afraid," says Deacon, smiling. "Speak up! We are here to support you."

"I'm Annie," she repeats, eyes still locked on the glass in her hands. "I'm fourteen. I'm adopted, too. From Taiwan. My mom and dad sent me here for . . . well, I don't know."

Then she looks up at Deacon. "What exactly is this place?"

"A prison," Julian says plainly.

Elena gasps. "Why would you say that?"

Deacon holds up a hand. "Elena, it's okay," he says. "We welcome doubt in this place, remember?"

He leans forward. "I'm sure you all see the similarities in one another. That is not by accident; it is God's design. This place . . . it is built to help children like you."

"Like us?" says LaShawn, a hint of worry in her voice.

Deacon nods. "You all *need* to be here," he explains. "And you will understand that by the end of the weekend."

"This place is beautiful," says Elena. "You're all going to love it."

But they don't appear to be loving anything. All three of them look . . . Well, a little terrified.

Was I like this when I was left here? In those first moments, was I afraid? Unsure? Uncertain?

I still can't remember. But I don't think that's important.

What's important is what came *after*.

This place came after.

I extend my hands out. "Deacon, can I lead our prayer?"

The smile he gives me . . . oh, it warms my entire body.

"Yes, son," he says, the words buttery.

I hold Elena's hand in my right, Deacon's on my left, then close my eyes.

"Heavenly Father," I say, "we give thanks for the bounty you have bestowed upon us, and for the gift of new friendship, new family, and new community. Please guide these souls to their righteous destination, and with your help, may they reconcile their bodies with their spirits. Amen."

I think LaShawn and Annie say amen back. I open my eyes, and Deacon is nodding at me. Eyes glassy.

"That was very good," he says, and he squeezes my hand once before letting go. Joy floods my body. I've made him proud, haven't I?

Maybe I won't be so bad at this.

But then I face forward. Julian is glaring at me. Then he gazes off. Inspects the ceiling. And all the warmth from Deacon's approval has vanished.

I don't get to say anything more, as Mrs. Thompson brings in a platter of various dips and a bright collection of freshly cut vegetables—vegetables I helped grow and harvest here on the grounds. I get up and help her, proudly telling the group that everything came from Reconciliation.

Am I doing what I'm supposed to? I'm still not sure; this is all so new to me. I glance up at Deacon, and he subtly gestures at Julian. After

LaShawn and Annie grab some food, I lift up the platter and place it near Julian.

"Try some," he says. "It's really good, I promise."

He doesn't look at me. Doesn't take any food, either.

"He's still adjusting," says Deacon softly. "Children like all of you . . . they are often not used to being treated well. They lash out. React like that to anything that is nice or holy or sacred. Give him some time, Eli."

LaShawn clears her throat. "But . . . what exactly is this place?" she says. "My parents also said it was some sort of retreat."

My heart races again. I could tell them. I could tell them what it did for me. But would they believe me? Would they call me a liar? I open my mouth to give them *something*, but nothing comes out.

Deacon doesn't seem discouraged by the questions at all, however. He smiles—in that warm, caring way he always does—and leans forward, resting his elbows on the edge of the table.

"I promise you will all learn more tomorrow morning," he says. "Elena and Eli here . . . they could explain it all. I'm sure they'd do a masterful job, too."

He winks at me.

Another jolt of elation rips through me.

"But I'd rather take my time with each of you," Deacon continues. "This place is not what it seems. Yes, it is a paradise, as I'm sure each of you have felt since you stepped foot on our grounds. It is not as unforgiving as the world outside. We know you are special, and each of your adoptive parents brought you here because they see potential in you."

He rises. "They want to give you a space to *actually* heal, away from a world that is determined to break you."

"Break us?" says Annie nervously.

Deacon nods. "None of you—Elena and Eli included—were born into *this* family. I created Christ's Dominion only five years ago, and that means you've all spent more time out there"—he gestures toward the direction of his front door—"than in here."

"But what's different about this place?" asks LaShawn, and she leans back in her chair while crossing her arms. "What's so special about Reconciliation?"

"And what *is* it?" asks Julian, furrowing his brow. "My parents keep saying that you promised to help me 'reconcile' myself."

"My parents told me you'd fix me," says Annie bluntly. When we all turn to look at her, she shrugs. "That's what they said."

Deacon puts his hands up. "I promise, this will all make sense soon," he says. "But I'll say this for now: You are here because each of your parents have identified something that's made it hard for you to fit in since you became a part of their family. And in order to help you heal so you can continue on your journey with God, you're here."

He smiles. "I think Annie's parents probably shouldn't have said they were going to 'fix' her. It's a little crude, but . . . the intent is there. I want you to be the best children to your parents that you can be. Reconciliation will help you achieve that."

There's an uncomfortable silence for a few moments. I resist blurting out what I want to say:

He's not lying!

This place will change your life!

I promise you, Reconciliation is beautiful!

But I'm still afraid I'm not good enough yet, that Deacon has put too much trust in me, that I won't be what God needs me to be.

Mrs. Thompson returns. Smiles. "Are you all ready for some dinner?"

I am thankful that she breaks the silence, that the smells of something from Deacon's kitchen have wafted into the dining room, that the others look excited about the prospect of a full meal.

I'm going to do this. I'm going to show them that this place is everything that Deacon promises it is.

Because I *have* to.

The Varelas bicker. Ricardo thinks we should just sleep in the van and get a room when we get to Los Angeles. Monica believes having the room will leave everyone well rested for the day of travel.

I've learned over the years that people hide themselves. They don't like others seeing the parts of them that are ugly. Sharp. Uncomfortable. Vicious. They'll turn their bodies away so you don't hear their phone conversations. They'll ask you to leave their homes. They all want to portray themselves in the most flattering manner possible.

I get it. It makes sense to me. In a way, I do that, too.

Monica and Ricardo don't do this. She tells her husband that he's too controlling of details. "Wasn't this whole hop-in-a-van thing supposed to be about spontaneity?" she says.

"You can be spontaneous without being a chaos demon," he says.

Monica sighs. "A demon. Is that how you really see me?"

"Come on. I was just playing."

"You're the one who wants to sleep in the van for the night!"

They go quiet. I watch as, moments later, he reaches over from the driver's seat. Grabs her hand. Brings it up to his mouth and kisses it.

"Ew," says Carlos.

"Your mom and dad are adults," drones Ricardo, still holding Monica's hand. "We're allowed to touch each other."

"Not on my watch," Carlos mumbles.

This is what they do. Endlessly. Argue and make up and clown on one another. It is normal for them, but I don't recognize it. Don't relate to it. Never seen it in others. Their flaws are out in the open.

Not mine.

We end up having to retrace both of our paths back up the 5 to the northern part of Stockton. By the time we arrive at the only motel Ricardo could find with adjoining rooms, I've disappeared into myself again. Shit. Just like Carlos says I do. I mean, I *knew* I did that, but it's weird to know that someone else can see it, too.

I still don't know how I feel about it.

At the motel, I discover the night's usual complication: two beds, four people. So I set up my sleeping bag on the floor at the foot of Carlos's bed, then sit with my back to it, too. Shove my duffel bag under the small desk and out of the way. I know Carlos is going to offer to have me sleep in the bed, but I know the rules. I know how this goes. Don't ever accept anything out of the norm. A person might be willing to change their routine once or twice, but soon, it will grate on them. They will quietly begin to resent you.

And I know what happens then.

Carlos eyes the bag on the floor. "You don't have to do that," he says.

I don't respond. It's part of the routine.

He sighs. Flips on his tablet. Watches something.

I guess we're back to the old Carlos again. That didn't last long.

Ricardo and Monica come in a half hour later. They found a Chinese takeout joint down the road and have returned with numerous Styrofoam containers packed tightly with food, and it smells good. My stomach rumbles.

And Monica hands me one of the containers and a smaller box with a little metal handle.

"I know we didn't ask, but I don't know anyone who doesn't like orange chicken and vegetables," she says.

I take it delicately, as if it will disintegrate. I don't understand any of this. Not one bit. I open it; steam hits my face. The first few bites are too hot, but I'm starving.

Yeah, Monica was right. This shit slaps.

I eat in silence while the Varelas talk about a Chinese takeout spot they used to frequent in San Francisco. Whenever they get like this, I do my best to fade into the background because I don't want to remind them I have no way to contribute anything. But this time, something is off. Different.

I want to say something. I want to offer some part of myself. Of my life.

Because I'm having to accept that no one has offered me as much kindness as the Varelas have. Is it going to expire? Is there a finite supply of it?

This is what they do, though, right? Monica said so. They find kids. Kids who were ejected.

God. That word. *Ejected.*

Never thought of it that way, but . . . it fits.

I should feel comfort over this new detail, shouldn't I? I somehow ended up in this place, with people who help others who have been hurt by places meant to comfort them. Except . . . why am I still so nervous?

Maybe I'm just another project for them.

After we've all devoured as much as we can of the food, Ricardo gathers up the trash. Tells me we'll head toward Los Angeles early the next morning and to get some sleep. "One step at a time," he says. "Don't sweat the details, okay?"

I don't have any details to sweat. It's just a collection of vague ideas.

Reconciliation.

Idyllwild.

Elena.

I think that's why this has me so messed up. What if that's all she is anymore? An idea. Because I haven't seen her in a year. What if she is nothing like my memories? What if my memories are all I have left of her?

Monica runs her fingers over my scalp. There's a soft layer of fuzz there; been a few days since I last shaved it. It feels good. Tender.

"Good night, Manny," she says.

Then she flicks off the light before shutting the door, leaving me behind with Carlos.

I can see the flashes of illumination from his tablet against the wall in front of me, but it's easy to ignore them. I've adapted to sleep pretty much anywhere. Anytime. Like . . . I don't know. A sloth.

I'm thinking of sloths and how great the Spanish word is for them. Perezosos. Great fucking word. I want to tell Carlos that. He's fluent like his parents, but then I'm thinking about how ridiculous that would sound, and how Carlos wouldn't care because he knows my Spanish is trash. "Basura," he would say, and then he'd shake his head at me, and it's right about this point that I am aware that I'm imagining a whole scenario in my head that's literally not happening.

Ah, the joys of being lonely and mentally ill.

I remain there, sitting with my back pressed against Carlos's bed. I don't move. I watch the flashes on the wall, and I wish I had the courage to stand up. Turn around. Talk to Carlos. Say anything to him. But I'm just so utterly convinced of my own awkwardness that this is the better solution.

I slowly slip into a dreamless sleep.

Someone taps me on the shoulder and my eyes pop open. It's dark in the room, but to my left, there's a small beam of light coming through a gap in the curtains.

"Yo, you gotta sleep like a normal person," Carlos says. His voice is close to me. Above my head. "I can't deal with you sleeping upright like that. It's creepy."

He rolls back to the head of the bed, and I rub my eyes. Shit. I fell asleep in this position.

I hoist myself up. Grab my small bag of toiletries. Head to the bathroom and shut the door. I stuff the bathmat under the bottom of it before turning on the light. Another trick I learned. Even little things can annoy others, and I know the light would be too bright in the room if I don't do this. Carlos is already annoyed at me, and I can't make this worse.

I still look exhausted in the mirror, so I turn around when I brush my teeth. Don't wanna see that. I think about a shower, but there is only one fresh towel. Can't inconvenience them. So no shower it is.

By the time I return to my sleeping bag, my heart is thumping loudly in my head. It's hitting me. Tomorrow, we go to find Elena.

Elena.

I allow myself to think her name. I want to say it again, to become practiced at the consonants and vowels, to speak it as if I've never stopped saying it.

But I did stop. For a year.

What if I've forgotten everything about her?

What if my memories are wrong?

What if what if what if

I flip to the other side. Tuck the pillow under my head. Blood's still racing, like I just finished a marathon. Tomorrow. Tomorrow. This is happening, isn't it? I should stop it. Shouldn't unearth this any further. I told them a truth; isn't that enough?

Lie lie lie lie lie.

I turn again. Mind won't go off. I think I can see Elena's face again, but . . . not all of it. Still too blurry around the edges, like I can't load the whole thing in my head. If that isn't her . . . what will it be like to see her again? To touch her again? To hear her voice, to talk to her, to ask her for advice, to . . .

I toss. Turn. Jump from one thought to another, looping back to names and faces, people I haven't thought of for years, wondering what my future is going to look like, desperate to know if I've taken the right step.

"Manny."

Carlos whispers my name in a harsh tone.

I freeze up. Hold my breath.

"Stop moving around down there," he says. "I can hear everything."

Shit.

"Sorry," I say, and I lie on my back, cross my arms over my chest. "Won't happen again."

He rustles the bed. Then his head appears above me.

"It *can't* be comfortable down there."

"It's fine."

"You don't even have a cushion under your sleeping bag."

I shrug. "I'm used to it."

"Doesn't sound like it," he grumbles.

I sit up. "I'll stay up then. Until you fall asleep."

In the darkness, it's hard to make out Carlos's face, but I think he scowls at me. "Man, will you just stop being weird and sleep in a bed? This one's big enough."

My heart leaps. "Share it?"

"What else could I have meant?" He rolls away, then to the left side of the bed.

I don't move. I haven't ever slept in the same bed as someone else. In the same room, sure, but . . .

My face burns.

Carlos sighs. "Just please hurry up. I would actually like to get some sleep tonight."

If I don't do as he asks, I inconvenience him. If I do, I could do the same.

Damn it, I hate this.

I push myself up after kicking off the sleeping bag. Walk to the opposite side of the bed. Peel back the thin blanket and top sheet. Slip underneath.

My whole body is on fire, despite how cool the room is. I immediately face away from Carlos, tucking my legs up, and yet I can still feel him. Sense him and his weight on the bed. Even without direct contact, I know how deeply close he is.

I want him. I have wanted him for a while. But I don't get what I want. So I simmer there, desire pulling me toward him, but I ignore it. Fight it.

His breathing evens out. Slows. I can feel that, too.

I have never been so still. So awake. So aware of my own body. I pull the blanket over me tighter.

He groans. Turns.

And his leg brushes against mine.

He's hairier than me. The hairs tickle, but I don't dare move. Was this an accident? It has to be.

I don't want it to be.

I remember a hand on my leg. Stan's. The squeeze. And perhaps it is just my lust speaking, but this is so much more tender, even if it is nothing but a mistake, an unconscious twitch of an appendage.

I don't move.

Carlos does once more, twisting so that his hand grazes my back, and then—

Nothing.

I am on fire, and there is no relief. I tense up and remain still until exhaustion claims me.

Diana Rogers was efficient.

I think that was good for her, but maybe not so good for the rest of us. It's easy to imagine that she was probably praised for the work she did. How quickly she handled her cases. How she always got right to the point.

But in the years leading up to her betrayal, I couldn't ignore how distant she was. How clinical she felt. She dealt with Elena and I as if we were problems to be solved, not . . . people.

When a family in Moreno Valley gave us back, for example, she seemed more concerned with how she could teach us to prevent this from happening than the fact that it happened at all.

The Bloomfields. They drove us an hour in traffic to return us. They were silent the whole way, which was uncharacteristic of the two of them. The husband was a lawyer and unsurprisingly loved to argue with his wife, who split time between staying home and working at an animal shelter a few days a week. I also remember that she wore cat ears all the time. Like . . . *all* the time. Little fuzzy cat ears attached to a headband. I think she thought they made her quirky or unique, but I assure you they didn't.

Because she was boring. She talked all the time, but she never said *anything*. She'd drone on and on about these terrible science fiction books she loved, oftentimes forcing us to try to read them. Even when Elena and I had homework that needed to get done. She'd introduce us to complicated board games with rule books as thick as bricks that she'd consult constantly because it was clear she didn't really get the rules herself.

And when her husband got home, they'd fight. Over the most benign, pointless stuff ever. A lot of it was the same nerdy shit she kept trying to push on us. Sometimes about food. Or parking spots. Or what needed to be repaired in their home.

After six months with them, even Elena was done, unable to keep up her usual positivity when it came to prospective families. So we sat in the back of the wife's hatchback, Elena's head on my shoulder, and I remember how she held my hand. I watched as all the familiar sights passed by: Alberto's. The colorful laundromat. The strip mall. The always-empty park. Each of them a signpost on the way to our inevitable destination.

There was the dogwood tree, growing out of a cracked and uneven slab of cement.

The car dealership with way too many inflatable men dancing in the wind.

The middle school with the crooked chain-link fence.

Elena leaned closer. Whispered in my ear.

The next one will be better. I know it.

I don't remember who was next.

Diana met us in the reception area. Had a look on her face that said: *Well, I expected this.*

Mrs. Bloomfield started complaining immediately. Said we weren't entertaining enough. That we wouldn't be her friends. That this wasn't what she thought being a foster parent would be.

I'm pretty proud of my response to that: I laughed. Said that I wasn't aware of her parenting us once during the last six months.

And it was the only one of my smart remarks that Elena actually laughed at.

Diana took us back into her office, the one overflowing with files and boxes and forms and papers. She'd thumbtacked photos of her kids along the doorframe. She had two of them. Cute kids, too. I always wondered if she treated them like us. If she ever sat them across from her like she did that time, then said to them:

"You guys really don't make this easy for me, do you?"

They always expect us to make it easy for the parents.

Who is making it easy for us?

I don't really remember Diana in the early days. I mostly remember Silvia. Silvia, who spoke in lilting, soft Spanish, whose English felt sharp and unpracticed. She was temporary, too, always the woman who took us in during the in-between. The time that unfortunately cropped up *between* placements. Now that I think about it . . . we definitely lived with her the longest. It just wasn't consecutive. Our time in her home, which smelled of Fabuloso, was a vacation. A respite.

She was the one who taught me how to wash my hair. Taught me how to braid Elena's whenever it was long enough. Stood me on a step-stool so I could mix a big pot of menudo with her. Read to me in Spanish. It made learning Spanish on my own years later so much easier.

I wish we'd stayed with her longer. I think she would have made a great mom. Unfortunately, after the Bloomfields, Diana fretted. Delayed us. Kept us in her office way longer than usual. This wasn't like her. Like I said: efficient. She always knew where to send us. Had another home or placement lined up.

I thought she had been in contact with Silvia. She wasn't, though.

Silvia died a week after we went with the Bloomfields.

We got a temporary placement somewhere. Don't remember.

Then we were in a noisy, chaotic home in Home Gardens that sagged and creaked. Rachel had four other foster kids. No real job because being a stay-at-home foster mom was a full-time gig for her, and she certainly had enough money from the six of us to keep us fed.

But I couldn't concentrate in that place. It was always so loud. And a couple weeks in, I picked a fight with Curtis and gave him a black eye. He hit on Elena during dinner. So I hit on him.

With my fist, of course.

Back to Diana.

Then: Gertrude and Sam.

And somewhere in there, the Sullivans. Somehow, they made it happen.

Why didn't Diana stop them? Why did she give us away?

By the time I'd met the Sullivans, we were already theirs.

There are protections in place. Red tape. Things have to go a certain way when you're in foster care. I had lost track of how many times a potential adoption or application for guardianship had failed over the years. So much so that it wasn't exciting anymore whenever Elena or a guardian told me that things were moving forward. I just couldn't get myself worked up over something that wasn't going to come to fruition anyway.

But Elena . . . she was *always* excited. It was like she couldn't help it. New guardians, new foster parents, potential adoptive parents? They all delighted her the same.

Until the Sullivans. I thought she was gonna explode when she first told me about them. We were walking back from school. There was a bounce in her step. An exaggerated smile on her face.

"We won't have to do this anymore," she told me.

"Do what?" I said.

"Live like this," she said. "Aren't you tired of it, Manny?"

I shrugged. "I dunno. I guess."

"Well, I've fixed everything. And I think you're gonna love it."

I grunted at that. Never really could muster up the same level of excitement that she had. "Whatever."

"You'll see. And I'm doing more than finding us a permanent home."

"Are you getting us out of school forever? Because I don't see the point in it anymore, either."

She stopped walking and beamed at me. "I'm saving our *souls*."

I rolled my eyes. "What if I don't have a soul to save?"

"Don't joke around about that."

I stuck my tongue out. "Just hollow and empty, Elena. Or maybe I'm like a ghost."

"You're meeting them today," she said, refusing to take the bait. "The people who are going to take us away from all of this forever."

"Take us away?" I stopped walking. "Elena, we are too old. No one is going to adopt us. Please, you *have* to stop thinking this is gonna happen."

Even though I wanted it to happen. I wouldn't ever tell her that.

Maybe I should have.

"There's no *maybe*," she shot back, and this time, her brow was furrowed. She was *angry*. "I already made it happen. There's no way they're backing out of it."

"Out of *what*?" I said, and my heart thumped hard in my chest. She was *serious*, wasn't she?

"I told you. We're being saved."

"Are you joking? Because I don't get what you think is funny about this."

Elena stepped forward, her eyes crinkled in concern. "Manny, I know how difficult our lives have been, but you won't have to worry about that anymore. I am not joking. I made a decision for us—for our family—that is finally going to give us what we've both wanted for so, so long."

Family.

That word.

We didn't use it. She was my sister, and I loved her to death, but we didn't call ourselves a *family*. We were missing every other part of what constituted one, so I just didn't use the word.

But now, she was.

They were waiting in the driveway when we got to our foster home.

A tall white man stepped out of a blue sedan, turned to stare at us as we approached, and his face broke into a wide smile. He was balding. Lanky. And a thought popped in my head as I took in the expression on his face:

He wants to devour me.

I thought of it as nothing more than one of the many cursed jokes swirling around in my head. But when the woman practically tripped as she got out of the passenger side of the car, she somehow had the same expression on her face.

They both looked . . .

Hungry.

She was about a half foot shorter. Reddish brown hair, though it looked like she dyed it that color. It contrasted too much with her pale skin. Her features were sharp, hawkish, and it only made the elated smile on her lips feel all the more sinister.

I could hear Elena's voice in my head, telling me to stop being so judgmental. But I had to be. If these were supposed to be our next guardians, I had to brace myself for the inevitable. To Elena, every potential parent or guardian was a promise, right up until that image of them in her head was shattered. It happened with Sam and Gertrude, who promised that they'd take care of us, but we rarely saw Sam. Gertrude treated us like an annoying inconvenience who interrupted her daily life. Both of them were quick to open the envelopes from the city and cash the checks they got for us, though.

Still don't think either of us ever saw a dollar from those.

I stopped just short of the sedan, but Elena kept going. The woman held out her hands.

"Elena," she said, her voice full of affection. And I realized that she did not say that as if she was confirming Elena's identity. It was as if she was greeting a longtime friend.

I watched as the woman hugged her, and then the man walked around the front of the car to throw his arms around the two of them, and he squeezed, and I didn't get it. I didn't know who these people were, and Elena had never spoken about them. Not once.

The man and the woman released my sister.

They all turned to me.

"I'm Frank Sullivan," said the man.

"And I'm Caroline," said the woman.

"Manny," said Elena, her smile stretching wider. "Come meet our new family."

The worst part was that when I first met the Sullivans, all the paperwork was done. It had already happened. There's no telling how many laws or policies were violated in the process, but it didn't matter. There was nothing I could have done to change it.

Nothing.

They took us out of foster care, and they did so by having someone break some of the rules for them. Plus: No one cared about where they were sending us. They just saw the perfect Christian couple, two white people who loved God and wanted to save us from the world, and the social worker just . . . gave us over.

I think Elena wanted the best. I do. I think I *have* to believe that, because the alternative is too grim.

They took us.

And then they took everything from me. And I'm certain none of them feel ashamed to have done so.

We left the home the same night we met the Sullivans. I expected Diana, the social worker who handled our case, to show her face. Make sure everything was done according to protocol. We usually had meetings with her in the weeks leading up to a new placement, especially if our current one wasn't working out.

She never showed. Like I said, it was all done. Over with.

Elena and I packed up all our belongings while Gertrude smoked in the courtyard of the apartment complex. Sam wasn't around, and I'm certain he wasn't going to notice we were gone for a week or so.

As I lugged my suitcase past her, Gertrude trailed behind me. Said only one thing:

"I'll find more of you."

We were always replaceable.

And that was it. I loaded my suitcase into the trunk of the Sullivans' sedan, my head spinning, still unsure that this was really happening. Elena had insisted that this was all done the right way, that we were about to be saved.

But why had no one talked to me? Why hadn't Diana asked me if I wanted this?

Shit, why hadn't Elena?

I was used to her excitement, but this . . . this was new. She was giddy in the backseat. Practically bouncing up and down. She wouldn't stop yapping at the Sullivans, who spoke to her with a conversational ease, as if they'd known one another for ages. Of course . . . they had. They'd been talking for weeks.

Caroline would occasionally glance up at me in the rearview mirror, but neither she nor her husband ever asked me anything.

It was like I was invisible.

I lasted a month at their home before they took me to Reconciliation.

I wake up before Carlos does. Smell terrible. I sweated through the sheets overnight. I take a quick shower and clean up. Cool myself off, too, because it's warm in the room and because I wake up thinking about the night before and . . . well, it's not good. Can't have that.

I use a hand towel to dry off so the bath towel will be there for Carlos. Sit in the early morning darkness at the foot of the bed until the first rays of sunlight peek through the blinds. Then I get up. Slip outside and into the chill. Breathe in the air of a new morning.

I might get closer to her today.

Don't know how to feel about that.

It is all still an impossibility. I can't imagine the whole; only the pieces.

And one of those pieces . . .

They're going to ask me what we should do first.

I don't know a first. It's all so jumbled in my head anyway. Where would I start? With the compound? With Reconciliation as a whole? With Christ's Dominion?

With the trip?

The Sullivans, the YouTube channel, our social worker, any of the other guardians . . .

I don't even know.

There's a creaking to my right. Ricardo comes out of his motel room, a Styrofoam cup of steaming coffee in hand. He's only wearing a pair of basketball shorts and one of those tight undershirts he likes a lot. He walks over to me. Leans against the side of the motel like I do. We just watch as the sun finally comes up over the hills far in the east.

Ricardo is a morning person. Self-described, I should say. I *can* get up early, and I often do out of necessity, but I don't really like it. Well, not all of it.

But the solitude. That part . . . that's the only thing I like. It's not the same as loneliness, though. Loneliness is being in a crowd and feeling isolated. It's watching this family act so damn healthy and mature around one another.

Solitude is just knowing you're alone. And being comforted by that.

Somehow, Ricardo's presence doesn't bother me. Doesn't upset my solitude. It works.

Don't know how to explain it.

Don't wanna question it.

By the time the sun has started to heat up the morning air, the rest of the world is waking up. Birds. A stray dog slinks by, watching the two of us warily, and a couple sleepily packs up a station wagon a few doors down. Drives off.

Ricardo finishes off his coffee. Glances my way.

And I blurt out the words forming on my tongue.

"Can I ask you something?"

He raises an eyebrow. Nods.

"Something your wife said."

"About the kids," he says. "And what we do."

"Yeah. That thing."

He chews on the inside of his lip for a moment. "Do you think that's what we're doing with you?"

I laugh, more a nervous reaction than anything else. "I mean . . . the thought crossed my mind."

"Well, in our defense, we didn't know anything about your story when we came across you last month. And we still took you in."

"But *why*?"

"Why not?"

I frown at him. "Come on. Look at things from my perspective."

Now it's his turn to frown. He gazes off into the sunrise. "I have to admit . . . it's a little hard for me to do so, Manny. I don't know that I've ever been through anything remotely like what you have."

I make to say something, but he raises the empty cup in my direction. "I barely know what you've been through," he says quickly. "I can't even say that I know what the tip of the iceberg is for you. And I respect that. You never have to tell any of us anything you don't want to. Okay?"

"Okay," I say softly.

"What I meant is that . . . well, I was never in foster care. Wasn't ever adopted. Wasn't taken in by a man like Deacon or attended a place like Reconciliation. Wasn't . . . abandoned, so to speak. So, imagining how you see this? It's really hard for me, Manny."

"Fair," I say. "I feel that way all the time. Like there's no one out there like me."

"I wouldn't be so sure of that," says Ricardo. Tips the coffee cup back to get the last few drops. "Some of these kids we find . . . their stories sound a little similar to yours. Some of their habits and behaviors . . . we've seen them, too."

"What happened to them?"

Ricardo's silence is longer this time. "Manny, it's . . . it's not entirely my story to tell. Some of it is, but we should have Monica and Carlos present for the whole thing."

I put my hands up. "No, no, it's okay, it's—"

"But I can tell you that I am here because I didn't listen. There were kids being hurt in the church I went to, and I didn't take it seriously. At least not until Carlos was targeted."

"Targeted?" My face flushes with fear. "What are you talking about?"

"Again: It's not my story, Manny. We will tell you everything, I promise. All I will say is that this whole idea was mine because . . . well, I wanted to do penance. To actually repair some of the damage I contributed to."

I scrunch up my face. This . . . this doesn't sound like the Ricardo I've come to know. Damage? What is he talking about?

"We adults are just as complicated as you are," he says, his voice quieter. "And I've been learning just how wrong I can be these last few years."

"So do you . . ."

I let the sentence fade out.

"What?"

"I don't know. It might be too personal."

He snickers. "I think we're way past that point, Manny."

I still hesitate.

Then:

"Do you still believe?"

Ricardo sips at his coffee. "Yeah," he says. "I do."

"How?"

He rubs his temples with his empty hand. "It's not easy, I'll tell you that. But I don't think my belief in God ever wavered throughout this. I had to change my perspective, though. I had to accept that *I* was the one who strayed. God was a constant, and I allowed myself to drift from Him."

Takes another sip. "Or . . . shit. Her. Them. I actually don't know. I think I've gotten to a point where I can accept that my problem was I tried to define God *too* much. And once I did that, things started falling apart."

"That makes sense," I say. "I guess I just don't even know how to start defining God."

Ricardo frowns. "You know, I believe that it matters a lot who introduces a person to God. That first interaction can mean a lot.

And so I take that to heart. I think about the kids in my old church who were introduced to God through us. Who had to find out the hard way how some people wield God like a weapon, not a force for love."

He shrugs. Peers into his now empty cup. "You good? You need breakfast?"

"Later," I say.

Ricardo starts to walk away.

"Wait."

He pauses. Turns back.

"Diana Rogers," I say, immediately breaking into a sweat.

"Who is that?" he says.

"She was our social worker," I say. "Elena and I . . . we were her case for a long, long time."

Ricardo steps closer. "Does she know what happened to you?"

The rage comes back.

Blurs my eyes with tears.

"She was the one who gave us to the Sullivans."

I see something settle on Ricardo's face. I don't know what it is. He just nods, then says, "Okay, Manny. Thank you for sharing that with me. It's . . . it's a first step, okay? I'll find out what I can, and then I'll bring it to you. And *you* can decide what we do next."

He steps closer. Puts both hands on my shoulders.

"Because you get to choose now, Manny. No matter what. We won't do any of this without your permission."

And then . . .

I collapse into his chest.

I put my own arms around him.

And I have never really done this. Never sought out comfort or affection.

But . . . I guess it feels right.

"Thank you," I whisper.

I don't know if he hears me.

He holds me.

A hug from Ricardo is different, but nice. He feels nothing like Deacon Thompson.

The Sullivans lived in Hemet. Didn't look all that different than Riverside, if I'm being honest. This whole part of California looked the same. Hot. Dry. Mostly brown. But there were more mountains looming all around, and I *did* like how they looked. They'd outlived everyone and everything around them. I respected that.

The Sullivans had no children, but their home suggested there'd been others. It was larger than what Elena and I usually lived in. Single story, painted white and blue, with a wide front lawn and spacious backyard with a dogwood tree towering over the grass. The inside was . . . sanitary. Only way I know how to describe it. Everything seemed so clean and plain. Few things adorned the walls aside from a framed photo of the Sullivans' wedding and a few crosses.

It was the other rooms that made me think that maybe they'd done this before. We didn't have to share a bunk like we usually did. Franklin took me to my room and left me to get settled. "We'll have dinner in thirty minutes, okay?"

"Sure," I said. I dropped my suitcase at the foot of an immaculately made twin bed and gazed around at the decor. Just like the rest of the house: almost nothing except an ornate cross directly above the bed. I wondered if they would get mad if I took it down.

In the closet, there were some towels, blankets, and sheets stacked neatly on a shelf. Lots of empty hangers. There was a Bible on top of a small oak dresser, and the drawers were empty, too. Never had had that much space, so maybe it wouldn't be too bad.

I laid out on the bed. I suppose I was used to the constant change.

What was any different about this? At least I had a bed. A roof. And something savory wafted into my room, so food would be happening soon. So I accepted reality for what it was.

I knew something was wrong at dinner.

I should have listened to my instinct. I should have gotten us out of there.

They'd picked up a meal from the prepared foods section of a local supermarket. Fried chicken, mashed potatoes, a broccoli salad. It was spread out perfectly over the table.

And as soon as I sat down, Caroline reached her hand out to me.

"We say grace in this household," she said.

I took it. No big deal. Wasn't the first time this had happened.

I grasped her hand, then Elena's on my right. Our hands linked, Caroline began, thanking the Lord for our meal and the bounty He had bestowed upon us. Franklin thanked God for giving them two beautiful children that he had fought so hard for.

My skin prickled.

I had known this man for maybe an hour. Fought for? I hadn't even met him before today.

"I prayed to you, God, and asked for the next child we could save, and you answered me by giving us *two* children."

My eyes darted up. Searched Elena's face. But her eyes were closed, her mouth stretched in a peaceful smile.

"We're just so happy that Elena answered our messages," Caroline added.

"Messages?" I said. "What are you talking about?"

As soon as I spoke, both Caroline and Franklin opened their eyes. Fixed me with an irritated gaze. "Son, do not interrupt grace," said Franklin. "Now we have to start over."

They closed their eyes. Bowed their heads.

"We thank you, Lord, for this bounty you have bestowed on us," said Caroline.

"And we thank you for these two beautiful children you sent our way," said Franklin. He continued, repeating everything he'd said before.

There was a pause. Caroline squeezed my hand.

"Manny," she said. "It's your turn."

"No, thank you," I said. "Don't really do the whole grace thing."

She did not hesitate. "You do in this household."

I balked. "Uh . . ." I said. "Well, okay. Thank you to the Sullivans for providing my sister and I with this meal and for taking us in."

I lowered my head. Waited for Elena to go.

"Manny, you have to thank God," whispered Elena. "Or else it doesn't count."

I glared at her. "I don't want to."

Franklin slammed his hand down on the wooden table, and I nearly jumped out of my seat.

"Now we have to start over," said Franklin. "Caroline, would you begin grace?"

She smiled. "Of course."

It took me two more times to get it right.

I was already on edge because of the grace.

But I was shoved over it when the Sullivans announced halfway through the dinner that Elena and I would be homeschooled.

"Absolutely not," I said. "No! I don't want to be homeschooled."

"Manny, it's going to be better for us," said Elena. "Trust me."

"You *like* going to school," I said. "I don't get why you're into this!

And can we even do homeschooling with our situation? I thought we *had* to go to public school."

"You don't want to be in public school," said Franklin. "Especially not with what they're teaching there."

My eyes went wide. This . . . this didn't feel real. We *had* to go to school. Was this a prank? Had Elena plotted some elaborate joke on me?

But she was smiling at me. Nodding. "Manny, please give this a try. For me? I think you'll appreciate what the Sullivans are trying to do for us."

I leaned closer to her. "And what is it that they're trying to do for us?"

"Save our souls," she said matter-of-factly.

It washed over me then. Something had been arranged here, and I had played no part in it. Not just the change in guardianship, but . . . something else.

I pushed away from the table. Heart raced in my chest. "What is this?" I asked. "Elena, who are these people?"

"I already told you," she said. "This is our new family."

"Our new foster parents? For how long?"

She *laughed*. Laughed at me like what I'd just said was the stupidest thing she'd ever heard. "No, Manny. These are our parents. They adopted us."

I didn't have words. My stomach dropped, and all the food I just ate threatened to come back up.

"Adopted?" I said. "How?"

"It's already happened," said Caroline. "Please don't be rude."

"But *no one told me about it!*" I yelled. "How is that possible?"

Franklin stood. Placed a hand on my shoulder. Pressed down. Hard.

"You will not disrespect your parents," he said, each word a dagger. "Those days are over. This is your home, and you'll live under our rules."

He pressed me into the seat.

I gaped at Elena in despair. Was this real?

But she was still smiling.

Still hopeful.

Still alight with joy.

"You'll see," she said. "I made the best choice for us."

Then she picked up her fork.

Pierced a piece of broccoli.

And ate like this was our new normal.

There's no TV in the room, so I head to the rental office at the far end of the motel. It's been a couple hours and Carlos just barely got up. He's showering, so the timing is as perfect as it's going to get.

9:05 a.m. Monday morning. Another chance. Another potential confirmation.

As soon as I push through the doorway, I see a small TV mounted on the wall. There's a woman behind the counter on the opposite side. Younger than I expected, with bronzed skin and dyed black hair. She's got headphones on, and I can hear something loud and angry buzzing out of it. I don't get to listen to music as much as I want—no way to play it, no means of collecting it—but even I know what I'm about to do is rude. I walk up to the counter. She doesn't see me, so I wave in front of her face.

She scowls. Takes off her headphones. "What, dude?" she snarls.

I point to the TV. "Is there any way I can use that? Just for a few minutes."

She raises an eyebrow. Reaches under the counter. Hands me the remote. Puts her headphones back on, and music blares out again.

I only have a minute or so until it starts. I turn on the TV, then start flipping through channels, hoping they have one of those corny local access stations that broadcasts Deacon's show. Don't know what the right station is in this part of the state, but I'm hoping it won't be hard to find.

I glance at the clock behind the woman.

9:04 a.m.

I flip. Past cartoon after cartoon, past an ad for a car dealership, past a weekend news broadcast, past a—

CHRIST'S DOMINION
WITH DEACON THOMPSON

The music is there. Louder than I expected. I quickly turn it down, and Deacon's face appears on the screen a moment later, and just as quickly as he's there, my hope perishes.

Deacon smiles.

And there are no children behind him at all.

I don't know what happened in Reconciliation this year, but there was a long stretch without children on that stage with him in the lodge. This is one of them.

So the video isn't new. Another repeat. Elena isn't in it.

It's her body.

The explanation comes so easily to me.

He's delaying episodes because his star is . . . dead. Gone. No more. For months on end, she was in *every* one of these broadcasts. For a while during the winter, it was *just* her. You could go to their YouTube page and see them all.

And now she's just . . . not there.

No. No no no.

Can't stand to hear his voice anymore. I turn the TV off. It's pointless, of course. I'm not gonna learn anything from this old-ass video.

I leave the office feeling a million times worse than when I entered.

A month.

That's all it took to unravel.

I wasn't sure if the Sullivans had jobs. I didn't think they were old enough to have retired, but they were *always* around. Maybe not both at the same time, but if one of them disappeared, it would be for a few hours at *most*.

It started slow. I can't even pinpoint when it all went awry. It just *happened*. Those first couple weeks, I thought I'd misjudged them. Our initial dinner had been uncomfortable, but once I accepted that we said grace at every meal, things got easier. I said the same thing every time: that I was thankful to God for the food, the family, and the home. It seemed to work. Both Caroline and Franklin appeared ecstatic over my eventual compromise, and at least I didn't have to see that forceful side of Franklin again.

The homeschooling was . . . I don't know. I had nothing to compare it to except for public school, which was . . . school. Sure, it was nowhere near as challenging as what I was used to. If I finished early, Caroline would send me into the backyard to read my Bible. I rarely did. Just pretended to. I mostly meditated. Stared up at the distant mountain. Tried to imagine a future outside of this place.

I believed it was possible back then. I just wanted to see new things. Wanted to travel. Wanted to have the things I'd never had. I thought that if I outlasted the Sullivans, once I turned eighteen, I'd be out of all of it. Out of the foster system, out of this family, and then Elena and I could go live the life we wanted.

But it became increasingly clear that this *was* what Elena wanted.

She wanted to learn about a history that never seemed quite right. Franklin loved teaching a version of America that simply didn't make sense to me. All that stuff about how God ordained the pilgrims to come here and take the land, to work with the natives until they became too difficult, too entrenched in their own sacrilegious beliefs—it felt like bullshit. So did any of the times Caroline taught us science. God created it all; evolution wasn't real; all that nonsense that I always thought was a bit of a joke, not something people really believed.

Even Bible study—which we did three times a week—kept getting me in trouble. I guess I liked all the wrong parts. I remember learning about Samson from a previous guardian of ours. Helen. But she said that Samson taught us the power of perseverance. Of faith and belief.

But what I remembered was how absolutely hardcore it was that the dude slaughtered a bunch of Philistines with the jawbone of a donkey. That's pretty metal.

Caroline didn't want to hear that. Said I didn't understand what really mattered.

Pretty sure I understood it quite well.

I wondered as we did our lessons—and Elena fell deeper into a bizarre, almost robotic enthusiasm—if my sister was faking it. If this was part of some grand plan to . . . I don't know. Pull one over on the Sullivans. Grift the system. Get us housing and food with people who at least had an abstract interest in us, rather than what we went through with guardians like Gertrude and Sam.

But maybe that's because it was what *I* was doing to survive everything.

Elena . . . Elena was always so *pure*. I never told her it, but . . . I admired that. Hell, I followed her through all her messy decisions because at heart, she really did want the best for both of us.

———

Fuck.

What do you do when someone you love keeps choosing to hurt you? She did it more than once. More than once, she chose someone else over me.

Fuck.

After a month of lessons I struggled through—
After a month of learning how to pray so that the Sullivans wouldn't keep making me start over—
After a month of spending nearly every waking moment in that house or in the backyard—
It was a boy.
A boy brought it all down.

He lived down the street. Nestor. He was a year older than me. Went to the local high school. Met him a week before it happened while I was taking out the trash cans to the curb. He froze at the end of our driveway and stared at me. Like . . . for way too long. I remember pushing the trash can up against the curb and turning to see if he was still there.
"You don't go to my school," he said.
"Uh . . . no, I don't," I said.
Started to walk away.
"When did you move here?"
I turned back.
He stood there, an eyebrow raised.

He was cute. Short. Hair cropped in a high fade. Had on tight jeans and an oversized Slayer T-shirt.

"Few weeks ago," I said.

"I'm Nestor," he said.

"Manny!"

Caroline called to me from the front door. I spun back, saw her watching with her hand on her hip.

"Inside, please!"

"Find me, Manny," Nestor whispered. "Two houses down. White with green trim."

He winked.

I stood outside his window that night. Guessed which one was his, which I was pretty certain of because I could see posters for bands like Opeth and Cave In on the wall. I tapped on it, and nothing came of it. I had turned to leave when Nestor wrenched the window open.

"You came," he said.

I nodded.

Nestor hesitated. "Gimme a second," he said.

Closed the window.

Moments later, the gate in the wooden fence to my left opened. Nestor was there. Frame shadowed by the light behind him on the side of his house.

I don't know why I did it. Up until then, boys had always been a fantasy. Used to be something I could talk to Elena about, too, but lately . . . well, she was in her own world. I couldn't penetrate it.

So I created my own world.

That first night, we just kissed. Didn't want to do anything else because I wasn't ready for that. But I pressed Nestor up against the siding of his house and I kissed him over and over again and rubbed against his body because I wanted to and because I could.

Because it felt . . . normal.

It wasn't lessons. Or prayers. Or regimented schedules.

I existed in the moment. Nothing else mattered.

I snuck out, over and over again. For a whole week, until I got sloppy, until I forgot to check behind me to see if anyone noticed me leaving. I met up with Nestor again, and this time, I took longer. We made out for a while, and then I got down on my knees because I was curious. I wanted to know if it was as great as everyone said it was.

We made out some more. He invited me to a party a couple weekends in the future. I told him I wasn't sure I could sneak out, but I would try.

"Your parents are too strict," he said.

"Not really my parents," I said.

He raised an eyebrow.

"I mean, legally, I guess. But they're weird. And super religious."

He kissed me on the forehead. "Well, sorry I've made you such a sinner."

We laughed together. He told me to come back soon. He said I made him feel good.

I drifted back home with my head in the clouds. So I didn't even notice that the living room light was on. I climbed back into my open window. As soon as I shut it, my bedroom door opened.

Franklin. Bright light behind him threw his body into shadows.

"Living room," he said. "Now."

I didn't think anything was going to come of it. I'd snuck out of plenty of bedroom windows to go to shows before. Sometimes, I just went on long walks to clear my head. And Elena definitely knew I did this, especially since we often shared rooms.

So I was thrown when I saw Elena sitting on the couch.

"Why did you leave?" she asked me. "Why couldn't you just stay here? These people *love* you. Why can't you see that?"

"What?" I said.

"You can't just sneak out anymore," she continued. "You belong here."

"Did you rat me out?" I sputtered. "Elena, oh my *god*, what is wrong with you?"

Caroline stuck a finger in my face. "Don't take His name in vain," she hissed.

"Who cares?" I shot back.

Franklin was pacing back and forth in the living room. "I can't believe you would reject us like that," he said.

"What are you talking about?"

"Where were you?" he demanded.

"Out," I said. That was all I was going to give them.

"Out *where*?" he said.

"Outside. You know, that place you guys never let me go?"

"Don't be smart, Manny," said Caroline.

"It's true! I don't do anything anymore. Ever since I was apparently adopted by you two, I feel like I'm a prisoner."

I stood.

Fixed a nasty sneer on my face.

"I don't want to be here."

Franklin stilled.

Glanced over at Caroline.

"I think it's time," he said, and the anger on his face washed away.

"Time?" I frowned at him. "Time for what?"

Caroline nodded, ignoring my question. "He did say there was precedent. They've done it before."

"What are you two *saying*?"

But it was Elena who stepped forward. "Manny, do you trust me?"

"What?" I rubbed at my eyes. "I mean . . . yeah. Yes. Why are you asking me that?"

"Because this family is going to save you," she said. "That's why I brought us here. It's why they're our parents. They know all about you."

"All about me?"

I stumbled back.

Dizziness swirled in my head.

They knew all about me? What the hell did that mean?

"It's time for you. For Reconciliation."

She said it as if it was the most sensible solution in the world. She said it as if this was a natural conclusion.

She said it like she believed it.

"Reconciliation?"

"Do you want to feel whole?" Caroline asked, and the rage I'd seen earlier . . . it was gone. She stared at me, beatific, as if in the presence of something holy. "Do you want to be happy for the rest of your life?"

"I . . . guess?" I said, scrunching up my face.

But how could I answer that truthfully?

How could I tell them that people like me . . . we didn't really *get* happiness?

Bounced from one home to another.

Never knew where we came from.

Nothing certain. Nothing stable. Nothing true except the chaos.

What they were asking of me . . . it just wasn't *possible*.

"Can we take you somewhere?" Franklin asked, and he reached for me. He hesitated for only a moment, aware of the chasm that existed between us. Then he smiled.

"One weekend," he said. "We want to show you a place where you'll never question yourself again. All it takes is three days."

"I've already been there," said Elena, and she stepped closer, too, her eyes glassy. "I've been there, and it'll change your life."

My stomach sunk. I looked to Caroline, too, and in that moment, they all gazed upon me with such *hope.*

I wish that I had resisted.

But I didn't.

I was flustered.

I was scared.

I was confused.

And Elena went in for a hug. Pulled me tight, and then said, "I would never do anything to hurt you, brother. Never. Please, come with us."

Despite my doubts, I couldn't see past her dedication. As soon as Elena promised that she wouldn't hurt me, I believed her. Like I always did—just as I had with every family that came before. She was the one who kept us together, who looked out for me. But . . . she believed. She believed that these new families would one day love *us* the way we loved one another. I knew without a doubt that none of these people actually cared about us. We were temporary fixtures in their lives. Even in Diana's.

In the end, she gave us up, too.

But I still agreed to go to Reconciliation, because Elena asked me to, because the Sullivans promised that everything would be different, that I would be loved and appreciated and would never have to worry about where I would belong ever again. That's what they said throughout the car ride to Reconciliation. The assurance was constant. It sounded real.

I should have known.

She fucking lied.

The parents arrive after dinner. I only see them briefly before Annie, LaShawn, and Julian are whisked off to their cabins. There's still so much construction to be done, and I wonder what it's going to be like when there are twenty families here at a time. Deacon says we're growing, that there are so many children who need to be adopted out in the world, all of whom will need this place.

I know that's what is best, but I can barely handle *three* new assignments. How am I ever going to handle that many?

I stand outside of the lodge. We had a group prayer tonight, and I think it went well. Annie seemed more open to this than the others; Julian was still deeply uninterested in anything that was being said; LaShawn struggled to keep up.

I was once ignorant. I tell myself that as my frustration builds. I was changed, but it still took time for me to become who I am today. I had to let go of who I used to be, and that's what awaits each of these people. Come Sunday, they'll be asked to shed their other lives and their other selves, and the process will be complete.

It worked for you, I think. *It'll work for them.*

Deacon says he welcomes doubt. But as a slight breeze blows over my skin, I shiver. I'm not sure I should feel this much doubt.

Is there something wrong with me?

Deacon closes up the lodge behind me. I twist around, and he extends a hand to me. I take it. He pulls me close.

His embrace is warm. He envelops me, holding me close.

"My miracle," he says into my hair. "You know you're special, Eli, right?"

"I do," I say, though I don't have the certainty he does. I still tell him what he deserves to hear.

"I can tell you are nervous," he continues. "It's just the first day, okay? Things will smooth out, especially as you spend the weekend with these children."

"I know," I say. "I just want to make sure I'm doing everything right."

He kisses the top of my head, and it sends an electricity through me. "I know you do, my son. Just keep in mind that this is important. God has put these young ones in your hands for a reason."

He lets me go. Holds me at arm's length.

"I want to create more," he says. "What happened with you . . . it was nothing short of a miracle. I think you are the key to what I've been trying to build with Christ's Dominion all these years. You are the way forward, Eli."

He kisses me on the forehead.

"You will change everything."

Then Deacon walks off toward his house. I think he meant that to be comforting. And in some sense, it is. To know that you are chosen? That you are special in God's eyes? It fills me with awe.

It also fills me with dread.

I stand there beneath the boughs of pine, beneath the sparkling sky, and I tremble. I try to remember what came before, but it's still fuzzy. That's the miracle, isn't it? I can't remember. I shed my entire past, free from the shackles of the old world.

I watch as the lights in the completed cabins go out, knowing that my future lies in each one. I was placed here for a reason, but the weight of it is so immense. It presses down on my shoulders, threatening to crush me.

What if I fail all these people?

I remain there in the darkness, listening to animals skitter in the distant underbrush. My heart thumps louder and louder.

I don't know how I'm going to bring about another miracle.

But I have to try.

Carlos's demeanor has changed. He's not angry or disinterested in me like he once was. When I climb in the van, he nods at me. Asks why I always wake up so early when I could sleep in "like literally everyone else our age."

It's certainly a step up from feeling constantly ignored by him.

"Your dad was up early," I say, clicking my seat belt.

He raises his hands in victory. "Exactly my point! Papi is inhuman. He *likes* getting up early."

"You will too one day," Ricardo says from the passenger seat. "Just wait. Soon, you'll be drinking coffee, and commenting on the weather to absolute strangers, and then you'll have an identical wardrobe to me, too. It's a rite of passage."

Carlos rolls his eyes at me. "Don't listen to him. Mom says he's been an old man for like . . . twenty years."

"Longer than that," scoffs Monica. "He was an old man in college, too."

Ricardo scowls. "So quick to throw me under the bus," he mumbles.

"And I was driving the bus, too," she adds, grinning.

There is a moment then, brief as it may be, when I don't feel the encroaching terror of doom. When it doesn't seem as if I've made a terrible decision. Where it suddenly appears possible that we might pull this off.

I wish this feeling—hope—lasted longer in me than it usually did.

———

Carlos talks to me the first hour, and we speak almost entirely about music. He is surprised that I know anything. Doesn't offend me, really. I so rarely let anyone know anything about me. He has a liking for things more on the electronic and pop spectrum than I do, but there's some overlap there in bands like Meet Me @ The Altar or Bad Religion or Paramore.

Ricardo interrupts us from the passenger seat. Says he has to ask me something about what we're doing next.

Next.

Just like that, the comfort washes away in the waves of terror and anxiety.

There's a next, isn't there?

"So, I kinda have a knack for finding people," he says. "And I wanted to ask you about Diana Rogers."

My heart leaps.

Even hearing her name still hurts.

"What about her?" I say.

"Well, first of all, I absolutely found her!" he says, and initially, there's an excited grin on his face. But it disappears once he sees that I'm not terribly thrilled about it.

"So . . . yeah," he continues, his tone much more even. "Turns out there are only two social workers named Diana Rogers registered in California with the Riverside County Department of Public Social Services. I eliminated one of them because until six months ago, she was working for Rutgers out in New Jersey, so she couldn't have been here when . . . well, when everything happened."

Ricardo grimaces. "Sorry. I swear, I'm not trying to pry by talking like that."

"It's fine," I say. A warmth spreads in me. I don't think anyone has ever genuinely apologized for prying before. People barge into my life. Demand to know all the lurid details. They want the pieces of my story, not because they're interested, but so they can fasten it into a patchwork narrative that comforts them best.

But . . . not these people.

"Are we heading to Diana's office?" I ask Ricardo.

"Well," he says, raising an eyebrow. "That's what I was going to ask of you. Do you want to do it this afternoon or wait until—"

"Today," I say definitively. "I've been waiting too long already."

Monica makes eye contact with me in the rearview mirror. "You sure, honey? You don't have to move faster than you're comfortable with."

Carlos watches me in anticipation.

"I haven't moved at all in a year," I say. "Please. I want to find Elena. I want this part of my life to end."

Carlos nods. "I get that," he says. Then, more to himself: "More than you know."

I don't understand what he means, but right then, I make a new decision.

I can unload some of this burden, can't I? Just a little bit to lighten the psychic weight.

Just a little.

"And there is something you need to know," I say.

Ricardo whips his head around.

Carlos leans forward.

Monica turns the music off.

"That place . . . those people there . . . it's *evil*."

Reconciliation. A word I didn't understand, a concept that made no sense to me, yet it was said so many times on that darkened ride. Reconciliation.

It was a destination. High up in the mountains. Elena said it was the most beautiful, peaceful place in the world. I would feel like I was coming home for the first time.

It was an idea. The Sullivans explained on the car ride that Thursday morning that the world was so hard to live in because we were fundamentally torn in two: There was our earthly body and its desires, and then there was our heavenly body, which is what God intended us to be. We were at constant war with our earthly body, which is why we were so sad. Angry. Confused. Lost.

Alone.

I knew that word. That concept. That idea. I would never tell Elena, but . . . I was so very alone.

Where we were going, Franklin explained, would allow us to repair our bodies. Would allow us to exist as one instead of two. And all it took was three days.

If I gave them three days, I'd be fine.

I didn't really believe them. God was another one of those ideas and concepts that worked for other people, but not for me. I'd prayed enough to him over the years, and he'd never responded, so I just . . . stopped.

But Elena had sounded happier than usual. Even as we climbed up a twisting, steep road, even as my head swam with nausea and nerves, I could hear it in her voice. Somehow, this place brought her *joy*.

That's what I believed. Nothing else. I believed that Elena was happy, and if I could get even a slice of that, I would be satisfied.

Three days.

I could do something for three days, then come back and continue living with the godly Sullivans, going along with this charade, for as long as I could.

The Sullivans made me wear a blindfold during the ride to Reconciliation.

They told me it was because Reconciliation was special. They told me it was because there were bad people in the world who wanted to destroy what they had found.

They told me they told me they told me they told me—

Doesn't matter. I did it. And I walked further into the trap.

A couple hours after we left their home, the Sullivans' sedan lurched to a stop. I felt hands at the back of my neck and winced, but they were gentle. Untied the blindfold. Removed it.

Light flooded in. I gasped for air.

Then gasped at what I saw out the window.

Tall pines towering over us on all sides. A meadow of wildflowers and grasses wafting gently in a light breeze.

I reached for the handle, shoved the door open, and the thick, earthy smell hit me first. I breathed it in. Felt it in my throat. Felt it embrace me.

"Holy shit," I muttered.

Elena was right there. Smiling. "I know, right?"

"Where are we?" I asked.

"Reconciliation," she said, then turned to walk off.

I followed after her. That wasn't what I had meant by the question, and I didn't understand why everyone was being so coy about where we were in a literal sense.

The Sullivans were walking ahead of us, and Elena and I caught up. I heard finches call out to one another. Some of the trees creaked in the wind. And that *smell*. I couldn't get over it.

They guided me to a clearing.

A ring of cabins surrounded it. A few of the cabins stood amidst the trees, basked in their shadows. I saw concrete foundations set in the ground. In other spaces, there were the outlines of frames for future cabins. *Lots* of future cabins. On the far side from the dirt road we were on, there was one enormous building. High windows. Arched roof.

A few people stood just outside the double doors. All of them were white; their pale skin contrasted in the greens and browns around them.

One was taller than the others. As we approached, he wore a wide smile. Had cropped facial hair. Dark blond hair slicked to the side.

Piercing blue eyes.

It was the man from those videos that Elena had been watching.

He stepped forward.

And she rushed into his arms.

"Elena," he said. "Welcome back, my child."

My child?

I wanted to say something sarcastic to him. To joke about what an obviously creepy thing that was to utter. To tell him that Elena was no one's child, just like me.

Instead, he moved toward me.

He opened his arms.

He wrapped them around me.

While he held me, he murmured into my hair.

"Manny," he said, "I'm glad you're here, and I'm sorry it took so long."

I didn't know where "here" was.

I didn't know what he meant about this taking so long.

I didn't even know his name at that point.

All I knew was that no one had ever hugged me like that.

Monica drives.

I tell them some things about Reconciliation. About how I got there . . . and how I left.

Monica drives, and they all listen.

Then there is a long, long silence.

I'm used to silence. Elena had always been the more talkative of the two of us, so I let her take the lead in the past. Besides, I'm too quick with a sarcastic comment.

But I'm unused to *this* silence. I have never revealed this much of myself to anyone.

I have revealed far less even than I could, and I'm still met with this:

A soul-shaking silence.

In a way, it's kind of affirming. It tells me: Yes, what you've gone through is pretty fucking awful, especially since I spend so much time shoving down the nightmare and trying to tell myself it isn't that bad.

It's pretty bad.

———

Monica is the first to speak.

"Jesus fucking Christ," she says.

Yeah.
    Pretty much.

No one is looking at me. I don't blame them. So I watch the land-scape rush by from the window. Wonder if I've said too much, revealed things about me that will change how the Varelas will treat me in the future.

I broke one of my rules, the one Cesar taught me, the one that kept me alive all this time. Have I fucked this up? Are they going to drop me off at the next rest stop or gas station or travel center? Will they decide that I'm too much?

Then Carlos surprises me.
    He's sitting sideways, staring out the window opposite him.
    He flings his right arm over the back of the seat.
    Seeks out my hand.
    Then he grabs it.
    Holds it tight.
    When I look up at him, his eyes are red. He's wearing a scowl.
    Is he mad at me?
    "They shouldn't have done that to you," he says in a low voice, his words laced with fury.
    Then.

Even quieter.

"They shouldn't have done it to me, either."

We drive for hours. No one says another word.

Carlos doesn't let go of my hand the entire time.

We make a necessary pit stop about half an hour outside of Los Angeles. It's later in the afternoon, but Ricardo assures me that we can still make it to Diana's office before it closes at 6 p.m.

Carlos peels his hand out of mine. Doesn't say anything to me when he does. Just climbs out of the van into the parking lot of the In-N-Out. I don't really feel like eating, but Monica insists that I have *something* in my stomach. "I know you're probably nervous," she explains. "But we can't have you nervous *and* starving."

At least it's In-N-Out. I don't get to eat it often—I consider it a luxury because I so rarely have money—but I take the opportunity to get my usual: Double Double with grilled onions, toasted bun, animal-style fries, and a vanilla milkshake. We sit outdoors in the heat at a table with an umbrella, and the Varelas make small talk with one another. I've never seen them do this, and I know it's because of me. None of them can talk about what they really want to discuss, which is me and what I just told them.

And I still haven't told them everything.

Probably won't. No need to. They have just enough to keep them interested. Why give them more? It'll only make this distance worse.

I just have to keep them around long enough to get to Idyllwild. To get to Elena.

To find out the truth.

So I can finally . . . what? What happens after? Really haven't thought of that.

Maybe . . . maybe I just want all of this to be over. To know that there *is* an after.

We load back into the van.

We pull out onto a major street, then hop back on the high-way, which seems impossibly wide down here in L.A. There are so many cars speeding along. I watch them. I imagine so many things:

What it's like to drive in one, to have the freedom to go any-where, anytime.

To drive alongside someone who likes me, who wants to be with me, as we go on a road trip.

To go on vacations.

To have a home on the hillside, looking out over an expansive valley.

Carlos holds my hand the entire time.

We make it to Moreno Valley nearly ninety minutes later. Monica says we lucked out and missed rush hour; the drive could have been a lot worse.

I don't feel lucky. There's still a part of me that wishes this wasn't happening, that I could run away like I always do.

I start recognizing buildings. Alberto's. The colorful laundro-mat. The strip mall. The always-empty park.

I haven't been here in ages, and my heart thumps painfully. I don't even realize I'm squeezing Carlos's hand hard until he shakes it.

"Dude," he says softly. "You okay?"

No.

No, I'm not.

"I'll be fine," I say. "Just nervous."

I'm not going to be fine, am I?

This is all going to fall apart.

There's no way out of this.

I'm sweating. Down my temples. Under my arms. My vision darkens around the edges.

"Breathe," says Carlos, and he reaches out. Touches my face.

I jerk away. Can't help the reaction; I wasn't ready for it. I let go of his hand. Tuck myself into the corner.

His eyes go wide.

Fuck.

Well, I fucked that up.

Carlos turns to face forward. "Sorry," he mutters.

Monica turns on the street.

I see the dogwood tree, still growing out of the cracked and uneven sidewalk.

The car dealership with way too many inflatable men dancing in the wind.

The middle school with the crooked chain-link fence.

I shouldn't be here.

I shouldn't be doing this.

Monica slows and turns into a massive parking lot that sits in front of a plain beige building. Rectangular windows spread evenly over the front. Lettering attached above the entrance reads:

COUNTY OF RIVERSIDE

DEPARTMENT OF PUBLIC SOCIAL SERVICES

There are people milling about outside. I've *been* one of those people before, either waiting for Diana or waiting to be picked up by a new guardian. Everyone looks tired or bored.

Monica pulls into an empty spot on the opposite end of the lot, far from most of the others. The side door opens, and Carlos is getting out, and I suddenly realize what is happening. I freeze.

Are they coming in with me?!

No! No, I *have* to do this alone.

Monica is there at the open side door, waiting for me. But then I sense movement to my left, and I watch as Carlos and Ricardo wander off.

"Where are they going?" I ask.

"You didn't think we were all going to go in there with you, did you?" She raises an eyebrow. "We have a little more tact than that."

I scoot sideways, then push my way out of the backseat and onto the asphalt of the parking lot. "I guess I did."

"They're going for a walk," she says, closing the door and locking the van. "Ricardo found a skate shop nearby, and Carlos needs a new deck. Early birthday present."

I can't tear my eyes from her. From the way she's looking at me, radiating warmth and tenderness.

I don't know what to do with that.

"So . . ." I say. "You're coming along, though."

Monica nods. "I promise I'm not trying to be all up in your business. I mean yes, I'm curious what these people are like, but I'm also trying to be useful. I do think it would be best if you had some kind of an adult with you—and for what it's worth, I have experience with this. Both Ricardo and I do. We've dealt with a lot of state and county agencies. Lots of red tape. So I can put pressure on people if needed, be someone they have to answer to—your adult, so to speak. Because I have seen far too many instances where these services for kids simply . . . don't listen to kids."

A breeze blows some of her hair over her face, and she flicks it away. And for a moment, she looks nervous. "Look, if it helps you get back to your sister, I'd like to help you."

"Why?"

Monica presses her mouth tight. "Why what, Manny?"

"Why are you doing this for me? I don't understand."

"Because I want to, first and foremost." She sighs. "And while I can't claim to know everything you've been through, I imagine that the bad moments and the bad people currently outweigh the good ones."

I don't respond to that, mostly because I'm trying to hold back a cackle.

"I'm right, aren't I, Manny?"

I rub the edge of my shoe against the ground. "Something like that."

"Ricardo told me that he shared a little bit more of what *we're* going through. I am not going to stand here and say it's exactly, precisely what you've gone through. But the three of us were hurt to varying degrees by an organization meant to love us. So I think we know the anger that comes with that sort of betrayal. The hopelessness, too, that makes it seem like nothing can ever repair what was broken."

Jesus.

That hits too close to home.

———

"So, we're just going to try," she says. "Is that okay?"

I tell her yes, even though I want to warn her:

I'm going to disappoint you.

"So, let me do this part with you, Manny," she says, and she reaches a hand out.

I hesitate.

And I fight the urge to spin around, grab my duffel, and march away from here, despite that it's what I want to do.

I take Monica's hand.

"Take a deep breath," she says.

I breathe deeply. Let it out. Again. Again. My nerves are alight with terror.

"Whatever happens in there, just know that I've got your back, okay?"

"Okay," I say, breathing out slowly.

She guides me across the parking lot. Toward the front door. Holds it open for me.

Mrs. Thompson stands at the front of the classroom. I wonder if she is as nervous as I am. My breakfast is sitting heavy in my stomach. She doesn't seem to be showing it, though. She stands upright. Proud.

And then she begins.

I've heard it all so many times before. The truth about the world beyond Reconciliation. The good news about this land that God has blessed. The chance to give it all up, to reconcile your body and mind as God intended it to be. But this is the first time these new souls are hearing it. It's the first time they're being exposed to the truth.

When Mrs. Thompson calls on me to speak, I tell them as much as I'm supposed to. I'm surprised when I don't stutter or hesitate. After a few moments, I settle into what they prepared me for.

I tell them that I once had a life of pain, misery, and suffering.

I tell them that once I gave myself over to God, all of that disappeared. Figuratively. Literally. It's all gone. My past did not matter anymore; I'd been given a new life in Reconciliation, and all I had to do was concede. Look what I had been given in response to that!

A home.

A family.

A sister.

Peace.

I falter on that last one, and I hope no one sees it. My pulse beats rapidly in my throat.

Do I have peace yet? My skin feels like it's crawling as Annie, LaShawn, and Julian stare at me. As they listen to me tell them that I found a way to get rid of all the terrible impulses and urges that plagued my life.

But I can't remember my life.

I just remember this place.

And I don't need anything else.

I gaze back at Julian, and a heat rises in my face. I like how his eyebrows look. He does this thing when he's frustrated–which appears to be all the time–where he chews on his bottom lip, deep in thought.

Why is Deacon so certain that I'm a miracle? That I can do what God is asking of me?

When I finish talking, the others fidget in their seats. Julian turns away as Mrs. Thompson thanks me for my testimony. "Elena?" she says. "Would you like to share more about how you came to this place?"

She glances at me. There's an odd look on her face, one I can't parse.

Then it happens:

The wall goes up.

I've seen it happen so many times since I arrived. For some unknown reason, Elena keeps herself from me. Maybe not everything, but there's a part she will not share, that she holds close to her heart. Am I not worthy of that?

Perhaps she is protecting me from the outside world.

"Sure," she says. "I can do that."

"Perhaps it will also help our new friends understand what it means to be brought to Reconciliation."

Elena stands up. I think I probably should have done the same. She's such a natural at this.

I notice then that it's warm in the classroom.

My training kicks in. I know what's happening. We are making these new souls *physically* uncomfortable. It is the only way to truly dislodge what is inside them. If they are catered to, spoiled, and protected, they will remain in their comfortable shells.

We can't have that.

How else can they experience the miracle of Reconciliation like I have?

My mind goes elsewhere as Elena starts to talk about choosing to come to Reconciliation. I've heard the story so many times; Mrs. Thompson has made her rehearse it, just like she's made me rehearse mine. She came here of her own volition, called by Deacon's videos online. Annie asks her what videos she's talking about, and Elena is thrilled she'll be able to share them. "They'll help your journey so much," she says.

She slips right back into it. Finding the Sullivans. Being called by God. Bringing herself to Reconciliation for a weekend that changed her life. Her adoption. Leaving her old family and her old ways of living behind.

Like Mrs. Thompson, she is so confident as she relates this all. I don't hear the same hesitation as there is in my own voice.

Why didn't God choose her? Wouldn't it be more effective?

Another uncertainty.

Another doubt.

Another sign that maybe I'm not made for this.

But what *am* I made for?

This. Deacon said that God created this miracle so that others would find their way.

So why do I feel so lost?

The new souls wipe sweat from their brows.

Annie fidgets in her seat.

Julian slouches.

LaShawn is struggling to stay awake.

Mrs. Thompson, Elena, and I remain as unbothered as possible. To show them what *is* possible.

I look over to the door.

I know it's locked. I know that we will be here until Deacon arrives, just at the perfect time, so he can free them.

It is a little white lie.

But they have to learn to trust Deacon—and that's hard to do in just three days.

I'm sweating, too. But I have to keep going. It's my sacrifice, another thing that makes me a miracle, and it will bring these kids closer to God.

So I push away the doubt and the darker thoughts, and I smile, and I listen as Mrs. Thompson tells them how this place is going to change their lives forever.

The world is broken.
    Reconciliation will fix it.

It's too loud inside.

Long, harsh lights overhead force me to shut my eyes for a moment. There's constant chatter. A child crying in a piercing wail nearby. Another coughing to my left, sitting in an adult's lap. Their mother? Foster parent? Social worker? I don't know.

We head to the high counter and the woman behind it—an older Black woman with her hair braided in an intricate pattern—asks if we have an appointment.

I don't answer. My gaze jumps from one person to another. To the cubicles and desks behind the receptionist, to the children waiting, to the signs on the walls and—

"Young man?"

I snap back. Monica squeezes my forearm gently with her hand.

"Go ahead," she says, nodding.

Deep breath.

Lie lie lie lie lie.

"I need some help," I say.

"Okay, honey," the woman says, adjusting her glasses. "What kind of help?"

Lie lie lie lie lie.

"I'm looking for my sister."

"Looking for her?" She frowns. "What do you mean by that?"

"I—I got separated from her. We were together most of our lives in a bunch of foster homes around here, but then . . . Yeah. I just want to see if I can find her again."

The woman raises an eyebrow and nods. "Okay. Well, let's do one thing at a time. Do you have ID?"

I shake my head.

"A name?"

"Manny."

"Last name?"

My mouth dries up.

I shouldn't be doing this.

The woman eyes me. "Son, I need your full name to continue."

"I don't know which one to use," I say. "I got . . . I got adopted a year ago or so."

"At your age?" she says quietly, and I don't think she meant for me to hear that. "Okay, do you remember your adoptive parents' last name?"

I can't form it. Can't utter it. Can't say it out loud.

"I don't mean to be cruel, Manny," the woman says, "but I have to have a last name to continue."

"Ma'am, I'm sorry to butt in," says Monica, stepping closer to the counter. Her voice is smooth as she talks. "But Manny here has been through a lot. I know you have your policies and such, and we're not trying to get around them. But he's . . . he's very overwhelmed by what he's been through."

The receptionist nods. "I understand. Sorry, it's just been one of those days where I've had to put out a hundred fires."

"Diana Rogers," I blurt out.

The woman's eyes lock on mine. "What did you say?"

"Diana Rogers," I repeat. "She was my social worker. She had my case. And my sister's."

Her demeanor changes. "Okay," she says, sitting up straighter. "I can work with that."

"Is she here?" Monica asks.

"She's been out in the field all day."

My heart sinks. Fuck. Well, this was pointless.

But the woman stands. Waves at me to follow her. "Come talk to one of the supervisors," she says. "You're sure you and your sister were with Diana Rogers?"

"Yes," I say, and I dart around the counter. "Yes, definitely."

"Well, that will narrow it down," she mutters.

We follow her down a brightly lit hallway. Past rooms with closed doors. I peek in one that's open. See a Black man with long locs hunched over a computer, typing away. Another room: vending machine. Coffee maker. One of those water dispensers with the big five-gallon jugs.

Then: into an office. It's small. One wall is filled with an enormous window. A calendar is tacked up on another wall alongside personal photos. There are posters with seemingly endless lists of rules and regulations, and the woman asks us to sit in two empty chairs opposite a wooden desk with metal legs. There's a boxy computer sitting to one side.

"Someone will be in shortly," she says.

Then she's gone.

We sit in nervous silence for only a few moments. Monica puts her hand on my knee after I immediately start bouncing it up and down. She smiles. Nods. I think it's her way of telling me that I'll be fine.

But I won't be. A thousand scenarios are running through my head:

They're going to know what happened to me.

They're going to know I'm a coward.

This is a mistake.

I'll never find her.

It's her.

A woman walks in. Tall, lanky, blond hair in tight little curls almost like a poodle's fur. She seems out of breath. Uncomfortable.

Doesn't make eye contact when she utters a low greeting. Can't even make out what she said.

She sits down—more like she throws herself into the chair—then drops a thick manila folder in front of her. When she looks up at us, I can see beads of sweat on her upper lip.

"Sorry," she says, "it's been a day around here."

"And you are?" Monica says immediately, her voice still as syrupy as it was when she spoke to the receptionist. "I don't believe you are Diana Rogers."

"I am not. Just the supervisor around here. Rachel Danforth."

Then Rachel turns her gaze to me. "And you said something very interesting to Jamiyah a few minutes ago."

"I just want to find my sister," I say. "Can you help me?"

"Could you tell me what you meant?" Rachel asks. She leans forward, sets her chin on top of her crossed hands. "Why did you say that your sister was *separated* from you?"

I glance at Monica.

She nods.

"Because it's true," I say. "I was taken away from her."

"How long ago?" asks Rachel.

"About a year."

"From *where*?"

There's a stone in my throat. I can't say the name of that place. The second I do, she won't believe a word out of my mouth.

I shake my head instead.

"Okay, well, can you tell me your sister's name? And yours? Jamiyah told me it was Manny. Is that correct?"

"Yes."

She pulls a keyboard out from under the edge of the desk and places it in front of her. "And your last name?"

I don't answer again. Just stare at her.

Rachel sighs. "I already found your file," she says, then pats the giant folder on the desk. "Sullivan, right?"

"I don't know if that's my name anymore," I say, and my heart feels as if it is about to burst.

This time, Rachel gives me a look that isn't annoyance. She tilts her head to the side. "Why do you say that?"

"Because . . ."

I swallow down the fear. I have to tell her *something*.

"Because the Sullivans gave me away."

"Gave you away," she repeats.

Types something.

Flips open the manila folder.

Her eyes go wide.

"This doesn't make any sense," she says.

And then the panic hits me in full, a tidal wave of terror and uncertainty bearing its weight down on me.

No. I can't do this. Oh, god, do they *know*?

"What doesn't make sense?" Monica asks.

Rachel narrows her eyes at Monica. "Exactly who are you?" she asks. "A guardian? His parent?"

"A concerned adult."

"But not *his* adult," Rachel says, pointing at me.

"It's . . . a lot more complicated than that," Monica says, and the sweetness in her voice breaks. She doesn't know what she's walked into, and it's all going to fall apart.

I stand up quickly. Knock the chair back, and it smacks against the wall.

"Let's go," I say to Monica, grabbing for her arm. "Now."

"Manny, what's happening?" she says, standing but taking a step away from me.

"Please, could both of you calm down?" Rachel asks. "Manny,

please don't leave. I'd love to resolve this discrepancy so I can help you."

Discrepancy?

"What do you mean?" I say.

She looks at Monica again, then presses her lips together tightly. "Diana filed reports on you. Your parents reported you as a runaway."

The fear dissipates.

In its place:

Rage.

"What did you just say?" I step toward the desk.

Rachel leans back. "She has all her reports in your file."

I sputter. I want to smash my fist through the top of the desk.

"I haven't seen her since she gave me to the Sullivans," I seethe. "It's been well over a year. She never checked in with me because my adoptive parents threw me out a month after they took me in!"

Rachel glances from me. To Monica. Back again.

"Do you remember the last date you saw her?"

"Not exactly," I say, my voice shaking in anger. "It's been a long, long time."

She types something.

Scowls.

Looks back up.

"Well, all the documentation is here. Why didn't you report this to us?"

The fury swirls in me, but Monica . . . Monica stops it. Rests a hand on top of mine, which I then realize is gripping the edge of the desk tightly.

"Miss Danforth, I promise you that is impossible," she says. "Manny couldn't have reported what happened to him to you because—"

"I'm sorry," says Rachel, "but who are you again? What's your name?"

"We should go," I say. "This is pointless."

Rachel quickly picks up the phone near her, hits a button, and I hear her ask Jamiyah for someone named Howard, and I don't need to hear any more. Monica is pulling me toward the door, but I don't resist. I follow her. Rachel yells my name again, but we keep moving. Past a closed door. Past an open one with a brown-skinned child crying in a seat all by herself while an older white woman observes impassively. Into the front area, and Jamiyah has her phone up to her ear, and she's looking at someone, then turns around to point at us.

There's a woman coming toward me.

Stringy blond hair. A blue cardigan over a white blouse. Short. Springs when she steps.

She freezes.

Stares at me as if I simply cannot be there. Should not be there. Because I shouldn't.

"Manny," she says. Almost breathless.

Diana Rogers grips the counter for support. Stares at Jamiyah.

"Where is Elena?" I say, my voice quiet at first, and then it pitches higher. "Right now. Where is she?"

She can't speak at first. The others in the waiting room, they're all staring at us, but I don't care. I just need to know. I need to know where she is.

Diana shakes her head. "Manny, where have you *been*?"

"Where have I been?" I scowl at her. "Why do you care *now*?"

"You ran away from your parents," she snaps back. "How would I know where you've been?"

"I don't fucking understand what's going on," says Monica. Then she looks around the waiting room. "Sorry for the language."

Diana sighs. "Manny, this isn't the time or place for this. You can't just waltz back in here, making wild claims and—"

"Wild claims?" I get right in her face. "Those nasty people you sent me to *without asking me* threw me away like garbage. *You* made it happen!"

"Please don't speak to me like that," Diana says softly. "I know you get emotional, but—"

"No, don't do that," says Monica, stepping in between us. "Don't try to discredit him for being emotional, and don't lie to him, either."

Diana scrunches up her face. "I'm sorry, who are you?"

"It doesn't matter," Monica shoots back. "Because this is bullshit. Manny did not run away. Why won't you just *listen* to him?"

"This is ridiculous," says Diana. She scowls at me. "When did you shave your head? Was that a recent decision?"

"No, it wasn't," I say. "Which you would know if you'd actually kept in contact with me! Why didn't you check up on us after you gave me and Elena away?"

I hope she'll reveal *anything* about Reconciliation, but instead, she shakes her head and says, "You're being absurd."

"That's all you have to say?" I scoff. "What does Elena have to say? When did you last talk to *her*?"

(I hold on to hope. I need to know.)

"Elena is eighteen now," Diana says, irritated. "We don't need to check in with her. Manny, this is a very serious thing you're saying. Do you understand just *how* serious?"

No. *No no no no.*

A tall white man with a close-cropped brown beard appears behind Diana. He has on a uniform: beige button-up, black slacks. There's a badge. Security. Maybe a cop. His hand is at his waist.

I think he's reaching for a weapon.

This is out of control. I can't do this anymore.

"I'll leave," I say, backing up. "Just tell me where Elena is."

"You know exactly where she is," says Diana, rolling her eyes. "She's right where you left her."

She glares at Monica. "How did you get here, anyway? This woman isn't your parent, Manny."

Then her face twists up again.

"Did she take you from the Sullivans? Because you know what I have to do next, Manny."

I groan loudly. "Please!" I say. "Just tell me where Reconciliation is. Please tell me where Deacon is hiding her at."

There is a moment when I think I've said what I need to, when she might actually tell me. Her face relaxes. A calmness passes over her.

"Oh," she says. "Okay, I understand now."

"Understand what?" says Monica.

"You're one of *them*, aren't you?" She puts a finger in Monica's face. "One of those activists or little citizen journalists who thinks that Christ's Dominion is evil, aren't you?"

It all falls away.

It all falls apart.

"You sent us away," I say, defeated. "You never should have given us to the Sullivans."

"I know exactly what this is," Diana continues, nodding. "Here is all I will say on the matter: I've made countless successful placements with families that Deacon has brought me. Every visit I've ever done for those kids has shown me that it was the right decision to make. Not once have I *ever* seen any evidence of what you people claim is happening."

"But—" I begin.

She raises a hand. "You're unbelievable. Both of you. I am not going to say that this department is perfect or that things don't go wrong, but we are trying to save children here. All you can see is a conspiracy, which says a whole lot more about you than it does me. There's nothing wrong with children going to good Christian families! What has this world come to where that's now a *bad* thing?"

The security guard steps closer. "Do we have a problem here?"

"No, Howard," says Diana smugly. "We absolutely do not."

She stares at me, irritated. "You've put me in a difficult position, Manny."

"Me?" I say weakly.

"The Sullivans . . . they gave up on you. They believed you would never come back, and it tore them apart."

Them?

The anger rages in me again.

"But I can't do anything unless you are detained by a police officer in the state of California. It's not against the law for a minor to be a runaway."

The white man behind her lifts his hand away from his waist.

"Do you want to go back to the Sullivans?"

I don't hesitate. "Never."

She glances at Howard. He shrugs. She turns back.

"Then I have nothing more to say to either of you," she says, and the look on her face . . .

She's disgusted with me.

And then Diana walks away from us.

I'm sitting in the backseat of the van, my chin resting on the seat in front of me. Monica slams her palm against the steering wheel. Once. Twice.

Then she gathers herself together. Glances up at me in the rearview mirror. Her eyes are glassy and wild.

"Sorry," she says. "I just . . . that triggered something in me."

"It's okay," I say softly. "Trust me, I get it."

It's a small moment:

She turns around. Locks eyes with me. And we share the sentiment.

We get this.

We know what this is.

We have both experienced it.

I don't know to what degree Monica is familiar, but that's what is on her face:

Recognition.

"For what it's worth," she says. "You deserve to be believed. You deserve to be treated as a person."

Then she makes a sound of disgust. "The way that woman looked at you . . . god, it was like you weren't human."

"I'm used to it," I mumble.

It's a step too far. Heartbreak tears at Monica's face. Maybe I shouldn't have said that, but it's the truth.

"But you don't deserve that. I hope you know that."

"Why do you care?" I say.

She shakes her head at me. "You're always asking some variation of that, Manny."

I shrug. "I'm a stranger to you. You don't need to be doing any of this."

"Says who? Why frame it that way? What if we *do* need to take care of one another?"

I don't mean to be cruel, but I look away. The anger is coming back, and her words . . . they're too close to something Deacon once said to me.

So the words come out.

"You sound like a preacher."

She clicks her tongue against her teeth. Faces forward. "That's because I used to be one."

I lift my head up. "What?"

"We both were," she says. "Me and Ricardo."

Shit. Me and my big mouth.

"I didn't know," I say. "Sorry."

She laughs. "It's fine, really. Ricardo is the more sensitive one about it all. I think he still wants to be one again."

"Do you?"

She waves a dismissive hand toward me. "No. I left that life behind for a reason."

"So you just . . . what? Don't believe anymore?"

"No," she says, without any hesitation at all. Then she turns back. "Do *you* believe anymore?"

I shake my head. "Kinda hard to after what I went through."

"Yeah, I feel you."

"I don't know if I ever did believe, if I'm being honest," I say.

A moment of silence. Her eyes drift downward, go distant.

"I don't know if you'll understand this," she says, "but I had a moment. Years ago, before we set out on the road and left our life behind. I realized that I'd been performing."

"Performing what?"

"Being a preacher."

But then she shakes her head. "No, not just as a preacher, but as a *believer*. My whole life, I'd been performing to a god I knew, deep down, I did not believe in. I acted like I thought he would want me to, and I assumed that one day, I would believe like everyone else. That faith would come to me, and it would all stop feeling so . . . fake. So artificial."

Monica faces forward once more.

"I don't think I've ever felt relief quite like being able to shed that performance for good."

She taps the steering wheel with one of her nails for a few seconds. Starts up the van. As we start moving, I stare out the window at the building. There are still people waiting outside. They look bored. Hopeless. Without direction.

I want to tell them all that they will not find what they need there.

I certainly won't.

Reconciliation was good for a very short period of time. The compound—enormous, stretching for miles in every direction, so far that I couldn't ever see the boundary—was gorgeous. Deacon Thompson introduced it to me as he introduced himself. As he explained how he'd founded this place a year ago when he realized that there was something specific that needed to be addressed.

"I know you are reluctant to be a part of something religious," he said as he walked alongside me, guiding me through the grounds. "At least that's what your sister told us."

I frowned at that, then looked back. Elena had stayed behind with the Sullivans. "I don't know what she's told you."

"That's fair," he said. "I'm not trying to make you into something you are not, and more than anything else, I'd like to hear from *you* about your life."

"Okay," I said. "But I don't know what this place is for or why I'm here."

"Reconciliation," he said, and he stopped walking. "Think of it as a place to finally be honest and vulnerable. A place where you can forget about the outside world and reconcile the two parts of yourself."

"I don't have two parts to myself, though," I said, and I scratched at my head. "At least, not how you guys think of it."

He started walking again. "So what do you think you are made of?"

"Made of? I don't know. Atoms and chemicals and water."

"But what about your *soul*?"

"Do I even have one of those? Pretty sure I was born without it."

It was kind of a joke, but Deacon gave me a stern look.

Ah, right, I thought. *You can't just say that kind of stuff around strangers.*

"Do you believe that, Manny?"

"I don't know. I guess."

We walked up to a large brick building with a wooden roof. Smoke lightly poured out of a chimney on top. Deacon showed me around the expansive kitchen. Three ovens. A fridge. A massive walk-in freezer. Four dishwashers. A pantry stocked with fresh veggies, fruit, canned goods, baking items. There were quite a few people whizzing about, rushing from one area to another. But each of them at least acknowledged us with a smile. A smile I'd seen before.

Took me a moment to realize it was the same expression I saw on the faces of the Sullivans a month earlier.

But another detail felt important enough that I couldn't ignore it.

All the adults were white, too.

I asked Deacon what they were doing.

"Each family that comes to Reconciliation gets their own home for the weekend," he answered. "We use community funds raised from online donations to feed everyone and just ask the parents to commit to a few hours of work around the grounds while their kids are learning. And your mother also runs the workshops with them during the day, too."

Wait.

"Kids?" I said.

Oh.

Aside from Elena and myself, I had only seen adults since arriving.

"They're in class with my wife," said Deacon, recognizing my epiphany. "You'd be there, too, but you got here later than the others. But I think you'll enjoy spending time with them. They're all like you."

I scoffed at that. "Like me?"

He merely smiled at that.

We stepped outside the kitchen. In the distance, through the tree line, I could see more cabins being built. I spun around. More behind me. "What are all those for?"

Deacon grinned. "My plan is to grow. We've been very successful with fundraising, and I know there are so many children out there who need homes. I want to be able to give that to them."

"So they'll live here?"

He shook his head. "No. Think of this place as more of a waystation. A place we can prepare adopted children for what life will be like for them in the outside world now that they're loved and taken care of. I consider it my greatest mission in life."

I was struck by how proud he sounded as he explained all of this. It did seem a bit too good to be true, though. It certainly didn't help that it all felt so vague to me.

Because what did kids *learn* here? And why did Deacon assume they were all like me?

He showed me the gardens, overflowing, vibrant, full of greens and tomatoes, squash on the vine, and watermelons.

He waved in the direction of his own home. "I stay at the end of that path," he said. "You'll see it tonight."

He had me peek in on the classroom. It was large. Rectangular. A plain-faced, brunette-haired white woman in a conservative blue dress and blouse spoke rapidly from the front. The kids all seemed pretty attentive to whatever she was saying. History, I think? She spoke rapidly about something that had happened in the past.

That didn't strike me as important, though. Maybe a little odd. No, it was the other detail that helped a piece fall into place.

Not one of the kids in that room was white.

Sometimes, you have to drift through these moments, questioning whether you're too sensitive, too defensive, too afraid of it being the actual truth.

But I wasn't imagining this. Every kid wasn't white. All the adults were.

It should have been a red flag. *Everything* should have been. But these questions about Reconciliation did not plague me as Deacon led me to the final place. They sat in the back of my mind, hiding in the shadows, because I kept telling myself the same thing: It was only three days. I just had to bullshit my way through this for three days.

Deacon walked up to a cabin. Opened the front door. Held it while gesturing for me to enter.

It smelled even more strongly of pine. Was mostly empty except for a modest couch, a coffee table, a medium-sized dining table. There was a hallway to the left. "Three bedrooms," he said. "Two baths."

"What is this?" I asked, running my hand along the smooth wood paneling.

"It's your new home," Deacon said. "At least as long as you're here with us."

"My home?"

I don't know that anyone had said those exact words to me in my entire life. My new home. Diana certainly hadn't. We always had "new guardians" or a "new placement."

Never a home.

Home.

The word, like so many others, did not seem to fit on my tongue. I walked down the hall, into a room on the right, and short rays of sunlight fell over a neatly made bed. An oak dresser. There was a small closet, too, and a trunk at the foot of the bed.

"Do you want this to be your room?" Deacon asked, standing

so close to me in the doorway that I could feel his breath on my neck.

I had an urge then. I wanted him to hold me again. So I backed up a bit. Brushed up against him.

He responded. Looped an arm over my shoulder. Clasped me tight.

"Yes," I said.

"It's all yours," he said.

I hated that I could see why Elena found Deacon so compelling.

There were six kids in Reconciliation by my final count that night when we gathered at Deacon's home for a welcome dinner. I sat across from Rakeem, a Black kid with a bushy fro, dark skin, and a septum piercing. He'd arrived not long after I did with his family, the Bradfords. Erin and Seth. I'd only seen them briefly as they ushered their son in. They were *young*. Maybe ten years older than Rakeem at best. It didn't quite make sense to me. I had already assumed everyone here was adopted in some form, but in all my years, I'd never seen guardians or adoptive parents younger than their mid-thirties.

I wondered what they were like. Was it easier to have younger parents?

I couldn't tell. Rakeem didn't exactly seem approachable. He sat at the table with his arms crossed over his chest. Didn't really ease up for the rest of the night.

Maybe it was Deacon's home. It was two stories, and a garish balcony sat over the wooden front doors. There was some sort of potted plant that had long grown out of its container, spilling a vine over the edge and snaking down the side of the house.

The whole thing looked fake, most of all because it didn't blend in with the surrounding forest at all. It gleamed white in the setting sun, which poured between the trunks of pines and oaks.

There was a giant chandelier hanging from the ceiling in the entryway. Every time the light hit one of the dangling crystals on it, it sparkled, brighter than the stars in the night sky. It sat over a large staircase that turned to the right and up to a second story. I could see it from where I sat in the dining room.

And the dining room. Jesus. The table, made out of some sort of dark wood, appeared to shine. And it was *enormous*. It was set with fancy silverware, plates, and napkins, but barely a third of it was being used for us.

Everything gleamed. Shined. Sparkled.

There were paintings on the wall. Of a beach scene, of a man being pulled out of the water as a shark lunged for his head, of a disjointed, angular portrait of a woman that's all lines and stark colors. They looked expensive. I wondered where he got them. How he afforded them.

Deacon sat directly to my left at the head of the table. He leaned forward. Put his hand on the small of my back.

"Your sister will be here soon," he said.

Then Deacon shifted his attention to the others, asked them to introduce themselves.

Simone. Originally from Haiti, adopted by the Loefflers. She had dark skin. Long hair in tight coils.

Omar. Originally from Mexico. Adopted by the Wilsons. Short. Dark brown skin. Short-cropped hair. Had dark eyes like mine.

Henry. Adopted from South Korea by the Gormans. Had his black hair combed to the side. Seemed super nervous sitting at the table and didn't really speak much.

There was Rakeem.

And . . . me.

What could I tell them? I wondered. Would it even matter? After three days, we'd all be strangers to one another again.

At least Elena had come in, finally, while Rakeem had introduced himself, and she was next to me, again.

"I'm Manny," I told them. "Elena's brother. We don't really know where we're from, because we've been in foster care our whole lives."

Elena looked at me expectantly, as if I had more to say.

"What?" I said. "It's true."

"And why are you here?" she asked.

I frowned. "Because . . . you asked me to come?"

"Because you *need* to be here," she said, then turned her gaze on the others. "All of you will understand that by the end of the weekend."

She paused and looked directly at Rakeem. Something passed between them, and it didn't look good.

I didn't get to ask about it, though. Elena reached over and grabbed my hand, talking just to me again. "This place is beautiful, isn't it?"

"I guess," I said. "It's very pretty."

She gripped my right arm. "You're going to love it. This place will change you, I promise."

I wanted to say:

Change me *how*?

I wanted to ask:

Why do you think I need to be changed?

Deacon raised his hands. Everyone fell silent.

"To our Heavenly Father," he said, "we give thanks for the bounty you have bestowed upon us, and for the gift of new friendship, new family, and new community. Amen."

No one but Elena said amen in response.

Deacon stood, and as he did, the parents began to pour into the room. They swarmed the table as Deacon stepped aside.

Wave after wave of food was brought to us, platters and plates stacked high with fresh vegetable salads and roasted squash, then Caroline brought in some sort of soup that was cold, but savory. She winked at me as she set it down.

Man, these people were *weird*.

While we ate, Deacon stopped by each person at the table to chat with them. By the time the third round of food came, everyone—except for Rakeem and I—was deep in conversation.

Multiple conversations, I should say. I couldn't follow any single one of them, as they looped around one another, collided with other bits and pieces of talk, all of it crowded with inside references. I think Simone and Omar had been friends on the outside. Henry spoke softly with Deacon, and Elena had stood to chat with one of the adults who had ferried in the food.

I was used to quiet, awkward dinners. Never got close with my foster parents enough to have nights like this. Plus, Elena and I rarely got housed with existing families because there were always two of us. Two was usually enough for a foster parent.

Is this what these kids' lives were like? Was this the norm?

A hand appeared in front of my face. One of the nameless white adults who was serving us smiled down at me. "Your plate?" she said.

I didn't get why we had to keep swapping them out. Couldn't we just put the new food on top of the empty plates?

By the time I turned back, Elena had moved on to Simone and Omar. Was introducing herself.

And once again, I was alone, left out like always. How did this come so easy to her?

She's been here before, remember?

All those times she disappeared for hours—days—at a time, she was with these people. She was becoming a part of their community. They were just welcoming her back, weren't they?

I looked over at Rakeem, who seemed to be having exactly the same sort of time I was. He picked at the plate of chicken and potatoes. Rested his chin in his left hand.

"Where are you from?" I asked.

He looked up. Raised an eyebrow.

"I'm not making friends here," he said plainly.

And that was that. Some luck I had with this group.

After I finished off the chicken, my plate was scooped away once more. Deacon Thompson finally made his way to me and Elena, and he squatted down between the two of us.

"How was the food?" he asked me.

"Good," I said. "Really good."

He offered a warm smile. "That's what I like to hear. This place is about goodness. Family. Community."

I glanced quickly over at Rakeem.

And when my eyes fell back on Deacon, I blurted out the question that had been sitting at the forefront of my mind the whole time.

"Right, but . . . what is this place *for*?"

The table fell silent. Every conversation died instantly.

"I already told you," said Elena, her eyes wide, pleading. "This is where your whole life changes."

I looked at some of the others.

They looked confused. Uncertain.

My gaze found Rakeem, who finally gave me his full attention.

"This is where they brainwash you," he said. "Don't listen to anything they say."

He scooted away from the table. Threw his napkin on his unfinished meal. Stomped out of Deacon's home.

"He's still adjusting," Deacon said softly. "Children like you . . . they are often not used to being treated well."

He rose.

"Manny, I know this is hard. But those of you who have been in foster care, who were abandoned as babies, who were born in countries less plentiful and less blessed than this one . . . you deserve better."

He gripped my shoulder. "That's what this place is for. To offer you something *better*."

"And then you'll change," said Elena, still smiling ear to ear. "All those things you worry about, Manny . . . well, they won't matter anymore."

I frowned. "Elena, you realize how *creepy* that sounds, right?"

She gasped. Pretty sure a few of the others did, too.

"Manny, don't—" she began.

"Actually, Elena, he's right."

My head snapped up to Deacon. "What?"

"Elena, we'll have you work with my wife tomorrow," he said. "If you want to start doing outreach, you have to work on your technique, okay?"

She nodded. As she looked downward, I saw that her face was flushed red.

"Manny, I promise you'll learn more tomorrow," Deacon said to me. Let go of my shoulder. Sat at the head of the table. "This place is not what it seems. It's not as strict, not as harsh, not as unforgiving as the world out there. You are *all* special. Rakeem included. You were brought here because your adoptive parents see potential in you, and they want to give you a space to *actually* heal, away from the nightmare of the outside world.

"None of you were born into Christ's Dominion," he continued. "It means that it might be a lot more difficult for you to mesh with your adoptive families. All we want to do is make that transition easier for you. To help you heal, so you can continue on your journey with God. And what better place to do that than here?"

He sucked in a deep breath. "You smelled it as soon as you got out of the car, didn't you, Manny? That deep, earthy aroma. That closeness to nature. That calm."

My skin tingled.

Deacon Thompson smiled. His blue eyes sparkled. Danced.

"You're going to do great things here, Manny."

I didn't believe him.

I didn't *need* to.

Three days. Three days in the mountains, among the finches and pine trees, and then I could go back to my life.

Easy. I'd given up more before.

So I smiled at Deacon. Gave him what he wanted.

"I look forward to it," I said.

Lie lie lie lie lie.

It's been hours since we left Public Services. Carlos had still wanted to skate around on his new deck, so Ricardo got a hotel in town because it was getting late. The place was a little bigger and fancier than the motel we left near Stockton that morning. As soon as they got their room, Monica and Ricardo darted off into it. I laid on the bed in the room next door and I could hear them. Talking frantically. Don't know about what. I assumed it was me. What had happened.

What Monica had seen.

I want to believe that they're going to stick around. The more I learn about the Varelas, the more interesting they are. The more I think I might be able to trust them.

But I still can't shake what happened the other times I chose to let anyone else in. Especially anyone who swore to protect and love me.

I should run away.

I should leave this all behind.

Lie lie lie lie lie. Do what you know, Manny.

Ricardo finds a taco joint for us for dinner that night. It has cooled down a lot, so I don't mind that we're sitting outside. I'm at a metal table that's been painted bright red, and Carlos has skated off again.

"How are you feeling after everything?" Ricardo asks me. He's spent hours resisting this question, even though I can tell he's been burning up to ask it.

"I don't know," I say. "Still a little numb."

"That's understandable," he says. "I mean . . . I know Monica talked about it, but I hate how familiar this all feels."

"She mentioned it."

Still don't know what "it" is, exactly.

Ricardo's mouth curls down on one side. "I think a lot of people simply cannot see the truth if they've invested their entire lives into a community like that. That Diana woman probably can't see the forest for the trees."

Carlos skates up to the table. "What are you guys talking about?" he asks. "Are you telling him about Lester?"

Monica's eyes go wide while her husband's mouth drops open a bit. "No," he says quickly. "Not yet, at least."

"Well, stop being all vague and weird about it," he says. "You wanted to know what happened to Manny, but now you're being all shy around him?" He rolls his eyes. "Make it make sense."

Ricardo rolls his eyes right back. "Oh, don't start with that."

"Am I wrong?" Carlos teases, then twirls his skateboard while balancing it on the nose.

"Why don't you go skate into oncoming traffic, mijo?" jokes Ricardo.

"I'll do it without a helmet, too!" he says, smiling. "Maximum danger at all times!"

Then he skates off.

"Who's Lester?" I ask.

I do want to know what big secret these people keep dancing around. But there's another reason for asking them about it:

I can direct the conversation away from me.

A staticky voice blares out of a nearby speaker. "Ricardo, your order is ready!"

"You tell him," he says to Monica, then jogs toward the pick-up window.

She frowns in discomfort. "Well, Lester Burton was an associate pastor at our church. We'd known him since high school, which is where I met Ricardo."

"So you two have really been together since high school?"

She nods. "Sometimes, it happens that way. I guess I just never really wanted anyone else. We got married at twenty-two, then started the Vine Fellowship after that."

"What's the Vine Fellowship?" I ask. "Like . . . a religion? A church?"

"A non-denominational church, yeah."

I blink at her. "Uh . . . I don't know what that word means."

"Sorry," says Monica. "It's basically . . . well, we were Christian, but we weren't attached to any of the specific denominations. Like Catholic, or Presbyterian, or Baptist. We didn't have any authority figures in our church either. Like the Pope, for example."

I can't help but think of Deacon. "So . . . no one was in charge?"

"Functionally, Ricardo and I were, which was part of the problem. Our church grew, and as it did, it took us away from home more and more. Media opportunities. Speaking engagements. God, there was a time when I thought that maybe Ricardo and I were going to become celebrities for what we were doing."

"Which was . . . what?"

Monica shrugs. "We tried to do something different. The Bay Area is pretty progressive, but we wanted to give others an experience with God that felt new. That felt open and accepting in a way that other communities attempted, but couldn't pull off. And it worked! For a solid decade, we kept growing. Kept accepting everyone under the sun and tried our best to make them feel loved. Like *truly* loved."

"But?" I say. "I feel like you're leading to that."

She sighs. "Yeah. Because our good work got us interviews. Other churches reached out to us to ask how we were able to draw in so many young people. So many people of color. So many queer folks. And we . . . shit."

Monica looks away. "We let it get to our heads. The notoriety was addictive. We started caring about that more than the actual work. So, as we spent more time away from Vine Fellowship, Lester filled the vacancy. Started doing what he wanted."

Ricardo returns then with two trays piled high with food, and she seems relieved that he's back.

She doesn't want to do this alone, does she?

Ricardo shields his eyes with his right hand. "Where's Carlos?" he asks. "I don't want his food to get cold."

He glances down at the two of us. Notes the somber mood.

"My timing was terrible, wasn't it?" he says, sitting down.

"No, mi amor," says Monica, reaching for his hand. "The opposite."

She looks back to me. "This part is hard to talk about, and at any point, Manny, you can tap out. We don't have to do this."

"Sure," I say. "But I don't actually know what 'this' is. What did that man do?"

Monica takes a deep breath. "A lot," she says. "Kicked kids out for any number of reasons. Was inappropriate with others. And when some of these things got back to me and Ricardo, he blackmailed and threatened the same kids into saying they lied to us. That they'd made up their stories for any number of reasons."

Ricardo frowns. "It's hard to accept that we made this worse," he says. "But it wasn't until Carlos came to us that we finally started to believe all the rumors."

"By then, however, it was too late," says Monica. "The damage was already done. That man . . . he tried to turn Vine Fellowship into his own little kingdom. He thought that what we believed in and put forth was too progressive. Too permissive."

"And of course, he went after the most vulnerable group of people first," Ricardo adds. "Children."

"It sounds like Deacon did, too," says Monica somberly.

"I don't even know what to say," I offer.

"Monica and I were out in the world," Ricardo continues. "Trying to spread the word about what we believed in and were doing. How it was important for the church to change with the times and with our greater knowledge of God. Meanwhile, Lester was quietly manipulating our church into a nightmare."

"We ignored children," says Monica, her voice defeated. "Children who were being sent to conversion camps that Lester's friends ran. Children who were being groomed and assaulted by Lester and his friends. Children who trusted us to take care of them and raise them in an environment of love, trust, and respect."

"That's what you meant," I say. "When you told me that you were traveling around to find the kids that were ejected from your church."

Ricardo nods. "That's part of it. You'll have to ask Carlos for the rest, though." He picks up one of the tacos and takes a large bite out of it. Chews. Swallows. "He has a big part in this, but . . . well, it's not our story."

Monica sips at her horchata. "We learned an important lesson in the worst way imaginable, Manny. We were all believers. We thought we were good people, that those we surrounded ourselves with were good people, too. Because we used that framing as an identity—we were *good Christians*, you see—we couldn't see the rot in front of our faces."

"Sounds familiar," I grumble, then roll my eyes.

Monica squeezes Ricardo's hand. "Diana said something like that. About how there is nothing wrong with kids going to good Christian families."

Ricardo groans. "I wish I could take that notion out back and put it out of its misery. It's just a convenient excuse. That's all it is."

Carlos skates back up to us. "Why didn't anyone tell me that the food was here?" he says, alarmed.

"How exactly was I supposed to do that?" Monica says, letting go of Ricardo's hand and picking up a carne asada taco. "Send up a taco signal so you'd see it?"

"I *am* Mexican," he shoots back as he sits down. "It probably would have worked on me."

"You and every other Mexican here," says Ricardo.

Carlos grabs a taco and wolfs down half of it in a bite. "Are *you* Mexican?" he asks me with his mouth full.

"I don't know," I say. "Elena and I have been in foster care our whole lives. We don't really know anything about our birth parents. Apparently, they're from Mexico, but even that's up in the air."

"Well, you can be an honorary Mexican with us," he says, shoving the other half of the taco in his mouth. "It's always good to have another one around."

The sentiment . . . that feels good to hear. I can't deny that.

But something else brews in me as we eat. As I fall back into my normal silence.

What these people have shared with me . . . it has opened up a possibility in me. Never met anyone who understands what it's like to have faith turned against you. I don't even know if I've ever had it to begin with, but that's not it. That place . . . Elena promised me it was about love.

(Lie.)

It's late. None of us know what we're doing after the disappointment that was Diana, so Monica suggests we brainstorm something the next day.

"As long as you're okay with that, Manny," she says.

Look, I don't know what the fuck I'm doing. I'm more than fine with waiting for tomorrow.

There is a TV in the room, anyways. It's still Monday, and so sometimes you can catch one of Deacon's programs at 11:35 p.m. Late-night showing.

This is a newer thing, though, and I wonder if that means Deacon is still trying to grow his community.

I don't care about that. I need a reminder of what Elena looks like. Of what I'm trying to do—why I should go back to Idyllwild.

Once more, I'm sitting at the foot of Carlos's bed, my back against it, the remote in hand. Flicking through channels at 11:36 p.m., hoping I see a familiar image.

It doesn't take long to find it. I've missed the music, the title card, the wide shot of Deacon on the stage in the lodge.

There she is, standing directly to Deacon's right, smiling as big as ever.

I lurch forward until I'm just inches from the television. I examine her:

Yellow blouse. Black skirt. Black hair pulled back. Is it still long? Shorter? I can't tell.

Deacon starts talking. Welcomes everyone to the day's message. Says that he has something important to tell the world.

I don't care, though, and disappointment deflates me.

Because I've seen this video before.

It's been a while, so I didn't recognize it at first. But his words . . . those bring me back. This is an old one, recorded long ago. He's saying that there's a war waging in the world between body, mind, and spirit.

I ignore it. It's all bullshit.

Elena is still smiling at his right side. Still beaming proudly, like she always did around him.

I wonder if there's anything here I could use to pinpoint Reconciliation's location, especially now that I know he's in Idyllwild. But there are no identifying details in these damn programs, except for the occasional shots of children on the grounds of the property. Even then, there wasn't ever anything in them to help figure out *where* the compound was. Deacon Thompson keeps everything vague. Non-specific.

Even his words.

"I have found the way to finally repair what the world has broken," he says, smiling.

No, you haven't.

"I know the secret to reconciling your damaged self with the self that God intended."

No, you don't.

"And Christ's Dominion will finally set this world on the right track back to righteousness."

No, it won't.

I reach out. Touch the screen. Wish so badly that I could feel her again. That I could yank her out of that nightmare, that I could remove her from those people, that I could save her and change her and make it so that she never, ever knew what Christ's Dominion was.

But . . . would she even want that?

Is this a fool's errand?

The lock clicks. The door flings open. I push myself back, I try to find the remote, but in my panic, I think I kick it under the bed.

"Is that him?" Carlos asks, rushing up to the television. "Again?"

Then he looks down at me. "What are you doing, dude?"

"Nothing," I say.

He grimaces. Raises an eyebrow. "Okay," he says.

Looks back to the TV.

"Manny."

He's not moving.

"Manny, is that *you*?"

The camera has panned out. Deacon is still droning on and on about saving the world, saving the children, and how he's only able to do so with the support of viewers like you, and there.

There I am.

Standing on the far left of Deacon.

Fuck. I'd been so focused on Elena that I hadn't even noticed *myself*.

"Bro, you look . . ." Carlos steps closer to the TV. "Why is your face like that?"

He points.

"Like you're happy, but . . . but *not*?"

There's a smile plastered on. Loose-fitting white T-shirt. Blue denim jeans. My hair is long. Well, longer than it is now. Curly-ish.

Smiling. Smiling. Smiling.

Carlos watches.

I can't turn away. Can't move.

I don't remember recording this with Deacon.

But that doesn't surprise me. I can recall most of the time I spent with him in great detail. Unfortunately, I guess. Some days, I wish I could forget it all. And yet there are times when my memory fails me, when things that happened fall through, as if I'm grabbing at blowing sand.

I stare at my smiling face on the screen, and heat rushes to my cheeks in the now.

I don't want Carlos to see me like this. Don't want him to see the truth of what I am—what I have been—what this is like, and what these people were capable of. How they could rob a person of their sense of self.

When was this? What part of that weekend?

Carlos points to the girl in the yellow shirt.

"That's her, isn't it?"

I don't answer.

I regain control of my body. Push up from the ground, and soon, I'm through the door, out into the hallway, running down the stairs, then out the revolving door in the lobby, and the air is cooler than I expected, and I welcome it. I suck it in, breathe deeply, but it's not enough.

No.

I can't do this.

I have to get away.

They can't know. They can't know any more.

Lie.

I didn't ask any questions that first day I was in Reconciliation because no one gave me any time to.

Thursday was basically an orientation day. Deacon caught me up, showed me what the schedule was going to look like over the coming weekend. Hikes. Classes. Prayer. Lots of community meals. Okay. I could handle that. Late that afternoon, after he'd finished running over everything with me, he said I had the rest of the day off. I could explore as I wanted, as long as I was showered and ready for dinner at eight.

I spent that time wandering the grounds. There were about five completed cabins, with the bones of about twenty more cabins spread around the clearing. I walked into the forest. Smelled the trees. Watched birds. Sat beneath a pine as the sun began to disappear.

It felt wonderful.

Who was I to question any of that? Nothing these people said could take away how gorgeous it all was.

Dinner was held out in the clearing between the cabins and the lodge. It was a huge picnic. Grilled burgers and sausages, potato salad, chips and guacamole, fresh cut fruit, brownies and cookies. All freshly made. I ate not because I was hungry—lunch had been enormous—but because it was there. Free. I didn't get this often.

The parents spoke to one another with ease. Showed off their children. Bragged about them. Even Caroline and Franklin got in on it, insisting that Elena and I were the smartest kids there.

I didn't call them on it, despite knowing that I hadn't gotten higher than a B my whole life. I let them claim it. Besides, I was enraptured by the starlight. So bright and brilliant. I leaned on Elena's shoulder as I watched more stars come out. As I told myself that I just had to get through the weekend. That's all that mattered.

I slept in a new bed that night. In my own room. No chores to do when I woke up, so I slept without an alarm. Couldn't remember the last time I'd been able to do that. Breakfast was provided for us. It was another feast. Scrambled eggs and toast and waffles with maple syrup—the really good kind. And when that was done, Deacon led us on a long hike through the land that Christ's Dominion owned, a large bag on his back.

It was beautiful. Magical. We waded through a cold stream at one point, then hiked uphill through the dense forest. Saw a deer. Don't think I'd ever seen one up close. We must have walked for four or five hours up that hill. Near the top of the incline, there was a massive waterfall that roared as it plunged down. Deacon set up there and revealed that the bag he'd been lugging up the hill was full of food. He spread out sandwiches wrapped in wax paper, sliced watermelon, and cookies that he bragged were baked that morning.

And as we ate, he told us that God had sent him to find this place.

I still struggled with that notion. It seemed odd to me that God would listen to Deacon, that he would help this one man, while so many other people didn't get one bit of his attention. It was a fundamental problem that no one wanted to talk about: How did God decide which prayers to answer?

He continued on, telling us how spiritual and holy this part of the world was. "You're closer to God on this mountain," he said. "This is why all of *you* are here."

Rakeem scoffed. Said nothing, though.

Deacon pushed past it. "I know you each probably have a bunch of questions."

I certainly did.

"And there will be time for that. But for now, I'd like you to appreciate this place. It is here that each of you will come to understand your *true* nature, that you will be able to shed your earthly self in reconciliation."

Even at the time, it sounded like bullshit to me. But I was in the middle of a forest. I was being fed. I had a roof over my head, and there were few things expected of me. I would say whatever this man or our foster parents wanted me to, not because I believed it, but because it would buy me time. I expected no permanence from the Sullivans, from Deacon Thompson, from Christ's Dominion.

They were another stop on my journey. At some point, someone would tire of Elena and me (probably just me), and we'd move on.

So why not take the good while I was able to?

I felt justified in this thinking an hour later as we snaked our way down the hillside. Simone asked Deacon how long this healing journey was supposed to take.

"Everyone has a different journey on healing themselves," he explained. "Reconciliation can take place quickly, and this weekend is an important first step for all of you. But for others, we have to give it time."

He glanced at Rakeem, who was hiking just ahead of us.

Simone brushed her long black hair out of her eyes. "Okay, but how *long*? When am I healed? How will I know?"

He laughed. Took her hand and helped her over some rocks. "The quickest we've seen someone heal . . . well, that record goes to Elena."

He gazed at her, and there was a look upon her face I'd never seen before. Happiness didn't quite cut it. Neither did joy. Or reverence.

Took me a while. But I figured it out.

I think she loved him.

She might still love him.

I don't know where to go. Don't know what to do. Don't know how to get out of this nightmare.

I should have grabbed my duffel. Should have been prepared for this eventual, inevitable moment when this was too much. When this good thing came to an end.

All good things come to an end. All things decay.

I remember a term right then, something I learned about in the last science course I ever took, before all of this happened.

Entropy.

Things always fall apart.

Things always remain a mess.

I walk to the left, sticking close to the building toward the parking lot. Not sure where I'm going. Maybe they'll come looking for me, and then I can sneak up to the room. Grab my stuff. Be gone.

Fuck. No. I can't. I don't have a room key.

I hear a car door slam. Turn around. See a man get out of a small blue sedan, a large bag hoisted over his shoulder. Realize I'm just being skittish.

I turn back and Carlos is *right there*.

I actually yelp. He jumps, too, probably because he didn't expect me to make that sound, either.

"Jesus, Manny!" he says. "It's just me!"

"How the hell did you get down here so fast?" I say, practically breathless.

He points to the right.

There's an exit door right there.

"Dude, you gotta stop with this bolting thing," he says, his hand on his chest. "I get that this is scary and weird and probably super uncomfortable, but you just . . . you just spaced out. And *left*."

"I know," I say. "I just . . . I can't do this."

Carlos fishes in his pocket. Pulls out a vape pen. Takes a hit, then exhales a thin blow of vapor. It smells earthy and thick.

"Don't tell them," he says.

"I'm not a snitch."

He holds it out to me. "You want some?"

I shake my head. "Nah. Not my thing."

He takes another pull. "Why not?"

"I don't like . . . feeling like I'm outside my own body," I say. "Like I'm not in control. I don't know why. Just how I am."

Carlos considers that for a moment. "I get that," he says. "I don't know that this would do that to you, but maybe we shouldn't find out right now."

"Thanks," I say.

"Though you might be less uptight if you tried it."

I scowl at him.

"I don't blame you, though. Your life . . . it seems pretty chaotic. So maybe you like feeling in control."

Okay, therapist, I think. *Bit on-the-nose there.*

Takes another pull. "I don't know if this makes sense, but this gives *me* control. Allows me to relax and think better. Stops my brain from going a thousand miles per hour."

"Shit, then maybe I *do* need it."

He offers again. I decline.

"Do you ever think about how weird your life is?" he asks before stuffing his vape pen in his pocket.

"That's a real direct question," I say, raising my eyebrow.

"It is," he says. "But I was just wondering if you think about it."

"I guess," I say. "I don't like putting too much thought into it, though."

"Because then it's harder to actually live your life, right?"

I purse my lips. "Yeah. I guess it is. How would you know that?"

"We're all made of secrets, man," he says. "You think there isn't shit I haven't told you yet?"

"I just didn't bother asking," I say.

He uncrosses his arms. "Why not?"

"I don't get to know people on purpose," I say. "I never stay with folks long enough. Sometimes, they overshare, but most of the time, they don't tell me shit. And I like it that way. It's easier."

"Easier than what?"

God, why is he like this? Nothing seems to satisfy him.

"It's just that . . . dude, I'm not used to people being interested in my life. They want to know my *story*, but to them, that's all it is. A story."

"It's separate from you," he says, nodding his head. "You're like a character in it, not a real person."

Bumps raise over my skin. "Yeah. Exactly like that."

"So . . . why keep moving? Why not settle down somewhere?"

"Settle down with *what*?" I say. "I own a duffel bag with clothes and toiletries. Where am I supposed to go? Or do? I don't have an ID. Or a birth certificate. The Sullivans have it all. I can't even prove I'm *real*."

"Shit, man," he says, and he takes the pen out again. "I guess I didn't think of it like that." Inhales. Holds it. Exhales. He's confident when he does. It's weirdly attractive.

Then:

"Those people really did you dirty."

"Yes," I say. "That's one way of putting it."

"And in the year or so since they kicked you out, you haven't found anyone?"

I tilt my head to the side.

"Anyone like Ricardo and Monica?" he clarifies.

"You mean . . . like *nice* people?"

He laughs. But then he fidgets with his pen in his pocket. Leans against the wall.

"No," he says. "Not like that."

And then he changes.

I've seen Carlos as a confident person. As someone who knows who he is. Who knows what he wants. Who is opinionated and funny and just . . . just a whole person.

Unlike me.

But something is crumbling there. He twists his face up. Looks away.

"You know they're not my parents, right?"

"What?"

He looks back quickly, panic on his face. "I mean, they *are*. The adoption went through a couple years ago."

"You're *adopted*?"

He nods. "I am."

"Wait, so that means . . . Shit. How old were you?"

"Fifteen," he says.

What the *hell*?

"I have a million questions," I say. "I don't know what you're okay with me asking."

"Oh, so *now* you're interested in me?" he teases, raising an eyebrow.

"Shut up," I groan. "Like . . . wait, how did this happen? *Why*?"

"My parents—my first ones, that is—they gave me up, too."

I feel like I'm going to pitch forward. My head spins. My heart races. Carlos does not seem nearly as upset as I expected, but . . .

When I told the Varelas about Reconciliation, I wasn't emotional. I didn't cry. Why am I not expecting the same of Carlos?

"Well, goddamn," I mutter. "That's awful."

"It was," he says. "They chose Lester over me. They didn't believe me when I said he tried to seduce me. When I told them that he touched me all the time. Little stuff at first. Like his hand on the small of the back. Lots of hugs. He used to do this thing where he kissed me on the top of my head. I guess I liked the attention at first, but it just kept getting worse. So I finally told him to knock it off."

"And did he?"

He rolls his eyes. "Of course not. Until he followed me into the church bathroom one day. Tried to make out with me in a stall."

"Fucking hell," I say. "I'm sorry, man."

"I mean . . . I'm okay now." He grins. "Lester wasn't. Especially not after I kneed him in the balls."

"Seriously?"

"If only that had worked," Carlos says, sighing. "He may have stopped with me, but I suddenly noticed things I'd never seen before. Him following other kids. Boys and girls and nonbinary kids. Gender didn't matter. And every time, these kids just . . . disappeared eventually. Sent away, or they moved, and I started piecing it together."

"Why didn't you disappear, though?" I ask.

"I think I was the only one he was actually afraid of." He gestures at his own body. "I'm a big guy. People have weird ideas of what I'm capable of."

Carlos frowns then. "But I told my parents after Jamal went missing. Like, one day, he wasn't at school or church. And he was my best friend, and I knew Lester had done something. So I told them everything I suspected."

"And it didn't go over well, I'm guessing."

He shrugs. "They literally said I made it all up for attention.

By the end of the week, they'd told Lester, and they all agreed: I'd broken some holy covenant. Lying and disrespecting my family and the church, and . . . that was that. I was out."

"And the Varelas took you in," I say, shaking my head.

He nods. "Pretty quickly after my parents threw me out," he says. "Once the news got to them, they found me at a park down the street from my house. I haven't left their side since."

"But . . ." I scratch at my head. "I don't get it. You said they adopted you."

"They did." He smiles, more a rueful thing than anything else. "Because my parents allowed it. I filed for emancipation from them when I was fifteen, and they gleefully agreed to it. Told the judge I was a demon who didn't belong in their home anymore, and the Varelas were more than happy to take me in."

"The others," I say, tears springing to my eyes. "You guys find the others. That's what you're all doing."

"Yeah," he says. "And we don't even know how many of them there are. He sent so many kids away—all with their parents' permission, mind you—and we also can't remember them all. So, sometimes, we're visiting these people to reconstruct how many are out there. Or how many need help."

"That's what we were doing in Redding," I say, and the pieces fall into place. My eyes go wide. "Yvonne was—"

"One of his victims," Carlos finishes. "We'd been trying to find her for six months. So, once we do, we help them. Get them papers, ID, food, housing . . . all that stuff that is exceptionally hard to get."

He winces. "Right. I don't need to explain that to you. You already know."

That's what he meant, then.

Why hadn't I found people like his parents?

I didn't have an answer to the question. My mind swirled in confusion. In shock.

Carlos knew. He knew what it was like to have your family reject you like that.

"I'm sorry," I say. "About Jamal. You were going to go visit him, and I—"

He holds a hand up. "I promise we're good, Manny. I really understand why you did what you did. And Jamal is fine! He starts college in the fall, he's got a cute-ass boyfriend he met while working, and we were just paying him a visit."

"Still," I say. "I didn't mean for that to happen."

"It's all good." He grabs part of his shirt and sniffs it. "Can you still smell the vape?"

I lean forward. Sniff. Inhale a sweet scent. I think he's wearing a cologne of some sort. I resist the urge to lean closer. To put my hand on his arm and pull him in.

"You're good," I say. "Can't smell it."

"Thanks," he says. "So . . . can we go back up to the room? I shouldn't be out too long or Papi will get suspicious."

So we head back in silence. I still don't know what to say to his confession, to the revelation that in this one way, he *is* like me.

I don't know what the fuck to do with that.

After we pass through the revolving door into the lobby, we see Ricardo at the front desk. He turns and smiles, then holds up a toothbrush. "Dropped mine in the toilet."

"I don't want to know how," says Carlos.

His dad looks from him to me, then back.

"So, this wasn't how I wanted to do this," he says, "but did you just share your weed vape thingy with Manny?"

Carlos actually gasps beside me.

Shit.

Ricardo raises his hands. "It's fine, papi. I'm not angry or anything."

"How long have you known?!"

"Six months at least."

"But *how?*" Carlos implores.

"Mijo, I can smell it on you *every* day."

Carlos nudges me with his shoulder. "You said you didn't smell anything!"

"I didn't!" I say.

"You both severely underestimate how much weed I've smoked over the years," says Ricardo. "Think I didn't notice after that first time outside Yosemite?"

"Ugh," Carlos groans. "Are you trying to be one of those cool dads?"

Ricardo rolls his eyes as he guides us toward the elevators. "Mijo, I'm an ex-preacher who travels the country with his homeschooled kid in a modified touring van while he rescues kids exiled from a church. There's not a single parent cooler than I am right now."

The elevator doors open with a ding, and we get in. "Well, shit," says Carlos. "Now I'm going to have to move on to harder drugs so you seem uncool by comparison."

"A brilliant plan, Carlos. Becoming a drug addict out of spite."

I laugh at that one. "You guys are too much."

Ricardo smiles at me. Rubs my scalp with an open palm.

And for the moment, it feels . . .

Normal.

I think it's almost midnight.

I can't sleep. Wide awake. I have been trying to avoid tossing and turning on the floor because I don't want to irritate Carlos. So I stare up at the ceiling. Count the tiles. Try to push away the mounting dread.

Tonight was nice.

It isn't going to last.

It's the thought my mind keeps coming back to. Our connection, no matter how significant, will ultimately sever.

I am in over my head. I shouldn't have initiated this, but it has a momentum of sorts. A mind of its own. One good thing leads to another, doesn't it? And now, I've broken so many of the rules that Cesar taught me, and where has it led me?

Ricardo spoke to me before he went over to his room; gave me his support. Said that he was glad I was in the family's lives. Said that they'd do everything in their power to reunite me with Elena.

When am I going to believe what people say? Because I don't. Maybe it's of my own making. No one should believe me. I lie to everyone.

Maybe at the end of the day, the person I really don't trust is myself.

The mattress squeaks. Carlos rolls over.

His head is above me.

"Sorry," I whisper. "Did I wake you?"

"No," he says. "Couldn't hear you at all."

Pause.

"Sleep in the bed," he says. "Please."

I could argue. Disagree. Tell him a lie about why I don't want to, how I'm more comfortable on the floor.

I sit up. Grab the edge of the mattress to leverage myself up. Quietly slip into the bed on the opposite side, then face away from him.

Look at the red alarm clock.

12:02.

"Happy birthday, Carlos," I whisper.

Silence.

Mattress squeaks.

Then.

A hand. On my right arm. He loops it around to my chest, pulls me. Squeezes.

"Thank you," he says, his voice deep, soft.

But his hug doesn't end.

It isn't a hug.

He holds me close. My body is on fire. Heart thumping. Blood rushing down there. Can't breathe.

He doesn't let go for the rest of the night. Just holds me like that.

I think I am imagining it, but it all feels real: the body heat. The sweat. The smell.

I fall asleep in someone's arms for the first time in my life.

It isn't love. It isn't a promise. It isn't anything but what it is.

But when you've wandered a desert for most of your life, you are overjoyed when it rains.

I'm watching Julian, Annie, and LaShawn head off to afternoon instruction after lunch when Elena grabs my arm. I stop just outside the lodge as the parents shuffle in.

"Hey, Eli," she says. "Do you have a moment?"

"Yeah," I say. "Mrs. Thompson says I have the afternoon off anyway." Elena smiles warmly. "Take a walk with me."

Mom waves at the two of us as she passes by to head into the lodge for the parent classes. "Deacon says you're both doing wonderfully," she says quickly, then winks before rushing inside.

The doors close. I wonder what she teaches in there. What does she tell them about us?

Elena guides me toward the gardens, which are beyond the cabins still under construction in the south. She doesn't say anything as we walk; she just breathes in deeply, slowly, deliberately.

"Is something wrong?" I ask her as we approach the nearest crop. Watermelon, I think. The vines spill out over the ground, and bumblebees dart in and out of the greenery.

"No," she says, her hands behind her back, her gaze on the rows of vegetables that are grown on the compound. "You did really good this morning, Eli."

"Thank you," I say. Then, after some hesitation: "It's harder than I thought it would be."

She nods, still examining the garden. "It was that way before, too," she says.

"Before what?"

She flinches. "Before you. You know, with the other souls who have come through this place."

"Does it ever get easier?" I ask. "Talking to strangers. Trying to convince them that this place really is what Deacon promises it to be."

She finally turns to me and smiles. "Yes, it does."

"How?"

"With practice," she says. "The more you tell your story, the more comfortable it becomes. The more you understand your purpose on this Earth, the more determined you are to help others find their path."

"What's your purpose?"

"To direct souls to God," she says without hesitation. "Specially, those souls born without parents. Those in foster care. The orphans. The ones who have been abandoned."

On the last word, Elena nudges me with her shoulder. "The ones like us," she adds.

She grabs my hand. "You realize that God made us special, right?"

"Special how?"

"The things we went through may have been hard, but they brought us to this place. We suffered so that we could be holy. We despaired so we could bring others joy."

"But I don't remember what I went through," I say.

Elena lets go of my hand. "Right," she says. "God made you special in a new way."

I sense something there. Not just hesitation. There's a space growing between us. Have I said something wrong?

"That's your miracle, Eli," she says. "You were given a true clean slate. That's never happened before. That's what you're going to give to these three kids: a fresh start."

"But how do I do that?" I say. "How does reconciliation actually happen?"

"Leave that up to Deacon," she says. "Just do what you've been called to do: Share yourself. Show the others what this new life has given you."

"I will," I say softly.

But Elena hears it: the lack of confidence in my voice. She turns to me. Raises an eyebrow.

"There's no one like you, Eli," she says. "That's why none of us gave up on you through your rehabilitation and training. We knew you were special."

The side of my mouth curls up. "I know," I say. "And you didn't have to take me in, but you did. I have a family now because of this place."

"We chose you," she says.

Then it's there: the wall. The barrier. Elena's eyes go distant for a moment, even though she's staring at me, even though she's still talking.

"Never forget that," she continues. "God loves to bless others with the gift of life, but there's nothing more sacred than parents who *choose* their children."

She steps closer. "Please, just think of that when you're in doubt. We chose you. And you don't want us to regret that choice, do you, Eli?"

Elena squeezes my upper arm. Drifts off, distant in every sense.

My heart is lead in my chest. I can't disappoint these people.

Before dinner, Deacon has us gather for a broadcast, standing on the small stage behind him.

It's important to show the world what we believe, he tells the new souls. What important work is done in Reconciliation. And these broadcasts . . . they reach people. They find those who need Christ's Dominion. That's what we're doing: spreading the truth.

"Consider it a preview of what's to come," he says as he assembles us on stage. "You'll all be my little stars."

I think Annie likes the idea of it. She blushes when Deacon positions her directly to his right. Elena absolutely does. She's all dressed up in a loose yellow blouse with a long black skirt. Says she wants to make a good impression. I didn't have anything as fancy as her; just a white shirt and jeans.

So I make up for it with my smile. I'm behind Annie and Julian on the left, and I stand up as straight as I can. I shove the doubt down. Away. Force it into a space in my heart no bigger than a grain of sand.

Mrs. Thompson handles filming. Deacon goes over the run of the show.

And every time the camera rolls, I stretch my mouth wide.

Smiling.

I will show the world what a miracle I am.

On that first day, Omar tried to ask what Reconciliation really *was*. But Deacon wouldn't really explain it. Just kept making references to the war between our spirit and our body, the same war I'd never heard about before I had met the Sullivans. It was a feedback loop. A repeating circle. We couldn't break our way out of it.

Why had this place made Elena so happy?

Why did the Sullivans want me here, too?

I was sure they saw me as some sort of delinquent, after all the sneaking out and moodiness. Someone dedicated to sin or evil or whatever antiquated belief they had. And this place would "heal" me.

So, was this like conversion therapy? I'd heard horror stories about the practice from other kids in the group home Elena and I had been in. A place kids were sent to by their foster or adoptive parents so that the gay could be "prayed" out of them. But as far as I knew, no one aside from Elena even knew that I *was* gay.

It didn't add up. Deacon's whole faith thing was odd, but he was kind to us. He seemed as if he genuinely wanted the best for our lives. There was no talk of fire and brimstone, of Hell and penance, of sin and deviance.

Shit. I was really naïve.

———

We got back to our cabin in the early afternoon. I sat on the porch. Stretched my sore legs in the gorgeous afternoon light. I can't lie. Life felt good at that moment.

Caroline approached me while I was there. "You seem to be fitting in here," she said softly, sitting in the wooden chair on the porch. She looked around quickly. "You seen the other chair? I swear there were two of them."

I shook my head. "Never really noticed another, to be honest."

And then, when I could tell she was waiting for me to respond to her first comment:

"Yeah, I guess I am. It's nice here."

"Good," she said, leaning back into the chair. "This place is Godly."

The question prickled my skin. I knew I shouldn't poke the hornet's nest—especially if I was trying to successfully bluff my way through the weekend—but I couldn't resist.

"Caroline, why am I here?"

She glanced over at me. "Because it's important to us."

"Right, but . . . is there something wrong with me? The way Deacon talks about this place, it's clear that he thinks the world out there is pretty awful."

"There's something wrong with *all* of us," she said plainly. "Reconciliation helps you repair yourself."

"Right," I repeated. "But like . . . what's wrong with *me*? I feel like that's the meaning buried under the surface. You and Franklin saw something in me the other night that made you want to bring me here, right?"

She didn't answer for a second. Picked underneath her nails.

"We don't know the world you came from," she said. "We don't know what you've been exposed to all these years. Think of this place like . . . like a cleanse. A detox. It will help you get rid of all your nasty impulses. See the world for what it is. And then, when we go back home on Monday morning, you'll feel . . . right. Like you're exactly where you're supposed to be."

She stared out at the forest, a warm smile on her face.

But it didn't warm me.

I finished stretching, then sauntered away to shower off the filth that her words left on my skin.

Nasty impulses.

I worried about what that meant.

Dinner Friday night was a smaller affair. More like light snacks. Deacon said the adults had been in classes led by my parents all day, so they hadn't had time to create a larger meal for us. It was fine, even though I was a little hungry because of our ten-mile hike. I ate the roasted corn and sausages quickly while Deacon played his acoustic guitar. He sang some pretty cheesy worship songs, but then he took requests and I was surprised he knew stuff like Social Distortion and Depeche Mode.

But there was still that odd familiarity: Elena knew some of the songs I didn't. The adults sang along—and even cried—as Deacon crooned about God's power or the sacrifice given to us or some other theological thing I didn't understand. Was this supposed to inspire me? Make me feel like the Holy Spirit was entering my body?

I just felt like an outsider all over again.

Elena, though . . . she was *enraptured*. She wept openly, but not in a sad way. She looked ecstatic. So did Omar, who fell into a rapid burst of Spanish as he prayed, spoken so fast that I could barely make out any of the words. Henry followed after, but his tears looked frightened. I had a dark thought: Was he crying because he didn't want to be the only one *not* crying?

I thought that I was just projecting. That I was imagining Henry's thoughts because they were actually mine.

But then I saw that Simone and Rakeem were just as confused or disinterested as I was. Simone had an eyebrow raised as she looked around the gathered families. She didn't sing along once. Rakeem had his hands behind his head, laid out flat on his back, and he stared up at the stars between the trees.

I didn't know what to do. What to say.

The singing rose to a terrible crescendo. Adults and kids cried and shrieked. Deacon yelled over it all. "He is here! Don't you feel Him?"

Yeah, I didn't feel anything.

And a new thought birthed itself in my mind:

Was there something wrong with me?

Why did this seem to come so easily to all these people? Why were there only three of us who weren't affected by the display? A part of me yearned to be a part, but most of me . . .

I just didn't get it.

And then it was over. People hugged, wiped away their tears, thanked Deacon, then guided their kids back to their cabins.

I had no fucking idea what had just happened.

I didn't sleep well Friday night.

The Sullivans and Elena stayed up to pray in the living room. I could hear them long after the crickets arrived, after Reconciliation otherwise fell into silence.

They were praying about me. Asking God to bless me and send me the wisdom to know what I was being given. Asking God to cast away all the doubt I'd been poisoned with.

It all felt so passive-aggressive. So *unnecessary*. But what could I do about it?

So I lay in that bed, counting the seams between the wooden boards on the ceiling. My stomach rumbled; I was still hungry. I thought about how the day had started off so well, and yet there I was, irritated and confused in a strange new world.

Where was I?

Why wasn't I allowed to know where Reconciliation was located?

What was so secretive about this place that no one would tell me outright what it was for?

I doubted that night. The Sullivans thought that was a poison in me, but I couldn't see why they *didn't* doubt all of this.

What *was* this place?

There was a moment at breakfast on Saturday morning where I became acutely aware of the change. Caroline led me into the lodge, where there was a basket of apples, carafes of orange juice, and some baked pastries. Nothing more. I only had juice and a Danish because Red Delicious apples are the world's true evil. They taste like toothpaste.

Afterward, the six of us were brought out into the clearing and Deacon met us there. Said that we'd begin to truly cleanse ourselves that day.

"Over the next forty-eight hours, your lives will change," he explained. "It will be frightening at times, but just know you're among your people. You will be taken care of."

We listened to Deacon tell stories of setting up Reconciliation. Of visiting faraway countries like Venezuela or Ghana or Chile or El Salvador and seeing how many orphans there were, and knowing that he could do something to help them, to give them a better life.

"That's why you're all here," he said. "You've been saved, but it's not enough. In order to truly make you God's perfect vessels, we must clean you. Think of finding the perfect plate or dish at a thrift store. It might be a little chipped or cracked, but you know it's the one. But you wouldn't immediately serve food off of it, right? No, you'd wash it by hand, taking care not to damage it while you scrub off the dried food, the dust, the filth."

His lips curled up in a smile. "That's what is going to happen. A cleansing."

I looked to the others. Once again, only Rakeem and Simone seemed disturbed by Deacon's words. The others . . . they were wide-eyed with excitement.

I realize now what it felt like.

Like summer vacation had just come to an end.

California is massive. It would be so easy to get lost here. To become anonymous. Just a brown boy with a first name and nothing else. I could reinvent myself. They do that here in California, don't they? I could become a musician. Front a band. Tour the world. Leave all of this behind.

I don't, though.

I'm not good at the aftermath of panic. Never have been.

I wake up in a sweat again. Peel myself from Carlos and head to the bathroom. Shower off the fear and the shame and the desire. Because as terrified as I am over what just happened, I also want it. I want it so badly.

I clean up. Look at the fuzz on top of my head and realize I need to shave it all off soon. I moisturize. Pack it all up, set it on top of my duffel under the desk, and the—

I think about crawling back in bed.

I think about what it would feel like if he welcomed me.

Pulled me in tight again.

I move on.

My body tingles like a thousand tiny bee stings as I sit across from Carlos at the diner we're at. They sing happy birthday to him, much to the annoyance of both Carlos and some of the other patrons. He gets a brand-new set of over-the-ear headphones. They welcome him to seventeen.

He looks at me once during this. Smiles like we share a secret.

Because we do.

It sets my body ablaze.

Carlos is the one who comes up with the idea.

I can't seem to eat, even though I'm hungry. Every bite of the waffle is lead in my stomach. Between Diana and Carlos, my mind is an unholy mess of anger, resentment, lust, and anxiety. Truly a fun mix. Invite me to your parties.

Monica and Ricardo are doing that thing where they are clearly talking *about* me, but I'm not part of the conversation. They're strategizing. Ricardo is convinced that Idyllwild is a small enough community that we can just drive there and figure out where the Reconciliation compound is. Monica argues that this is the worst idea her husband has ever had, especially when she points out just how large the wilderness is on Mount San Jacinto.

"Do you think we should just don backpacks and camping gear and wander a forest until we find a group of creepy Christians?"

"Maybe!" Ricardo says. "I mean . . . okay, that doesn't sound great when you put it like that, but I was thinking of it differently. You know, ask around town. See what the locals know."

She narrows her eyes at him. "And a bunch of brown people asking about a church compound that's a big secret isn't going to look suspicious?"

Ricardo gives her something in between a grin and a grimace. "This is why I married you, isn't it?"

She reaches over and grabs his hands. "And don't you forget it."

"Well, now that you two are being all gross and straight again," says Carlos, "what if we abandon that idea and we just go to the Sullivans' house?"

We all turn to look at Carlos.

"What?" he says. "Isn't Hemet super close to here? Maybe Manny's shitty parents will be there, and we can just *ask* them where Elena is."

My mouth drops open. I mean . . . it's not a terrible idea.

No. No! It's an awful one. I haven't seen the Sullivans since—

The images are swirling back.

What they said to me, did to me, what they chose, what she chose—

"Manny."

Carlos.

Carlos has his hand on my arm.

"Hey, it's okay," he says, and I find his eyes. Dark. Soft. "Take a deep breath. We aren't going *anywhere*."

"Not without your permission," adds Monica. "You're leading this, remember?"

I don't want to lead anything.

I want to disappear.

"I'm sorry I was so casual about that," says Carlos. "It's not just a 'good idea' to you. This is your life."

"I know," I say, and I wipe away the sweat that's now appeared along my hairline. "It just . . . all came back. All at once."

Carlos takes his hand back. "Yeah. That happens sometimes."

Then he smiles. "Welcome to being mentally ill!"

It undoes me in the best way. All four of us collapse forward onto the table, and I laugh until there are tears. I'm certain we're the most annoying table in here, but I don't care.

Wow.

I don't care.

"Let's do it," I say. "Fuck it. Let's go to that house."

That cuts their laughter short.

"Wait, are you serious?" says Ricardo.

"Man, why *not*?" I say. "After all this. Like . . . I'm just now realizing how satisfying it would be if I show up. They're not expecting to see me ever again."

"Surprise, bitch!" says Carlos. "I bet you thought you saw the last of me."

Not sure what Carlos is referencing, but he seems pleased with himself, so I smile.

And I'm also smiling because . . .

Shit. I'm afraid.

There is a part of me that wants to see the shock on Franklin's or Caroline's face.

That wants to hear what possible excuse they have for what they did to me.

That wants . . . revenge.

One fantasy at a time, Manny.

"Do you remember the address?" Ricardo asks. "That's the easier option. I could probably find them through property tax information or the county clerk and—"

"Please don't bore him with details," Monica interrupts. "I know you get excited for this part of the research."

"It's okay," I say. "We don't need any of it."

I tell them exactly where to go. It was the last "regular" home I had before . . .

Well, before all this.

Ricardo plugs it into the GPS for Monica. "Less than an hour," he says, then turns back to me. "Do you really want to do this, Manny?"

To be honest, I don't know what "this" is.

I think they have an idea of what's going to happen. I'll show up. Maybe one of the Sullivans will be there. There will be a confrontation. We'll either get more information on Elena, or we won't.

The problem is, they don't know everything. They don't know that once Franklin or Caroline sees me, I'll be an instant reminder of what they did to me. Of how they abandoned me in the middle of nowhere. Of their own culpability.

There's a chance that I'm not the one who will erupt in anger, in violence.

It might be them.

"Yes," I tell them. "We should try it. We should go there."

"We've all got your back," says Carlos, nodding.

"All of us," adds Monica.

First time in a long, long while that I believe it. There's another possibility here:

That we get the information that we want.

That I find out the body is not Elena's.

That I rescue her.

That we all get to escape Deacon's clutches.

"Then let's do it," I say.

I met Mrs. Thompson—*really* met Mrs. Thompson—for the first time that Saturday morning.

I'd never been around someone so confident. So sure of everything they said or did. I ended up walking to her classroom with Rakeem after our paltry breakfast. While my stomach rumbled, Deacon marched us over to her himself. "Try to keep an open mind," he said. "She has a lot of brilliant things to share with you."

Rakeem looked up at Deacon. Gave him a smile that seemed genuine, too.

"No," he said.

Rakeem and I sat in the back of a room that felt stuffier than it did when I first peeked in on one of Mrs. Thompson's lessons. The others shuffled in afterward.

Except Elena. Apparently, she didn't need to learn anything.

Mrs. Thompson rose from the small desk tucked in the corner. Wiped her hands down the front of her long skirt. "Good morning, children," she said. "I've met most of you before, but let's all welcome Manny Sullivan, who missed our orientation class on Thursday."

The group offered a paltry welcome to me.

"Uh . . . thanks," I said. "What did I miss?"

Rakeem yawned. "Nothing you need to know," he said sleepily.

"No more interruptions today, Mr. Bradford," snapped Mrs. Thompson. "I know it's your thing, but please let the other children have a chance to learn."

And then she began to talk.

It was rambling at times. Incoherent. Dramatic, though. I had to give her that. Mrs. Thompson had a cadence to the way she spoke, kinda like her husband did. Highs and lows, and she was so good at emphasizing words and key phrases, but as for what those words and phrases *were*?

She started off by reminding us that the world was bad. That outside Reconciliation, unless you were healed and ready to face evil, we would fail.

(Fail at *what*?)

She said that everything that went wrong in our lives happened because we hadn't been brought here. Rakeem chuckled.

"It's true," she said. "Everything."

"My last foster parents called me a slave," he said matter-of-factly. "How did that have anything to do with Reconciliation?"

I expected her to falter.

Instead, she grinned as if she'd just been handed a victory.

"Because the world in here is not like the world out there," she said. "We are trying to strip all evils out of you. Out there, people are spoiled by the poison of racism. In here, we are closer to God's true purpose and mission."

I watched Rakeem narrow his eyes at Mrs. Thompson. "You said that yesterday, but you're a bunch of old white people trying to teach *us* about how to make racism go away. So . . . how exactly does that happen?"

"Through instruction," she said. "Even though it's only a day or two, I'm giving you the information you need to let go of who you've all been."

"That's your answer?" said Rakeem.

"No," she said confidently. "You are all constantly teaching us about the world beyond Reconciliation. What *we* are doing is building a new one within. You can live in a world without race, where you get to be part of God's family. God does not care about skin color or country of origin. You are all His children, and *that* is why you experienced what you did. You simply were never close to Him."

"What the hell?" Rakeem whispered.

Truthfully, it did nothing for me, either. Like . . . it was bullshit, right? So I chuckled, too.

"Okay," I said. "I agree. That doesn't make sense."

"Do you think you know more about Reconciliation than I do, Mr. Sullivan?"

Irritation flared in my head. I didn't like being called that. Yes, that was my legal name, but it had only been the case for *maybe* a month. It didn't feel real or genuine. But I didn't call her on that.

I simply said, "No, I don't. But I think I *do* know more about racism than you do."

"That's simply not true," she said confidently. "For who would know more about that evil than the people who perpetrated it?"

That time, Rakeem laughed. "Did you just admit to being an expert in racism?"

That caused some light laughter around the room.

"Enough," said Mrs. Thompson. "Would you like to be excused, Mr. Bradford? I won't tolerate more interruptions from you."

"Absolutely," he said as he stood. "I don't want to be here at all."

"Sit," she ordered. Strode over to him.

"No," he said, and then he glanced down at me. Grinned.

I thought that maybe he realized I was on his side, and it felt like a victory.

A victory that was short-lived.

Because Mrs. Thompson backhanded him.

The silence that followed was horrific. Simone gasped, and then:

Nothing. We didn't move. Even Rakeem, wide-eyed, could not believe that she'd done that.

"Do not think I am not willing to do anything to maintain the proper atmosphere," she said. "And before you think about whining to your parents, know that each of them expressly gave me permission to do anything I needed to in order to help cleanse you."

"You're lucky," Rakeem said, rubbing his face where she slapped him. "Lucky I don't beat your ass right now."

He walked away. Shoved on the door.

It didn't budge.

He grabbed the doorknob. Tried to twist it.

It also didn't move.

He spun around. "What the hell, Harriett?"

"We're here until we're done," she said matter-of-factly. "And you would be wise to call me Mrs. Thompson."

Walked back to her desk. Opened a drawer, then held up a phone.

"Until I call Deacon, that door is not unlocked."

She put the phone back. "Things had to change, Mr. Bradford. Too many interruptions. Too many times you've derailed me this year."

This year? I thought.

Was this not Rakeem's first time here?

"Now, are we going to learn or not?" she said.

I watched Rakeem return to his seat, defeat and anger twisting up his face.

He sat down, and the others—Simone, Omar, and Henry—turned back around. Faced forward.

I glanced over at Rakeem.

A rage burned from those eyes.

Mrs. Thompson smiled. "Excellent. Now, what was I saying?"

She began a new cyclical, incoherent line of reasoning about why God had turned His back on the rest of the world. I couldn't concentrate on much, though, because . . .

What the fuck had just happened?

"Would you agree, Mr. Sullivan?" she asked.

"What?" I said.

"Would you agree?"

"With what?"

She clicked her tongue against the roof of her mouth. "I could tell you were not paying attention," she said. "Do you not think this is important?"

I swallowed down my gnawing frustration. "I don't know what *this* is," I said. "Any of it. I'm lost."

"Well, of course you're lost," she said. "That's why you're here."

I groaned. "I mean . . . ugh, it's like everything you say is a circle. It hurts my head to think about it."

There was sweat on my brow. I wiped it off. Damn, did it feel hot to the others?

"My child, I understand it might be confusing to hear all of this at once," she said. "But you need to hear the truth. Did the Sullivans not tell you more about Christ's Dominion?"

"Not really," I said. "They never really spoke about it."

For the first time that morning, Mrs. Thompson seemed confused. She paced at the front of the class. "I think perhaps we need to do something differently," she said, then looked to the other three kids. "What about you three? Do you know what this place stands for? What Deacon has built?"

All of them were reluctant to speak until Henry raised his hand.

"My parents have shown me Deacon's videos," he said, his voice shaking. "We watch them all the time."

"That's good," said Mrs. Thompson. "What does it make you feel?"

Henry looked back to me and Rakeem.

"No, Mr. Gorman. Eyes on me."

He hesitated. Trembled.

"I don't get it," he said. "Christianity is . . . it's a whole thing in South Korea. And I thought I was getting away from that."

She turned to Omar. "And you?"

"My birth parents raised me Catholic before they died," he said softly. "So, that's basically what I believe."

"And you, Ms. Loeffler?"

"Why did you strike Rakeem?"

I couldn't help gasping, and Mrs. Thompson shot me a dirty glare.

"Rakeem is a troublemaker," she said after a moment. "He must be dealt with accordingly."

"But you're an adult. And *white*. Why are you hitting him? Are you going to hit the rest of us?"

My heart raced, but I was emboldened by Simone's bravery. "It's a fair question," I said.

The heat pressed down on us.

Mrs. Thompson stared back. She sat at her desk. Continued staring.

And then she started talking again.

Every new thing out of her mouth was more absurd than the last. She said that we needed to know the basics, that without a foundation, our buildings would crumble.

It didn't seem to end. She jumped from one topic to another:

Said that we masturbated because no one had told us that our bodies belonged to God, that our souls were just renting them so we could do His work. We were stealing from the Lord.

Said that anxiety and depression were what filled the vacancy left behind when we refused God's love.

Said that any act of sex outside of procreation in marriage was one of deviancy, meant to draw us away from the holiest of unions.

Said that God had sent each of us to our adoptive parents as part of His plan for changing the world.

I had heard variations of these things over the years, sometimes from foster parents, from teachers, even from Diana.

Never from one person. Never all at once.

———

The temperature rose in that room. Henry's face was bright red. Simone was slumped over in her chair, and she fanned herself with her hand.

She asked us to tell her the truth.

"The truth about *what*?" Rakeem said, his voice barely more than a sneer.

"Yourself," she said. "You know this part, Mr. Bradford. In order to understand our own shortcomings, we must admit them. So tell me, Mr. Bradford, since you know these courses so well: How do you fall short of God's glory?"

"I don't," he said, then smiled. "I'm perfect the way I am."

"Bro, *please*," said Omar. "Just tell her something so we can get out of here."

"Is there any water?" Simone asked. "It's mad hot in this room."

Mrs. Thompson ignored them again. "Mr. Bradford, I asked you a question."

"And I'm not answering it."

She glared at each of us.

Settled on me.

"Tell me, Mr. Sullivan," she said. "How do you fall short of God's glory?"

"I don't know," I said. "I guess . . . I guess I don't really believe in him, so technically, if he's real, then I fall short in every way imaginable."

Omar groaned. "We're never getting out of here."

"That's the point," said Rakeem. "It's only going to get worse."

"I am afraid!"

Henry has his hand raised again.

"What was that, Mr. Gorman?"

"I'm afraid of Him," he said. "God. And what He could do to me."

"Well," she said, and she approached Henry. "I've never heard that answer before. Why are you afraid?"

"Because . . . what if I'm wrong? What if I don't do what He wants? Is He going to punish me?"

And Mrs. Thompson *smiled* at that.

"See, children? You can be honest about yourselves here."

She placed a hand on Henry's shoulder.

"Thank you, Mr. Gorman. That couldn't have been easy to admit."

I watched him deflate, sink farther into his seat.

The sweat rolled down my back.

The blood pumped in my temples.

Pain thumped behind my eyes.

What the fuck was happening?

And then, as if God himself timed it so, the lock on the classroom door clicked. The door swung open. Light poured in around the form of Deacon Thompson.

He immediately reared back. "What the—"

Then Deacon stepped inside. "Harriett, why is it so warm in here?"

"I'm just doing as instructed," she said. "Trying to do years of work in just a few hours."

"Everyone out *now*," he said, and he held the door open with one hand. "Head straight to the lodge. I'll make sure that there's water and food available as soon as possible."

They all rose quickly. Bolted for the door. I swayed as I stood, and if I hadn't had that moment of dizziness, I don't think I would have heard Deacon.

"What are you *doing*?" he whispered sharply. "You can't make them suffer. They won't learn."

"But I'm just—"

"Not like this, Harriett!"

And he turned. Looked straight at me.

"Go, Manny," he said. "Please."

I got out of there as quick as I could.

My legs were even more sore than the night before. I hobbled toward the lodge. Could see the others not far ahead of me.

I didn't get it. Why Mrs. Thompson had treated us like that. I welcomed the coolness of the lodge. Watched as a cooler with water and ice was brought to us along with sliced watermelon. I was thankful that even Deacon had realized how absurd her behavior had been.

What the hell is this place? I thought. *How can Elena possibly think I would enjoy any of this?*

The theory came back again: conversion camp. Fuck. Is that what this *actually* was?

Caroline passed by and saw us in the lodge. Tried to give me a hug to comfort me, but I pulled away from her. I was still too hot. Too shaken.

She said she'd heard that Mrs. Thompson was too strict on us. That maybe she'd gone overboard. "I'm going to give her a piece of my mind," she said, then stormed off.

It was the first time I'd seen her act so fiercely in defense of me.

But as I sat there trying to cool off, I couldn't stop thinking of what Mrs. Thompson had said:

That our parents had given her permission to do what she needed to.

Was this the kind of mom Caroline would be in the coming days, weeks, months? As I drank down more water and grabbed another slice of watermelon, I realized I couldn't answer that question.

Because I didn't really know anything about her *or* Franklin.

It wasn't necessarily *that* weird, given how often Elena and I hopped from home to home. What did we really know of Gertrude and Sam? I don't know shit about cars, so I couldn't tell you the first thing about what kept Sam out of the house, except that he always came back to the apartment in Riverside covered in motor oil.

There was Heather Hopkins, who we lived with for a couple weeks a long-ass time ago. She was a nurse. I remember that. She liked Reese's Pieces. And extra butter on her popcorn, which she made as a snack in the middle of the night when she got off her shift. The sound and the smell always woke me up, and sometimes, I'd sit at the table and she'd share it with me. Tell me stories about the wildest patients she had.

I liked her, at least. She couldn't keep us long term because she got promoted, but the time we spent with her wasn't so bad.

I remembered almost nothing about Rosalie, who ran the group home we lived in before the Greenes. Elena and I both got lice there, and it was the first time I ever had my head shaved bald. Rosalie was just a shape in my mind. Blond and short and always seemed frazzled. I mean . . . she watched over like nine kids at once. I didn't blame her.

But did I *know* her?

What about Jennifer Cartwright? She took over the group home the next summer. She loved reading paperback mysteries. Drank iced chai lattes like they were water. Wanted to be a mom but told me once she couldn't have babies of her own, so this was the next best step.

I don't think I really knew her, either.

But the Sullivans . . .

I didn't know anything about them.

I hadn't seen Franklin since Friday night at the weird picnic thing. Had no idea where he went during the day. Had no idea what he did in general. What was his middle name? What were his interests? Any hobbies?

Who the hell were *any* of these people?

My desperation grew on Saturday afternoon.

Deacon invited us to stay in the lodge while he filmed one of his videos for YouTube. "It's important that you see this," he explained. "It is not enough to be cleansed. We are putting you back out in the world to save others. These videos . . . they are our life preserver. I toss them out into the chaotic sea, and I hope to save as many people as possible."

Elena was there, too. She was quick to join Deacon on stage and stood at his right while Mrs. Thompson set up a camera, a laptop, and a fancy lighting rig a few feet from the stage.

She said nothing about what she'd done.

Deacon waved in the five of us newcomers. Said that we could practice a few times being a part of the video. Rakeem remained behind, which didn't surprise me, but I figured that I could use this to convince Deacon and the Sullivans that I was still game for whatever this little retreat thing was.

But as I approached, Deacon held up a hand.

"Not this time," he said somberly. "You're not ready yet."

Then he walked up to the stage, leaving me behind.

Rakeem chuckled as he walked up to me. "Guess you're not good enough for him," he said.

"I guess," I muttered.

And god, it pissed me off.

It made no sense. I shouldn't have cared that Deacon wasn't letting me be in one of his videos, but the quick rejection hit hard.

I wanted to be a part, even if I was faking it.

I stewed there in anger, deep within the contradiction. Why did Deacon's refusal sting so much? Maybe . . . maybe it was because of Elena.

Shit, I thought. *Am I jealous of her?*

I watched as Deacon ran through his intro multiple times.

Told Elena, Simone, Omar, and Henry to smile wider or else no one would believe them. Didn't they want others to know how happy they were?

Said the same thing to the camera four times. Children are the most important source of God's love in the world. We must protect them. We must save them. For the world is broken, and here is why.

He didn't get to the list. Kept snapping at his wife about the camera.

The contradiction grew.

I wanted to be a part.

I didn't want to be here.

I wished Deacon had chosen me.

Didn't anyone aside from Rakeem see how *weird* all of this was?

I moved to the back of the lodge. Rakeem followed me. I thought of leaving out the double doors, but some instinct told me to stay put, that if I washed Deacon in the light that would spill in through the doorway, he would snap at me like he'd done to the cameraman. I didn't want to anger him or annoy him.

Or disappoint him.

Instead, I watched Elena. All smiles. All joy.

And I resented her. It always came so easy for my sister, didn't it? The positivity. The opportunities.

The love.

I shouldn't have wanted it.

It's all I wanted.

Rakeem sighed beside me. "Look how stupid they look," he whispered. "Like puppets."

"It's not that bad," I said. "They're trying."

"You're not," he shot back. "And neither am I."

"Gentlemen, *please*," snapped Deacon. "We don't need your commentary while we're filming."

"Fuck this," said Rakeem, and he turned around and shoved his way out of the lodge.

And this time, I followed him. I didn't care that Elena gazed upon me with disappointment on her face, or that Deacon appeared frustrated.

I had to get away.

"I know you keep trying to be my friend," Rakeem said as I trailed behind him. "But it's not going to work."

"What are you talking about?"

He kept heading toward his family's cabin. "Don't act like you don't know."

"Humor me, then! Pretend I don't actually know!"

He whirled around, fury on his face. "I don't trust your sister," he said.

"Elena?" I shook my head. "Okay, I am *genuinely* lost."

"Oh, come *on*, Manny," said Rakeem. "I know you play that whole naïve thing to your benefit here, but it doesn't work on me. You can't possibly say you haven't noticed how close she is with Deacon."

I grimaced. "I've noticed," I said quietly.

"This place is *death*," Rakeem said. "It is meant to kill your spirit. The sooner you realize that, the sooner you'll do everything in your power to ignore it."

"Ignore it?" I scoffed at him. "Why do you say that?"

He stepped closer to me. "Anything would be better than this."

"So why are you even here?" I said. "Why don't you just leave?"

Rakeem grabbed me by the arm. Tugged me toward the path that led to Mrs. Thompson's classroom.

"What are you doing?" I asked.

"Come with me," he said. "Just this once."

I gazed back at the lodge.

There was nothing there for me, so I went with him.

We left the trail once it passed the classroom. Trudged through undergrowth for a few minutes until we intersected with another dirt trail, one I'd not seen before. Rakeem turned right, and I rushed down the incline to catch up with him.

"Where are we going?"

"You'll see."

That's all he said.

We pushed on, and soon, the path snaked farther away from the compound, deep into the forest. The trees grew closer together out there, and it wasn't long before I couldn't hear anything other than the wind in the boughs. The chirping of birds. Our shoes on the dirt.

Rakeem stopped. Looked to his left. Nodded. Walked off the path and crunched through the underbrush.

And still I followed.

Moments later, a thick patch of trees sat in front of us. The trunks of the pines were bent over, and it provided the perfect natural hideaway from the sun.

There was a blue blanket spread out. Rocks on the corners. Two of the wooden chairs that usually sat outside of each of our cabins.

"I had to take the chairs one at a time," Rakeem said, then plopped down in it. "And I didn't want them to suspect it was me, so . . . sorry, Manny. I stole one of your family's chairs."

I laughed. "What is this place? How did you find it?"

"On one of my many walks," he said. "I tell the Bradfords that I need to meditate to find God or some bullshit, and they eat that shit up. Then I wander. Found this place a few weeks ago and I come out here all the time now."

I sat in the other chair. "This is really nice," I said.

Then:

"But why did you take *me* here?"

He was silent for a moment.

"I just needed someone to talk to," he said.

And then Rakeem started talking.

He was born in Oakland. In foster care his whole life—just like Elena and me—bouncing from home to home. The Bradfords adopted him a few years back. Said they weren't all that different than other foster parents had been, at least not until they started watching Deacon's YouTube videos. It became a family obsession, and then they were convinced that they, too, were suffering from the great disconnect that Deacon spoke of, that they wanted to heal their earthly bodies. It wasn't long afterward that they brought Rakeem to Reconciliation to weed out his "sinful" tendencies.

"Tendencies?" I said.

"Wish I could tell you I understood," he said. "Could be that I'm queer. Could be that I wear this." He gestured to his septum piercing. "Could be my hair. I'm pretty sure they mean my skin color, too. All of it together paints a 'portrait of deviancy' to the Bradfords."

"Gross," I said.

He sighed. "Didn't matter to my social worker. She asked if they were abusing me. If they touched me. I said no. She said, 'Well, then what's the problem? You don't like that they're religious?'"

I thought of Nestor then, the boy down the street I hooked up with. It felt like it had been ages since that had happened.

It had been less than a week.

Rakeem gently snapped in front of my face. "Sorry, I seem to have lost you there," he said. "I'm guessing what I said sounds familiar."

I nodded. "There was a boy. I used to sneak out to see him. They never caught me with him, but earlier this week, they caught me sneaking back in the house."

It hit me then. Completely.

"Then my sister asked me to come here."

I wanted to slump over. To bury myself in the dirt, never to be found again.

She asked if I trusted her. She told me Reconciliation would change my life.

Rakeem didn't have a snappy remark for me. "I'm sorry," he said. "Seems like you love your sister a lot. But . . . she's gone, dude. I think this place claimed her, just like it claimed the others."

"The others?" I said weakly.

"The kids who leave," he said. "This place is meant to break you down so that you accept their version of the world. And then they do that reconciliation ceremony, and you're supposed to feel your body coming back to life, but it's all a fucking scam, Manny."

"But how do you *know* that?" I asked. "You keep talking about this place like you have history with it."

Rakeem gave a bitter laugh. "This is my fourth time here," he said.

"*Fourth*? What the hell?"

"It's always the same," he continued. "I was in the very first group brought up here like . . . I don't know. Don't even remember how long ago. And while Deacon and his wife have changed their techniques, it hasn't really been any different. They try to butter you up. Make you feel loved and appreciated for the first time in your life.

Like you belong to a community. You do group activities. You bond with all the other adopted kids. Then Harriett starts 'teaching.'"

He used air quotes around the last word. "It's not really teaching, is it?" he asked me.

"No," I said.

"So then you learn about how broken the world is out there, and little by little, they offer explanations for why our lives are so shitty. It isn't because no one really cares about foster kids, or because the adoption industry is a complete fucking mess. No, it's because *we're* broken."

He rolled his eyes. "I'm not gonna sit here and say being in foster care is a breeze. I'm sure you know it's hard. But the truth is that these people break you. It's all on purpose."

I swallowed the lump in my throat. "So what's 'reconciliation,' then?"

His bitter laugh came back. "Nothing. It's literally nothing, Manny."

"What?"

"Oh, Deacon and the adults put on a spectacle in that lodge of his, but it's loud music. It's adults screaming at you to let go of your sinful, non-white, non-straight self. The music gets louder and more intense. They basically traumatize you into a confession, everyone weeps and hugs, and then . . . you're healed. You've given yourself over to Christ's Dominion, and you're ready to go back out in the world! Ready to be a soldier for God."

There was a sarcastic smile on his lips. "And if you're lucky enough, you'll end up in one of Deacon's videos."

"That's it?" I said.

Rakeem leaned back in his chair. "It's all a scam, Manny. And you'd be better off accepting that now."

———

We walked back once darkness started to fall.

Rakeem talked a little more, as he guided us through the trees. About living in Oakland, then moving to Pomona. He wanted to get out of California once he turned eighteen.

"The Bradfords can't stop me then," Rakim said. "I'll head east. Probably Atlanta. Heard it's a good place for people like me."

"Why do you stay here, though?" I asked. "If you want to leave so badly, why don't you just walk out of Reconciliation?"

He stopped as we entered the clearing. Clicked off his flashlight. Stared at the lodge, which was illuminated from the inside.

"You've never tried to leave, have you?" he asked me.

I shook my head.

"We're fenced in," Rakeem said. "Found that out the hard way."

Held out his hands.

I reached out. Ran my fingertips over the scars on his palm.

"Electric fence," he said. "Around the whole perimeter."

Rakeem walked back to his cabin alone. Left me there, illuminated in the glow coming from the lodge. Put a question in my mind I never would have thought of on my own.

Was the fence to keep people out or to keep us in?

It's coming back to me.

I remember this neighborhood. The small park tucked between some of the houses. And then I see Nestor's house. Does he still live there? Would he remember me? Is he even aware of what was set into motion that night?

The neighborhood looks the same. Everything does.

How has nothing here changed, and yet I have?

Monica pulls the van over just beyond the Sullivans' plain home. The sight of it sends tingles down my spine. Terror. Anticipation. Uncertainty.

"Are we here?" Carlos asks.

I nod.

Here. I'm back here.

I turn around. Stare at the home. Still painted white with blue trim. Still has an immaculate manicured green lawn out front. Dogwood tree still towers over it all from the backyard.

"We just wanted to make sure you're prepared for this," says Monica, and I twist back to her. "That you still want to actually do it."

"And if you need to bail, no one is going to judge," Ricardo adds.

It's almost comedic. They have no idea how badly I wish to do just that.

"Would you prefer if I go with you or Monica?"

I don't hesitate when I blurt out the answer.

"Neither of you."

They both are taken aback. "Manny, are you *sure*?" asks Monica.

"Yes," I say.

I do not tell them:

You've gone too far.

You know too much already.

This will only make your lives worse.

"I need to do this alone," I add.

A version of the truth. A placation. An offering. An act of desperation.

"Is that okay?" I say. "Just let me speak to them at first. If something happens, then I'll come back. And get you."

"That's fair," says Carlos.

Ricardo and Monica briefly glance at each other, do that thing they do where they seem to communicate volumes without a word spoken aloud.

"Of course," says Monica. "We'll just wait in the van while you're outside."

"Thank you," I tell them. "I appreciate what you're doing."

It's just enough. I should feel terrible, but this doesn't faze me anymore.

Alone is always better.

I'm standing next to the van. Staring. Unable to move.

There's a breeze. Like the universe is trying to push me toward that home. To face them. To face the inevitable.

What if they're actually there? What am I going to say? What am I going to do?

What I'm supposed to do.

Find her. Find out if she's still alive.

And get her out.

———

I walk. Allow the momentum to carry me because I'll never make it if I stop.

This is a mistake.

Maybe. But I have to try.

What if it is her?

Then I have to know.

I walk up the driveway. Go to the door. Raise my hand. I hesitate for only a moment, then knock. Once. Twice.

And then I hear Monica yell something behind me.

I turn.

Carlos is barreling across the lawn.

"Get back here!" Monica cries.

But he doesn't stop.

I shake my head furiously. Rage and terror surge, and then—

The bolt unlocks.

The door squeaks as it opens, and I spin around and—

There's a woman there. Her pale face wrinkled, her wavy black hair pulled back, and she looks upon the two of us suspiciously.

I've never seen her in my life.

She squints. Pushes the door open wider.

I can't move.

I don't understand.

Who the hell is this woman?

I sat on the steps of the porch of our cabin after Rakeem left. Fireflies darted between the trees, floating and glowing. Don't think I'd ever seen them before that. I watched them for a while.

A shadow fell across the forest, though, and there she was.

Elena approached. Her gait was confident. Assured.

"Manny," she said, drifting up to me. "Where did you go?"

I didn't answer her at first. Rested my chin on my left hand. Elbow propped up on my knee. I watched the fireflies illuminate themselves.

"This doesn't feel right," I said. "I don't get this place."

She sat next to me. Leaned her head on my shoulder. For the briefest of moments, I was taken back: to all the car rides we'd been on together, traveling to a new guardian. Traveling back to the group home. Traveling together because we were all we had.

Each other.

But that image dissipated when she pulled away. When she made a *tsk, tsk* sound at me.

"Manny, this is important," she said. "What Deacon is doing here is going to change the world."

Rakeem's words echoed in my head.

This place is death.

"Elena, will you just tell me the truth?" I asked.

"Yes," she said.

"What is it that Deacon is doing here?"

"He's saving—"

"Don't bullshit me, please," I said. "I'm lost. After listening to

Mrs. Thompson today, I can't understand why you'd choose to be around these people."

"Because they're right," she said. "Because Deacon changed my mind."

I groan. "What exactly did Deacon do to change your mind?"

"He simply showed me the truth of the world. We are broken. He puts us back together."

I actually laughed. "Yes, I get that. It's all very metaphorical, Elena. But what does it *mean*? What exactly is this reconciliation process he keeps talking about but never defines?"

"You're in it now," she said plainly.

I tried to laugh it off, but the hairs raised on the back of my neck. I didn't like how she said that.

"It's not a single act," she continued. "It's the whole thing. It's confronting yourself and the world outside the boundaries of this place and realizing you don't fit in. And there's a reason why."

"So you believe all that garbage that Mrs. Thompson 'taught' us?" I said, using air quotes on "taught."

She crossed her arms over her chest. "She's just telling us the truth."

Damn it, it was like arguing with a circle. Everything was right because *they* were right. "You don't believe that, Elena."

"Sure I do," she said, smiling.

"That God doesn't care about race?" I said, incredulity dripping out of me. "That we were mistreated in foster care because *we* were broken? That I'm a *deviant* for liking boys?"

"You're looking at it the wrong way," she said, and finally— *finally*—I could hear frustration in her words.

It was something.

It was *human*.

"What's the right way? Deacon's way? That's just the answer?"

"After all we've suffered through, Manny, don't you just want to let go?"

The frustration was gone.

In its place:

Sadness. Pity.

"You've made it your whole identity," she continued. "Suffering. You've been hurt, and now, you can't see any way out of it. So you make your terrible jokes, and you bring everyone down with you."

My heart sank as Elena stood. "What are you talking about?"

"Do you think I haven't noticed?" she said, her voice rising. "All the comments about our past guardians or foster parents. Your refusal to try to get along. Your belief that no one would care about us long enough to actually go forward with adoption. Well, here we are! You were wrong, Manny, and you can't even admit it!"

"Do you think those people care about us?" I said. "Caroline and Franklin?"

"You don't even want to give them a chance!"

"And why should I?" I yelled, then stood up. "Everyone disappoints us in the end anyway!"

"Well, I am *tired* of it, Manny," she said. "Tired of refusing to believe there's a better life for us, tired of always assuming the worst of everyone around me. Aren't you *tired*, too?"

She stormed off.

Left me there with the fireflies.

With my shame.

"Can I help you?" The stranger is waiting in the doorway still.

I don't know what to say. Carlos nudges my shoulder.

"I'm looking for Franklin," I try. "Franklin Sullivan."

The woman looks directly at me.

"Are you one of the kids he's working with?"

"Yes!" lies Carlos excitedly, which makes my heart race. "We definitely are."

She rolls her eyes. "I told him not to send any my way today, but that man . . ." She sighs. "He can be so forgetful. Can I get you boys something to drink?"

Carlos doesn't hesitate. "Sure!" he says. "What you got?"

And then he's going inside.

I have to follow because I'm not going to stand on the stoop by myself. I glance back at Monica, who looks just as confused as I am.

I shrug. Follow after Carlos.

Inside, memories flood back. It's . . . the same. Plain as the outside, without character, without detail. A couple crosses on the walls. It's still just as sanitary as before.

But as I pass through the living room and into the kitchen, I realize one thing *is* missing.

The photo from the Sullivans' wedding day.

There's something else tacked on the wall near the dining room. I approach it.

It's another couple on *their* wedding day. White and older, like Franklin and Caroline, but definitely not them. I get closer, and one is definitely the woman who answered the door. Between the couple, there's a young girl. Her skin is light brown. Black hair to her shoulders. She looks Latinx. Maybe Filipino.

Shit. This woman is another one of them. Do the Sullivans no longer live here?

I don't fucking understand what's going on.

Carlos is near the refrigerator, and the woman hands him a pitcher full of some sort of liquid. Lemonade, I think. He brings it over to the table next to me.

You okay? he mouths.

I give him a weak reply, somewhere between a shrug and a grimace.

"Tell me, then," the woman says, walking over with empty glasses in her hands. "Are you here for the local recruitment drives? I wasn't expecting any of you until tomorrow, like I said."

"I'm sorry," I say. "I hope this isn't rude, but I meet a *lot* of people nowadays. Could you remind me what your name is?"

She looks at me in admiration. "Of course, sweetie!" she says. "It's Paula. I don't think we ever met before. It's a good thing that you're getting out in the community and doing the hard work."

"Exactly," says Carlos, and he pours himself some lemonade. "How do you think it's going?"

What the hell is he doing?! I think.

But as Paula talks, I realize how brilliant that question was. She tells us that she's so impressed that we're seeking out other children at schools. That we're spreading the good news of Christ's Dominion to the very people who need it most.

That we've brought in more kids who need to be saved than ever before.

"I know the Lord is proud of our growth," she says. "He is always ready to welcome more to his flock."

"Agreed," says Carlos, and I have never seen him smile in such a ridiculous, exaggerated way before. "Praise Him!"

———

Was this what he was like?

Before. When he was in the Vine Fellowship.

Is he merely unlocking that part of himself again?

Is he doing it for *me*?

Paula focuses on me. Stares a bit as I sip on lemonade.

"So . . . what did you boys need?" she asks. "Training is tomorrow."

"I know," I say. "I guess . . . we're just overachievers. Wanted to get a head start."

"Right," says Carlos. "Because there are these kids at school we wanna reach out to, but like . . ."

He sighs.

It's so terribly perfect that I have to hold back a laugh.

"We just don't want to mess it up."

She seems to melt before us. "Praise Him," she says. "I'm just so lucky that He found two willing soldiers like you."

I twist around. Stare at the kitchen. Remember my first meal in this house. Grace. I messed up grace multiple times.

I realize it then:

The Sullivans showed me who they were that very first day.

I am thinking about this when Carlos makes it a million times worse.

"So, what do you know about the dead body?"

———

Paula stands up. Fast. Knocks the chair back.

"What did you say?" Her brows furrow. "Why would you ask that?"

I look between the two of them. Can see Paula's anger growing. Can see that Carlos realizes that he's miscalculated. That he's just set this whole conversation on fire.

She looks back to me.

Studies my face.

"My Lord," she says.

I'm on my feet.

Backing away.

"Carlos," I say. "We have to go."

"What's going on?" he says, twisting around from his seat.

There's a loud sound.

A door slams shut.

A voice rings out.

"Paula, are you still here? I left my phone somewhere."

I know that voice.

I know it, I know it, I know it.

I spin around.

He's there, in the space between the living room and the dining room.

Tall. Lanky. His hair is more salt-and-pepper than it was before.

He can't seem to process me. He looks at me, but words aren't forming on his lips. He struggles. I can see it all over him.

———

"Manny?" Carlos says. "Manny, what's happening?"

He takes a step back.
"You're . . . alive," he says.

I don't feel alive. Not after what they did to me. Not after he left me behind so very far from here.

My skin is on fire. Rage burns in my stomach, and I think I'm gonna throw up.

Carlos touches my arm. Says something. I think he asks me who this man is. I don't answer him. I can't.
Instead, I turn and run away.

My head buzzes. I scramble into the van, and both Ricardo and Monica are screaming at me, begging me to tell them what's happening. Carlos practically throws himself in after me.
"Go! Go!" I scream.
"Was that him?" Carlos asks, breathless.
I turn back.
Look out the rear window.
He's on the lawn. Staring at me. Looks like he's seen a ghost.

Because he has.

We're gathered around the fire that night in the clearing, and all I can think about are Elena's words:

And you don't want us to regret that choice, do you, Eli?

I don't.

Deacon Thompson has his guitar out. He's singing a dc Talk cover. "Between You and Me." I know all the words because Mrs. Thompson taught it to me months ago, and every so often, she looks my way, making sure I'm singing along.

Annie seems to know the chorus. LaShawn and Julian sit there, eating their s'mores with wide eyes and blank faces. I don't think this is reaching them yet. It's supposed to, though. Mrs. Thompson said that music is one of God's gifts. A powerful vehicle for His love. So I raise my voice. Sing louder. Pray deeply that this message reaches them.

Reaches me.

But at the end of a few songs, Julian rises. Wipes the crumbs from his hands. Then he just . . . leaves. Doesn't say anything. No good nights, no thanks, nothing.

LaShawn looks to Annie. "Where's he going?" she asks.

Annie shrugs.

Deacon strums out a chord. "Eli," he says, then jerks his head in the direction of Julian.

"Yes, Deacon," I say, and I stand. Jog after Julian. I see him on the other side of the clearing; he's on the porch of his family's cabin, just standing there. Facing the door. As I approach, though, he rounds on me.

"What do you want?"

I put my hands up. "Just to talk," I say.

"I'm really tired of talking, Eli," he says. "That's all anyone seems to do here."

For a moment, a familiarity spreads in my chest. I feel like I've been here before. Done this exact thing. I shake it off, though, because I have work to do. God's work, to be specific.

"Is something bothering you?"

He frowns. "I mean . . . yeah? Isn't it obvious?"

"Well, maybe I can help."

Julian laughs. "I very much doubt that," he says. "Unless you can get me out of this place."

"Why would you want to leave?"

For a moment, he's stunned. "Why would you want to stay?"

"This place is beautiful, and—"

He doesn't let me finish. "There are a lot of forests in the world. This one isn't special."

"But it's—"

He raises a hand in my face. "Stop. I already know what you're going to say. I've heard it so many times from you and your sister, and my parents, and that creepy Deacon guy."

"Don't call him creepy," I snap. "It's rude."

"But am I wrong?"

The familiarity tugs at my perception again.

No. No, I have to remain focused.

"You hesitated," says Julian.

"Because I'm thinking. About how to prove to you that you're wrong."

He purses his lips. Steps away from the door, and the porch light casts across his face.

"Why do you care? Like . . . honestly. I'm a stranger. You have no idea what my life is like. Why do you want me to be here?"

"You were brought here because God brought you here," I say.

"Do you really believe that?"

"Yes."

"What does He want with me?"

"Reconciliation."

He groans. "Yet none of you will just tell me or Annie or LaShawn what reconciliation actually *is*."

"Do you want to know the end of every book you read after the first chapter?"

Julian actually takes a step back, and I'm impressed with myself. Mrs. Thompson told me that one, and it seems to have worked.

"No," he says. "But most books don't involve being blindfolded for an hour and brought to a creepy compound in the forest."

"Why are you so insistent on calling this place and the people here 'creepy'?"

"Dude, are you serious?" Julian scrunches up his face. Removes his glasses to clean them on the front of his shirt. "You just told me earlier today that you don't remember your *entire life* prior to coming here. That's . . . that's not normal."

"Because it's a miracle," I say quickly.

"What kind of god would want you to erase everything about yourself?" he counters. "Don't all those experiences make up who you are today?"

My hesitation is not short-lived this time. I open my mouth. Close it.

"I don't get this place," he says, his tone much less sharp than before. "I don't want to change who I am. I *like* myself, Eli. And yeah, the world is fucking terrible a lot of the time. It's not easy being an orphan or being adopted, but like . . . I don't want to be a blank slate. That's what this whole reconciliation business feels like, man. Like a giant eraser."

"Don't you want to stop hurting, though?" I say.

For the first time since he's arrived, Julian looks at me with something other than irritation or disinterest.

There's only sadness on his face.

"Don't *you*?" he asks. "Because I don't believe for one second you're not in pain right now."

My heart drops. My face burns. The world drops away underneath me.

"I don't think this place is what you think it is," he says sadly.

Turns away.

Heads into his cabin.

The light on the porch stays on for a few moments. Then it disappears. Darkness shrouds me.

I start walking away, slow at first, then my feet are rapidly carrying me from the semi-circle of built and half-built homes, of potential made and promised, and I rush into the darkness. Beyond the pines. Deeper into the forest. I stray from the path because I just want to get lost. I think of the stories that the Thompsons have taught me, about Jesus's sacrifice, about him wandering the desert for forty days, and I wonder if I'll get my answers if I disappear, too.

Who am I?

What does God want with me?

I slip. Grab the trunk of a pine to keep myself upright. Ignore the pain on my scraped palm. Deeper into the darkness I go. An owl hoots at me, and I hear something scamper off.

It appears suddenly. Even in the darkness, I can tell this shouldn't be here: a dense pack of trees, hunched over a couple chairs.

I approach it cautiously. Spin around, certain someone is watching me.

It's a test, isn't it?

But after a while, I hear nothing but the occasional breeze in the trees. The calls of owls. Some creature prowling by.

I sink into one of the chairs. Stare up between the branches. I can see starlight up there.

I pray to God. I ask Him to give me a sign. To tell me what I'm supposed to do, how I'm supposed to make Him happy.

I'm met with the sounds of a forest coming to life.

Nothing more.

Monica starts up the van. Pulls away from the curb.

He's still there. Still staring.

Fucking hell, did I just screw everything up?

"What happened?" Monica shrieks as she speeds off. "Jesus, you two scared the hell out of me."

"I don't know!" says Carlos. "That man showed up, and the woman was already acting weird, and then Manny panicked, and I am very, *very* confused. But wow, this is the *wildest* birthday I've ever had."

"What man?" asks Ricardo. "What woman?"

"Just keep driving," I say. "Get away from here."

I screwed it all up.

We don't know if Elena is still alive.

We still don't know where Reconciliation is.

There's still an unidentified body out there, somewhere.

Not one bit of that helped.

We're on the far side of town in a parking lot of a massive shopping center. I'm outside the van, pacing back and forth.

"Manny . . ." Monica says. She's sitting on the step at the side door of the van, watching me.

I can't stop my mind racing. Can't stop all the thoughts.

I messed this up. I'll never find her. She's already dead. They'll figure it all out.

"Just tell us one thing," Ricardo says from the passenger seat. His door is open, too, and he's hunched forward, staring at me. "Are you okay? Did anyone hurt you?"

I freeze.

"No," I say. "I mean . . . no, I'm not okay, but no, no one hurt me."

"Well . . . that's a start," says Monica. "I can work with that."

Carlos walks up with two plastic bags. "Supplies," he says, holding them up.

He digs inside one. Hands me a sports drink.

"Just drink," he says. "Don't worry about talking. Is it okay if I tell them what I saw?"

I nod.

So he does that. Stands next to me, tells them what little we learned.

"She just changed, Mami," he says, then glances at me with a sad look on his face. "It was like . . . like, I don't even know. It was *weird*."

He shakes his head. "Then the man arrived."

"We saw him," says Ricardo. "In fact, we called you, Carlos, but you didn't answer."

He balks for a moment, then pulls out his phone. "Damn," he says. "I didn't even notice."

"It was him," I blurt out.

They all look to me.

"Franklin," I continue. "My . . . dad. I guess."

I laugh then. "Man, what do you call someone who is your legal dad but who rejected you? Doesn't want you around?"

Carlos gives an awkward grin. "Mami, Papi, can I swear? In Spanish?"

Doesn't matter because Ricardo lets loose a long string of insults in Spanish.

Carlos points to his father. "That. That's what you call him."

"Did he say anything to you?" Monica asks.

"Yeah. Just . . . 'You're alive.' That's it. Nothing else."

"Jesus," Monica mutters. "He really thought you'd be dead after what they did to you."

"Wouldn't you?" I say. "They abandoned me with nothing. Half the time, *I'm* surprised I'm still alive."

"I'm glad you are."

Carlos doesn't say it in a joking tone. Just stands there, concern on his face.

Oh.

He meant that.

My face flushes red. "Thanks," I say.

"So, you wanna go back and light that house on fire?"

"Carlos!" chides Ricardo. "We're not committing arson!"

"It would be a public service," he mumbles.

"I'm sorry," I say. "For being chaotic. For . . . dragging you all into this."

"Nope, stop that," says Monica, and she rises. "We're not doing more of that, okay? Remember, we talked about this yesterday, Manny. The whole thing about other people caring for you. We chose to be here."

Carlos nods. "All of us."

"But—"

"Are you seriously about to ask why *again*?" she cuts in. "Because we want to."

"Because it's right," says Ricardo.

"Because I like getting revenge on people like these Christ's Dominion fools," adds Carlos.

"So, this didn't go like you wanted," says Monica. "You're not a coward for leaving. You protected yourself. I'm sure the second you saw Franklin, your whole body was set alight. You getting out of there was an act of protection, Manny."

"But what do I do now?" I ask. "I didn't get anything I wanted."

I catch it again: Monica and Ricardo. Trading a look.

"No," she says.

"Mi amor, it's a possibility, and he should know."

"What are you talking about?" asks Carlos. "What's a possibility?"

"It's not fair that he doesn't know," says Ricardo quietly. "He deserves to make an informed choice."

They gaze at each other.

Then at me.

"Well, what the fuck is going on?" I say. "I don't get it."

"We can get you some form of an answer," says Ricardo. "But it might be disturbing. Traumatizing. And it could go very, very badly."

"Worse than *this*?" I say, my hands behind my head, my chest heaving. "It can't be worse than never knowing."

Another look exchanged.

Another silent communication.

"Yes," says Monica.

Ricardo sighs.

"I found out where they're keeping the body."

There was no dinner that night.

My stomach ached as I entered the lodge. No one had come to my cabin to tell me dinner was ready. I hadn't seen the Sullivans since I'd gotten back from my little excursion with Rakeem either. Darkness had fallen long ago, and I couldn't escape the feeling that something terrible had happened.

I half expected to find the parents setting up dinner for us, but I was met with a different sight. Deacon was on the small stage in the back, pacing back and forth. As soon as he saw me, his face lit up.

"Come, Manny," he said, then beckoned me forward. "There's a special activity tonight that you need to take part in."

"What kind of activity?" I said.

I didn't get an answer. The others arrived then, first Omar and Simone, then Henry. I watched them go through the same epiphany: Dinner wasn't being served.

"What's going on, Deacon?" Rakeem asked. "We haven't eaten since this afternoon."

He smiled at us. "My children," he said, "I am glad you are all here with us."

"What's up?" asked Simone. "Where are our parents?"

"What?" I said.

"Yeah, I couldn't find mine, either," said Omar.

"Same," said Henry.

"Before we get started," Deacon said, ignoring all our questions,

"I just want each of you to know that you're special. That you're here for a reason. Not just because God sent you, but because you are all standing on a precipice. Your lives are about to change."

Rakeem snickered.

Deacon ignored that, too. "Tonight, I will be giving you a nudge. After the events of today, we will need to delay reconciliation for all of you. Normally, it would happen here, tonight. But in one form or another, each of you needs my help, and I am answering the call to help you repair yourselves. To truly fix what has been broken."

"Let us venture into the forest," said Deacon, smiling at each of us. "All I ask is that you bring yourselves and an open heart. I will provide everything else."

"How about some food?" Rakeem asked.

Deacon knelt down. Picked up a large canvas bag, then patted the side of it. "You will be fed," he said.

Rakeem grumbled something, but I didn't hear it.

We followed Deacon. Out of the lodge, then past it, then onto a wide path that I had never taken. It narrowed to a trail, and he stopped. Handed out flashlights from the bag he carried.

"Keep close," he said. "There are still wild animals on our property."

I fell in step with Rakeem in the very back. "So what part of the whole reconciliation thing is this?" I whispered to Rakeem.

He didn't answer.

"Don't go all secretive on me now," I said. "Come on. What is this?"

He reached out. Grabbed the back of my left arm. His words were pointed, afraid. Said through clenched teeth.

"I don't know," he whispered. "I've never done this part."

My heart sank. "What do you mean?"

"Deacon never took us out in the forest in the middle of the night. This is *new*."

I pulled away from Rakeem, glared at him as we walked. Flashed the light in his face.

Which was drenched in sweat.

"Stop it," he hissed. "Pay attention."

Pay attention to *what*? Where exactly was Deacon taking us?

We walked. Omar and Simone spoke in hushed tones. Henry nervously shone his flashlight all over the forest, and it made me feel worse. I tried not to give in to panic, give in to my nerves, but as we trudged deeper into the forest—deeper into a seemingly impenetrable darkness—I felt as if I was being marched to my end.

This place is death.

The trees thinned out. A clearing appeared.

In the center of it was a pile of logs. Deacon set his tote bag down. Dug around in it. Pulled out a box, then lit a match by striking it against the side. Soon, a fire illuminated the entire clearing.

Illuminated five faces unsure of what was coming next.

We turned off our flashlights while Deacon searched around in the bag. Pulled something out and handed it to Rakeem. Omar and Simone were next. Then he got to me. It was a pencil and a notebook. I took it with one hand. Stuffed the flashlight in my waistband with the other.

"I know that I brought you all into Reconciliation to serve a purpose," Deacon announced once he had handed out supplies. "And each of you has proven to me that I was right about starting this place. Christ's Dominion needed it. We needed somewhere where children who had been brought into our family through adoption could be healed after the world so thoroughly broke them."

He paced around us.

"I hope, however, that none of you think that because I started this place, I am perfect."

He stopped.

Stepped between Henry and Rakeem toward the fire.

"I think I've spent a lot of time building a very specific image of myself for you, but it isn't fair to expect perfection of *anyone*. We all stray far from God's grace, and some of you have shown me that today."

He reached into his back pocket. Pulled out a smaller notepad and a pen.

"That also includes me."

Opened the notepad.

"So I want to be honest with each of you, not only because I love you, but because I need to lead by example."

Deacon started writing in the notepad, and as he did, he spoke his words aloud.

"I did not trust God's guidance, nor the instinct he gave me," he said, and upon finishing, he held the pad up for us to see.

What he'd spoken was written there.

"What does that mean?" said Simone.

Deacon's smile to her was a bit sad; only one side of his mouth curled up. "God sent me a very clear sign. He's done so for a while now. I tried to rationalize it away. Thought my imperfect, mortal mind was greater than His, that I could solve this on my own. But I'm a fool."

He started writing again.

"I allowed poison into our community on more than one occasion."

Held out the pad.

Kept writing.

"I thought I could purge it. I thought I was good enough to fight evil alone."

He kept going.

"I am impatient," he said. He wrote. He showed us.

There was a wetness on Deacon's cheeks. He rubbed at it with the back of the hand that held the pen.

My shame flared again.

I don't believe him.

Elena's words came back. Why? Why was I assuming the worst of this man all the time? Here was a full-grown man, crying to a bunch of kids, telling us he was imperfect.

Had I gotten this wrong?

"I am impulsive."

He flipped to a new page and scratched at the notepad.

"I have betrayed God more times than I could ever count."

His voice broke on the last word. I clung to it. There was something there.

Was Deacon finally telling the truth?

He continued. "I snapped at two members of Christ's Dominion today."

Looked up at me. "You saw that, Manny. With my wife."

I nodded. Said nothing.

Then he flipped to yet another new page. Wrote one more thing:

"I have to make a decision to protect this place, and I have avoided it."

Deacon tore the pages out of the notepad in one swift motion. Folded them in half.

"I give myself to God," he said. "I will repair this body. I will reconcile my earthly desires with my heavenly ones."

He held the pages over the fire.

Dropped them.

They fell quickly, landing in the midst of burning logs. Embers ate at the edges. Soon, the pages shrank as the fire consumed them.

"Gone," he said. "Purged."

I watched them disappear.

"This is what I ask of you, my children," he said, his eyes red. Glassy. Puffy. He sniffled. Rubbed his nose on his forearm.

He looked so very human in that moment.

It terrified me. I didn't want to trust him, but it had seemed so *real*.

Elena loved him. Rakeem hated him.

Who was right about Deacon?

"I want us all to cleanse ourselves together," Deacon said. "I know that each of you are, in your own way, struggling with what it means to be here at Reconciliation. Omar, we spoke earlier about your doubt, and I want this to be the thing that finally quells it."

He turned to Henry. "Henry, you believe you're not trying hard enough. Let this be what helps you gain your confidence."

Henry nodded at Deacon.

Deacon continued. "Simone, you told your parents earlier that you worried you weren't good enough," he said.

"I'm trying," said Simone softly.

"And yet, at home, you disobey," he said. Moved closer to her. "You assert your own worldview on your parents, who are trying to build a life for you free of all the prejudices and harms."

"But that's not what—"

"And you're doing it now," he said, cutting her words off. "Why do you insist you know more than your elders?"

"Why do you think you know more?"

Rakeem said this plainly. Loudly. Confidently.

Deacon smiled. "Rakeem Bradford," he said. "You are disobedient in nearly every waking moment. Surely you see the value in this, right? You can finally confess to what you are and then . . ."

Deacon mimed releasing a page above the fire.

"Poof. All gone."

Rakeem smiled. Laughed. "Whatever."

"Humor me, then," Deacon said, spinning to look at each of us. "Do as I ask, and I am willing to bet that each of you will feel better once you have done it."

He raised a finger. "But you must be honest, or this doesn't work. God wants honesty."

272 • MARK OSHIRO

Turned back to Rakeem. "Give Him this one thing, Rakeem. Just one. And let me make it more appealing."

He addressed the whole group. "None of you have to read your confessions aloud. When you are done, deliver your impurity to the fire. What transpires here will be between God and yourselves. That's it."

Rakeem smiled bitterly. "Fine," he said.

I glanced over at Simone. At Omar.

They were writing. Slowly at first, and then more words poured out of them and onto the pages.

I looked to Rakeem. He shrugged. "What's the worst that can happen?" he whispered.

He wrote.

The wood cracked from the heat. Pens scratched against paper.

They were confessing.

All of them but me.

I couldn't move. Couldn't write. Because what the hell was I supposed to say? What was I supposed to confess to?

That I didn't believe?

That I was using this place to survive?

Shit. I could try.

I wrote them down.

I'm a liar.

I think the worst of everyone and everything.

The others were writing faster. Even Rakeem.

"Having trouble, Manny?"

My head snapped up. Deacon loomed near me.

"Sorry," I said. "Just thinking."

"Maybe put that down, too," he said. "You overthink a lot. And I need your dedication right now. *He* needs your dedication. Your focus. Your commitment. Can you give Him that?"

"Yeah," I said.

But I did not feel God in that moment. Hadn't felt him before, either. Instead, I was overwhelmed with dread.

What if I was wrong? What if I had closed myself off to everything that these people believed, and because of that, I had doomed myself?

No. That couldn't be possible.

Humor me.

So I wrote.

I don't believe a word Deacon says.
    Reconciliation is a fraud.
    They've stolen my sister from me.

And then it all came out.

I'm never going to be good enough for these people.
    I want to escape.
    I want my sister back.
    I don't like the Sullivans. They're creepy little robots.
    I have failed everyone who has ever depended on me.
    I'm too negative.

I am I am I am I am

Who would ever love someone like me?
I am broken.
No parents, no sister, no boyfriend. I have nothing.
No god up in the sky to love me.

I spiraled. Wrote so fast that I tore one of the pages. Flipped to a new one. Kept going.

This is all my fault.
I should have said no.
I never should have come here.

Flipped to a new page. Paused.

Then wrote the truth.

I think I'm going to die alone.

There was a tearing sound. I looked up. Saw Henry standing proudly, his pages held up.

"I did it," he said. Sounded thrilled with himself.

Folded them up. Approached the fire. Held them aloft.

And just before he tried to drop them in the fire, Deacon snatched them from Henry's hand.

Henry lunged. Swiped for them.

And Deacon shoved him away.

Henry stumbled. Cried out.

"What are you doing?" Omar yelled.

Henry stood frozen, his mouth agape, his face burning red.

Deacon unfolded the pages.

"No," Henry said, his tone defeated, terrified. "I thought you said—"

"I know what I said," Deacon snapped. "We saved you from darkness, Henry. Just like all the others. And yet, you constantly hesitate. You're so nervous that you practically vibrate. Why do you hesitate before God?"

"Deacon, I don't—"

"'I steal food from the corner store all the time.'"

Deacon read with no emotion. Like it was a grocery list and nothing more.

Henry sputtered. "I get hungry!" he said, looking to us in a panic.

"'I don't pray because I don't understand it.'"

That wasn't even my own confession, and yet a flash of guilt rushed out from my chest.

I understood. I knew what Henry meant.

But this was not about comfort or understanding.

"'I think about going back to South Korea all the time.'"

"Please," said Henry to Deacon, his hands clasped together. "You weren't supposed to read that!"

Deacon pressed on. "'I wish Reconciliation never existed.'" He shook his head. "We saved you, Henry," he said.

"Oh, shut the fuck up, Deacon," sneered Rakeem. "No one saved us from anything."

Deacon lowered Henry's confessions. Glared at Rakeem. "Apologize. Now."

"No," said Rakeem.

"Excuse me?" he said, then crumpled up Henry's pages, turned back to him. "There's more, but I think we've all heard enough. Henry, you can rest easy knowing that the other secrets are between you and God for the time being."

He tossed the pages in the fire. The flames devoured them as Henry fell to his knees, sobbing.

Then he strode over to Rakeem, and for the first time since I arrived at Reconciliation, I saw rage on Deacon's face.

His features were twisted. The warmth was gone.

He looked capable of anything.

"You're going to read my list, aren't you?" Rakeem said, a scowl fixed on his face. "I don't care. I'm not a coward like Henry is. Do it."

"Apologize to Henry," Deacon commanded.

"For what? What are you going to do if I don't?"

"I'm going to do whatever I want because I have God on my side," Deacon shot back. "Who's on your side, Rakeem? Who's really telling you to disrespect your sibling like that?"

"He's not my sibling. I don't even know him."

Henry gasped from the ground. "What?" he said. "Why would you say that?"

"Well, you're not!" Rakeem screamed. "None of you are! We're all strangers! Why are we even here?"

"It's clear you're upset, Rakeem," said Deacon, and he slipped back into that voice. The one where he sounded like he cared. Like he was truly our father.

"Don't patronize me, Deacon," Rakeem said. "I know exactly what I'm saying."

And then Rakeem held up his own list of confessions, his face curled with spite.

"'I don't want to be here,'" he read. "'Every day, I dream of escape. I wonder what it will be like when I walk through the front gates and never come back.'"

Omar stepped forward, transfixed. Hung on every word out of Rakeem's mouth.

"'I am disgusted by this place.'"

"Please, *stop*," Henry begged. "I don't want to hear it anymore."

Deacon raised a hand to silence him.

Rakeem tore the pages in half. Once. Twice. Again. He held them up.

"'I long for the day,'" he said, reciting his last confession from memory, "'when I can dig my thumbs into Deacon's eyes and end this nightmare once and for all.'"

Rakeem held his head high. As he tossed the scraps into the fire, his hand shook.

"You're evil, Deacon," he said. "What you do is evil. Everything about this place is evil. No one here seems to see it. They lap at you like dogs, begging for leftovers, and you *want* them to."

Tears poured down Rakeem's face. The long streams glistened in the light of the fire.

"I'm not afraid of you," he said defiantly.

Deacon was still as stone. There was nothing on his face.

He turned away from Rakeem. Walked up to Simone. Plucked the folded pages out of her hand as she stood still, horror on her face.

"Don't," said Rakeem. "Punish me, but leave her alone."

Simone didn't fight it. She was frozen. Her eyes were wide, and she trembled.

Deacon mumbled as he read, and I couldn't make out what he was saying until—

He frowned. Stitched his eyebrows together.

He held a page high.

"'Dad made me get an abortion.'"

Tears poured down her cheeks. She wasn't moving at all. My heart raced.

"Please, stop it," seethed Rakeem. "What are you doing?"

It overtook me. I didn't let Deacon react; I reached over and grabbed Simone's list as she cried out, and then I turned to Omar, who had already figured out what I was doing. At the same time, Omar and I tossed our pages in the fire.

Deacon jerked toward them, but the flames claimed the confessions.

We watched it all burn away.

"Manny," Deacon said, and I could hear the edge of a threat in his voice. "What have you done?"

I held my breath.

"What you told me to do," I said.

His face loomed in front of me. A lip curled in fury.

"You told us to cast our confessions in the fire," I said.

My heart was in my throat.

I thought for a moment that this was it. He was going to attack me. Do something worse than what he did to Henry or Simone.

And then he broke into a smile.

"Good," he said. "You are correct. I did tell you to cast them in the fire."

His face was so close to mine. I could feel him breathing on me.

He finally twisted away. "You've all purified yourselves," he said. "I'm proud of you. *All* of you. We did this for our community, didn't we?"

There was a long silence. We looked to one another, uncertain.

"Yes, we *did*!" Deacon yelled. Pounded his chest with a fist. Breathed heavily.

A bone-chilling smile appeared on his face. "I'm glad we had this moment together, my children."

Then he turned around. Pulled a large canister out of the tote bag, upended it over the fire, and the light was gone. The darkness of the forest immediately swallowed us, so I reached for my waistband.

Deacon got to his flashlight first. Flicked it on. "Let's head back," he said.

And with no word about what just transpired, Deacon marched back in the direction of Reconciliation.

There was a brief hesitation among us.

"What the *fuck*?" Rakeem muttered.

I didn't understand. How had he gone from such a raw display of vulnerability to . . . *this*?

We started walking. Simone's movements were jerky, so I held up the rear to make sure she didn't get left behind. We all said nothing until we reached the point where we could see the lodge in the distance.

"I'll see you tomorrow, my children," said Deacon. "I'm so very proud of you."

Then he left.

In the terrible nothingness that followed, Simone sucked in a breath.

"It was his," she said.

"What?" said Rakeem.

"My dad's."

I stared at Simone, unable to hide my horror.

She nodded. "I just needed you all to know the part that Deacon didn't read."

Then she walked off to her family's cabin.

I'm underneath the stars.

No motel tonight. Ricardo felt too paranoid to go the traditional route and book a room for the night, so they chose to do some camping.

The Tucalota Springs Camp is sprawling, tucked into a set of rolling hills off a two-lane highway. We're surrounded by trees on all sides. Oaks and mesquites. It's the first time I've camped with the Varelas. They opened up the rooftop carrier. Set up a tent. There's a fire going, and we dine on Thai takeout.

My hair is still damp from the shower. They had a small bathroom facility near the entrance, and I used it to wash away the stickiness of sweat and terror from earlier.

Ricardo and Monica are setting up the sleeping arrangement in the tent. Carlos and I are going to be in the van so things aren't as cramped. It's a three-person tent, but Carlos says he's too old for it. "That's kid's nonsense," he said. "I'm seventeen now."

"Of course," said Ricardo, nodding knowingly. "Would you like us to pass along your homeschooling bill to you now? Since you're practically an adult."

Carlos groans. "Your superpower is ruining jokes," he says.

Ricardo looks proud of that.

I sit off to the side. Watch the three of them joke with one another about the impossibility of assembling tents. Monica said I didn't need to help, but . . . I suspect she sees me differently. They all must. Ricardo speaks to me in clipped sentences. Monica keeps glancing my way, and I don't think she knows I've noticed it.

The context might be different, but this is nothing new. This has happened to me time and time again. Every person I meet slowly has this realization. I'm not the image of a poor, abused kid that they have in their head. I'm someone else. Someone more complicated.

Guess it won't matter. Tomorrow, I'll know. I'll know the identity of the body. There was a part of me furious that Ricardo had not presented me with this option, but . . . what was he supposed to do? Stop me from going to the Sullivans? Surprise me with a dead body?

No. He made the right decision.

I was the one who messed it up. Not Carlos. *Me.* I could have found out so much more if I hadn't froze. If I hadn't been such a coward.

I sit there, under the stars, aware of how close I came to ruining it all.

I think: It's probably time to part ways. Always better on my own. Maybe after I find out the truth about the body, I can set out on my own for this last bit of the journey.

But . . . it's nice. Being next to Carlos when all the stars come out and twinkle brightly in the sky. I remember doing this before. Might be the only good memory I have of Reconciliation. I'd never seen them so brilliant before.

I wonder if I'll get to do that again.

It's her body.

It's not her body.

"You boys make sure to put out the fire correctly, okay?" Monica says. She pulls a blanket tighter around her shoulders. "Let's not burn down the entire campsite."

"Yeah, I will, Mami," says Carlos.

She leans down. Kisses him on top of the head.

Looks at me. Hesitates.

"Good night, Manny," she says. Then walks away and ducks inside the tent.

Ricardo waves at me. "Tomorrow," he says. "I know today was probably disappointing, but tomorrow, we'll try something new. We're not giving up."

"We never do," Carlos adds. "No matter the setback."

"Thanks," I say.

Even though I want to say: You can't protect me from what happened.

Even though I want to say: You can't promise you won't give up, because you don't know what this is.

Even though I want to say: Please. Please give up on me.

Ricardo heads into the tent, and then Carlos and I sit in silence. A good silence, though. I don't feel a compulsion to say anything, and I don't think he does, either.

So I just stare at the stars for a while.

Tomorrow.

"Where will you go?" Carlos says softly.

He fidgets in his chair. Picks at his nails.

"Go?" I say. "What do you mean?"

"What comes after? If you find your sister, one way or another?"

One way or another.

Well, it's blunt. But he's not wrong.

"I don't know," I say. "I haven't thought that far ahead." I gaze back up at the stars. "I rarely think far ahead."

Carlos is silent for a moment.

"Because all you can focus on is the now. Right?"

"Yeah," I say. "Exactly that."

"I remember feeling that way," he says. "After all the stuff around Lester came to light. After the retaliation. It got so overwhelming that I couldn't see a way out of it."

The fire crackles. He stares at it. Eyes distant.

"That's been most of my life this past year," I say.

I'm breaking Cesar's rule again. *My* rule.

But . . . I think it's okay with him.

"I just try to survive to the end of the day," I say. "It's easier."

"I honestly get that," says Carlos.

Silence.

Then:

"Will you leave us?"

My response is immediate.

"I don't think I can stay."

"We have room," he says. "An extra seat in the van, and we can figure things out if we get your sister."

"That's not what I mean."

I lean forward, hold my hands closer to the flames.

"I need to figure out a life. Something other than this. I don't think I can wander around anymore. *Especially* if my sister is still alive. Like . . . what kind of life am I bringing her into?"

"I don't know, but—"

"Truck stops and truckers who can't keep their hands to themselves?" I whisper. "Jobs that last a week, that don't pay me because to them, I don't exist? Days without food unless I steal it?"

I stand up and the camp chair falls back. I wobble. The world is spinning.

Oh, god, what *am* I doing?

Running headfirst into traffic.

Off a cliff and into my dark abyss.

Into another nightmare.

I want Elena back. I want to rescue her. But . . . what am I giving her in return? I don't even have a home for us to go to.

I can't offer her anything that Reconciliation already grants her. Fuck.

Carlos stands, too. "Hey, don't think of that stuff yet," he says. "Just . . . we have to focus on one thing at a time, okay? Just like you already do. There's no sense trying to figure everything out now."

"But what am I supposed to do?" I say, panicked, and my voice rises. "What am I *doing*, Carlos? Like honestly, what the fuck am I doing?"

Carlos casts a gaze at the tent, then grabs my arm. Drags me toward the van. The seats are laid down, my sleeping bag laid over the one in the rear. He pushes me inside, then darts back to the fire. Puts it out with water and dirt. Then climbs into the van. Quietly shuts the door behind, and then we kick off our shoes.

"Sorry," he says. "I just don't want to wake them."

I crawl to the far corner. Pull my knees up to my chest. Eyes blur with tears.

"I shouldn't do this," I say.

"Shut up, dude," says Carlos. He lies on his side, faces me, props his head up on his arm. "You've come so far. No sense giving up now."

"What if it goes like today did?"

He looks away.

Great. I fucked this moment up, too. Vision blurs. Hot tears run down my face.

Carlos looks back, his dark eyes sorrowful. "He was terrible to you, wasn't he?"

"Yes," I say.

"You only told me a little bit," he continues, "but what I heard was enough."

"Enough for what?"

"Enough to understand why you ran today," he says. "Do you think everything I did with Lester was all bravery all the time?"

"I don't know," I say, looking away. "You called him out, right? You set this whole thing in motion. I could never do something like that."

There's a hand on my arm. I turn my head toward Carlos, and he's lying on his back, his right arm out, his fingers on my skin. His eyes are soft. A little sad.

"What?" I say.

"I think you are a thousand times braver than I could ever be," he says. "Because you survived this last year *alone*."

Then his eyes explore my face, but not in that way others do. When they're trying to dissect me. Dice me up. Make me more palatable to their comforts.

His are warm. Exploratory. Full of wonder and admiration.

"I had the Varelas," Carlos says. "Almost immediately. They took me in when my parents threw me out. When I began to tell my story. And yeah, they've probably told you how bad they screwed up by not paying attention to all the rumors and stories, and I get that. I get their guilt. But they stepped up the second I needed it. And I didn't have to do any of it alone."

His hand moves down my arm.

His fingers loop into mine.

"I don't know what happened after your parents abandoned you. But from then until now, you didn't have anyone. You survived all of this *yourself*."

He squeezes.

"It doesn't feel like a big thing," I say softly. "It's just . . . living."

"Man, *I'm* impressed," he says. "Take the compliment, you weirdo."

I smile at that, and his face lights up. "See? You don't have to be so dour all the time."

"Shut up," I say.

And I look down at our hands. Locked together.

This is real. This is happening.

"So like . . . have you thought about how you're going to get her?" Carlos asks. "If she really is still there?"

"No," I say. "Because—"

"Because you don't think that far ahead," he finishes.

I smile at that. "Yeah. I don't like thinking about things that I don't know are happening. Makes me anxious."

"Maybe you could disguise yourself," he says. "So that you can get in and get your sister, then get out."

"How would I do that?" I say, and my heart skips. "Wouldn't Deacon or the Sullivans recognize me in a heartbeat?"

"That's a good point," he says. "Well, you also have the three of us. Maybe we can pretend to be prospective new members and try and spot her."

"Maybe," I say, uncertain that that would work, either.

"Do you . . ."

He doesn't finish at first. Then he breathes deeply.

"Do you think that body is hers?"

I don't want it to be. But I can't be sure.

I wonder if this is all going to collapse soon. If this charade will crumble.

I swallow. "No," I say. "I don't think it is."

He shrugs. "I'm sure we'll figure out something."

We. He says that so casually. Like it's a certainty. The future . . . it is not an unknown to him, is it? I'm alone in this.

Like I always am.

"You're thinking of leaving again, aren't you?"

I raise my eyebrows. "What?"

"You got that look on your face the other day," he says. "Right before you took off."

I sigh. "I'm always thinking of leaving. Can't stay anywhere long."

"Why not?"

"Usually, people don't want me around. I'm a nuisance. A charity case they can feel good about at first, but eventually, they all tire of me. I move on."

I stretch my legs out. Let go of Carlos's hand. Spread the sleeping bag over my body. Lie back.

"It's just how it goes."

Silence.

Carlos twists around. Can feel his eyes on me.

"I want you around."

I scrunch up my face. Glare at him.

"You're serious?"

"Yes."

"Because some days, it didn't feel like it. I thought you hated having me around."

"I did," he says plainly. "But . . . not for the reason you think."

I roll my eyes. "What does it matter, then? I still don't feel good about it."

"I didn't like how you made me feel, okay?"

"Made you feel?" I push myself up on my elbows. "I didn't *make* you feel anything."

"I thought my parents saw you as another problem to solve," he says. "I didn't get why they kept you around so long! We never did that with anyone from Vine Fellowship, so I didn't get what made you special."

He squeezes his eyes shut. Presses his lips together tightly.

"God, I hate saying it like that, because I know you're special. And I'm so glad you're still here."

He puts his hands on my face. Gently tugs my head forward. And then his lips—warm, soft—are on mine. He presses them, moves them open and shut. Don't know what I'm supposed to do.

But maybe I do. Because I put my hand on the back of his head. Pull him closer. Press myself into him. Then he uses his left hand to press me back, back onto the seat. His weight is on me. Feels good. Feels *right*. His tongue flicks into my mouth. Frightens me. It's all so new. So foreign.

I don't reject any of it.

Wrap my arms around his back.

Lie lie lie lie lie.

Hold him tight.

Lie lie lie lie lie

He kisses my neck. No one's ever done that.

No one's ever done any of this.

Not like this.

I am afraid, but not of *him*. Beneath him, I am safe. I don't panic. I feel every part of him against me, and my body responds. Writhing. Hard.

I don't stop him when he removes my shirt. My jeans.

Don't look away when his shirt and shorts come off, too. Run my hands over his stomach. It's soft. Big. I like it.

I like him.

He guides me the whole way. Not like an expert, but like someone on the same path as me. Someone doing this for the first time. I can tell because he shakes. Trembles. And when my hand goes into his underwear, he shakes a whole lot more.

He tells me it's my turn, but I shake my head. Not yet, I tell him.

He cleans himself up. Searches his bag for a change of underwear while I redress, then . . .

He brings his blanket over to me. Spreads it over the two of us. "Is this okay?" he asks.

Yes.

Yes, it's okay.

Nothing has ever been more okay than this.

He turns me to the side so that my back is to him. Wraps his arm around me. It is not a mistake. Not an unconscious move while asleep.

Kisses on the back of my neck. Shudders down my spine.

Then he pulls me closer.

"I'm sorry I was a dick," he says. "I guess I didn't know what to do with what I was feeling after you arrived."

"It's okay," I say.

"Not really," he shoots back. Embraces me tighter. "Will you at least consider sticking around?"

I know he will not be able to accept the final truth. But I lie. It's what I do to survive, and one more lie won't hurt.

"Yes," I say.

I fall asleep in that warmth.

Our breakfast the next morning is short: just a few freshly baked pastries, a bowl of fresh fruit, and either juice or water. During my training, Deacon explained to me and Elena that this was by design. As the weekend progressed, less and less would be given to the new souls under our care. "We need to make sure their bodies are in a state of hunger so that they hunger for God," he said. "If they have everything, they'll never realize that they truly have nothing."

I eat what I can without giving away to the others what is about to happen. Julian picks at his Danish, while Annie and LaShawn devour their food quickly.

"Are we ready, my children?" Deacon says as he arrives, clad in shorts and a tight-fitting athletic shirt. "Today, we're going to do a little exploring and get closer to God's creation."

"What does that mean?" asks LaShawn. "I don't do hiking."

Deacon laughs. "It's not hiking, per se. Think of it more as a holy journey."

LaShawn frowns. "Where there will be hiking."

"It won't be so bad, I promise," he says. "My wife has some water bottles for you outside, so grab one out of the cooler, and then we'll get started."

I hear Julian mumble something as he stands up. He gives me one quick glance, and for a moment, I think he's going to say something to me, especially after the previous night's conversation.

He remains quiet. Marches out of the lodge.

"He'll be a difficult one," says Elena at my side. "But I have faith in you, Eli. You can get through to him."

After last night, though . . . I'm not so sure.

Our hike along the trail is quiet. Tranquil. I take the time to commune with myself. With God. To build up the fortitude I'll need as we approach Sunday's reconciliation ceremony.

Today is the prep work. The marinade, as Deacon puts it. We are doing what must be done so that these souls are ready to receive what is coming to them tomorrow night.

I beg God to help me. To put this right. To make it so that I succeed in guiding these souls to reconciliation.

But it all collapses an hour later.

As Deacon leads the five of us deeper into the forest and through a cold, ankle-height stream, he tells the others how he came to find this place. How God challenged him to make it a place of devotion and worship.

"I assumed this would be the home for a new church," he explains. "But God had called me for another plan."

"A much better plan," Elena adds, and then she grins at me. I only offer a weak smile back.

"I saw a world full of orphans," Deacon continues, sloshing through the cold water. "Full of children in foster care. Full of young souls who needed to be loved and returned to God."

"I don't get it."

I turn.

Annie is standing in the middle of the stream, her face red from exertion.

"Don't get what, Annie?" Deacon asks, stopping in place.

"I don't *need* that," she says, then glances nervously at Julian and LaShawn.

"My child, *everyone* needs to find their way to God."

"Yeah, I know," she says, then shakes her head. "But . . . I'm already a Christian. Like, that's what I believe, too. So . . . yeah. I don't really understand why I'm here."

Deacon smiles. "That is not the same."

"Why not?" asks LaShawn. "And what's with all the weird stuff your wife was saying in class yesterday?"

"Weird stuff?" Deacon says, twisting up his face. "You mean the truth about the world?"

LaShawn scoffs. "I wouldn't call that the 'truth.' "

"Why not? It's true the world outside is corrupt. That it has molded you in a way to prevent you from being what God wants."

"Even if that was true," says LaShawn, who then points to Annie, "she's already a believer. She has a relationship with God. So what does this place *do* for her?"

Annie steps out of the stream. "Is it the gay thing? It has to be, right?"

Deacon sputters, but before he can respond, Julian lets out a peal of laughter.

It reminds me of something. Someone.

"What's so funny, Julian?" asks Deacon.

"I can't believe I didn't see it," he says. "It's so obvious."

I watch the frustration spread over Deacon's face, and I back away from him. "See what?" he says.

"This is one of those conversion camps, isn't it?"

"No," says Deacon. "Not in the slightest."

"Maybe not exactly," says Annie, "but you are basically teaching the same thing. All that stuff about how impure we are, how the world poisoned us, how we need to be *fixed*."

Julian steps closer to Deacon. "We've imagined all these problems in our life because we don't have a relationship with God? Like God doesn't see color?"

And then Deacon casts a glance my way. I know what he's doing. What he means.

He's asking for help, isn't he?

"It's not like that," I say. "You're twisting it all up."

"Man, no offense," says LaShawn, "but I don't think any of us are going to believe you."

My mouth drops open. "What?"

"Dude, your whole thing is . . . weird," says Annie. "Like, *really* weird."

"Do you *really* not remember your life before this place, Eli?" LaShawn asks. "And if so, why the hell would any of us ever want to experience that?"

"Because I'm *happy*," I say.

But my voice wavers. It's uncertain.

I feel Julian's eyes on me, and the pity is back. He's shaking his head. He feels sorry for me.

"We don't believe you, Eli," he says. "And I think you mean well. At least, that man"—he gestures toward Deacon—"wants us to believe you do."

"Please don't speak of my brother like that," Elena warns sharply. "He's a miracle."

"And you support this?" Julian cries. "Your brother seems like he's an empty vessel most of the time, just regurgitating whatever he's been told. Who *is* he? Do any of you even see him as a person?"

Something is there. Coming back. It's on the edge of my consciousness.

Who was I?

Who was I before?

"My children," Deacon begins.

"We're not your children," Julian snaps.

Deacon actually flinches. "Don't correct me," he says. "It's rude and disobedient."

Julian ignores him. "We decided," he says. "Last night."

"We're not doing this reconciliation thing," adds LaShawn.

"At all," says Annie.

"So you can tell our parents, and we'll all go home," Julian says, crossing his arms.

Elena gasps. "You don't know what you're saying," she says. "You're just . . . tired. Hungry."

Julian narrows his eyes. "And why is that? Could it be that there was no breakfast this morning, and then Deacon immediately took us on a long-ass hike?"

My head spins, and I look to Deacon again, hoping he'll provide me with guidance. I didn't train for *this*.

Instead, his mouth curls downward for a moment.

Then:

It's gone.

His face is blank.

"It does not matter," he says, and he starts walking back the way we came. When none of us follow, he spins around. "This isn't up to any of you. We will be going through with the ceremony tonight regardless of your feelings. God will not wait for you."

Tonight?!

"You can't *force* us to do it," says Annie softly, and her face goes red again.

"Do you think you can stand in defiance of God, Annie?" he says.

"Deacon . . ." Elena says, and she steps toward him, a hand raised. "Maybe we should just take a moment and—"

He fixes her with a scowl I've never seen from him before.

Elena shirks away. "Sorry," she says.

And in that moment, something crosses her face. Something I've never seen from her, either.

Doubt.

Her brow furrows. Her mouth is open slightly.

She is uncertain.

Elena, my sister, my foundation . . . she doesn't know what to do.

And it terrifies me.

The walk back is excruciating.

There's too much I'm thinking about: Elena. Deacon's anger. The fact that the others must have discussed me at some point.

I'm something they dissected. Analyzed. Came to a conclusion about.

They don't trust me. They find me bizarre.

I'm an empty vessel.

I want to be offended by that. I *should* be. But it hurts in a different way.

Who am I without this place? What opinions do I have about the world? A world I don't even remember.

It's there again. Something just out of reach.

We trudge through undergrowth. We rejoin the trail. We walk in silence. When the bones of the northern cabins appear, Deacon stops. Waits for us to catch up.

"Shower," he says. "I will tell your parents about tonight's ceremony."

"But—" LaShawn says.

"No," he says, his finger in her face. "You have no idea what's about to transpire tonight. You will be *begging* for forgiveness once you realize what I am capable of here."

Then he stands up straight. Smooths down his hair. Smiles.

"I'll see you all later," he announces. "I have a broadcast to give, and then . . . then I'm going to change your lives."

He drifts away from us, so certain, so steadfast.

And he leaves me nothing but uncertainty.

The van door slides open.

I bolt upright. Cool air hits my face. Brightness. Rub at my eyes. There's a figure in the doorway.

Monica.

"Sorry," she says. "Didn't mean to wake you up."

Carlos's hand slides off me. He yawns. Turns over. Blinks a few times, then . . .

"Ah, shit," he says. Sits up.

Monica has a wide smile on her face. "Well," she says.

"Mami, it's—"

She raises a hand. "Whatever it is, it's fine, okay?"

And she doesn't look at me like she did yesterday. She isn't afraid.

She's beside herself.

She grabs her bag of toiletries. "We should head out in half an hour," she says. "You boys get ready, okay?"

Then the door slides shut.

"I'm sorry," I say. "I didn't know she'd—"

"Shut up, Manny," he says.

And then his lips are on mine.

And I actually shut up.

My stomach rumbles, both from hunger and fear.

Ricardo found a Mexican restaurant on the edge of Hemet that makes breakfast burritos. "An art form," he said. He asked to take my order. Told him that the very idea of eating made me sick. I was too nervous. Monica tried to sell me the same logic as she had yesterday, but I wouldn't budge.

I feel terrible.

There's a pit growing in me, ready to devour my entire self.

There's no possible outcome today that *won't* change everything about my life.

It's her body. I lose my sister. I lose it all.

It's not her body. Someone else is dead, and my sister is still lost.

Even if I was somehow able to find Reconciliation in Idyllwild, I still have no plan to get her back. Even worse, I remember our last argument. I remember what happened at the end of the ceremony.

I remember that she did not choose me.

She chose *them*.

What if she doesn't want to leave? What if she's slipped even deeper into that horrible place? What if Christ's Dominion is better than the world outside of it?

The Varelas eat. I watch them. The fear bubbles and grows.

I knew something was different when Elena sat next to me at breakfast that last morning, rather than next to Deacon's reserved spot at the head of the table. She just had two slices of buttered toast on her plate. Nothing else.

They hadn't offered anything else, of course.

Simone didn't speak. Ate her toast quickly, then excused herself without any eye contact. Omar arrived late and sat alone. He didn't talk, either. Henry was next; he took one look at the three of us there and immediately bolted.

I remembered gazing at Elena. Wondering if she would say anything to me about what had happened. Had Deacon told her? Did she know? Was she still convinced of the goodness of this place?

She gazed back at me with glassy eyes, distant. She was somewhere else.

"What?" she said.

"Say something. Anything."

She pressed her lips together. Took a bite of toast. Chewed slowly.

"Where's Rakeem?" she said.

I looked around the table in the lodge. I watched the Bradfords enter and putter near the toast platter. Saw the Loefflers chatting over coffee.

Rakeem wasn't there.

"I don't know," I said. "You didn't see him around this morning?"

She shook her head. "I only got here a few minutes before you did."

I walked over to Omar at the end of the table farthest from us.

"Hey," I said. Crouched down next to him.

He didn't react. Like he was in his own world.

I touched his arm.

He jumped in his seat.

"Sorry," I said. "Have you seen Rakeem? I think the Bradfords have a cabin near you."

He shook his head.

I wanted to say something more.

I said nothing because I was afraid.

Afraid of the terrible feeling crawling over me. Afraid of what would happen if I openly confirmed what had happened to Henry.

Elena made eye contact. I shook my head.

"Everything okay, Manny?"

I turned to find Mrs. Thompson standing near, a plate of scrambled eggs and bacon in hand. Where had she gotten *that*?

"We haven't seen Rakeem," I said to her. "I don't think he came to breakfast."

"Who?"

"Rakeem," I said. "You know . . ."

She didn't react.

I narrowed my eyes. "Rakeem?"

"Is he one of the newer kids?" she asked, then gazed down the table. "Sometimes we get children who can only attend a single day."

"No, Mrs. Thompson, he's not," I said, raising my voice. "Rakeem Bradford. You know exactly who I'm talking about. He's been here a million times."

She scrunched up her eyebrows. "I don't think I know him," she said. "Where did you meet him? Maybe Deacon hasn't introduced him to me yet."

I backed away from her. "What?"

"Maybe you can do that," she continued. "I would appreciate it!"

"Is this a joke?" I said.

Elena rose up from the table. "Manny, what's going on? Didn't you see him last night?"

Last night.

I made eye contact with Omar, and the color rushed from his face.

Elena didn't know.

She didn't know.

"If this is a joke, it's not very funny," said Mrs. Thompson.

"What's happening?" asked Elena as she approached.

"She says she doesn't know who Rakeem is!" I said.

Elena gave her the same suspicious look as I did. "Rakeem," she said. "We all know him. You literally once told me he was the worst student you'd ever had."

I immediately wanted to ask Elena about that, but there wasn't a chance to.

Mrs. Thompson shook her head. "That doesn't sound like me. I don't speak ill of our students." She looked between the two of us. "Are you sure you two aren't confused or something?"

My stomach lurched.

This wasn't happening. It made no sense.

"I don't get it," said Elena.

"We just saw him last night," said Omar. "After . . ."

Silence. He couldn't bring himself to say it. I didn't blame him.

Mrs. Thompson tilted her head to the side. "So . . . a new entrant, then."

"No, Mrs. Thompson!" said Elena, and that time, *she* was yelling. "We all know him! Rakeem! How can you say you don't know who we're talking about?"

Omar looked ill as he stood up, as he tried to steady himself with the table. "What are you doing to us?" he said.

I turned to the Bradfords. "Where's your son?" I yelled.

They looked at me. Mr. Bradford raised an eyebrow. "Our what?"

"No," I said, shaking my head. "This isn't funny."

"We're just here to help," said Mrs. Bradford. "We don't have a son."

Then she beamed at her husband. "One day, though! We hope God bestows a child upon us."

I was ready to let a shower of curse words pour out of my mouth when a shadow fell across the doorway.

I knew the shape of that figure.

"Please stop interrupting breakfast for the others."

Deacon's voice boomed in the lodge. The entire room froze.

He strode forward, then sat at the head of the table. "Good morning," he said to everyone. "Everything fine?"

The adults offered gentle affirmations. The rest of us stood there, dumbfounded.

"Remember that we have class this morning," he said as Mrs. Thompson placed a full breakfast plate in front of him. "Is everything all right, my love?"

"Of course, Deacon," she said, smiling warmly at him. "Some of our children were just a little confused."

"I'm not confused," I said forcefully. "Where's Rakeem?"

Deacon made the exact same face as Mrs. Thompson had. His confusion . . . it looked *genuine*. Real.

My stomach sank in terror and anticipation.

"Who's Rakeem?" he said.

I rushed from the lodge to find Rakeem. Went to his cabin, but the Bradfords' belongings were gone. It was just another bare, sparsely furnished home. Where were their things? I didn't understand. It looked like . . .

Like it was ready for the next family to come through. Ready for the next family to be broken.

I turned around in that empty space.

Rakeem was gone. And they were all acting like he had never existed.

He was real. He had been here.

They couldn't take that from me.

I skipped class. I ran from Rakeem's cabin, followed the path we'd taken just a day before. Didn't remember all of it at first because my heartbeat was ringing out in my head, thumping so loudly I thought it would burst out of my ears.

Missed the first cut off the path. Doubled back and tore through the underbrush. It scraped up my bare legs, but I didn't care. I had to know. I had to look.

I must have looped back around. Gone in circles. Took me an hour to find the pines, bent and huddled over, and beneath them were the two chairs. The blanket.

No Rakeem.

He was gone.

I collapsed in one of the chairs. I cried. Hard at first, until my throat hurt, until my eyes were puffy, and nothing felt real.

This was not happening. This was not happening. This was not happening.

Rakeem could have been a friend. There was potential there, especially after the day before. But I knew I wouldn't ever find out. Had Deacon finally had enough? What had they done to him?

He wasn't ever coming back, was he?

I wondered then, as I had before, if there was something wrong with people like Rakeem and I. Were we so fundamentally broken as people that we couldn't receive the blessing that Deacon offered? Is that why we doubted? Is that why we struggled with faith? With what Christ's Dominion offered?

No one else seemed to have this problem. This *struggle*. They all eventually . . . believed.

I stayed beneath those trees for hours. Couldn't bring myself to stand until I had to. Was thirsty. Had to pee. Relieved myself nearby, and then I made the slow walk back. Pretty sure I got lost a few times, but that was mostly because I just didn't care.

No, that's not right.

I was afraid. Afraid of what I would find when I returned.

Deep down, I knew something was wrong. It all felt so obviously cruel.

And yet: I couldn't ignore the pull. I was caught in the orbit that Deacon had created. I despised what he had done, but a part of me still wanted his approval. Still wanted his acceptance. Still wanted to understand why everyone was so ready and willing to become a part of this community while I doubted.

I was split in two. And it hurt.

It was nearly noon when I got back, and Elena was on the porch, pacing. When she finally looked at me, she did not seem surprised or shocked.

Mostly . . . annoyed.

"Where have you been?" she said. "Henry said you weren't with Mrs. Thompson today."

"He's gone," I said. "Rakeem."

She shook her head. "It had to be for a good reason, Manny."

"You can't possibly believe that."

She stopped pacing. "Maybe Deacon was right," she said. "He needed to go."

She hesitated.

"I saw how he was affecting you."

"Affecting me?" I said. "Elena, you have no idea what Deacon did last night. We can't trust him!"

"He told me everything, Manny."

I faltered for a moment. Sputtered nonsense. "Everything?"

She nodded. Looked away. Looked back.

Her eyes were empty. Dead.

"We have two bodies," she said. "Deacon was right about that. And Rakeem refused to listen to him. He would have poisoned even more of the kids here."

"Even more?" I shouted. "What are you *saying*?"

Elena stepped forward. Held herself straighter. "He poisoned you, didn't he? Poisoned you against this place."

"I *never* liked it."

"You seemed to when we went on hikes. When you were served meals by the others. When it was all about *you*. But as soon as you started becoming friends with Rakeem, you resisted. You questioned. Why don't you want to do the hard work, Manny?"

"What hard work?" I said, scowling. "Mrs. Thompson's awful fucking classes?"

Elena's eyes went wide. "Stop it. She's trying to—"

"She's trying to manipulate us," I said. "Trying to water us down. You know what she's saying is bullshit. All that nonsense about how race isn't important, or how all our problems are because we haven't accepted our Godly bodies or whatever. You know it isn't true! You know how we've been treated all our lives."

"You just don't want to let go of being hurt," she said. "Just like I said yesterday! It's the same problem it's always been with you. You whine about our foster parents, but refuse to open yourself up to them. You whine about racism, but what are you doing to change it? Or change your mindset?"

I threw my hands up in the air. "Do you know what you sound like?" I said. "Change my mindset? Racism isn't in my head. It happened *to* us. To both of us! All those shitty, disinterested parents. The ones who treated us like servants. Like paychecks. That wasn't in our heads, Elena! It happened!"

"Because we *let* it happen!" she shrieked. "You can't see it because you're so brainwashed by people like Rakeem."

"*I'm* brainwashed?" My mouth dropped open. "Look what *you've* done. You brought us out to the middle of nowhere for . . . for *what*? Who is Deacon? Where did he come from? What does he actually want from us?"

"To save us," she said plainly. "To save us from the world outside."

"And are we *saved*, Elena? Do you feel *saved*? Because I don't. I feel like I was tricked. Tricked into coming here because of the Sullivans. Because of *you*."

"But—"

"Rakeem told me everything. He told me what reconciliation is. That it's just prayers. Manipulation. That we're asked to change who we are to fit in with what Deacon *wants* us to be. It's all bullshit, Elena, isn't it?"

"You haven't even given this place a chance," she said, her tone defeated. "You don't know anything about it."

A wave of frustration crashed into me. "You're literally not listening to what I'm saying," I said. "You're always coming up with a defense of Reconciliation or of Deacon rather than just *listening* to me."

"And you're always latching on to everything negative! How is that any better?"

"Because it's *reality*!" I screamed. "Our lives are messed up, Elena. And this whole positivity-until-we-die shit is *exhausting*. You can't seem to actually see what we're going through!"

"I see it every day!" she said and she lunged at me. "God, Manny, are you that short-sighted? Do you think I'm just naïve?"

I hesitated. "Y-yes?"

"I know what we've been through," she said. "I know every day that we've been chosen by some of the worst people. That to so many of these white foster parents, we are a story. We aren't human. We are a piece of *their* puzzle. I know that living in one foster home after another is chaotic. I know that we can't make friends, I know that our lives aren't normal, and I know that *I'm exhausted*."

She stepped forward again, and I backed off the porch.

"I'm so tired, Manny. I'm tired of fighting everything. I'm tired of seeing the world as a collection of things that can hurt me. *That* is why I brought you here. Because they have the answer I've been searching for my whole life."

Elena was so close that I could feel her breath on my face.

"The rest of the world is broken. Deacon repaired me, and now I don't have to be sad or scared or broken anymore. I gave up the rest of the world, and soon, you're going to as well. You will see the truth, and reconciliation will come to you."

"No, it won't," I said, shaking my head.

"It happened for the others."

"The others?"

"While you were gone," she said, holding her chin higher. "All of them. Henry, Omar, and Simone. They've all been saved."

"No," I said. "There's no *way*."

"Reconciliation happened. You can't deny it. All you can do is accept it."

"You're joking," I said. "They don't want this. There's no way they gave in to Deacon."

She smiled at me. "It's beautiful, Manny. To be able to see the world through God's eyes. There's nothing more I want for you than that."

And then she walked off.

Sometimes, I wonder if I could have changed things.

Was there something I could have said to show her the truth?

Or was she right? Was I so hopelessly committed to seeing the world as an awful place that I couldn't see what a paradise Deacon had built?

He came for me not long after that.

I headed to the lodge. No food. No people. Where were the others? I frantically ran from one cabin to another.

All of them were empty.

Elena was right. They'd had their little ceremony *without me*.

I panicked. Fled from the last empty cabin to ours. No one was home there. There was no food in any of the cupboards. Nothing in the small refrigerator, either.

The whole place felt *fake*. An approximation of a home. A poor imitation.

The front door creaked open.

I froze. Was met with silence.

"Elena?" I said. "Is that you?"

The floorboards in the living room groaned.

I stepped forward. Peered around the corner.

Deacon stood in the middle of the room.

"We built this cabin first, you know," he said. "Out of all the others, this was the prototype."

I swallowed down my rising terror. "I didn't know that," I said.

"It's not shaped like the other cabins. I believe it's actually much, much bigger. We learned, though. Over the months, I helped streamline this place. These families . . . they don't need luxury. They just need the basics. There shouldn't be any distractions."

He finally moved toward me, and I fought the instinctual urge to run. To shove past him. To never stop running.

"I don't like distractions, Manny," he continued.

Took another step toward me.

"The act of reconciliation—of repairing the body that God gave us—is a delicate thing. It requires focus and attention."

Closer.

I backed up.

Hit my hip on the counter behind me.

"Because there are simply so many things outside the boundaries of this place that distract us. That try to pull us back into the world."

I had nowhere to go.

"Rakeem is gone," he said. "He's never coming back."

"What did you do to him?" I whispered.

"I did nothing to him," he said. "He made his choices, over and over again. It was finally time for him to stop distracting my children from their goal."

Stepped closer.

"Where is he?" I choked out.

"He left." Deacon frowned. "Focus, Manny. I need you to focus."

"Focus? Focus on what?"

"Our goal."

Another step.

"It's time for you to let go," Deacon said. "You have a firm grasp on the world, my child. Your loyalty to Rakeem proves that. And you need to let it go."

He reached out. Rested his hand against the side of my face.

"Tonight," Deacon said. "Tonight is your reconciliation."

• Back in the van.

I remember the feeling of Carlos's body against mine last night. And I know for certain: It's all going to end today, isn't it?

The longer I stayed with the Varelas, the more inevitable this became. The more the fabric frayed. The more the seams stretched. Threatened to burst.

We pull away from the restaurant, then head west to Perris.

Deacon has not called upon us yet. I've taken to pacing the cabin, but Mom tells me that it is making her nervous. "You're going to do fine tonight, Eli," she says from the kitchen, where she's pouring herself some iced tea. "Just remember that this is our first retreat since . . . since you, truthfully. Things were bound to be complicated."

Dad nods his head in agreement from the couch, where he sits beside Elena. "Your mother is correct. All that matters is that your faith is unwavering, okay?"

"Okay," I say.

"We chose you," Mom adds. I stop pacing and gaze at her. Her eyes sparkle. "We brought you into this family because God gave everyone a miracle."

"I know."

But she shakes her head. "One day, you might fully understand, Eli. But for now . . . just know that you're the sign we'd been praying for since joining Christ's Dominion years and years ago."

Elena looks downward.

I'm seeing it again.

Doubt.

"I need some air," I tell them.

I step out onto the porch. Head for the clearing. It's still warm out, so I lower myself. Lie on my back. There's a spot near the center where the pines give way to an almost perfect circle of a view of the sky above.

It's cloudless tonight. The sun is gone. The stars are out.

I watch them. They appear slowly. Sparkle.

I feel distant, like they are. As if I am not just far from God, but far from . . . myself.

Every waking moment in this place has been dedicated to my rehabilitation. To my training. I've devoted myself to it. I want to make my parents proud. My sister. Deacon and his wife.

But . . .

I don't think of myself. Almost ever.

Who am I?

What am I outside of this miracle?

I am God's soldier. Deacon told me that once. We are fighting a war for the souls of the young.

But this doesn't feel like a war.

An empty vessel.

I think about how much Julian is able to see right through me. How LaShawn is unnerved by me. How unbelievable I seem.

Maybe I am not the miracle Deacon thinks I am.

But this is all I want. To make them happy. To be loved by them. To be part of this incredible, holy family.

Why don't I want anything else?

I breathe in the earthy scent of the forest, and I beg God for guidance. I want to be His vessel. If that's what He's going to make me, then I want to be the best version possible.

But I lie there, met only with an inescapable maw of silence.

What am I doing?

I didn't leave that cabin for hours.

In my mind, the moment I stepped outside of it, I would be swept away. Swept up into whatever awaited me beyond the door of my home.

Home.

No.

No, this wasn't a home. Never was. Neither was the house in Hemet. Or any of the places before.

I had no home.

I had nowhere to go.

I sat on the couch, desperate to calm the spiral inside me. Tried breathing it out, like Diana had once recommended to me. But then I remembered that Diana had been responsible for all of this. Had approved the adoption and had helped the Sullivans take me and Elena away from the world.

She gave us up. She let it happen.

I wondered if Elena was right. I wondered if I had resisted change because I was so deeply, deeply flawed. What if I tried? What if I let myself go and gave this whole thing a chance? What was the worst that could happen? A little peace? A little quiet? A little love and acceptance?

I tried to remember what Rakeem had said. That "reconciliation" wasn't anything. Just another round of indoctrination, only louder. More intense. I could resist that. I knew I could. Then I could get out of this place. Get Elena away from Deacon. I could stop her from becoming . . . whatever she was turning into.

The fan in the living room spun. Squeaked as it did so. I used the sound to try and further calm my nerves. But the heat in that room . . . it grew. And grew. I was bathed in sweat. I knew I should get up, get some water, take a shower, do *something*. But I couldn't.

What had I gotten myself into?

I didn't want to be a sanitized version of myself for these people. That world, that reality . . . god, it seemed so fucking *boring*. And then what was I supposed to do? Return to life outside of Reconciliation and do . . . what? Be a "soldier" for God? What did that even *mean*?

No, I told myself. *I will resist.*

I doubted.
I hoped.
I rejected.
I desired.

What if you're wrong?
What if you're right?

Franklin found me there, sitting on the couch.

I hadn't seen him in days. When he stepped into the cabin, I finally accepted how much of a stranger he was. He'd been my parent for less than two months. He was barely around. Didn't do much of anything a parent was supposed to. In that sense, he was more like my foster parents prior to him, wasn't he? He was an *idea* of a father.

He was a complete nobody to me.

"Manny," he said. Let the door close behind him. Smiled. "I heard the news."

"What news?"

"Tonight is the night," he said. "Your reconciliation! Your mom and I are so proud."

I laughed. A bitter, harsh thing. "Who told you that?"

He scrunched up his face in confusion. "Deacon did," he said. "Did I get that wrong?"

"Do you believe him?"

He walked over to the couch. Sat next to me. "About what?"

"Do you believe what he says?"

His bewilderment grew. "Of course I do. Do *you*?"

I ignored his question. "So you think I'm ready."

"If Deacon says you are, then yes. You're ready."

"But I didn't ask that," I said, twisting away from him. "I asked if *you* thought I was ready."

"I don't get where this is going, Manny," he said.

"What do you know about me, Franklin?"

His brow furrowed. "About you?"

"Anything," I said. "Who am I?"

"You're my son."

I shook my head. "No, that's who I am to *you*," I said, and my voice cracked. "Do you know anything about me? Because you and Caroline spent no time with me before you adopted us. You didn't get to know *anything* about who I was."

He stared at me with furrowed eyebrows, like what I was saying was spoken in another language.

"Why did you and Caroline adopt me?"

He balked at that. "Because," he said. "We were supposed to."

"What does that *mean*, though?"

"It means God told us to," he answered. "We prayed. And Deacon helped us to answer God's call."

"But why did *you* adopt me?"

He sputtered. "I don't understand."

"You're telling me why God wanted me to be adopted. Why did *you* adopt me?"

"Because God told me to!" he said, exasperated.

"So that's all you had to do?" I said. "You and Caroline signed a few papers, and you fulfilled God's will. Is that it?"

"Well, I wouldn't put it like that" he said, and this time, his own voice pitched higher. "God called us to—"

"To just pick any two random kids to make your own?" I said. Stood. Backed away from the couch. "Why would God want that?"

Franklin rose, too, and I could see a thin line of sweat on his brow. "Manny, I don't know what's going on, but I promise, reconciliation will make it all better."

"Why did you bring me here?" I shouted.

"Manny!" he boomed. "Don't yell at me like that. I'm your father."

"No, you're not!" I screamed back. "You're never around. I don't know anything about you. I came along for the ride because it was a place to live. Food to eat. I didn't want the rest of this! And I certainly didn't want you or Caroline."

He raised his hand.

Hesitated.

"I know you want to," I said. "Do it. You're proving my point already."

His hand came down.

"I'm sorry," he said. "I let my emotions take hold of me, Manny."

"Why am I here, Franklin? What do you want from me?"

"To be healed," he said.

"From what?"

"The world."

"What did the world *do* to me, exactly?"

His eye twitched. "You know. Mrs. Thompson has taught you."

I groaned loudly. Once again, I was arguing in circles. "How can she teach me about my life? She doesn't know me any more than you do!"

For a moment, I saw the anger build on his face. Twist his features.

And then, it all passed. A tranquility came over him. He smiled, much like Deacon had hours earlier.

"You wanted to know if I think you're ready," he said. "And I know in my heart that you've never been *more* ready."

He rested a hand on my shoulder. It felt like lead.

"Your life is going to change forever tonight," Franklin said. "You'll never be the same."

I hate that he was right.

My view of the stars goes dark.

Someone's there.

Elena extends a hand out. "Come on, Eli," she says. "It's time."

I've been here before.

It's time.

It's time to pull the errant thread.

I take Elena's hand, and she pulls me upright. I brush off some grass and dirt from my back, and catch her gaze.

She's worried. Her brows stitched together, her bottom lip curled in, her fingers playing with the ends of her hair.

This means something else to her, doesn't it?

I want to ask, to finally penetrate this wall, but I don't get to. Mom and Dad are coming for me. The lights are on in the lodge. I see the other families bringing forth their own children. LaShawn. Annie. Julian. They are marched along the clearing with me, and we arrive at the double doors. Annie is escorted in first, and I finally get to see all their parents. I don't know their names. Don't know their faces. Annie's parents look like . . .

Like . . .

I don't know.

They look like my parents.

They look like Deacon and Mrs. Thompson.

They look like LaShawn's parents.

Julian's parents.

They all look the same to me.

Nameless faces that blend together, that gaze at me with anticipation, as I enter the lodge last with Deacon Thompson and his wife on my heels.

They stare at me.

There's hope there, yes, but also . . .

Hunger.

They look *hungry*.

———

There are three chairs, one for each of the new souls.

LaShawn in the left one, Annie on the right, Julian in the middle.

Julian adjusts his glasses. Looks to me as if he's waiting for an answer to a question he asked.

I know the question, don't I?

What's about to happen?

I don't know the answer.

I think.

I move toward the three of them.

The gathered parents close in around us.

Deacon places his hand on the small of my back. Leans in. Whispers in my ear.

"It's time, Eli," he says.

Time for *what*?

Night had fallen. The shadows stretched across the cabin floor.

"Are you ready, Manny?" Deacon asked me.

I thought about what Rakeem told me the day before.

Electrified fence. All the way around.

I could still feel the scars on his hands if I thought about it.

Rakeem was real. I told myself that again and again.

Deacon extended his hand out to me.

I wanted to cut it off.

"Are you ready to reconcile your body and spirit?"

Elena, Caroline, and Franklin walked behind me, and Deacon led. He spread the double doors open, and I stepped inside. It was darker inside. All the tables had been cleared away. There was a lone chair in the middle of the space.

I knew that chair was for me.

I shuffled my way inside. The Sullivans followed. Elena took a spot standing between Caroline and Franklin.

I sat. Then the other parents came, but without their children. They gathered around me. White faces threatening to drown me.

How many kids had sat in this exact chair? How many of them

doubted what was to come like I did? How many feared what this ceremony was like and wondered if it was going to work?

I couldn't have been the only one.

Deacon closed the doors.

Walked over to me.

Placed his hands on the back of my chair.

"It is time, my family," he said. "For reconciliation."

The Riverside County Coroner's office sits across from an open, barren field. There's something deeply unsettling about that. Life only exists far from this place. I stand in the parking lot, staring at that field. The grass is dead, the color of hay. Maybe even a little more yellow. There are hills in the distance, and behind them, the San Jacinto Mountains.

Idyllwild is up there.

Elena might be there.

It's her body.

Or she could be here.

It's not her body.

"Come on," says Monica.

She's at my side, staring out at the field, too. She's holding my hand. Then she lets go and pats me between the shoulder blades. "It's now or never," she says. "At least you'll know."

There's something in the darkness.

I feel it.

It's waking up.

I twist around and look into Deacon Thompson's piercing blue eyes.

"I don't know what I'm supposed to do," I say.

"Pray," he says, and I know he's trying to be comforting. But it sounds like a command.

"Pray for *what*?" I whisper back.

"Their souls," Elena says, butting in. "Pray for them to accept what God gave them and to make a choice."

She pauses.

"To make the same choice you did."

I turn back to the others. Annie looks at me, eyes wide. "What's happening?" she asks.

The parents raise their hands.

They begin to mumble prayers. I can't make out specific words. It's just a low buzz in the room, but they all seem to know what they're supposed to do.

Mom. Mom taught them, didn't she?

She's there, to my right. "Go ahead, Eli," she says.

"We believe in your miracle," Dad says, and his hand is on my shoulder.

But what is my miracle? What happened to me?

"It's time!" Deacon calls out.

LaShawn gasps in the brief silence that follows.

And then the parents close in on their children.

Mom and Dad are there, too, their hands on the three children, and their prayers are loud, forceful, so much so that they bounce off one another in the lodge, but Deacon is the loudest, imploring these souls to run toward God, to cast out their impurities, to choose choose choose choose choose

Choose *what*?

Annie shrinks away from their hands.

LaShawn shoves one of the men off of her.

And Julian . . .

Julian looks at peace.

His eyes are closed, his body rocking from side to side as the adults press their hands to his shoulders, his arms, his head, telling him to accept his fate, to choose to let go of his old life.

LaShawn tries to stand up, but her mother pushes her back down.

I stand there. My mind swirls.

I remember something.

Hands on my body, pushing me down.

"Just let go," Elena calls out. "You can accept this miracle, just like Eli did!"

Just like I did?

"No."

LaShawn says it. I almost don't catch it among the chaos and roar of prayer, but Dad steps away from her.

"No," she says again.

Dad looks to Deacon.

Then to me.

"Pray," he demands. "Pray for her, Eli."

"No."

Annie stands up and swats her parents' hands away. "No," she repeats. "I don't want this. I don't want to choose *anything* you are offering me!"

"Pray for them, Eli!" Mom commands.

Then Julian shakes his head. "No, I won't do this, either," he says. "I don't want to give up who I am."

He glances to me.

There is nothing but sorrow there.

"I don't want to become like him."

My heart sinks. His words sting as they lash at me. As they force me to ask myself: Is he wrong for saying that?

Why would anyone want to become this? Half a person. A vessel without identity, a soldier without a war, a question without an answer.

What exactly am I supposed to do here?

———

"You've done it before," says Deacon. "Eli, help them choose. Help them cast out what is not needed. What is unwanted!"

Before.

What was before?

What did I choose?

"I don't understand," says Elena. "Why isn't it working?"

"You promised us," says a woman, her finger in Deacon's face. "You told us they would *change*."

I can see myself. Here. In this room.

I've done this before.

"Eli, I need you to focus," says Deacon. "I need you to pray and bring about the miracle that changed you."

"*What miracle?*" I yell. "No one will tell me what it is!"

The room goes silent.

"You're the miracle," says Mom, and she's at my side. She grabs both sides of my face. Turns me toward her. Caresses my cheeks. "You chose that day, and we chose you back. You gave up your sinful impulses, your disobedience, your constant need to ask questions, your refusal to accept God's will."

Dad is close, too, and his eyes are red. "That day, you became our son."

"We believe you can give that gift to these parents, Eli," Mom says, and her eyes plead with me. "Call on God. Let His power work through you."

"This is reconciliation," says Deacon, and I see him smile over Mom's shoulder, watch as he turns to the parents and their children. "Repairing the body and soul."

He extends a hand out to me. "Who you were before does not matter when you are here," he says. "All that matters is *now*. The choice you make *now*."

Then he waits. His anticipation is thick and blunt, pressing down on me like hands on my shoulders.

I've been here before.

"Who was I before?" I ask. "Do you know, Deacon?"

Julian stands up. He reaches over and grabs LaShawn's hand and helps her to her feet, then holds his other hand to Annie.

"We don't want this," he says. "Whatever it is you're offering . . . Keep it."

"Who was I before?" I repeat.

Deacon wavers.

For just a moment. It's a twitch. A small tell.

"No one," he says. "You weren't anyone before you were here."

The parents are yelling. At Deacon, at their children. Julian shakes his head, and he leads the others out of the lodge, ignoring the shouts of the adults, and then they're just . . . gone.

I think Deacon is going to follow them out, but he's transfixed. Staring at me with those horrible eyes of his.

"Honey, what should we do?" asks Mrs. Thompson.

"Go get them back, Harriett."

"But how—"

"Now!" he snaps.

She spins away and chases after the others.

Deacon hasn't broken eye contact with me the entire time.

"Who was I before?" I say again, my voice pitched higher.

Elena is trying to reach me.

A noise escapes her. A gasp, I think, but . . . no. It's a sob. She covers her mouth and I pull away from Mom.

"Don't," says Dad, and I think he's talking to me, but he steps toward Elena, grabs her shoulder. "Don't."

"Why do you ask that question, Eli?" Deacon says. "You haven't in a very, very long time."

I don't know how to answer.

"I think we were wrong," Elena says, and tears spill down her cheeks.

"Don't say another word," Deacon warns, and his features twist in fury.

But she says it anyway.

"I think I was wrong."

It's a plain, flat building. Looks a lot like the Department of Public Social Services from the other day. No character, no individuality. I guess I get it. This is a place of death, of sadness, of the violence of loss. Why make it look nice? Doesn't explain why the other county building is so boring, though.

Monica takes me forth. Opens the door for me and holds it open.

Ricardo and Carlos stay behind. It isn't by request; they both think it's best that just Monica is with me. But Carlos does gaze at me with those big brown eyes of his as we pass the van, head toward my destiny.

I think he's sad. Or anxious. Or both.

Because none of us know what comes after.

Monica tells the man behind the front desk—thin mustache, blond hair slicked back—that she had called the day before. That we were there to make a potential identification.

He nods. Asks us to sit. Picks up a phone.

I can't stay still.

My legs are shaking. My stomach roiling. I'm glad I didn't eat. It all would've come up. Ended up on the scuffed, dull tile underneath me.

"Deep breath," Monica says.

I try.

The air here is stale. Clinical. I think I smell something sour. It's the bodies, isn't it?

It's her body.

It's not her body.

A man is coming toward us. He's short and plump. Thick-framed glasses. Balding on top. There's a patch of sweat in the middle of his chest.

And in his hand is a manila envelope.

The dark blot in my mind . . . it throbs.

Something's wrong. There's a part of this . . . a part of this that's still in the darkness.

He beckons us to follow him. Does a double take, then shakes his head, keeps heading deeper into the building.

Don't know how I get my legs to work, but we're moving. We're taken around a corner to a small, cramped office. Two mismatched chairs sit across from a metal desk.

"I know it's not much," he says, "but hopefully this is quick."

He stares at me again.

"We haven't had much luck with this case. Someone else is supposed to come by today to give it a crack, but honestly . . . we'll take anything."

He places the folder down on the desk before sitting behind it, and when he does, I can see the edge of what's inside it.

Photos.

That's it. The answer is right there.

Monica extends her hand. Introduces herself. Says she's here to accompany me just as support.

"What's your name, young man?" he asks.

I don't answer.

"I'm Walter Grant," he says.

And he stops. I think he believes that was going to make me more comfortable, but I still don't give him my name. He stares at me, long and hard. Then: "Have you ever done something like this before?"

I shake my head.

"Monica here tells me you think you might know who this is."

"Maybe," I say. Then: "I used to be there. Reconciliation."

He studies me. Narrows his eyes. Doesn't react, though. Just . . . stares. Like he's trying to figure me out.

"And do you think you know who the deceased is?"

The deceased.

My heart is in my throat. It's her, isn't it? That's what's happening. He sees it. The resemblance.

It's not her body.

"I think so," I say, my voice cracking. "My sister."

There's a reaction. He relaxes. Sits back. Is he relieved? No. Stressed? No.

"What is it?" Monica says.

"Well, I can confirm it's definitely not your sister," he says.

My heart leaps. "What?!"

"The deceased is definitely a young male."

He pushes the folder closer.

"Maybe you can help, though," he says. "Maybe you recognize who he is."

No. Oh, no. There's a possibility. One I didn't think of. Another person this could be.

"I'll show you the sketches our artist did first," says Walter. "The body was pretty badly decomposed by the time it was found, so these are just an approximation of who John Doe was."

John Doe.

Something is happening. The hair raises all over my skin.

I'm on the floor of the lodge.

My chest hurts. I hold a hand over it as my heart thumps faster and faster.

What's happening?

Walter flips the folder open, and then starts spreading the

sketches out, but I don't need it. I don't need to spend one second further to identify that face. It is not exact. It's wrong in some ways. But . . .

Intake of breath.

A terrible silence.

"Take a look at these," Walter says.

I can't.

He looks up at me again, his expression pointed. He glances back down at the sketch, then at me again. I can tell it's happening. He wants to say more. He is putting the pieces together. But all he says is:

"Do you think you know who this is?"

Everything is a blur. Sounds. Images. Colors. Lights. There's a hand on my shoulder. Wrapped around my waist. I stumble, and my hands are on the ground. In grass. I think it's wet. Damp.

Elena. That's her. She's here.

Someone has my other hand as I throw up into the grass, and she's moving my hair out of my face.

Caroline.

No.

Mom. That's who I want her to be.

I want her to love me.

They lift me up. Carry me across the darkness. It's hard to see, and my chest hurts. I try to turn back and look where I came from, but it hurts too much. I'm exhausted, and it takes every bit of willpower not to crumple to the ground.

Something pulls me back, though. I shouldn't be doing this. I shouldn't–

Go back go back go back go back

But they guide me forward. Through a door. I fall forward onto a couch, and sweat drips off me.

Something is wrong with me.

My eyes blur with tears.

"No," I say. "I'm sorry. I don't know who that is."

Monica is looking. Leaning over the desk.

"Manny . . ." she says. Scrunches up her face.

"We need to go," I say, standing up.

She's picked one up. Can't stop staring.

I am both in this office and in the lodge.

The darkness is floating away.

The veil is lifting.

I run.

Out of the office, out of the reception area, out into the bright morning light, and I see Carlos and Ricardo, walking toward me, but they're not alone.

There's a couple walking alongside the Varelas. I don't recognize them—both of them are Black women. Tall. One has her head shaved; the other has long locs that hang to her waist.

But between them—there's a boy.

A boy I know.

I freeze. Nearly stumble at the edge of the lot.

He rushes toward me, but I can't move, even though I should. I shouldn't be here. I can't let this happen.

It's all closing in on me. The truth. Everything that I've ignored, everything that I've buried, everything I've denied for so long, it's all returning.

I've pulled the thread.

It's unraveling.

"Manny?" the boy says, and then his arms are open, wrapped around me, and he's sobbing. "Oh my god, Manny, I thought you were dead. I thought it was *you*."

The fucking irony.

"Manny?" Rakeem says. "Manny, say something."

My mind spins. I'm crying again.

"Manny," Rakeem says, grabbing the sides of my face. "I thought I would never see you again."

Can't really see him through the tears, but it's his face. His hair is different. Cut shorter. Sharper.

It's him. It's him. It's him.

Deacon gets in Elena's face.

"Don't say that," he commands. "Do not question God's miracle."

"His *miracle*?" She groans loudly. "If Eli is His miracle, then why did they all leave? Why haven't they given up their old selves?"

"He must lack faith," says Deacon.

"How can he?" sneers Elena. "That's why we got rid of the *other one*!"

The other one.

The way she says it.

Those words are a curse in her mouth.

"The *what*?" I say.

Mom grabs my arm. Pulls me away from Elena. "Stop it!" she screams. "Don't speak of *him*. We agreed!"

"Does it even matter?" she cries, then points at me. "It's clear he's not a miracle at all!"

"Elena, no," says Deacon, and I don't know how it's possible, but it's like he *grows* standing in front of her. He puts his hand in her hair. Strokes it until he reaches the end, then grabs a fistful of it. "Eli is my miracle. My greatest work. You will not sully that."

He pulls.

"Stop it!" Elena yells, and she tries to free herself, but he only seems to grip harder.

I lurch forward.

And Dad stops me. He puts a hand to my chest. "No," he says. "Let Deacon deal with it."

Elena yanks herself out of Deacon's grasp. "What are you *doing*?"

He brings his arms up, like he's going to lunge at her again.

"Deacon!"

Mrs. Thompson is at the door, her face flush with fright. She looks from Elena to her husband.

"What is it, Harriett?" Deacon says, his voice practically a sneer.

Her eyes are panicked; her chest rises and falls rapidly.

"Spit it out!" he yells.

"They're *gone*."

His arms drop to his sides. "Gone?"

"The Munro family already left," she says, panting. "Julian grabbed his bag and ran down to the car."

"Forget him," he says. "What of the others?"

"Annie's family doesn't want to go through with this anymore. They said they don't need another church. And the Robinsons . . ."

Mrs. Thompson freezes up, and her gaze is distant.

Deacon crosses over to her. "What is it?"

"They canceled their donation," she says. "They think . . ."

She doesn't finish.

Because she's staring at me.

"Tell me," Deacon orders, and he grabs his wife's chin, forces her gaze back to him.

She swallows.

"They think you're a fraud."

The wooden floorboards creak under Deacon.

"A fraud," he says.

"Honey, they're just disappointed," Mrs. Thompson says, running her hand up and down Deacon's arm. "We have plenty more members of the church and—"

"I don't care about them, Harriett," he seethes. "I care about the children. Our future. The only way we're going to win this war against evil."

He wheels around.

Points at me.

"If anyone here is a fraud, it's *him*."

I've been here before.

I struggle with this distant epiphany. I can't grasp the edges of it, can't pull it out of the darkness. But it's there.

"Who was I before?" I ask.

Deacon's pale face goes red.

He strides over to me, his boots pounding on the boards, and I don't even see it coming. His hand is around my throat, and I never knew how strong he was, never knew he could crush the wind out of me like that, but I'm swatting at his hands, trying to break away, and his eyes bulge as he lifts me up, as dark blots appear in my vision.

"You were a waste of life," he says. "You were a disobedient little shit who spat in the face of God's mercy, and you corrupted nearly every person who came into contact with you."

He throws me down.

My head cracks against the floorboards, and there's a brightness at first, then a searing pain.

It shakes something free.

———

I've been here before.

Elena screams. I think she comes for me. Not sure. I can't see right, and the shapes blur in the light of the lodge.

It's Deacon. He's standing above me.

"Why couldn't you be more like your sister?" he screams. "She came to me all on her own. She left her terrible foster family to be with the Sullivans. She gave up on the other one because she *knew* what God required of her."

He kneels down. Grabs the back of my head. Then brings his hand into view.

There's something on it.

Red.

He shakes his hand. Disgusted with me.

I push myself up on my elbows, pain and nausea swimming in me. "I don't understand," I say. "I chose this place. I chose *you*. Didn't I?"

"It wasn't enough," he spits back. "You embarrassed me tonight. You took God's miracle, and you destroyed it. All you had to do was show your loyalty. All you had to do was give them the same gift you received!"

He turns about. Kicks a chair. It flies toward the small stage.

"Why couldn't you be like Elena?"

"Please, stop," Elena says, and then she's at my side, cradling me. "Please, he can try again."

She locks eyes with me.

"You'll try again, won't you?"

"No," I say, the pain at the back of my head growing. "Not if this is what Deacon is."

I've been here before.

The door to the coroner's office swings open again.

"Monica?"

Ricardo rushes forward. Rakeem lets go of me, and I see that she's swaying. She's going to fall, but Ricardo steadies her.

She looks at me.

She looks at me like she's seen a ghost.

Because she has.

"Monica, what happened?" Ricardo says frantically.

"Mami?"

Carlos is there, too.

They're all here. The Varelas. The strangers. *Rakeem.*

And Monica cannot stop staring at me.

"How?" she says. "How is that possible?"

"How is *what* possible?" Ricardo asks.

"How, Manny?" she shrieks, and there are tears in her eyes, tears pouring out, tears tracing down her face. "Manny, *how?*"

"What is she talking about?" Carlos demands. "What happened?!"

I've unraveled.

I devoted my life to him and this church. I did my best. I did as I was *told*.

But it's not good enough, is it?

Was I ever good enough?

Another wave of nausea rolls through me and I can't keep myself upright. Elena holds me. Screams for someone to help.

Where are Mom and Dad? Why aren't they doing anything?

A shadow falls over me. Deacon.

"You were my greatest disappointment, Eli," he says. "I thought it had been the other one. Manny."

Manny.

"The body," I say to them. "It's mine."

I tell them everything.

   Because I finally remember it all.

   I remember . . . him.

No one says anything for a long while. Because what can you say to all that? What possible response is there?

There was no music like Rakeem had said.

The Sullivans began praying, low murmurs at first, until:

"It's time!" Deacon repeated.

And then they closed in.

It happened so fast that I couldn't stand up. No chance to react. The space around me was gone, and they put their hands on me, and they began to pray.

"Lord, open his spirit!" Franklin begged, and spit flew from his lips, fell upon my face.

Another hand, on my shoulder, and another voice in my ear: "Cast them *out*!" Caroline shrieked.

More hands. On my arms. My face. My chest. They squeezed my biceps. Franklin slapped an open palm on my chest; Mrs. Thompson wrenched an arm back. I thought I heard something pop. Was it me? Had that been my body? Elena screamed, prayed louder than them all.

Their voices beat at me. One after the other. They prayed. They excoriated. They implored. They begged.

I squirmed. Swatted them away, but each time I did, there was a new hand, a new prayer, a new person begging me to accept what God had destined for me. Someone scratched at my face.

"Stop it!" I yelled.

And they did not.

I couldn't breathe. They swarmed in like ants on a carcass, shad-owing me, swallowing me in their darkness.

Then they stepped aside.

I gasped for air. Blinked away tears as I was temporarily blinded by the overhead light in the lodge.

"He's resisting," Deacon said, but I couldn't see where his voice was coming from.

I rubbed at my eyes, and I thought to stand, to bolt out of that place as fast as I could.

Caroline and Franklin stood in my way, each of them with a hand raised, and they put them on my head.

"Are you ready?" Franklin asked.

"No," I said. "No, I'm *not*."

I stood up.

No. *Tried* to.

And they both shoved me back down.

I tried to stand up again, but they held me. Pressed me down harder.

"What are you doing?" I said.

Elena was there. "Just let *go*," she said. "Manny, this doesn't hurt. Nothing is going to happen to you but *peace*. You just have to accept reconciliation."

"I don't know what that *means*!" I said.

"One body!" Deacon screamed.

The lodge went silent. The singing cut out. He strode forward, a tower of anger and rage, and when he placed his hand on my fore-head, I reared back. The chair nearly tipped over.

"We are trying to repair your body, Manny!" he cried. "Why do you resist it? Why have you fought this every step of the way? Don't you want this?"

This?

"Don't you want to be *loved*?"

Yes. Yes, I do.

"Don't you want a family?"

Yes. Yes, I do.

"Don't you want a community you can call your own?"

More than anything.

"And yet, you question. Your body belongs to the world, Manny. You do not see what God has given you. You cannot know the true nature of your soul and its desire to be reunited with what God intended."

They were just words. Words with no meaning to me.

How would they help me? Heal me?

Fix me?

"Don't you want what everyone else has?"

"Yes!" I screamed. "Of course I do!"

"Then why do you fight this process?" he said, then pressed me down further. Further. My neck ached from the pressure. "Why do you question my wife? Why do you defy your parents and tell them they don't love you? Why do you refuse your sister?"

"It's been *three days*!" I shouted. "You are asking me to give up some huge part of my life after *three days*."

"It's never too soon to turn to God," Deacon shot back.

I pushed myself up and screamed as I placed my hands on Deacon's chest.

I *shoved*.

He stumbled, his eyes wide with shock.

"None of you ever ask me what *I* want!" I cried, then pointed at the Sullivans. "They didn't even ask to adopt me!"

"You sound like a *child*," Franklin said.

"Because I *am* one," I sneered at him.

"Then why can't you *be* one?" Deacon said. "Be our child. Be a part of a family. That's all we're asking. Accept this, and you'll be a part of everything."

"Please," Elena begged, and she came forward, her hands clasped in prayer and desperation. "There's nothing I want more than for us to be a family."

I knew deep down that I wanted that, too.

I couldn't say that to Elena out loud. I was ashamed: ashamed to have buried that feeling for so long. Ashamed to have fought so much against what she wanted. Ashamed that she'd probably been right.

Being suspicious of everyone *was* exhausting.

But how? I wondered. How could I make *this* my family?

"I can see you are confused, my child," said Deacon. "That you are still torn. That you still cannot choose."

He knelt in front of me. Put his hands on my thighs.

"What part of the old world still gives you pause? What did it give you that this place cannot?"

I didn't know how to answer him.

350 • MARK OSHIRO

———

Because what *did* I have?

A home? No. Nothing permanent. Nothing stable. Nothing real.

A family? Maybe. Elena, for sure. But Christ's Dominion had taken her away from me. Would doing this bring me back to her?

A community? Never. Never thought I'd ever get one. Not for someone like me.

What did I have?

Nothing.

And here was a whole group of people offering me *something*.

But at what cost? They wanted me to give up who I was. They wanted me to be someone that was easier to . . .

To devour.

They were devouring me, weren't they?

"You must choose," Deacon demanded.

And I couldn't. I wanted both. I wanted freedom. I wanted love. I wanted choice. I wanted certainty.

———

"I don't know," I said. "I don't know what to do. I don't know what this *is*."

Elena knelt in front of me. Brought my head down with both her hands. Pressed them against my face.

"Yes, you do," she said. "Deep down, you've always known, brother. You know what you want."

The praying continued.

Began to rise in volume.

Like a chant. Like an invocation.

"Take what you've always wanted, Manny," said Deacon.

He laid his hand on the top of my head.

"God is awaiting you. *We* are awaiting you. Choose, my son."

My son.

No one had ever said it like that before.

I wanted it.

I hated it.

Franklin rested a hand on my right shoulder.

Caroline's went on my left.

They pressed down.

Sent their willpower into me.

Choose choose choose.

What did I want?

I couldn't breathe. A pain stabbed into my chest, right on my sternum, and I cried out, a wild peal of terror, and they only got louder, louder, screamed back at me, and I rose up—

No.

No no no.

It tore out of me.

My chest split open. Or it didn't. I don't know. It felt like it did, but there was no blood, no gore, no fluids, nothing. But it was open, and something grabbed my ribs as it burst forth, as it slithered to the ground, and they cried out, backed away from me, and my head rolled back, far enough that I could see Deacon above me, his hand still on my head, but his eyes locked on the impossibility before him.

He watched the birth.

I felt it kick its way out.

I felt it slide down my body.

I heard it hit the floor of the lodge with a sickening thud.

And I fell to the side.

Gasping.

Couldn't breathe.

My hands went to my chest, but it was whole. Unblemished. My shirt was drenched, and I expected to find blood there.

Just sweat.

Someone was crying. Whispering. Murmuring. My vision blurred as I looked up, and I reached for the wooden chair, grasped it hard, tried to heave myself up and—

There was a new person there. On the ground. Curled up.

"Help me," I moaned, but no one was looking at me. No one.

I was no longer the center of attention or focus.

He was.

I rested my chest on the chair, my arms strewn over the other side, and he turned over.

He wore the same clothes as I did: a green T-shirt over black jeans. His hair was black. Wavy.

He turned his head.

Looked right at me with dark eyes.

I slid off the chair.

"Deacon, what *happened*?" Elena said.

Her voice sounded so far away. All of them did. And I couldn't take my eyes off of him.

Off of me.

I crawled forward.

I reached a hand out.

Toward . . .

Me.

It was me.

———

I saw myself from the outside for the first time.

He wore a terrified look on his face. Brows together in shock, his mouth slightly open. His eyes were dark. Practically black.

He had my face.

My hair.

My jawline.

It was me.

I scooted closer.

Reached out.

I needed to touch his waxy skin. I needed to know he was real. I needed to know this was happening.

I stretched my hand out.

And he yanked his hand back.

"Elena," he groaned.

In my voice.

"Elena, help me up."

Caroline backed away. Vomited. Wiped at her mouth with the back of her hand.

"No," she said. "It's not possible."

Then she glanced at me. Back to him. At that impossibility made real.

Mrs. Thompson cried out, fell into sobs. "My Lord," she slurred. "Deacon, what *is* that?"

"Elena, *please*," he said.

But they made no move toward him.

Toward me.

Their gaping stares said everything.

This was impossible.

This was evil.

This was an abomination.

Until.

"Deacon," he said. "You saved me."

Deacon blinked. "What?"

Mrs. Thompson clung to her husband's arm as her legs wobbled. "No," she said.

"You saved me," he repeated.

Then he lifted a hand up. Extended it toward Deacon.

Deacon looked at me once. Long enough for me to know what was about to happen.

"No," I groaned, and I flopped onto my back, my head swimming, pain radiating down my torso.

Deacon approached him. His steps were cautious. Uncertain.

"Deacon," the boy implored. "Please."

He held his hand out.

"How?" Deacon said. "How are you here?"

The other one looked at me. Back to Deacon. His lips moved without a sound. Then, the words came, soft and slurred.

"I chose."

I tried to push myself up, but another burst of pain flared on my chest, and I collapsed back down.

"You chose?" Deacon said.

No. No, this wasn't happening.

"What did you do to me?" I wheezed.

An anger filled me then, and I ignored the pain in my torso. I pushed myself upright and swayed and—

Elena took a step away from me.

"Elena," I said. "Please."

Deacon wasn't even looking at me anymore. He placed a hand on the impostor's forehead.

"Do you choose reconciliation?" he said. "Do you choose to accept the reconciliation of body and soul?"

He smiled. "Of course I do," he said.

Deacon turned. Beckoned his wife over. "Come," he said. "Come see our miracle."

No no no no no

"What are you *doing*?" I slurred, then lurched forward.

And Franklin did what he wanted to earlier.

He struck me. Right across the face.

"Get away, you *demon*!" he hissed.

I stumbled, but stayed on my feet. "Stop this," I said. "I don't understand what's happening!"

Caroline looked to Deacon, then knelt at the impostor's side. Took his other hand.

"Are you our son?" she asked, tears brimming her eyes.

He gazed at them, his expression empty. A thought struck me then:

He did not seem human.

But a warmth returned to his face. His eyes softened.

"Of course I am," he said, and he smiled.

It was as if he'd never smiled before. Like he was trying it on.

But then it grew.

And it looked real.

Happier than anything I'd ever worn on my face.

Franklin was last. He rubbed his hand—the one he'd hit me with—and then he walked away. Came back. Twisted his face up.

"What is this, Deacon?" he cried. "Who is that?"

Deacon didn't answer, because he did.

"I'm your son," he said.

The words I couldn't ever say.

Franklin stepped closer. Tears in his eyes. He embraced him.

"And you are my father," the boy said.

I said.

Deacon stepped away as they hugged, and his eyes were alight with ecstasy.

He was thrilled.

But Elena . . .

She still stared at me, the color drained from her face.

"Manny," she uttered.

To *me*.

"Manny, what is this?"

"I don't know!" I said, and when I moved toward her, Franklin raised his hand again.

"It's *me*," I begged, then wobbled in place. "I don't know who that is."

"Isn't it obvious?" said Deacon, his face alight with joy. "Reconciliation happened. Two bodies. He did it. He gave us the miracle I've always wanted."

My copy smiled.

A rush of horror and sickness roiled through me. "Stop it," I said. "Stop this."

"I chose," he said once more.

Elena stepped up to him.

She placed her hand in his, and she tried to smile, but it didn't quite happen. Her lip quivered as she gazed at me.

I thought I saw uncertainty.

"I'm tired," she said, gazing my way.

She pulled him close, clutched his left hand tightly.

"I choose," she said.

She stepped away from me. Caroline took his right hand, and the two of them walked away, and Mrs. Thompson followed. None of them looked back at me.

I already didn't exist.

We are all in a hotel.

The two women I didn't know are Ameena and Vera Samuels. Rakeem met them somewhere in Nevada, which is where he'd hitchhiked to after he ran away from the Bradfords. I don't know anything else, but I imagine there must be some similarities in our stories. What we went through.

What we survived.

Carlos is on the couch next to me, his hand still locked in mine. He held it the entire time. The Samuels are on one bed, the Varelas on another.

And no one says anything. They stare at me. At the impossibility. I don't know what they must think of me. Of what I remembered. It's just . . . silence. A terrible, terrible silence.

Ameena is the first to break it.

"We set up here because of the news we saw last week," she says. "Rakeem wanted to help."

He wipes tears off his face. "I thought it was you, man. I really did."

Vera finally speaks. "Rakeem told us everything that happened. What that place was like. And he sometimes watched Deacon's broadcasts, just to see if he could get glimpses of you."

"It's so ironic," I say, and a nervous smile breaks out on my face. "Because that was never me. I never got to be in one of Deacon's videos or broadcasts. I just . . . couldn't remember."

"Trauma," Monica whispers.

"Huh?" I say.

"I'm not a mental health professional," she says. "And I'm certainly no expert in what you just described to us, but . . . shit. I bet that was the only way for your mind to survive the experience. You just . . . forgot."

"It was always *him*," Carlos says softly.

"Yeah," I say. "So . . . you've seen him already."

Ricardo swears.

I look at Rakeem. "How, though?"

"How what?"

"Your parents," I say. "The Bradfords. What happened to them?"

Vera rolls her eyes, and Ameena fixes a mean scowl on her face.

"Sorry," I say. "You don't have to talk about it."

"It's okay," says Vera. "It was just a hell of a process."

"There was a private investigator we hired to find them, first of all," says Ameena, and she wrings her hands together. "And once we did, they wouldn't meet with us. Wouldn't sign over parental rights. Nothing. We tried to get into Reconciliation to find them, but . . . no luck."

"The only thing we ever got out of them was one sentence," says Vera.

"'We never had a son,'" says Rakeem. Shakes his head. "I still don't exist to them."

"If you don't mind me asking," says Monica, "what changed? We work a lot with kids who have been . . . well, targeted. Abandoned. Thrown out."

"We don't know," says Ameena. "One day, the Bradfords sent the signed papers to our house."

"Didn't give them our address, either," Vera mumbles.

"And then it was done," says Rakeem. "I could finally start over. Like *really* start over."

It dawns on me.

"You didn't exist," I say to him.

He shakes his head. "No ID. No birth certificate. Just a first name."

"Just like you," says Carlos.

Just like me.

There's no one just like me. I can't ignore that anymore. I am alone in this.

"Manny," Deacon said.

"What is happening?" I sobbed, my eyes on the doors to the lodge, hoping they'd come back, hoping that this was a terrible joke.

"Manny," Deacon repeated, and he grabbed my head. *Hard.*

"You were given a chance to prove yourself to me and this community," he said. "You didn't choose. And God has no mercy for those who are indifferent to His love."

I struggled to squirm out of his grip.

"You had so many opportunities to do us right, and yet you failed. If you chose anything or anyone, it was that wretched friend of yours. Rakeem."

The tears came, hot and bitter. Spilled down my cheeks.

"God performed a miracle tonight," Deacon said. "An actual miracle. And you have given us a gift that will be returned a thousandfold to God. So while you no longer have a place here, I must thank you, Manny."

He placed a kiss on my forehead.

"I wish it didn't have to come to this."

Someone grabbed my arms. Wrenched them back. I screamed and tried to spin around, but I lost my balance. Hit the ground with a sickening pop. A shooting pain in my shoulder. I cried out again, and a figure was on top of me, and the pain was blinding. They grabbed my wrists. Slapped a zip tie around them and pulled. I screamed out as it bit into my wrists, and then I was yanked up, my hands bound in front of me. Shoved forward, toward the double doors.

The last words Deacon said to me, standing in the middle of the lodge:

"We don't need you anymore, Manny."

"Stop struggling."

I recognized Franklin's gruff voice.

"Where are you taking me?" I asked.

He didn't answer. He brought me close to the porch. Held me in place. Called out to his wife.

Caroline came out. Glared at me. "What are we doing?"

"What God wants us to," he said.

"What's happening?" I sobbed.

She ignored me. "What about our son?"

"*Our* son?" I coughed out. "Who am I?"

"Can Elena care for him? This is important."

Caroline nodded and went back in the house, returning half a minute later. She carried something in her hands. Gave it to Franklin.

The door was open. I could see her over Caroline's shoulder. Kneeling next to the couch. He was sitting upright on it, staring in my direction.

"No," I sobbed. "Please, Elena!"

I could . . . I could feel him. Something tugged deep inside, but—

Franklin yanked me away. And Elena didn't answer.

They led me past the cabins. Down the road, and then I saw the cars lined up on either side of it, and something called me back, pulled me away from these people.

Go back go back go back.

We came to a stop. Caroline held something out. Something I hadn't seen since I first came here.

The blindfold.

"Caroline, what's happening?"

Still wouldn't look at me.

"Mom, *please*—" I began.

Her rage-filled eyes flicked up to me. "Don't call me that. You had all this time to treat me like your mother, and *now* you say it?"

I tried to pull apart my bound hands. Didn't work. Could feel the blood trickling down them.

"You're despicable, Manny," she said.

"Caroline," said Franklin gently. "It's over. Now we'll get the son we wanted."

Him.

They meant him.

But the image of that other one . . . it was fuzzy in my head. I kept trying to see it. Kept trying to remember.

It was faded. Blurry.

They put me in the passenger seat. I explored their faces as they did so. I wanted to see anything in them that I recognized.

But I was a stranger to them.

Caroline leaned forward, held the blindfold out between the seats. "Bring your head to me."

"You don't have to do this," I said.

She froze.

"You're getting exactly what you wanted," she said.

"What I wanted? I didn't want *this*!"

"You never respected us, did you?" she shrieked. "What were we to you? Did we ever mean anything?"

What exactly had they done for me?

There were the basics: a roof. Food. Homeschooling.

What else?

Had they ever said that they loved me?

Had Franklin ever tossed a football in the yard with me, or whatever the fuck fathers did with their sons?

Had Caroline ever kissed me on top of the head? Or thrown me a birthday party?

What had they done for me?

They plucked me out of foster care.

They cast me into a monstrous abyss.

It was a futile, bitter fury that erupted out of me. I wanted to hurt them. I wanted to make them suffer.

So I locked eyes with her in the rearview mirror.

"No," I said. "I feel the same about you as I did before I ever met you and Franklin."

She smacked the back of my head. Hard. The echo of it rang out in the car, and then she started crying, and Franklin was suddenly there at her side. He rubbed her back, told her that everything would be okay.

"God gave us our miracle child," he said.

"He just has no idea what we sacrificed, Franklin," she said through her sobs. "No idea!"

I took a step out of the car. Wasn't sure what I was trying to do. Escape? Attack them? I don't know. I swung my other leg out. Used my bound hands as leverage as I tried to stand, grabbed at the side door.

Franklin reacted quickly. He rose from my right. Pressed his filthy boot against my chest and kicked. I smacked my head on the steering wheel when I fell back.

I saw stars.

They were taking me away. Away from this place where the stars were so close.

I thought: They're going to make me disappear. Just like Rakeem.

"Don't," I slurred, and my vision twisted as I sat up, leaned forward.

"I don't care what you want anymore, Manny," Caroline said, hatred dripping off every word. "I don't care what happens to you. Ungrateful bastard. You want to leave this place so badly? Then we'll give you that. We don't care about you. You can do whatever the fuck you want."

Then Caroline tugged the blindfold over my head, and I was in darkness.

"Remember what he said, Franklin?"

Franklin sat in the driver's seat. Put on his seat belt.

"Wherever God leads us," he responded.

The engine came to life. The sedan reversed. Then turned.

He drove me into an uncertain future.

———

I didn't speak. Wasn't just that I didn't know what to say. The silence allowed me to disappear. If I stayed quiet, I could almost believe that this wasn't happening.

I was not blindfolded and bound. I wasn't sitting next to my father, in front of my mother, as they took me somewhere to get rid of me.

I had not been split in two.

They had not chosen the other one.

They had chosen me.

I just wanted someone to choose me.

I tried to think about him again. My chest throbbed, but as we moved away from Reconciliation, so did my memory.

I knew something had happened. My body ached because of it.

I couldn't see his face anymore.

In that terrible silence, I could sense the descent. Could sense the growing speed. Could sense the sharp twists and turns.

We were leaving the mountains.

I was leaving.

I was really leaving.

———

The irony hit me in full: I *had* wanted to leave. I *had* wanted to escape that place. And now I was getting exactly what I wanted.

I saw one face, over and over again in my mind, in all that darkness.

Elena.

I wanted to hate her. It would have been so easy to.

I saw her face at the exact moment she chose. Her lip quivering.

She wasn't sure. She couldn't be. She wouldn't do something like this.

She wouldn't have chosen these people over me.

The abyss grew darker. Deeper.

We were no longer descending. No longer twisting down a mountain. Just on a highway or a freeway somewhere, and I knew then that I probably wasn't going to see Elena again.

I started crying, a quiet, soft sound at first, but then the enormity of what awaited me overtook my whole body, and I couldn't breathe. The blindfold was too tight around my head. I thought I was going to die in that passenger seat.

I tried to stick my thumbs under the edge of it, but Franklin ripped the blindfold off and threw it in my lap.

"Calm down!" he ordered.

I gasped, then gazed out the window.

It was dark out, so the lights from cars blurred past me.

"Stop being so dramatic. This'll all be over by tomorrow."

"Tomorrow?" I twisted my head toward him. "What does that mean?"

He remained silent. Stared straight ahead at the road.

"Where are you taking me?"

He didn't answer.

I tried to stay awake. Tried to remember all the signs we passed, but they were nothing but nonsense in my brain. The darkness, the fear, the exhaustion—it all lulled me into a fitful, uncomfortable sleep. I awoke later, in an even worse darkness. Few street lamps lined the highway where we were, and Franklin was speeding. Could hear Caroline snoring softly in the backseat.

I looked for anything to tell me where I was. Only saw a few billboards advertising rest stops, gas stations, and restaurants. Another for a divorce lawyer. Nothing else.

"Put the blindfold on," Franklin said.

"No."

Without any hesitation, he reached over and dug his thumb into the sore spot between my shoulder and my chest. I screamed.

"Put it on."

I grabbed the edges of it. Slipped it over my head. Darkness returned.

Caroline still said nothing from the backseat.

I slept.

Came back into consciousness a few times. Only heard the sound of the car gliding down the highway.

The Sullivans remained silent.

———

I woke up to darkness again.

Reached up. Pulled off the blindfold.

There was only one car on the dark road ahead of us. No headlights. The land beyond the highway, illuminated by moonlight, was flat. Dry. It rose up in an incline on either side. Dotted with these scraggly, wispy trees I'd never seen before.

There were no pines or firs. Probably none of the siskin finches or foxes or mountain lions like there were in Reconciliation. Everything under the light of the moon and stars looked dead. Desolate.

Where were they taking me?

"Where are we?" I asked, turning to Franklin.

He actually jumped in his seat. "You startled me," he said. Then quickly glanced over. Glared at me. "Put the blindfold back on."

"No. Why do I have to wear it?"

He reached over to make a grab at it, but I snatched it out of the way.

"Put it on," he demanded. "Deacon required it."

"What's he gonna do? Kick me out a second time?"

Franklin sighed, then put his hand back on the steering wheel.

"So you're really just going to ignore me this whole drive?" I said.

"Stop talking. I need to concentrate."

"On *what*?" I gestured ahead of us with my bound hands. "There's nothing out here!"

"God is telling me where to take you," he said plainly.

I squeezed my eyes shut. Shook my head. When I opened them, Franklin was still focused on the road ahead.

"You're saying that God is speaking to you right now?"

He didn't answer.

"Is this the same God that told you to adopt me?"

"Please don't—"

"God actually wants you to drive out to the middle of nowhere and . . . what? What are you going to do to me?"

"Must you argue and question *everything*?" he snapped. "Why can't you just accept things?"

"Maybe I wouldn't have had so many questions if you and Caroline hadn't denied me so many answers!" I screamed back. "You *tricked* me into going to that place. You told me that I would be happy for the rest of my life if I went."

He slammed his hand against the steering wheel. "You were so annoying the day Caroline and I chose you," he continued. "Couldn't you see what we were doing for you? That we were saving you from that filthy place? From a terrible life? We took you there to help you escape from the world, and here you are, running right back into it."

I held my hands up. "Do you really think this is a voluntary choice?"

"Shut up," Caroline said from the backseat.

"*You* gave up this opportunity, Manny. We saved you, so it's only fair that we toss out the trash where it belongs."

We sit in silence again. Let it swallow us whole.

And then Carlos asks the question that's been on the tip of my tongue for the last few minutes.

"So . . . what now?"

I don't know.

I don't know anything at all.

No. That's not true.

I know that in some small way, I feel . . . better. Because now, these people know the truth. None of them seem to be questioning it. If they are, they're keeping it to themselves, even though I'm certain they all want to know more.

Want to know how it is possible that there was once two of me. Once.

No longer.

———

He's dead.

Carlos's question sits there, and then nervous laughter spreads around the room. The Samuels ask if we'd like to get dinner some-where, and then Ricardo immediately jumps into planning mode. He's good at that. Starts looking into restaurants nearby that could fit seven.

I can't think of that stuff right now.

All I'm thinking about is him.

What was he like? Did he act like me? Talk like me? Have the same dark humor as me? I was only in his presence for a few minutes.

(They chose him.)

But did they prefer him over me?

His dead body suggests ... maybe not. I mean ... someone there killed him.

I've been given an answer: The body is not Elena's.

But it has unlocked a thousand new questions.

What is happening in Reconciliation?

Where is Elena?

What next?

It has to be her.

"We have to go back for Elena," I say. "She is probably still alive. And maybe she has something to do with . . . him. Me. Whatever."

"She hasn't been in a broadcast for a while," Rakeem says. "But . . . what do you think happened?"

"I don't know," I say. "I have no idea, but I can't just sit here, knowing that she doesn't have *anyone* up there."

"Dude, she gave you up," says Rakeem. "Are you sure you want to do that?"

I frown and stand up. "She . . . it's not that simple."

"Sometimes, it is."

It's Carlos who delivers that one. I turn back to him, and he's shaking his head. "I know you want to believe that she regrets her decision, but . . . some people are too far gone."

"Carlos," Monica says gently, her eyes sad, pleading.

I don't get it at first.

Then:

"Your parents," I say.

He nods. "Just like Rakeem's, they want nothing to do with me. It's been years. They still think Lester is God's chosen one."

Rakeem grunts. "God has a lot of chosen ones."

Carlos nods. "And pointing that out does nothing for some people. I don't think there's any amount of logic or appeal to reason that could ever sway them. Some people are just . . . done with you."

He gives me a sad look. "All I'm saying is that . . . well, what if you got all the way up to Reconciliation, and she still doesn't want you?"

I hate that he's vocalized my fear.

"Well, what if this is a sign?" I say. "What if she somehow did this to send me a message? To tell me to come back to her?"

Ricardo is shaking his head. "Manny, I don't know," he says. "That's . . . complicated. Never mind that this whole situation is already complicated as hell. But it just doesn't make sense to me."

"So what am I supposed to do?" My voice jumps higher. "I came all this way, and now what?"

"We should tread carefully," says Ricardo. "There's so much we don't know here."

"Not only that," says Vera, twisting one of her locs in between her fingers. "But Manny, these people are *powerful*. Reconciliation has exploded in the past six months. Deacon has lawyers now. People watching out for his best interests."

"And there's that fence," says Rakeem, twisting his hands together. "So, like . . . you can't just waltz into Reconciliation if you want to."

"But isn't this what you guys *do*?" I say to the Varelas. "Travel the country, trying to find all the people your church hurt?"

"Yes," says Monica hesitantly. "But this situation . . . it's a little different."

"How?" I say, knowing the answer already: me. I'm the difference.

"This isn't our home turf," says Ricardo. "We weren't ever part of Reconciliation."

"We only have a vague idea of what they're capable of," continues Monica.

"We don't, though," says Ameena. "We have spent the last year trying to deal with them. To say they're a pain in the ass is an understatement. Deacon has amassed a ridiculous amount of power and influence with his little online empire."

All I can hear is:

No.
No no no no no.

Carlos grabs my hand. Pulls me back down onto the couch.

"I'll help," he says. "What do you need?"

My heart warms, but it doesn't last.

"Carlos, please," says Ricardo. "Let's take a moment to consider our options before we go promising something we can't provide."

"So now we *can't* help someone?" he says.

I can see the frustration building in the Varelas. Can see it in the way they silently communicate with one another.

They start arguing. Then the Samuels join in as well, and soon, all four of the adults are measuring the merits of legal action. Invoking the Public Social Services Department. Contacting law enforcement. Local news networks and journalists.

My head swims.

No no no no no.

Because I can see what's developing. What's growing before me.

It's happening again.

I am becoming a burden. Something to be discussed and debated. A thorn in their side.

I am a problem.

And when that happens . . .

I think it's time.

I stand up. Carlos tries to pull me down, but I yank my hand out of his.

"I'll figure it out," I say.

I swipe the van's key off a nearby dresser and dart out of the hotel room. Run down the hallway. I think someone's following me, but I can't stop for them. I can't stop for anyone.

I have to do this.

I run out of the lobby and head straight for the Varelas' van. My head is swirling with ideas. I could head back to the coroner's. Find out where the body was found. Get up to Idyllwild and ask around.

This isn't impossible. Hard, but not impossible, just like this last year.

At the van. I yank open the side door after unlocking it. Head for my duffel in the backseat, but realize it got moved to the rear. I rush to the back and pull open the double doors, and I see it, sitting right next to the red gasoline canister.

This is the right decision.

It *has* to be.

"Stop."

A breathless Carlos rushes up to the van.

"Please, don't go," he begs.

"I have to," I say, and I turn away from him. Grab the strap on my duffel and pull it toward me.

"No, you don't," he says. "I'll go with you. I don't care."

"Your parents will never let you."

I hoist the bag up on my shoulder.

"That doesn't matter."

"Yes, it does," I say. "You have parents who love and care for you.

They're not just going to let you leave. All I have left is Elena. I have to *try*."

"Then let me try with you!" he cries.

"Why?"

He rushes forward.

He kisses me.

It's sloppy. Uneven. He presses his lips against mine, and then I press them back. His arm loops around me.

Pulls away.

His eyes are red. Glassy.

"Because *I* don't want you to leave."

Fuck. It feels nice.

He holds me, and I can feel his stomach pressing against mine. He is . . . safe. That's what I'm feeling.

"Come back," he says. "Just give them a chance. I think they're still processing." He laughs. "And maybe freaking out a little."

"Why aren't you?" I say, leaning into his chest. "I am a freak, after all."

"Shut up," he says.

Then:

"There might have been two of you. But I like *you*."

I don't know what this is. Or why it's happening, especially amidst such an unending nightmare.

"You don't have to do this alone anymore," he tells me. "I know why you've done all this by yourself. But come back. Let us help you."

"I don't know," I say.

"Can we just *try*, at least?"

How do I get used to this? How do I accept people who want to do nice things for me?

I think I . . .

I think I need to believe in the possibility of a future.

"Okay," I say.

Carlos guides me back to the hotel room.

They all look at me when the door swings open.

And Rakeem holds up his phone.

"Glad you came back," he says. "Because Deacon finally posted a new video."

Rakeem hooks his phone up to the TV in the room. Broadcasts it for us.

The music swells.

The words appear.

CHRIST'S DOMINION

WITH DEACON THOMPSON

His face fills the screen.

It looks mostly the same. Piercing blue eyes. His facial hair is a bit longer. Bit more unkempt. He smiles. It is like ice in my veins.

The camera pulls out as he says, "Welcome, my family. It has been a long time."

He's in his chair on the small stage in the lodge. There are children on either side of him. All strangers, all smiling, all young and brown and Black and—

"Oh, Jesus," says Rakeem.

It's her.

She's . . . thinner. Visibly so. She stretches her face in a smile. Wide.

It has never looked so fake.

But it's her eyes that chill me.

They look dead.

"It's her," I mutter.

Deacon spreads his arms wide. "Our community continues to grow, my children, and today, I welcome a new member to our family."

A young girl steps forward. I don't think she's older than ten. Brown skin, long straight black hair.

"Welcome, Maddie," he says, and she giggles as she runs into his arms for a hug.

"That sound you hear is the sound of love," he says over her shoulder. "One of our families managed to adopt this little angel from China. Called by God to save her from such a godless, sinful place. And now . . . she is here."

Maddie turns around.

Smiles with perfect timing.

Runs off camera.

And I catch another glimpse of Elena. Smiling from ear to ear. Looking like it is taking every ounce of her energy to stay upright.

It cuts back to Deacon, seated in his chair upon that stage like it is a throne.

"We cannot do what God has destined us to do without your support. We know it is not possible for every God-loving member of our family to adopt, but our agents are standing by. With your support, we can better navigate the complex world of adoption. Every dollar you give us goes to them."

The camera zooms out wide again.

The six children—three on each side—stand there, smiling.

The image cuts away.

There are scenes from life in Reconciliation. Children frolicking and playing in the clearing in front of the lodge. Mrs. Thompson teaching one of her godawful lessons. Dinner around a campfire.

Shots of children in their families' homes.

It all looks so normal.

And then:

An image I've never seen before.

"Pause it," I say.

Rakeem does, and then he's approaching it, too.

It's from inside the lodge. A wide shot, clearly taken from the side. On the right: Deacon, on the stage with Elena, Simone, Henry, and Omar.

On the left:

Me.

Standing next to Rakeem.

We look like we're concentrating. Studying. Completely enraptured with what's unfolding. I know exactly what day that was. Didn't even know that Mrs. Thompson had filmed us.

And unless you were there, you'd never know. You'd never know what we were feeling.

Rakeem sniffles. Closes the video on his phone. Sits on the edge of the bed.

"We escaped," he says.

"What?"

"You know what makes it easier some days? To rethink it all. We *escaped*. We got out of that place."

"We did," I say.

"And maybe we should give Elena that option."

He stands.

Turns to his parents.

"We have to try," he says.

Then, to the Varelas:

"You saw her. Manny is right. We can't just sit here."

"She looked terrible," says Carlos. "She might die in Reconciliation."

She might die.

Pieces fall into place.

A wild idea possesses me.

I grip the edge of the dresser I'm next to.

"I know what to do," I say.

"What?" says Monica. "About what?"

"I know how to get to Elena," I say.

I smile.

Oh, it's so deliciously evil.

"How?" says Carlos.

"You have to kill me."

Mom's face hovers into my field of vision, and a burst of pain shoots through my chest.

"I'm sorry," I blurt out. "I'm sorry I didn't believe you."

She tells Elena to get a wet cloth and a bag of ice, then turns back to me. Runs her hands over my face. "It's okay, Manny," she says.

"Manny," I repeat.

She leans away. Takes the wet cloth from Elena, who crouches beside me.

"That's who you were," says Mom. She wipes away the sweat off my forehead, then places the cool cloth on it. "But you can be who you want now."

There is something within that's tugging me. Telling me to go back.

"I want to be a good son," I say. "A good brother."

"You are," says Elena, running her fingers through my hair. "You have been. You just needed . . . you just needed an extra push."

"A push that Reconciliation gave you," adds Caroline.

Mom. This is Mom.

Go back go back go back

"Will Franklin . . . will Dad love me, too?"

I cough as Mom kisses my cheek. "Of course, my son. Of course he will."

I hear a voice. It calls out. Caroline.

"I'll be right back," she says. "Your father and I have to go do something that's very important. I know you are probably confused, but will you be okay staying here with Elena?"

"Yes," I say. "As long as you're happy."

She looks upon me as if I am the greatest gift she's ever received.

"I love you, Manny," she says.

She stands and heads to the door. Elena scoots into the space she left, and I stare into my sister's eyes.

Go back go back go back.

"What about . . . him?" I ask. "Where is he?"

She studies my face. Runs her fingertips over my nose, my cheeks, my chin, then down my arm until our hands are linked together.

"You're him," she says. "You're my brother. That's the choice I made."

"But—"

"No," she says. "I prayed for this. I prayed for my brother to finally accept God, to accept this place, and then . . . you arrived. You are a miracle, Manny."

She squeezes my hand.

And I sit upright, so quickly I almost slam into Elena. My head spins. I feel it.

I feel him.

The door opens. Caroline is there. No. Mom. Mom is there, and she smiles as she walks into another part of the cabin.

They're beyond the door. I can only see their outlines. Dad.

Him.

Mom comes back and rushes outside. She stands in the way for a moment, then shifts to the right.

He's there. I know him.

It's me.

"No," he cries out. "Please, Elena!"

Dad pulls him away, and when he does, a part of me wants to leap up from the couch. Follow him. I shouldn't be here. This shouldn't be happening.

The sensation dissipates. I lean back into the couch.

It's gone.

"Everything is going to be okay," says Elena. "He's gone."

I squeeze my eyes shut. Open them. My head swims. I can see the out-line of his body in the shadows on the porch, but . . . his face. His face when he first saw me . . .

"Okay," I say, but I'm grasping. Grasping on to images that seem to be running away from me. People and names and places. Where were Elena and I before this? The house. Hemet. Silvia. I remember a woman named Gertrude and then I don't.

I put my free hand on my head. Wince. "I want to remember," I say.

"Remember what?" she says.

I shake my head. I'm unsure. It all feels like a jumble. Every house, every guardian, every meeting with . . . whatever her name is.

"What do you remember, Manny?"

My heart is in my throat. "Bits and pieces. Reconciliation. This place and . . ."

My eyes go wide. "Where is Rakeem?"

"Shhhh," she says, and she puts a finger to my lips. "No, you don't have to do that. You don't have to remember any of it."

"Why not?" I ask. "Isn't that who I am?"

Tears spill out of her eyes. "That's the beauty of the miracle, isn't it?" she says. "You don't have to remember any of it. You get to start over. Let them go, Manny. Let them all go."

She gently pushes me back until I'm lying on my back on the couch.

"You don't need any of it."

The darkness is there. I don't know how, but every moment that passes is another moment that my memories fade away.

It's comforting.

It's bliss.

"This will be better for you. Accept the miracle, Manny. It's what God wants."

She's happy. I can see it all over her face.

This is what she wants.

And I suppose . . . I think it's what I want, too.

I want her to be happy.

I want her to love me.

An image appears in my mind. Elena. Her head resting on my shoulder. We're in the back of a car. She's holding my hand. It feels safe. A reminder that we're always in this together.

And then:

It evaporates, too.

"There's a story in the Bible," says Elena softly. "About a father. Someone who has two evil sons, who couldn't choose between himself, his love, and the love of God. He reminds me of you."

"But I chose," I say. "I chose you. Mom and Dad. Deacon."

"Yes," she says, smiling wide. "And I want you to remember that forever. Not that other person. Not the one who was disobedient and argumentative, who rejected God."

"What was his name?" I say.

It seems so obvious what I should say next, so I do. Because I want to do what she wants.

"What is my name?"

Elena squeezes onto the couch with me. Rests her head on my chest.

"Eli," she says.

She speaks it into my heart.

Eli.

I'm God's miracle.

Franklin drove.

And I sank further and further into despair.

I dozed off. Too tired to try to stay awake and figure out where we were going. Why even bother?

I was woken up by heat. It was warmer inside the car. Could feel the sunlight on my bare arm. Sweat dripped down my nose. Down my back. I squirmed.

Fell back asleep.

Then the car stopped.

The driver-side door opened. Shut. Then, moments later, my door was yanked open. I opened my eyes, then shut them frantically when bright light poured in.

"Out," Franklin said.

I shielded my eyes. Stared out the windshield.

There was a row of electrical wires on tall wooden poles over us. I stepped out, and a flat dirt road stretched from right in a straight line out to a mountain range in the distance. The sun was rising above the peak, so . . . east. That was east.

Another step away from the car. On either side of the road was dead grass. Bushes without foliage. No greenery; everything was yellowed and brown and gray.

Franklin grabbed my arm, and I flinched. He held my wrists up. Used a pocket knife to cut me loose.

I was flushed with relief as I walked to the trunk of the car and saw a larger paved road running perpendicular to the dirt one we were on. Saw squat houses, all shaped like rectangles, set upon cinder blocks or stacks of wood. Most were white. Some painted in soft, pastel colors.

And in either direction off the main road, the horizon stretched as far as I could see.

"What is this?" I asked. Rubbed at my sore, bloody wrists. "Where are we?"

"This is where it ends," said Franklin.

He wasn't looking at me.

Caroline wrenched open her door. Stood next to her husband.

"Well . . . *go*," she said.

And she shooed me.

Like I was a stray dog.

"Here?" I shook my head. "You're just leaving me on the side of a random road?"

"It's not random," Caroline said. "God directed us here. This is where He wants you."

"You can't possibly believe that," I said. Stepped toward them.

They both took a step away from me.

"You really don't get it, do you?" said Franklin. "This isn't a trick. Or a lesson. We are not going to put you back in this car and drive you back. This is it for you, Manny. You lost it all."

"You have no idea how selfish you've been," added Caroline, and her face twisted with disgust. "After what you just saw? After the miracle that God gave us? You *still* think we'd want you?"

The miracle.

What was the miracle?

I spun around. Saw no other cars. No other people.

"But where am I?" I cried. "What am I supposed to do?"

"Why would we care about that?" said Franklin. "You're a spare. You're the unnecessary refuse left behind after God created something beautiful. You're of *this* world."

"You're not special anymore, Manny," said Caroline. "You never will be. You have no soul. That other version of you . . . *that* is the one God intends to be loved. Why else would He have blessed the act of reconciliation like that when He has never done so before?"

I knew what they meant. Deep down. There was something there. But it evaded me as I tried to pin it down.

My head spun.

I was truly alone.

Caroline grunted. Smiled bitterly. "You know, he warned us about you," she said. "Before he left. Made a big scene in Deacon's house. Said you were probably the next one to refuse the gift of reconciliation. Said that if we knew what was good for us, we'd get rid of you, too."

Tears sprung to my eyes. "Shut up. Don't say that."

She moved quickly, closing the distance between us in a few long steps. "And he wasn't wrong. You betrayed our love and our family, and you will *never* be forgiven for it."

Then she turned. Spat on the ground. Got back in the car.

"You can't leave me here," I pleaded weakly. "Franklin, *please*."

I reached for him.

He yanked his arm away, like I could have infected him with my touch.

"This is it," he said. Gestured to the dirt road beside us. "I have no interest in explaining this again. This is your new life."

He turned.

Walked to the other side of the car.

Then he turned back.

"If you somehow—God willing—find your way back . . . don't. Don't even bother. Because from this moment on, you're a stranger. Dead to us and everyone who knew you. Act like it."

"But what am I supposed to do? Where do I go? How do I eat? I don't even have anything!"

He froze then. Shut his eyes, then lifted his head a bit. He was muttering a prayer. Then he reached back, pulled out his wallet.

He held it out.

A single twenty-dollar bill.

"A parting gift," he said. "It is an act of charity. God tells us to love orphans and widows."

I approached. Gingerly took the money.

The door slammed as I stood there, shocked. Numb. Unable to move. The engine started. He nearly ran me over as he backed up, and I stumbled. Fell to the dirt.

The wheels kicked up dust into the air. The blue sedan turned left on the main road, and I watched it get smaller and smaller and smaller until I couldn't see it anymore.

I stood there.

Thought it might come back.

I remained in that spot until the sun burned the back of my neck, until I couldn't tell if they were tears or sweat on my face.

They're gone.

They left me here.

I finally stopped crying. It was as if a switch turned it off in my mind.

I didn't cry. Didn't scream or shout. Didn't beg God to help me.

They're gone.

They left me here.

———

She chose him.

A part of me wanted her there with me. I had done everything in my life with her. Relied on her. Looked to her for guidance.

She was gone, too.

So I turned that off in my brain, too.

It all extinguished. All of it. I should have been panicking. I should have been terrified.

It was all gone.

I stuffed the twenty-dollar bill—now slightly soggy from my sweat—into my pocket. My stomach grumbled in response.

Food. Hadn't had food or water since . . .

Couldn't remember.

I stood. Wobbled. Head still throbbed, but after a few deep breaths, I stabilized.

Then I started walking.

Up to the main road first. There was a street sign at the intersection. Duncan Highway and Fletcher Road.

I had three choices.

East on Fletcher, into the sun and distant mountains.

Right on Duncan Highway, toward some homes and nothing else.

Left on Duncan Highway, into what looked like a neighborhood and some small businesses.

My skin prickled. I didn't know where I was. Didn't know where I was going. There could be nothing in all three directions.

But I had three choices.

Three choices that were mine and mine alone to make.

A silver lining.

No one could choose for me.

I went left.

More and more homes. Cars parked off the road. A sign for a motel.

Throat parched. Stomach rumbled.

Had to focus. Couldn't think about the before. Just the after.

Passed an RV park. Some abandoned buildings. Wondered if I had made a bad decision.

But then the houses got bigger. And then I saw someone across the street. A woman. Dark hair, brown skin like mine. Small bag on her back. I didn't know where she was walking to, but . . . it was a person.

I wasn't alone anymore.

The road sloped down. Passed under two bridges. One was clearly a highway, and more cars meant a better chance of finding something.

The road looped around. No real safe place to walk, but I kept my head down. Stuck to the edge. Cars zipped by. One honked at me.

Kept moving.

Once the road straightened out, I saw it on the left.

A gas station.

If I hadn't been so exhausted, if my shoulder hadn't ached, I would have run to it.

I kept moving.

I kept living.

I was blasted with cold air when I pulled open the glass door. There was a middle-aged woman behind the counter scrolling through her phone. She glanced at me. Tanned. Thought she might be white, but her skin tone was close to mine.

I walked into the first aisle to my left. Faced with so many choices. So many snacks and treats I hadn't had in days because—

No.

There was a dark hole there. A fresh wound still bleeding.

No.

I touched a bag of chips. Then some brownies. Then thought maybe I should get water. Or something to wash with. Where would I even do that?

"What ya lookin' for, honey?"

The woman from behind the counter stood off to my right. She smiled, and one of her teeth was capped with silver.

"Just . . . hungry," I said. "Thirsty."

She looked down. I did, too, and saw the dirt and filth on my clothing. The dried blood around my wrists.

She didn't say anything about it, though. Just:

"When was the last time you ate?"

I shook my head. "Don't really remember."

She walked past me to the refrigerated section. Opened a door, grabbed two water bottles, then handed them to me on her way back. "Hold these."

She then disappeared down another aisle.

Doubled back.

"Don't just stand there," she said. "Follow me."

I did as she asked. She grabbed other things. Granola bars. A bag of tortilla chips. Donuts. Piled them up on the counter, then started bagging them up.

"You like hot dogs?"

She pointed at the glass case where they rotated on a metal tray.

"Sure."

"Go get a couple."

"But . . . I only have like twenty dollars," I said. "This is too much."

She popped some gum in her mouth. "I know." Then she waved me toward the hot dogs.

I got a couple. Put them in buns, poured some ketchup, mustard, and relish on them, mostly because I was hungry and I needed every calorie.

Because I realized then I didn't know when I would get any more.

I returned to the woman, and she smiled at me. "On the house," she said.

I shook my head. "No, that's . . ."

"It's already done. So take it and enjoy."

Then she picked up her phone. Started scrolling again.

I could feel the wound.

Could feel myself gnawing at it.

My eyes blurred. I grabbed the overflowing plastic bag and stuck my arm through the loops. Held a hot dog in each hand. Went for the door. I didn't look at her because I knew it would just make it worse. I shoved the doors open with my uninjured shoulder, then made a beeline to the left. Headed around the building. Slumped there in the shade.

I cried.

Because the darkness felt so impossible to push away.

Because it was growing.

Because it was going to suffocate me.

I was in the middle of nowhere. Didn't even know if I was still in California. No one knew who I was. What I'd been through. I'm nothing. No one. Completely invisible.

I downed a bottle of water then. Nearly threw up because it was too much, too fast. Head still ached. Couldn't lift my other arm too high.

I ate a hot dog. My stomach roiled, but it was food.

Ate the other.

Then she was there, right at the edge of the building, staring at me. Smacked her gum.

"You okay, kid?"

"Fine," I said.

"You don't look fine," she said, then walked over to me.

I glanced up at her. Saw she had a name tag on.

Em.

"I'll be okay," I said, looking away.

"You look like you rolled around in the mud."

"You're really observant."

"That's what my wife says, but I think it's a good thing. She thinks it's kinda annoying."

I didn't respond.

"Do you need help?"

"No. I'll figure things out."

"What things do you need to figure out?"

"You're very persistent," I said.

"Wife says that, too."

"Fine," I said, and I turned my head up to her. "Can you tell me where we are?"

"We?" She grunted. "Well, we're outside my store."

I narrowed my eyes at her. "Are you always like this?"

She flashed her silver-capped tooth in a smile. "Lordsburg."

"And where is that?"

"'Bout an hour west of Deming. Maybe two from Las Cruces."

"Which is . . . where?"

It was her turn to fix me with a suspicious look.

"New Mexico?"

I nodded.

Turned back to the bag of food and water and pretended to search through it so that she couldn't see the tears in my eyes.

New Mexico.

The stone in my throat grew.

"What's your name?" Em asked me.

I gazed off at the horizon. "Manny," I said.

"Well, Manny," she said, turning away from me. "If you're around later, I can see about helping you figure out some of those things."

"Thanks," I said.

She rounded the corner.

I gathered up that plastic bag.

I started walking.

Past the gas station, back the way I came. She had mentioned that there were towns that way. Maybe even a city.

I walked because I didn't want her help.

I didn't want her to know anything about me.

Monica follows the directions that Ameena gave us. It's late in the afternoon before we begin the trek to Reconciliation; the Samuels needed time to do their part.

And once it had been completed, we set out to finish it.

It isn't until we hit the incline at the base of the mountain that I realize I've never seen this. Both times I traversed this road, I had a blindfold over my eyes.

It really does seem so absurd now. So much of it does. I tolerated things no person should. And for what? What did it all amount to?

The drive is steep. Twisting. The highway snakes through canyons, traces the edge of sheer cliffs. The farther up the mountain we go, the more trees.

I ask Ricardo if the windows can be rolled down. He doesn't ask why. Soon, the earthy pine scent hits me. Memories flood back. Most aren't pretty; they're sharp, piercing. But I recall the first moment I stepped out of the Sullivans' car over a year ago. It was a moment where I chose to believe in possibility.

I'm doing that again.

Except this time . . .

This is better. This is real.

This isn't going to shatter me into pieces.

I inhale the scent.

Carlos holds my hand.

We drive.

Closer.

Closer.

I wonder what I'll feel when I see the trees. The cabins. The lodge. Terror? Revulsion? Something more complicated? Am I now too far gone to ever appreciate it? Probably.

No. Definitely.

The nature around Reconciliation is beautiful. But that place is a cancer.

A cancer that must be excised.

That must be brought into the light.

We drive through Idyllwild. The town is tucked delicately among the trees and hills. It's still hot up here, but the shade helps. We pass motels. Convenience stores. Small strip malls. A diner with flashing neon lights in the large windows.

This is all a first, too. Idyllwild seems quiet. Calm. It's certainly beautiful.

Too bad I'll never associate it with anything else.

When we are before the gate, I wonder if this is all going to fall apart.

There are too many pieces. Too many variables. Too many things that can go wrong. It is natural for me to consider them all. It's how I've survived.

What if Deacon never lets us past the gate?

What if he doesn't believe me?

What if the Samuels' contribution backfires?

What if she doesn't want to leave?

I have a back-up plan. A way to ensure that I get what I want. But I worry about the others and what it might do to them. But the Varela family . . . I believe they'll take care of it for me.

I hope.

It's so hard to hope. It is not an instinct natural to me anymore. Maybe that other version of Manny took the rest of it away from me. I don't know.

Still. Can't stop thinking of some of the things that Elena said to me before she chose. About how I can't seem to choose anything but misery and negativity.

She can be right about that and still wrong about everything else.

I have to know.

The gate is right where Ameena told us it would be.

At the end of a long, uneven dirt road, it blocks our way. It's higher than I expected—about ten feet or so—with a dense, complicated metal mesh design. The fencing then stretches out in either direction for as far as we can see.

"Yeah, we're not getting through that," says Ricardo.

I scoot across the seat. Pull on the handle and open the side door. Leap out of the van.

"Manny," says Monica. "What are you doing?"

There has to be something here. Something I can do or use to get their attention.

I grab a branch on the ground near the dirt road. Without a second thought, I toss it against the fence.

There's a light beeping sound. Then a spark. Then the branch falls to the ground, smoking.

And then:

Nothing.

Ricardo gets out of the van. "This was a possibility," he says. "It doesn't mean there's nothing you can do, but we might have to regroup. See what else we can do."

"Just wait," I say.

Aside from the occasional breeze through the trees, the forest is silent.

I pick up another branch. Toss it against the fence. Same beep, same tiny spark.

Same nothingness.

Carlos steps out of the van, too. "Do you think that'll work?"

I don't give him a response because the answer is: It *has* to.

I pick up another. Toss it against the fence. Then another. I do this over and over again.

Until.

Ricardo hears it first. Shushes us. I freeze in place and—

Yes.

Tires on dirt.

I watch the road ahead of us. At the top of the incline, a red truck appears. Comes slowly down the hill. Stops about twenty feet from the gate.

I hear Ricardo breathe deeply. "Here goes nothing," he says.

I recognize her first. The driver.

Mrs. Thompson. She steps out of the truck, a hand to her mouth. I think her hair is dyed. Looks fake.

Doesn't matter. She's not who I'm here to see.

Deacon Thompson steps out the other side.

I am struck by how much older he looks compared to his videos and broadcasts. As he approaches, I see bags under his eyes. Wrinkles at the corners. His facial hair is still evenly cut, but there are whites and grays in it. His blond hair is also fading away.

He walks with a limp.

Stares at me with disbelief.

He stops, just a few feet from the gate.

"Manny," he says. My name is breathy in his mouth, just as unsure as he is.

I move in front of the Varelas' van. Get about a foot away from the fence.

He's shaking his head, his mouth has dropped open a little, and those ferocious blue eyes are locked on me.

"Manny," he repeats again.

"Hello, Deacon," I say.

"You're here."

I nod.

"How did you—"

I decide not to let him control this. It's the only way this is going to work.

"I know, Deacon," I say. "About my . . . other half."

His lips twitch. He blinks, repeatedly, then casts a glance at his wife, then turns back.

"How?" he says.

"It's not important. I—I came back."

"I can see that."

"I think I was sent here."

He processes that. "Sent," he repeats.

"I know it must be hard to believe me," I say. "Especially after what happened. But the series of events that brought me here— right back to Reconciliation—I can't ignore them. I think I was *meant* to come back."

"Meant by whom?" he asks, raising an eyebrow.

"You know."

"I need to hear you say it."

"God," I say, without hesitation. "I think His will brought me right here."

He looks over my shoulder. "And who are they?"

"A family I've been traveling with for a while," I say.

I turn back. Look at each of them.

"I think God sent them to me, too. So that I'd find my way here."

Monica is at the side of the van now. "We've seen your videos," she says. "Have watched a lot of them together. And . . ."

She hesitates.

Looks away, then back.

Sells the lie even better than I could have expected.

"He told us what happened to him. What *God* did to him."

"Is it true?" says Ricardo, his voice both frightened and hopeful. "Did God give you a miracle?"

Deacon's face is like stone as he considers what they've said. My heart leaps. What if he doesn't believe us? What if he turns us away?

What if this is all for nothing?

He finally looks to me. "Tell me, then," he says. "Why are you here?"

I gulp down the terror.

Lie lie lie lie lie

"It's obvious I was wrong," I say.

Lie lie lie lie lie

"About before. About what you're doing here."

Lie lie lie lie lie

"I can't explain what's happened, and I don't know why he isn't . . . why he's not here anymore."

Say it, I tell myself.

"Why he's dead."

Deacon narrows his eyes.

"But I think that's the biggest sign of all," I say. "I think God got rid of him because I'm supposed to be here. He wanted to win *me* over, not that other one. And that's the whole point of this. I am the soul He actually wants."

He turns around. I think he's about to leave when he waves at his wife.

"Harriett," he calls out. "Open it up."

Holy shit.

It worked.

And then:

"But they stay behind," he says, gesturing to the Varelas.

I knew this was a possibility, though.

"No," I say.

He glares at me. "Manny, how can you say that you were wrong about before, and yet you openly defy me like you used to do?"

"I'm not defying you," I say. "I want to *ask* you. Take them in. Show them the truth. Maybe they aren't ready for reconciliation, but they're certainly ready to learn. I accept that the Sullivans . . . they did what they had to. I am not asking them to forgive me. I'm moving on."

I wait for the reaction. But Deacon merely stares at me suspiciously.

I hope I've read this correctly. I hope it means Franklin said nothing about our run-in.

I put a hand on my chest. "This is me moving on and accepting that I lost the right to my parents. These are . . . I don't know. My new ones. And I'm bringing them here to *you* as an offering. To show you I'm not messing around. That I'm serious."

"An offering," he says.

"If you are going to change the world, you have to invite others," I say. "There are so many more you could reach, but you're not getting to them."

"We used to be pastors," says Ricardo. "This isn't new to us. We think we can give Christ's Dominion some new blood."

He stares. Blinks. Keeps his face still and impassive.

"Open it, Harriett."

The wound tears open again once I'm in the clearing.

We're on the far side of it, near the cabin where I once lived. The Varelas are walking behind me and Deacon. I have my duffel slung over my shoulder.

My back-up plan is inside it.

I let him lead. I let him think that he is in control. I let him tell the story.

And I can tell the story is already being spun.

There was Deacon, at the front of a procession. Behind him was a ghost.

There are more cabins now. Lots more. Some are occupied, and then one of the adults approaches me. Takes me a moment to place her.

It's Erin Bradford.

"How?" she whispers. "How could you let him come back?"

She must know something, but Deacon shoos her away. "Not now," he says. "Soon."

He leads me forward.

Beyond the doors of the lodge.

There's a woman folding up chairs, leaning them against the far wall. She turns.

Shit.

Wasn't anything that could have prepared me for this.

————

Caroline drops a chair. It clatters against the wooden boards, echoes in the lodge. She wobbles and sways.

The duffel bag falls off my shoulder.

Shit.

"Caroline," Deacon says softly. "Focus on my voice."

"No," she says, eyes wide, all color draining from her face. "This isn't happening."

"My voice, Caroline. Focus on it."

"Deacon . . ." She clutches a hand to her mouth. Stops a sob from escaping.

"Look at me," he commands, his words sharp.

She does. Even from here, I can see the tears spilling down her cheeks.

"I saw his body," she says. "We *all* did."

"Caroline."

He reaches back for me.

I extend a hand. He takes it. It's wet. Clammy.

"Caroline, it's not him," he says.

It takes a moment for this to register in both of us.

She realizes who I am.

And I realize that Franklin did not tell her about seeing me yesterday.

She presses her lips together. Wipes away the tears.

"No," she says. "Absolutely not."

The rejection stings, if only for a moment. Because then I hear someone gasp behind me.

Monica.

Who would never do anything like what Caroline had done to me.

I turn and look for the Varelas, and the three of them are standing silently just past the door.

Watching this unfold.

"I need you to listen to me," Deacon says, and he begins to approach Caroline, his hand still out.

Like she's a wild, skittish animal.

"Your prodigal son . . . he has returned."

"Returned?"

"Yes, Caroline." He gazes back at me. "And I believe that God sent him to us and has given us an opportunity for a second miracle. The one we were denied."

I see it then, so plain and pure that I don't know how I didn't see it before:

The utter devotion on Caroline's face.

It's that smile. The way her eyes light up when she looks at him. Before, I thought that was hunger, but it's more than that.

She doesn't doubt at all.

I am thrilled, if only for a second, that the lie I have told has worked on these two, but the moment does not last. I don't have time to react to how quickly she crosses that space, throws her arms around me, and squeezes.

"It's so good to have you back," she sobs, pressing her face into my shoulder. The same shoulder that was once injured. "I missed you. *I missed you.*"

I have to sell the lie.

So I embrace her back and whisper, "I missed you, too."

She holds me.

And holds me.

And holds me.

He gathers the others.

The Varelas help Caroline set up the lodge. Monica and Ricardo talk to her so easily. It's not that I couldn't see them as pastors prior to this, but watching them smoothly go back and forth with her? It is practically magical.

And every moment sells the lie more and more.

A single chair is placed in the center of the room. Across from it, there's a small wooden table. The laptop. The digital camera. The microphone. Wires and cables string between them all, and an extension cord snakes off toward a nearby wall.

I set my duffel bag on the floor. Still heavy. Still ready. I tap my front pocket, too, and feel the small box.

Just in case.

Caroline excuses herself. "I have to go get your father," she says to me, and her eyes water again. "I have to tell him."

She brushes the side of my face with her palm. "You're here."

"I am," I say, nodding.

"It almost seems too good to be true," she says.

And then she walks off.

Carlos comes up to me. "I gotta say, this is one of the weirdest days of my life."

"And mine," says Monica.

"Mine, too," says Ricardo.

Carlos nudges my shoulder with his. "I can't imagine what this is like for you."

A fucking nightmare.

"Just keep it up," I say. "Keep them going a little longer."

As if on cue, they begin to pour in.

First: Mrs. Thompson. She has a hard time looking at me. Only gives me furtive glances. She walks over to the table. Fiddles with the laptop and the camera.

Others follow. All of them are strangers: parents of children who are currently attending Reconciliation. I keep a mental count. Including the Bradfords, I get to ten. Ten is a good number. Means there are maybe five kids somewhere on the grounds. At most, maybe six or seven.

The Varelas can deal with that.

I, however, need to deal with the rest.

Like seeing the Bradfords again. This must be why they finally gave up Rakeem.

They have a new child.

I sit in the chair. Stuff my duffel underneath it.

Franklin arrives next, his wife just behind him. He looks around the lodge until he spots me.

His reaction is not as dramatic as Caroline's. He scowls. Shakes his head. Moves closer to me, then stops, about ten feet away.

Then he just stares.

For a long while. I watch him process. Observe. Accept.

I wonder then:
Did he do it?

God. They're all capable of it, aren't they?

"Manny," he says, very similar to how Deacon vocalized my name when he saw me standing outside the gate. "You're alive."

Still don't know what to say to that a second time. I fidget. Look beyond him because there's still someone else I need to see.

She arrives.

Tears prick my eyes.

It's her.

It all swirls inside me: I miss her. I hate her. I want her back. I wish she'd never brought us here.

One emotion overpowers them all: horror.

Because Elena looks *terrible*.

It's like she hasn't eaten in days. Weeks. Her long hair is matted on one side, as if she just got out of bed. I can see her cheekbones from across the room.

She seems to be near death.

Yet in that moment, I imagine: the shock on her face. The emotional outburst. The way she crosses the room to embrace me, to say that she missed me, too, and then she cries on my shoulder, welcomes me back, begs me to take her away from this place. It's what I want, isn't it? The perfect reunion. The confirmation of my desires.

The fantasy fizzles. Extinguishes. She walks toward me as if I am a random stranger. Says nothing. Keeps her face emotionless.

Perhaps the sight of me is too much; I have to remember that she's now lost me *twice*.

She chose him.

Deacon is last. He closes the doors to the lodge, then strides straight up to me.

He's changed.

Combed his hair back. Switched into a crisp shirt over dark jeans. He almost looks like how he did before. Confident. Self-assured. Powerful.

The room falls silent, the gathered crowd's eyes locked on him.

Which is why none of them notice the Varelas sneaking out the lodge doors.

"The prodigal son returns," he says, repeating the phrase he used with Caroline earlier. "Welcome back, Manny Sullivan."

I nod at him. Then point to his wife.

"Are you streaming this?" I ask.

He pauses. Glances over at Mrs. Thompson and the camera equipment.

"No," he says, looking back to me.

"Why not?"

"You have fooled me and this community before. Do you think I've forgotten that? This is being recorded as *evidence*. I won't be betrayed again."

These people know nothing of betrayal. They know nothing of the suffering I've been through.

I hit my heel against the duffel bag.

"Sorry," I say. "That wasn't what I meant. I was just . . . nervous."

"I'm sure you can appreciate our precarious position," he says. "It is why the children remain in their homes. I cannot trust you yet, Manny. I don't want you corrupting them."

Deacon nods at his wife.

The camera flicks on.

Mrs. Thompson raises her hand as Deacon takes his place behind my chair. Counts down from five. Then points to Deacon.

I think my heart is going to burst out of my chest.

"My family," Deacon says. "Today is a momentous occasion. I know many of you are confused and shocked. As am I. But before we continue with this, I must ask a few questions from our visitor."

Visitor. The word is a weapon in his mouth.

"Manny," he says, and then he puts his hands on my shoulders. Grips them.

Hard.

"Why are you here?"

I can't hesitate.

I can't show him that I'm terrified.

"Because God sent me here," I say. "He guided me back."

Deacon doesn't hesitate.

"No, He didn't."

I twist around. "Yes, he did."

"Do you think God would use you as a means of validating this place *without* me? Who exactly do you think you are?"

I look to Caroline and Franklin, who now watch me with concern.

"I'm Manny Jimenez," I say.

And then I swing wide and hard.

"I'm not the prodigal son," I say. "I'm the resurrection."

"That's why I wanted this broadcast," I say. "I believe God sent me here to create another miracle."

He hesitates. Comes around the chair to look at me.

"The resurrection," he says.

"I'm dead, aren't I?" I say.

"Dead?" says Erin. "What does he mean?"

I don't smile, even though I want to. *She doesn't know*, I think. Deacon has kept Eli a secret.

It's all the confirmation I need that he was the one who killed me.

But then:

"He shouldn't be here," says Elena. Her voice sounds dry. It comes out more like a croak than anything else. "He's dead. We all know it."

There is a moment there when panic crosses Deacon's face. He knows the truth. He knows what happened to me.

I glance at the gathered parents. They seem confused. Seth whispers something to his wife.

"We should listen to him," says Caroline. "Deacon, he came *back*. Isn't that a miracle enough?"

"No," he says.

Then: "Manny, why are you here?"

"Because of God," I say.

"Bullshit."

Some of the adults in the room gasp.

"I need your trust, my family," he says, spreading his arms and turning about. "We cannot accept just any old charlatan who waltzes in here and says they've been ordained by God."

"Why don't you believe me?"

"I wanted to," he says, spinning back to me. "When I saw you at the gate, I couldn't believe my eyes. But something happened. God protected me and us. He protected this place."

Deacon pulls out his phone. Unlocks it. Holds it up to my face.

It takes a second for my eyes to adjust.

Fuck.

It's an article from *The Press Enterprise*. Breaking news.

I see my face.

I see the headline.

It identifies the body found outside the Christ's Dominion property as seventeen-year-old Manny Sullivan.

They killed me, just as I asked them to.

Deacon is inches from my face.

"What the fuck have you done, Manny?"

———

I smile. I knew that this could have happened, that the news would beat me here. But that's not why I smile.

I smile because I did not anticipate this:

Feeling utterly pleased to see Deacon so *angry*.

"I'm bringing you into the light," I say.

I know it's time. I can't wait anymore.

I stand up, and Deacon jerks back. Caroline is asking what he meant, and Franklin frantically searches on his phone.

Elena is . . .

Cracking.

Her lower lip trembles. She looks to the Sullivans, then to Deacon, whose eyes haven't left my face. She's looking for guidance. Understanding. She doesn't know what's happening.

None of them do.

"What have you done?" Deacon repeats.

"Shut up," I say.

I reach down. Grab the duffel bag that's under the chair. Tear it open.

Inside is a red plastic canister.

Deacon recognizes it instantly.

"Manny . . ." he utters.

I ignore him. Hoist it out of the bag.

"I don't know if God sent me here," I say. "I don't even know if God is real. I chose to come back here, Deacon, so that I could finally speak the truth to you."

I unscrew the cap. The vapor of gasoline hits me. Intoxicates me.

I stare at the Sullivans first.

"You abandoned me," I say, and I step toward them quickly. Caroline actually yelps. Clings to Franklin. Elena ducks behind both of them.

I don't care.

"You two drove me to the middle of nowhere and abandoned me. With nothing. No extra clothing. No way to prove who I was. Nothing but twenty dollars. It was fucking *evil*."

"No," says Franklin, and I see that he's trembling. He sniffs the air. "No, it wasn't like that. You—you weren't him and—"

"It doesn't matter!" I scream. I make eye contact with the nameless strangers in the room. "That's what Deacon told them to do to their child because I didn't do what I was told."

I slosh the gasoline in the direction of the Sullivans, and a tiny bit spills out.

"He told us to do it," Franklin says softly, echoing my words.

A new rage boils in me. "But you still could have said no," I snap at him. "Do you realize how monstrous it is to abandon your child?"

"Please," says Deacon. "Be reasonable, Manny."

There is no reason in this place.

———

I roar at Deacon.

Others scream. Franklin reaches for me, and I run for the door, knowing that they'll try to escape, and I can't have that. I make it there before anyone else. Spin around. Hold out the canister.

And I pull out the book of matches with my other hand.

"Tell me the truth," I say, and I place the canister of gasoline at my feet. "Tell me who killed me."

Deacon has a fit of coughing, then glares at me. "What?"

"Tell me who killed me," I repeat. "Give me that, and then give me Elena. Let us go, and you'll never hear from me again."

The Sullivans are at Deacon's side in the center of the room. My empty duffel is at their feet.

"Manny, stop it," Franklin orders. "This is absurd. You can't do this!"

I watch him. Can see him grasping for straws in his mind.

"What about your future?" he says.

I bark out a laugh. "I'm dead now, Franklin! Completely dead. In the eyes of the state of California, I don't exist anymore. I don't have a future! At least not as Manny Sullivan anymore. So I'm going to take my sister, and we will never come back to this place."

"Give me the matches," says Deacon, slowly stepping toward me. "End this ludicrous charade. Then leave. No one wants you anyway."

"Elena does," I say. "Don't you?"

I finally stare into her wide eyes.

"No," she says quietly.

"You can leave now, Elena," I say. "You don't have to be here anymore."

She shakes her head.

"No, that's not it," she says. "You have it all wrong."

"No, I don't," I say. "This isn't your family. I am. And I came all this way to say I am willing to forgive you for bringing me here in the first place, but you *have* to leave with me."

She hesitates.

And then the door slowly swings open behind me.

Carlos pokes his head in, sees me immediately.

"You good, dude?" he says.

Sniffs.

Looks around.

"Is it done?" I ask.

He nods, his eyes wide. "Three," he says. "And all of them were more than eager to leave with us."

"Three?" says Deacon.

And then he gets it.

"Manny, I swear to God above—"

He takes a few furious steps toward me.

I light the first match.

I can hear their breathing stop. Can sense the silence filling that space.

"You heard that?" I say to them all. "Your children want to leave. They don't want to be here anymore."

Some of the parents start crying.

And I don't care anymore. I just need one more thing.

"Elena," I say, holding out my free hand. "Come with me."

"You have this all wrong," she says, and her eyes fill with tears. "This is my family."

"No, they're not," I say. "You know what they did to me. What they convinced you to do."

"They love me," she says.

"I love you, too," I choke out. "Even after everything you did. *Please*, come with me."

"You didn't love me," she sobs.

"Yes, I did!" I scream.

The match goes out.

I toss it behind me.

Light another one.

"No, you didn't," she says.

"How can you say that? I trusted you. I came to Reconciliation *because* I loved you so much that I believed what you said."

She's still shaking her head. "I wasn't talking about *you*."

Wait.

No.

"He stopped loving me," she says. "Stopped loving our family. Stopped loving this community."

She sighs.

"So we all killed him."

Carlos grabs my arm. Steadies himself.

"Quiet, Elena," warns Deacon. "Just let him leave."

She turns her head slowly toward him. Shakes it.

"But you told me to do it," she says.

The match goes out.

I don't move.

I don't understand.

This isn't happening.

"Stop talking, Elena," says Deacon.

"Shut up," Caroline says, and she twists up her face.

The color drains from Franklin's face. Looks like he's going to pass out.

"He started turning into *you*." She says this so plainly. As if it isn't the most absurd thing I've ever heard.

"I don't get it, Elena," I say.

"He started questioning," she says. "Me. Deacon. This place. He was so devoted at first to every part of it. He was . . . everything. Everything we wanted."

Elena approaches slowly. "But he doubted. Just like you. And he messed it all up."

She sobs.

"Just like you."

Hot tears spill down my cheeks. "Elena," I say. "Please tell me this isn't true."

"We all killed him," she says. "Me and Mom and Dad and—"

She points back at Deacon.

"And *him*."

I've been here before.

No.

I've been him before.
  Before.
  Before.
  Before.

"Manny," I say, his name a prayer.

"I should have realized my true miracle was here all along," says Deacon.
"It was you, Elena."
  He crouches once more. Reaches over me. Puts a hand to Elena's face.
  "I will never hurt you again," he says.
  "Stop it," I say. "Don't touch her."
  But they don't seem to hear me.
  "You are the key to Reconciliation," he says. "No one has ever de-
voted themselves to God as quickly as you. As thoroughly as you."
  "Please help him," she says. "He's bleeding."
  "Will you promise to continue fighting in this war?" he asks.

She doesn't hesitate. Doesn't look my way.

"Of course."

He takes her free hand tenderly. Runs his fingers over it.

"Where is he?" I ask. "Manny. Where is he?"

Deacon places Elena's hand over my nose and mouth.

I don't know what is happening at first. I think he is trying to get me to stop moaning and crying. My face is wet. My hair is soaked.

"We don't need him anymore, Elena."

She removes the hand from behind my head as she starts crying. "What do you mean?"

"Caroline? Franklin?" Deacon turns to them. "Hold him."

And then he presses her hand down hard.

I squirm beneath the two of them, and I try to kick myself up, but the heels of my shoes slip on the boards, and then Caroline has my right arm pinned to the ground, Franklin has my left, and I can't move anything but my legs. I twist from side to side and Elena's tears fall onto my face.

"I don't want to!" she shrieks.

"You have to!" Deacon screams back. "Together, we will get rid of this blight. We will never lose another soul in this place!"

I think she's trying to pull away from him.

I think she wants to leave.

I think she wants me to live.

The pain rises in my lungs. The darkness fills in.

"Stop!" Elena cries.

I struggle. I try to live.

But then Deacon removes his hands. Steps back.

And Elena pushes down harder.

"You were given a miracle," she sobs. "That's all I wanted. I wanted what you got."

She lets go.

I gasp for air and start choking.

"Do you love Deacon? Do you love God?"

A rage builds in me. How can she ask me that? How can she doubt my loyalty all these months?

You're never going to be good enough.

That's it. That's the truth.

I was never going to be good enough.

I can see his face in my mind.

I spit in the direction of Deacon Thompson.

"No," I say. "I only love you, Elena."

Elena puts her hand back on my mouth. Presses down, as the pain returns, as the darkness comes roaring back. She cries and cries and I
try to bite her hand, try to get out of this nightmare, but I'm losing. I'm

losing. Mom and Dad are screaming at me, holding down my arms and legs, and I can't move.

She finally turns her head away.

Deacon doesn't.

He stares down at me. Blue eyes boring into my skull.

He's smiling and smiling and smiling and smiling and–

I light another match.

Elena turns and glares at Deacon. "You said he had to go. You said he was a waste of life."

Panic spreads across Deacon's features. "She's distressed by the return of Manny," he says. "She doesn't—"

"You *told* me to get rid of him!" she screams. "My parents held him down, and *you* put my hand over his mouth and— Don't you remember it? Because I can't forget it! Every waking moment, I think about it!"

"Elena, *shut up!*" he bellows.

She tears at her hair. "Deacon, he's back. He's standing *right there*. How? How can God be wrong about this *twice?*"

She falls to her knees, slams her fists against the wooden boards. "You told me I was the miracle. I was the answer to your prayers. But you've kept me hidden. I don't get to talk to the kids anymore. I'm not in your videos and broadcasts. I don't get to save souls anymore."

"You haven't been well," says Caroline tenderly, but I hear the tremble in her voice. "That's why. We've just been trying to get you better."

But Elena cries out again. "*Why is he here, Deacon?*"

"I don't know, Elena!" he shouts, backing away from her.

"You don't know?" She wipes at her face. "But you *always* have an answer."

———

The match goes out.

I light another.

"Elena," I say. "Come with me. You don't have to be here with these people. None of this matters. We can get as far away from Reconciliation as you like."

"Why would I do that?" she shrieks. "The world out there is poisoned. Look at what it did to *you*. You're standing there, threatening to set this place on fire while we're all inside it. How is that any better?"

I feel it.

Just the tiniest squeeze in my hand.

Carlos.

It is a reminder, even if he didn't intend it that way.

Because behind me, the Varelas have rescued the children in Reconciliation. Carlos is standing at my side. The Samuels freed me.

How can I explain that to her? How can I show her that there is more to family than the Sullivans? Than this nightmare?

We have another choice.

Extinguish.

Ignite.

"Get out," Deacon says bitterly. "Leave us here to heal the wounds *you* wrought, Manny."

"Not without Elena," I say.

"Elena isn't going anywhere," he says. "She's made her choice."

But has she?

An eternity seems to pass as the old match singes my fingers. I blow it out. Let it fall to my feet. Realize that this can't be the end. It just can't. Not after everything I've been through.

"Leave," Elena says. "Leave me here, Manny."

"What about our children?"

A man with dark hair and a bushy mustache steps toward me. He is yet another stranger. Another adult willing to give their child over to this machine, to be ground up, to be reshaped into something less than human.

"They're not yours," I say. "They never should have been."

And then Deacon laughs. It's hearty. Deep.

"You think you can defy God?" he says. "This is a holy mission. Who else will save these children if we don't? Who else will build God's army if not me?"

He pushes Caroline out of the way. "You can't stop any of this! You're nothing but a lost, confused child. A *coward*. You can't stop what's coming. What God has deemed necessary."

"Let's go," says Carlos. "Please. We need to get out of here."

"Not with our children!" says the man with the mustache.

"We'll get more," growls Deacon. "There's always more, Travis! Let him *leave*."

Elena, still on her hands and knees, sobs profusely. Tears and snot drip to the floorboards. "Leave me," she says. "Please."

"Fine," I say aloud. "We'll leave."

I blow out the match.

A collective sigh is exhaled in the room. Everyone stands there, numb, confused.

"Leave," says Deacon. "You've done enough harm, Manny. Let us *heal*."

I approach Elena. She rolls over onto her back.

"Go," she says. "Don't come back."

I crouch down. Grab her hand and hold tightly.

"I found you," I say. "After a whole year. You can find me, too." Then:

"I'm sorry these people broke you."

Because I mean it.

Reconciliation broke so many children. Not just me. Not just Elena. Not just Rakeem or Simone or Omar or Henry. There are so many more.

I think I need to go with the Varelas and find them. Add more kids to their list because there are too many children in this world that have been taken advantage of. Rejected. Cast out.

I have to do *something*.

Elena clutches my hand tightly.

"Get as far away from here as possible," she mutters.

"I will," I say loudly, turning my head to glare at Deacon. At the Sullivans. At all these human monsters.

"Good," sneers Deacon.

He doesn't see me pass the box of matches to Elena.

Doesn't see her realize what I've given her.

Doesn't see her tuck them into her pocket.

"Remember," I say to her. "Deacon told you. He told you about our confessions that night."

She tilts her head to the side.

"Remember that we get to make our own choices."

I stand up and look upon the others with disgust.

"You're not my family," I say. "You never will be."

I hear the van pull up. Glance out the open doors, and there it is. The side door opens, and Monica is there.

Darkness is falling outside.

And it's time to bring this place into the light.

"Let's go," I say, grabbing ahold of Carlos's hand.

Choosing him. His family. My own future. Because it's so obvious now. This is my choice. Rakeem was right. I escaped. I've been free, and I never truly knew it until this exact moment.

And before I leave, I kick the canister over. Gasoline splatters forward and pours into the willing wood, spreads closer and closer toward Elena.

One of the kids is crying.

I recognize her when I climb into the van. It's Maddie, the girl from the most recent broadcast. Monica is holding her, whispering to her that everything is going to be okay.

"I'm so hungry," Maddie says, sniffling. "Do you have any food?"

I know then that I've made the right choice.

The van speeds across the clearing, away from the lodge. We hit the dirt road as I make it to the rear row, back corner, and then we start the descent as Ricardo speaks in rapid Spanish to the boy sitting behind him, the one with bruises on his arms. There's a third kid in the back row between me and Carlos. She's Black. Her hair is in a braided set of pigtails. She isn't talking. Eyes wide. Heart racing.

"What's your name?" I ask her.

She stutters it out.

"Cora."

Looks up at me.

"Am I safe now?"

I don't know. The world outside of Reconciliation can be terrible. I know this.

But there's some good. And it's always because people *choose* to be good.

"Yes," I say. "You are."

I have to choose.

I have to choose to find the others. I know they're out there, and they have to know that there's another option.

I have to return to the Samuels.

I have to figure out who I'm going to be now that Manny Sullivan is dead.

I have . . . Carlos.

The future is unwritten. He's going away to college. He might be leaving me. He might want me to stay. But he wants me around.

Isn't that enough, sometimes? Isn't it enough to want to be desired?

When you've lived your whole life in the desert . . .

I look to Carlos.

To the rain cloud.

"We'll figure this out," he says. "I promise."

We. There's still a we in his mind.

And maybe he's right. I gave Elena a choice. I couldn't convince her to leave. Couldn't force her. She has to do it on her own. All that matters is that *I* am free of this place. Free of the burden of Manny Sullivan, the son they wanted me to be, the impossible boy. I get to be whoever I want to be now.

Do I pick a new name? I wonder if they ever gave him one or if he just continued on as me, their me.

An even bigger reason to change now. To choose a future that I want.

I have so many choices ahead of me.

God, it's fucking invigorating.

And then the van comes to a lurching stop.

"Holy shit," Monica says.

I turn around.

The forest is glowing behind us. Bright oranges and yellows, leaping up into the sky.

I've never seen anything like it.

Carlos holds me.

When I look at his face, there is awe upon it.

I think he understands.

It means the world to me.

We watch in silence until I see a figure. A shadow in the backdrop of light. It's walking toward us down the hill.

I smile.

There is a warmth in my heart.

It is holy.

Righteous.

I think this must be what God feels like.

AUTHOR'S NOTE

Dear Reader,

This book is about six years in the making. I first got the idea for a spooky mystery back in the summer of 2017 while at a convention. (Shout out to CrossingsCon!) However, I was not emotionally ready for the subject matter. It took me writing five other books before I could fully dive into the world of *Into the Light*.

When I was a teenager, I survived something that no one should have to go through, but which countless teenagers here in the States (and unfortunately, around the world) have also experienced. It shaped me into the person I am today. I think you can see bits and pieces of this story spread throughout the books I've put out into the world, because I know I've spent my entire adult life grappling with what it meant to be rejected by the very people who were supposed to love me the most.

I might be thriving now, but I find that life is beginning to repeat itself. Many of those very things I faced as a teenager are being forced upon kids all over again. Dogma. Repression. Hatred. Queer and trans kids are being targeted, rejected, stigmatized, deliberately misunderstood, and cast as monsters.

It is hard not to see this cyclical nightmare for what it is.

This book is my attempt to bring these things into the light. To be honest about a segment of the American experience of Christian nationalism and adoption that some of us know all too well.

For those coming here from the dedication: This will be a difficult read, but know that Manny's journey through the darkness is all about the light at the end of the tunnel. Because it's there for all of us. I believe that. Take care of yourself as you read this book. If you are particularly sensitive to depictions of **parental abuse (especially** from adoptive parents), religious abuse, conversion therapy and depictions of abusive techniques from conversion therapy camps, parental rejection, teenage homelessness, and predatory adults, this book may trigger you. This is not an exhaustive list of triggers, but should cover most of the broad categories.

While it is unfortunate that a large portion of this book is auto-biographical in nature, I still did a lot of research regarding the intersection of the American adoption system, foster care, and Christian evangelism. If you are interested in further reading on the subject, these books all helped guide me. Some stuff never made it into the final manuscript at all, but all contributed in some part to this story.

The Child Catchers: Rescue, Trafficking, and the New Gospel of Adoption—Kathryn Joyce

American Baby—Gabrielle Glaser

The Girls Who Went Away—Ann Fessler

Cultish: The Language of Fanaticism—Amanda Montell

Taking Children: A History of American Terror—Laura Briggs

Finding Fernanda: Two Mothers, One Child, and a Cross-Border Search for Truth—Erin Siegal

Blessed: A History of the American Prosperity Gospel—Kate Bowler

Torn Apart: How the Child Welfare System Destroys Black Families—and How Abolition Can Build a Safer World—Dorothy Roberts

Terror, Love, & Brainwashing: Attachment in Cults and Totalitarian Systems—Alexandra Stein

Kinship by Design: A History of Adoption in the Modern United States—Ellen Herman

Thank you for taking this journey with me. I wouldn't have had the courage to write this book unless I felt my readers would support it.

Let's go into the light together.

Mark Oshiro

ACKNOWLEDGMENTS

I'll keep these brief because this book is already long enough. (I promise I'll write a short young adult book someday!)

Thank you to my agent, DongWon Song, for your endless support and brilliance. My career is what it is because of you.

Thank you to Miriam Weinberg, for our absolutely unhinged collaboration on this story. It's hard to believe that the proposal I gave you years ago was a supernatural *comedy*. You have helped shape this story into what it is by giving me guidance, but also allowing me to be feral. I still remember that frantic phone call I gave you in the spring of 2021 when I figured out the general idea of the "twist" of this book, and you encouraged me to throw myself wildly into uncertainty.

Thank you to Sarah Gailey for the continued brainstorming/writer's block sessions we have. You are truly the best friend I could ever ask for, and this book wouldn't have taken the shape it is without you.

Thank you to the incredible team at Tor Teen for so many things! Your patience, first of all, as this book was rewritten THREE TIMES over the course of a year, so many of you couldn't even read it until it was very, very close to its due date. Secondly, I know how much each of you have lovingly supported my vision and my art over this project and my past ones; I couldn't ask for a better support team.

So, thank you to Michelle Foytek in Operations, Lani Meyer for the brilliant copyedits, Greg Collins for your design magic, Tessa Villanueva (editorial assistant extraordinaire!), Lesley Worrell for designing the jacket, Carolina Rodríguez Fuenmayor for the cover illustration that took my breath away, Rafal Gibek for your managing editor support, and Ryan Jenkins and Steven Bucsok for all things production (even as I continue to make your jobs harder I PROMISE I WILL WRITE A NORMAL, LINEAR BOOK FOR YOU ONE DAY). And then there's the rest of the team, like Isa Caban, Anthony Parisi, Kayah Hodge, Jocelyn Bright, Eileen Lawrence, Lucille Rettino, and Devi Pillai, who are the best folks to EVER have promoting and marketing your books, I ADORE ALL OF YOU.

Special shout-out to Saraciea Fennell, my forever publicist boo, who continues to change my life and my career. Love you.

Thank you to the group chats: Adam Silvera, Patrice Caldwell, and Dhonielle Clayton for your support, advice, gossip, and general shenanigans. To my Deadline City wives, too: love you, Zoraida and Dhonielle. The original homies: Justin A. Reynolds, Kwame Mbalia, Saraciea, Patrice, Ashley Woodfolk, Jalissa Corrie, and Tiffany Jackson. May we all continue to shine bright in this world.

To all the folks—educators, teachers, librarians, book bloggers, BookTok, Bookstagram, students, writers, readers, authors, booksellers, book buyers, indie bookstores—who have championed and supported my books: thank you for still believing in me. My books have been banned collectively more times than I can recall at this point, and you still haven't given up on me. I appreciate you all.

To Rian German, for your light and wisdom and brilliance.

And to my Georgia folks—there are simply so many of you that I keep editing in new names, so I'll just say that y'all know who you are—thank you for welcoming me to your state, letting me write in your homes or in cafes or restaurants, and for generally helping me feel like this place is now *my* home.

With light,
Mark